The House of Mammon by Fred M White

Fred Merrick White was born in 1859 in West Bromwich in the Midlands of England to Joseph White and Helen Merrick who had married the previous year.

Joseph was a solicitor's managing clerk, who by the time the family moved to Hereford a few years later, had become a solicitor's article clerk.

Little is known of White's early years but what is known is that he followed in his father's footsteps and worked as a solicitor's clerk in Hereford. His father by now had also become a solicitor and times seemed quite prosperous for the family.

However in the late 1880's something went badly wrong for his father and he was imprisoned.

White had by now decided that writing was a more preferable career for him than the law. By 1891 Fred M. White, now 31 years old, was working full-time as a journalist and author, earning enough to support himself and his mother, Helen. By this time Fred's younger brother, Joseph A. White, had left home and working as a glass-blower.

In 1892, White married Clara Jane Smith. The wedding took place at King's Norton, Worcestershire, and the couple went on to have two children; Sydney Eric White (1893) and Ormond John White (1895).

As the century closed Fred's father had been released from prison and was living as a "retired solicitor", together with Helen, in Worthington in West Sussex.

By the time of the 1911 census, Fred M. White, now 52 years old, and his wife Clara were living at Uckfield, a town in the Wealden district of East Sussex. As the ominous shadows of the First World War gathered White had established himself as a popular and extremely prolific author. Indeed whether it was novels or short stories they flowed from his pen with a startling speed and many of them were initially serialized in the popular weekly and monthly magazines. His clever use of science to create imaginative and highly adventurous story lines was a particular talent of his.

During the First World War, both of his sons served as junior officers in The Royal Inniskilling Fusiliers.

The titanic struggle of the First World War and his sons' war-time experiences in it greatly influenced this phase of his writing. His novel The Seed of Empire (1916), describes early trench warfare in great and gritty detail. He went on to describe how the social changes after the war created many problems for returning soldiers as they attempted to fit back into a now peaceful society.

Fred and Clara spent their twilight years in Barnstaple in Devon, an area which also provided the backdrop for his novels The Mystery Of Crocksands, The Riddle Of The Rail, and The Shadow Of The Dead Hand.

Fred Merrick White died in Barnstaple in 1935.

Index of Contents

CHAPTER I

FATHER AND DAUGHTERS

On either side of the road for the best part of a mile stood the Marlton beeches, which were among the glories of the Grange. This was one of the show drives for visitors staying in the neighborhood of Sheringham and Cromer; they came and admired these glorious beeches, with the tangle of fern and heather behind them, and mildly envied the fortunate possessor of Marlton Grange. Farther along the road a drive had been hewn out of what centuries ago had been a stone quarry, and here was a quaint thatch lodge built so far back as the time of Charles the Second. Beyond this was the park, with its herd of dappled deer and glimpses of the singular, twisted chimney-stacks of the Grange itself.

If the curious visitor asked—as was frequently the case—who lived there, the answer was to the effect that the place belonged to Mr. John Sairson, a London business man. He had purchased the property some five years ago, after Sir George Lugard, the last of his family, had been found dead in the library, with a revolver in his hand. If further details were needed, they were cautiously and grudgingly given. There were folk who said that Sir George had been badly treated. He had been robbed of his property by John Sairson in connection with some transaction. No; Mr. Sairson was not at the Grange very often. He kept up the property, but he did not shoot, or hunt, or play golf. He had a wife and daughters, and there was some talk of a son, but nobody seemed to be quite sure as to that. Mrs. Sairson appeared to be kind and generous, but the young ladies kept themselves to themselves, and practically there were no visitors at the Grange. Half the year Mrs. Sairson and her girls were abroad.

Now here was the making of a romance. Here was the grand house transferred at the end of three centuries from the old family to a new order with the mystery of a suicide hanging over the scene like some sinister shadow. Here were rich people deliberately avoided and shunned by neighbors who were quite ready in the ordinary way to hold out the right hand of friendship to trade itself. The Gilettes, for instance, owed everything to Leicester, and ready-made boots, and the Sylvesters were "in" provisions. Nevertheless, they had the freedom of the cover-side and the golf links and the ballroom, but the Sairsons remained beyond the pale. Nobody precisely knew why, nobody could lay a finger on anything definite, but such was the state of things. There are worse drawbacks than open scandal, and this was one of them.

Mansion and surroundings were very refined and beautiful. The grounds and gardens had never been so well kept, the splendid old furniture in the Grange was intact and undisturbed, a few good modern pictures had been added to the old ones, a new conservatory had been put up here and there. Sairson's collection of enamelled armor stood in the great hall, possibly the finest specimens in Europe. The Grange was essentially the hiding-place of gentlefolk, and it must be confessed that the Sairsons, mother and daughters, were part of the picture.

The long grey front of the house slept in the misty sunshine, the velvet sheen of the lawn was pierced here and there by the crimson and gold and pallid blue of the flower beds. Beyond lay the park, a diaphanous study in emerald hues. Here and there were glimpses of the sea. The stone terrace was a tangled mass of yellow roses. Over all brooded that suggestion of mellowed peace and dignified detachment which one associates with age and happiness. Below the terrace, with its drip of bloom and wreath of foliage, Mrs. Sairson sat with some silken fancy-work in her hands.

She was not more than middle-aged, the masses of her hair were abundant, a beautiful grey, giving a note of distinction to the ivory tint of her face and the dark brown of her eyes. A quiet and delicate face it was, suggestive of resignation and suffering, mental more than physical. There was some trace of passion in the lines of the sensitive mouth, a reminiscence of tempestuous youth, of a soul that had fretted itself out against the bars of life. The slim hands were working restlessly and nervously, and the voice in which Mrs. Sairson spoke was clear and refined.

"My dear Nest," she said, "what is the use of talking like that. I am sure you have a great deal to be thankful for. Your father—"

"Mummy, I believe there are times when I hate my father!"

Mrs. Sairson shuddered. A curious pallor increased, if possible, the whiteness of her cheeks, and a look of scorn crept into her eyes. She should have recoiled in horror from such an outburst. Glancing at the girl standing by her side, she could see, as in a glass dimly, the picture of herself some score of years before. Only two-and-twenty years! Surely, it must be longer than that! She saw a tall, slim girl, a defiant head poised under a mass of shining chestnut hair, a dark, wilful, beautiful face, tinged with exquisite coloring, a pair of sorrowful brown eyes, and a little mouth that quivered passionately. Here in the flesh was one of the reasons why Mrs. Sairson had learnt to control herself.

"My dear Nest," she said, "I cannot permit you to talk like that."

"Why not?" the girl went on rebelliously. "Don't you hate him sometimes? If you were not the dearest, sweetest, most delightful old darling in the world—"

Mrs. Sairson smiled; She was not lacking in a sense of humor.

"I was exactly like you at your age."

"Were you really, dearest? And yet to look at you now! What am I saying! But when I get restless and miserable, as I am to-day, I am ready to say anything. What is the matter with us, mother? Anyone can see that you are a lady, and I'm sure there is nothing the matter with Angela and myself. Why does everybody avoid us as if we had the plague? Why does nobody call? Why don't you go and see some of the new people? Why does everyone stare at us in that furtive way when they meet us in the road. If father had ever been in gaol—"

"Your father has never been in gaol," Mrs. Sairson smiled.

"Well, prosecuted, perhaps, escaped by the skin of his teeth; mixed up in some shady business in that horrid city where he spends most of his time!"

"I have never heard anything so absurd," Mrs. Sairson answered.

"Well, if you say so, of course," Nest admitted. "All the same, you are keeping something from me. You don't know how sad and weary you look at times. And I am convinced that Angela knows. If there is any trouble, I have a right to share it. I'm twenty, remember, and haven't forgotten what happened to Angela and Captain Barr three years ago."

"Angela has not been alluding to her—her disappointment?"

"She his never said a word to me, mummy. I was seventeen at the time. I daresay you thought I was quite a child at that date, but I wasn't. When you live under a cloud, as we do, you get—well, precocious; and if ever I saw real happiness it was that night Angela told me she was to marry Jack Barr. They were going to live at Dower House, and all kinds of good times were before me. I was in the drawing-room the night Jack came to see father. I shall never forget his face as long as I live—a sort of sad sternness, as if he had been told that his life was over. Angela, as white as a ghost, told me afterwards that it had all been a great mistake, and that she was not going to be married ever. She said she was glad, and cried herself to sleep as it was getting light. Mother, what does it all mean?"

There were tears in Mrs. Sairson's eyes as she bent over her fancy work.

"Why did Jack Barr behave so badly?" said Nest, cruelly insistent.

"My dear, he did not behave badly at all. There—there was no alternative. The fault was entirely mine. I have never ceased to regret it. My child, why cannot you be content to leave well alone? You are happy, you are under no shadow—"

"Under no shadow, mother! Why, we live in the shade. It is only when we go abroad that we can be said to have any time at all. But for these few months every summer I should go melancholy mad. Then we see other people and exchange ideas. But nothing ever happens here."

A neat parlor-maid, dainty in her black and white uniform, came out with a telegram on a salver. Mrs. Sairson read it with a certain vexed amusement in her eyes.

"There is no answer, Palgrave," she said. "Here is a change for you, at any rate dear. You father telegraphs from London that he has found a prospective tenant for the Dower House. The gentleman will be here to lunch and will stay the night. Your father will be back in time for dinner. It will be a change for you."

"It sounds promising," Nest said dubiously. "But I must not build any hopes. Probably the new tenant will be middle-aged and devoted to business. What is his name?"

"It looks like Lugard," said Mrs. Sairson, consulting the telegram. "Yes, it is Lugard, Cecil Lugard. Strange it should be the same name as the old family who—"

"Not at all," Nest interrupted eagerly. "Probably a relative of the family who wants to come back to the old neighborhood. Well, I shall be glad to see him, anyway. It is possible he may be an interesting person, a good talker. If he is young, so much the better. I like the name of Cecil. It does not suggest a fat city man in a white waistcoat."

"You can never tell," Mrs. Sairson said sapiently. "Mr. Lugard will arrive about half-past twelve, your father tells me, and I am to send the car for him. Afterwards he will probably want to look over the Dower House, and you can take him."

It was nearly one o'clock when Nest crossed the terrace in the direction of the drawing-room, with an eager curiosity she felt just a little ashamed of. She could hear someone talking easily and pleasantly in a mellow, baritone voice. She stepped through the open window and stood there for a moment, a pretty and graceful picture.

"This is my daughter, Nest," Mrs. Sairson said. "Mr. Lugard."

The stranger held out his hand. His expression was at once pleased and puzzled.

"I fancy we have met before," he observed. "Have you forgotten me, Miss Nest?"

"At Berne," Nest said with a dazzling smile. "But you did not call yourself Lugard then?"

"No, I was a Franklin at that time. But there was money, you see, if I took the family name. It is very delightful to see you again—and in such a lovely old place as this!"

CHAPTER II

THE ONLY MAN

The ivory pallor of Mrs. Sairson's face deepened, and she raised her hand to her heart as if conscious of some physical pain there. The beauty of the place, the wide sweep of the lawns, the deer in the park, all seemed to mock her. In a sense Marlton Grange was a prison. There were times when its very grandeur oppressed and saddened her. Hitherto she could console herself that the prison was her own. Escape might be impossible; but, on the other hand, it was not possible for others to get in. And here was the intruder she had always dreaded. He came in desirable shape—in the form that all mothers who love their girls pray for—yet he filled Mrs. Sairson's soul with dread. She marked the look of pleasure in Lugard's face, the keen delight and admiration of his eyes. She saw the flush on Nest's face, the smiling curves of her lips. She began to see with a startling clearness the hidden meaning of certain incidents when they had met this young man at Berne some time ago. Like all true women, she scented the delicate flavor of romance, but the mere suggestion of it filled her heart with terror.

"Mammy, aren't you going to say something more to Mr. Lugard?" Nest asked.

A graceful phrase or two came from Mrs. Sairson's lips. It was pleasant to meet Mr. Lugard again. They had been very agreeable days at Berne. Nest often spoke of them.

Lugard smiled as he wondered whether Nest had remembered everything—had mentioned everything. He was under the impression that Mrs. Sairson had deliberately spirited her girls away. He had not connected Mr. John Sairson with his charming acquaintance at Berne; he had dismissed the chance with a smile. The name was the same, of course, but John Sairson did not suggest the proud father of a lovely daughter. He suggested nothing but money.

"Positively I had no idea I was to have this delightful surprise," Lugard said. "Quite by chance I saw that the Dower House was to let. It occurred to me as a good idea to take it. Though this used to be the family seat, I have never seen it before. I saw that a certain Mr. Sairson was the owner, and I went to see him. That is why I am here."

"Your idea is to settle in the neighborhood?" Mrs. Sairson asked.

"I think so, dear lady. I want an old house with some shooting and fishing. As a Lugard on my mother's side I am pretty sure of a welcome here. I'm not a millionaire, but I daresay I could manage to be comfortable at the Dower House."

Mrs. Sairson hoped so; indeed she could say nothing less. She could like this young man with the frank and handsome face in ordinary circumstances. But there could be no ordinary circumstances here; there could be nothing but trouble and humiliation and despair. And the worst of it was that nothing could be done. .. Nest was full of pleased associations; she chatted gaily. There were so many things to admire about the house, and Lugard admired them frankly. The view from the big west window of the drawing-room attracted him greatly.

Angela Sairson watched the pair from under the fringe of her long lashes. Her beauty was purer than that of her sister, the white, subdued sadness of her face suited the perfect profile. She had all the softness and sweetness of the nun—there was a suggestion that the world was hard for her—and her pose one of resignation. It was such a lovely face, too—a face that poets and painters would have raved over. A tender, wistful smile crossed her face as she watched Nest and her companion in the window with the sunshine on them.

"Poor mother!" she murmured. "Poor mother! Did you think you could stop it."

"And poor, poor little Nest! We would have both died to save her if we could."

"God knows, we would," Mrs. Sairson sighed. "But, perhaps, after all, we are anticipating—"

"No, we are not, mother. I saw it coming at Berne. That is why I was anxious to get away before it was too late. We might have saved Nest if Fate had not played this trick upon us. Don't interfere, mother; don't blame yourself for the inevitable."

Mrs. Sairson brushed the tears from her eyes. It seemed to her that she was drifting hopelessly. Yet it was good to hear the brightness of Nest's laughter. She was but a child, and perhaps Providence would provide a way out of the situation which threatened to become tragic. As the gong was sounded in the hall, the sun shone brightly out of doors. Cecil Lugard came forward and offered his arm with an old-fashioned grace and chivalry.

"What a lovely place this is!" he exclaimed, as he unfolded his napkin. "My mother used to tell me what a delightful room this was. The carvings exceed my expectations. I am not surprised my poor old uncle was fond of it. It was very hard times to be cheated out of the place by a scoundrel of a money-lender."

"I—I don't quite follow you," Mrs. Sairson gasped.

"Oh, that was before your time, of course," Lugard went on. "I am talking of the period before that rascal disposed of the property to Mr. Sairson. It had nothing to do with your husband, who doubtless paid a fair price for the estate. But that man, John Blaydon, the money-lender, is one of the most loathsome reptiles that was ever allowed to live. I have heard things about him that make my blood boil. Such a shameless villain, too. Well, my dear lady, he got hold of my uncle and fleeced him of everything. My lawyer says that if my uncle had not lost his nerve he could have prosecuted that scamp for conspiracy and saved everything. The unhappy man committed suicide instead—murdered, really, by John Blaydon. But I have not done with that reptile yet."

Mrs. Sairson sat white and still, while Angela listened with her eyes cast down. Only Nest looked frankly and admiringly into the face of the speaker. There was something in his set face and the determination of his square jaw that moved her to admiration.

"I like to hear a man talk like that," she cried. "You have my good wishes for your success, Mr. Lugard. If there is one creature on earth more detestable than another it is a money-lender. I could be friendly with a released convict, but with one of these wretches, never! I hope you will punish the scoundrel as he deserves."

"Oh, I am going to," Lugard said grimly. "A little time ago certain papers and documents relating to my uncle's affairs reached me anonymously. Evidently they had fallen into the hands of somebody who had cause to detest Blaydon. Another link or two and the chain will be complete. I will not rest till Blaydon stands in the dock."

Angela glanced up from her dessert plate, her black eyes gleaming against the pallor of her face.

"Pardon, me," she said, "but I'm afraid my mother is not feeling well."

Lugard paused and stammered. He blamed himself for an unobserving brute. Possibly his chatter had been too much.

Mrs. Sairson forced a smile to her lips. "I feel the heat," she murmured, "though I love the sun. It was foolish of me to sit out so long this morning. A few minutes' rest in the drawing-room will put me right. But you are not to leave the table, any of you. I shall be distressed if you worry over me."

All the same Angela rose and followed her mother in her silent, sympathetic way.

"I'm very sorry," Lugard said. "What a beautiful face your sister has—and how sad! He dark eyes positively haunt me. I don't want to be impertinent, but—"

"Angela had a disappointment," Nest explained; "an unfortunate misunderstanding. I was only 17 at the time, but I remember it perfectly. Oh, no, you must not think that Angela kept the reason to herself. She won't hear a word against the man, nor will mother. She says the affair could have had no other ending. In a sense my mother declares that she was chiefly to blame. I was very sorry, for I liked Jack Barr."

"What! Jack Barr, of the Northern Rifles?" Lugard exclaimed. "You don't mean to say—"

"Indeed I do, Mr. Lugard. Do you know him?"

"Know him! Why, he was my greatest friend at one time. Three years ago he chucked up everything to go out West. All I could get out of him was that he had had a serious trouble. But that he ever did anything mean or dishonorable, I refuse to believe."

"Of that I am certain," Nest rejoined. "I am not quite sure whether I ought to have told you this. You won't mention it to Angela, will you? No doubt you think it a pity to waste this glorious afternoon. There is a caretaker at the Dower House who will show us everything, and I hope you will take the place. We have no callers and seek none. My mother does not care for society. But it is very dull for me."

Lugard smiled down at the pretty face lifted to him. He was selfishly glad to hear this. Those deep violet eyes had never ceased to haunt him; in his day-dreams he had seen that wild-rose coloring and that hair with the threads of sunshine in it. If he were only allowed to have his way Nest should not be dull any more. The stars in their courses were fighting on her side.

"I shall be only too delighted, if I can," he said. "It is awfully good of you to feel all this interest in me. I had no idea I was going to have so happy a time. The mere pleasure of seeing you again.....Do you remember that evening on the hill near Berne when we lost our way?"

Nest's eyes deepened—Lugard could never make out what their exact hue was—and a soft flush crept over her face. She did not like to confess how well she remembered.

"It was a very, very pleasant time," she admitted.

"And many more to come, I hope?" Lugard smiled. "Are you ready for our expedition?"

It was tea-time before they returned, Nest happy and gay, and full of the merriest spirits.

The adventure had been a success in every way, the house charming, and needing little in the way of repair. So far as Lugard was concerned, the tenancy was as good as settled. Nest dashed into her mother's room with the good news. They were to have a really congenial neighbor at last.

"Come over here and kiss me," Mrs. Sairson said. "My child, how happy you look! I only pray you will not allow yourself to—"

"Let me whisper to you," Nest said, with her head buried in her mother's hair. "Hold me tight and think the best of me, because there never has been and there never will be another man who—who—Now, isn't that a shameless confession for a girl to make?"

With a broken laugh Nest hurried from the room. Mrs. Sairson's lips quivered piteously.

"I can do no more," she murmured. "God's will must be done."

CHAPTER III

A MAN OF BUSINESS

John Sairson and Co.'s premises were situated at St. Martin's House, one of the newest blocks in the city, and here the successful man of business made his money. The building itself was a large one, and, as a matter of fact, was Sairson's property. His own suite of offices was modest enough, consisting of two rooms on the first floor, with an extra apartment for a couple of clerks. The rest of the fine structure was let out to various commercial enterprises.

Sairson was supposed to be a kind of general commission agent, and he was rightly looked upon as a man of considerable substance. Shrewd and successful, he was a keen hand at a bargain and a hard taskmaster. It was a difficult matter to picture John Sairson as a country gentleman taking an interest in a fine old estate. He looked remote enough from Marlton Grange as he sat at his desk; his mind was far from the grey house bathed in the sunshine, the brown pools of the lake where the lilies bloomed under the shadow of the beeches.

He was a big, loose-limbed man, with a heavy face and pendulous cheeks. His red-rimmed eyes were shifty and unsteady, unless money was being discussed, when they focussed themselves like those of a cat watching a bird's every movement. Sairson's dress was a compromise between that of the business man and the country gentleman. In expansive moments he was fond of boasting of his place on the east coast. But he rarely put in more than a week-end there, and even that at intervals.

He turned over a mass of papers impatiently and rang his bell. A clerk entered and waited respectfully for his employer to speak. Sairson looked at him sourly.

"Have you got those contracts ready for me?"

"Yes, sir," the clerk replied. "They are on the desk by the bookcase, sir. I have seen that everything is in order. If you would like to go through them again, sir—"

"Of course I should like to go through them again," Sairson growled. "It's an important matter, as you know, Partridge. It will take me an hour or more, and I am not to be disturbed. No matter who calls or desires to see me, I must not be disturbed. If any clerk dare knock at the door before 12 o'clock, out of the office he goes."

Sairson spoke in the loud dominating tones of the bully. The wretched clerk listened meekly. He was a struggling man with a family, and used to the kind of thing.

"Very good, sir," he said humbly. "It shall be as you say. If anybody calls you are out and not expected back till midday. Anything else, sir?"

Sairson dismissed the man with a gesture, and put the latch of the door down after the clerk departed. It was a strong door fitted with a Yale lock framed in steel. To appearance it was no more than an ordinary office door, but in reality it was nearly as strong as that of a safe.

Sairson smiled with the air of a man who is pleased with himself, took a cigar from a box on the table, and lighted it. The office was lined with books of various kinds from floor to ceiling. Sairson touched one of the books, and immediately a portion of the centre of the wall slid back and disclosed a room beyond. Sairson stepped into it and then shut the false partition behind him. He had entered another office which was back to back with his own, and opened into another corridor. It was a private room, and the door was fitted with a similar steel frame and Yale lock. Once more Sairson smiled with the air of one who is not displeased with himself.

This was a different room altogether. It was far more luxuriously furnished. The apartment was almost extravagantly furnished, the pictures on the wall were good, and the carpet was real Persian. Sairson put up the catch of the lock and rang the bell sharply.

There came in prompt answer to the summons a tall man with a faint suggestion of the athlete about him. He was fat and puffy, like his employer, but had the air of one who has been intimate with the covert-side, the cricket-field, the river, and the racquet-court. Under his collar he wore the colors of a famous cricket club. With it all he had the air of a man broken down and beaten in the daily conflict with the world. A certain quivering of the lips and shakiness of the hand told their story.

"Now, Gosway," Sairson said curtly. "Anything doing?"

"Not very much this morning," Gosway answered with a touch of familiarity. "Some half-dozen applications I have gone through. For the most part they are no good. I thought perhaps you might like to see two of them. Both for biggish amounts."

"All right," Sairson said. "I'll look at them presently. Better make appointments this afternoon for the two likely ones. I'm glad there isn't much doing, for I want to get away into the country as soon as possible. No more of those anonymous letters, I suppose?"

A gleam of malice glistened in Philip Gosway's moist eyes.

"No more letters," he said significantly. "You were foolish not to consult the police. You could have managed it easily enough. Nobody would have recognised you if you had appeared before a magistrate. Not a soul in England could connect John Sairson with—"

"Except yourself and one other man," Sairson interrupted impatiently, "and the other person happens to be the very person whom you advise me to prosecute. We shall have to buy him off. After all, it's only a question of money. If he should presume to come here—"

"My dear sir, he has been here," Gosway said impressively. "He was here an hour ago. If I had not been a bit of an athlete still there might have been trouble. And you may clear your mind of cant as far as your previous money is concerned. He would not hear of it. From what I can gather, money is the last thing he is thinking about. He scoffed at the suggestion."

"Then what the devil does he want?" Sairson asked testily.

"Revenge! The man is more or less mad. He has brooded over his wrongs till they have turned his head. He looks to me as if he had been drinking heavily as well. It's that or drugs. He looked like a lean and hungry wolf. I had great trouble in persuading him that you were not here. Goodness knows where he got the information from. If you meet him alone in some dark corner late at night, look to yourself!"

Sairson blinked uneasily. His big face was white and flabby, and he glanced suspiciously at the man before him.

"You're not in the infernal game?" he asked hoarsely.

"You know I'm not," Gosway replied. "I'm too much under your thumb for that. If I had been a man of that sort I should have stuck a knife into your ribs long ago. When I came to you first I was a happy man with a good record in my regiment; I went in first wicket down for the good old club whose colors I still wear. When you had sucked me dry I was a broken man with nothing to cling to but my little girl, who does not know how her wretched father gets a living. I do not forget that you could send me to gaol if you wanted to—if I were likely to forget it your constant reminders would keep the fact before me. Men I used to know at one time come here and sometimes recognise me. That is part of the punishment of my folly. But you are safe from me because my girl has to be thought of. Otherwise I believe I'd have broken your neck long ago. For the sake of the child I am loyal to you. All the same, unless you help yourself—"

Gosway paused and shrugged his shoulders meaningly. The cold contempt of his words seemed to arouse no feeling in Sairson. He pulled nervously at his cigar, and his brow knitted in a frown.

"All the same, it is a confounded nuisance," he muttered. "It won't avail me to pursue that matter I was talking to you about so long as that man knows anything."

"Not a bit," Gosway grinned. "You are known here as an elderly man with black hair and beard. Your spectacles and white waistcoat are quite artistic in their way. And it is a bit rough after you have planned everything so carefully to find yourself cornered by the one man you have to fear."

Sairson did not appear to be listening. He chewed the end of his cigar savagely.

"Did he say he would call again?"

"No, he didn't," Gosway explained. "He led me to understand that he had another scheme. He said he was going to the country for a day or two; would spend his money on a ticket to some place on the east coast. You can probably guess what that means!"

Sairson's florid face assumed a sickly green hue.

"I don't like it," he commented. "I don't like it at all. Leave the office to Griffin for an hour or two and go and find the fellow. Take a fiver out of the petty cash and spend it freely if necessary. Before I go out of town to-day I must know the movements of that man. If you have done your duty by me you will know where to put your hand on him."

"I have done all I have been asked to do," Gosway protested. "You can rely upon me to let you know something definite before the afternoon is over. Where shall I send it to?"

"Oh! send it to my club. Let me have a telegram or an express letter. If anybody calls, say that I shall not be back till Monday."

Gosway retreated into the outer room, carefully closing the door behind him. The Yale lock clicked, and Sairson was alone once more. He crossed over to a cupboard and produced a flask of liqueur brandy. He drank two glasses of the red spirit, and the florid red came back into his face again.

"Curse the follow to all eternity!" he burst out presently. "Why does he carry on like this? He lost his money with his eyes wide open, but could have got it back again but for his idiotic pride. As if it mattered in the least! No one need ever have known that the girl— But it is idle to speculate as to what might have happened. The fellow is a dangerous lunatic, and will do me a mischief if he gets the chance. There's one way yet—"

Sairson returned presently into his own office again and closed the false door behind him. He pulled back the catch of the lock and rang the bell.

"I can see nobody to-day, Partridge," he remarked. "I am going into the country at 5, and shall probably not be back till Monday. I'm not feeling at all well, and a day or two in the fresh air will set me up again."

Partridge received certain further instructions and departed. It was nearly 5 o'clock before Sairson had tea at his club, and then rose with the intention of summoning the dining-room waiter to call a taxi-cab to take him to Liverpool street. At that moment another waiter entered with an express letter on a tray which he handed to Sairson.

"Just come for you, sir."

Sairson snatched up the letter and tore off the envelope. There was only one significant line.

"Don't go home to-night. Dangerous for you to travel on the East Coast."

With a savage execration Sairson strode over to the writing-table and grabbed a telegraph form.

CHAPTER IV

THE OPEN WINDOW

It was very pleasant to linger in the wide panelled hall by the tea-table watching Nest's slender hands as they played over the cups and silver. It was delightfully cool and pleasant after the heat of the afternoon, and the green of the trees was refreshing and grateful to the eye. Cecil Lugard lay back in his chair, smoking a cigarette and looking at Nest with the yellow sunshine on her hair. The girl's face was radiantly happy; there was a soft glow in her eyes. In the course of that afternoon ramble to the Dower House and back, Lugard had made up his mind. He had told himself more than once at Berne that if ever he was in a position to marry, this was the one girl for him. He had not spoken then for many reasons; Nest was rich, and his prospects were not encouraging. He had longed for some miracle to happen so that he might have the chance to—

And behold! the miracle had happened. He was in a position to speak now, and had met Nest directly after his good fortune had come to him. It all seemed like some favored dispensation of Providence. Surely there never was a romance like it before! He felt pretty sure of his ground, too; he knew that Nest cared for him; and Dower House would make a perfect nest for him. They sat talking confidentially for a long time. Mrs. Sairson had retired under plea of a headache, though heartache would have been a more fitting description, and it was Angela's usual custom to take the dog for a run after tea. By and bye Mrs. Sairson entered the hall with a telegram in her hand.

"I have just heard from my husband," she said. "It is very unfortunate, for he has been detained at the last minute by most important business and cannot be here to-night."

"Is that really so, mother?" Nest exclaimed. "He is not coming? How—"

She broke off abruptly, her face a delicate pink. It seemed to Cecil that he knew what was passing in her mind. If she meant anything, she was glad her father was not coming. She ought to be ashamed to admit it, but the fact remained all the same. There was no mistaking the sparkle of pleasure in her eyes. She turned awkwardly to her mother.

"I suppose he will be here some time to-morrow, Mummy?"

"It seems exceedingly doubtful, dear," Mrs. Sairson explained. "It is quite possible your father may not be here for the week-end at all. I am very sorry Mr. Lugard. If you can put up with our company for a day or two, perhaps you would not mind. You see, your business—"

"Dear Mrs. Sairson, I shall be delighted," Cecil exclaimed. "Nothing would give me greater pleasure. I'm sorry to miss my host, of course, and in any case I should have gone to the village hotel. I have quite made up my mind to take the Dower House. It is exactly what I need. Let me thank you again for your kind offer, which I am very grateful for."

Nest's eyes flashed at Cecil. She was telling him of her pleasure as plainly as words could speak. Her beaming glances set his heart beating, yet he was conscious of a certain dullness in Mrs. Sairson's manner. Why did she not want him to stay? Why was Nest so delighted to hear that her father was not coming? What was the cloud of sorrow hanging over Angela? With all its beauty and refinement and evidence of wealth, the Grange was a home of tears. So far the blight seemed to have passed over Nest's very head, but it might not be for long. It should not come at all so far as he could help, Cecil determined.

"Are you sure it is convenient?" he asked.

"Oh, I hope you don't imagine that you are in the way!" Mrs. Sairson cried. "It is a great pleasure to myself and the girls to see anybody in these days. I mean somebody.. .. You follow me, I know. I will telegraph to my husband that you are staying till Monday."

She faded from the hall as gently as she had entered, leaving a subtle sense of constraint behind.

"Your conscience troubles you," Nest smiled. "You think that perhaps you ought not to stay."

"I'm sure that I want to," Cecil replied. "But your mother—"

"Would rather you didn't? I don't really know. I am puzzled at things at times. This is a most extraordinary household. Mother is most kind and hospitable, and would be very miserable if you did not remain. There's a skeleton in every cupboard, they say; and if I blunder upon the cupboard that contains our family skeleton I shall burn it. As to my father, I am glad he is not coming. Oh! I know all about duty to one's parents. But we have never hit it together, and never shall. The longer he stays away from here the better I like him. We ought to have a real good time between now and Monday. I hope you are going to have the drawing-room in cream and gold."

"The drawing-room of the Dower House will be as you please," Cecil said. "If you like we will spend the whole of the next few days in planning it out. Only I must have a say about the dining-room and the library. I want you to scheme out the other rooms exactly as you please. You know why, Nest!"

The girl flushed and trembled, and laughed unsteadily.

"It would be delightful," she whispered. "Every girl worthy of the name loves the planning of a home. I have in my room a most delightful book with colored plates, designed by a French artist. There are plans for a house just like yours. May I fetch it for you?"

Cecil begged her to bring the volume, and she returned with it in a few minutes. Nest drew up a chair and opened the book. Cecil sat so close to her that he could catch the fragrance of her hair, could feel the warmth of her slender young body. She laid her hand upon his shoulder and he did not move.

"Now, what do you think of this?" she asked. "I should like a drawing-room like that, and a morning-room like the one on the next page. And that doesn't seem a bad scheme for a hall. Oh, Mr. Lugard, I do hope you can afford to indulge in such expenditure."

"The money is all right," Cecil said grimly. "Have no fear on that score. I am going to adopt your suggestion as to everything. I want you to feel that it is all your own."

"Only it must be a secret from the future Mrs. Lugard," Nest laughed. "It would never do for her to feel that somebody else had been consulted."

"She would not be jealous," Cecil said. "My dear Nest, don't you know why I have asked you to do this for me? Don't you know that I wanted you to feel that nothing had been done without your consent? Because I hope—it is my fervent desire—that the Dower House will be—not mine, but ours."

The red and pink flamed in the girl's cheek again. Her eyes were moist and blurred, so that the colors on the diagrams were misty. A new happiness filled her heart, and she was conscious of a sense of pride that she had never experienced before. She knew that his love was dear to her. She felt herself drawn towards him with a tender, lingering pressure.

"You are going to share it with me, darling?"

Nest looked up quickly. The glad eyes in her crimson face brimmed with happy tears. "You really and truly mean that?" she whispered.

"Of course, I mean it. My dear, you know I mean it. I believe you know that I loved you from the very first day we met. I did not tell you so at Berne, because I was not in the position to ask you to be my wife. What do you say, darling?"

Nest lifted her face and kissed him.

"What is there to say?" she asked, "except that I am the happiest girl in the world. I knew all along that you cared for me, and I understood, too, why you could not ask me to be your wife. It was very fine and very noble of you, Cecil, but it vexed me very much, because I did not care how poor you were; I did not care about anything so long as you loved me. I would have shared a cottage with you. I believe I would have married anybody to get away from a hateful life like this."

"My dearest girl," Lugard protested "surely you don't mean—"

"That I could ever think of anybody else after you," Nest sobbed. "Oh, no, no! There never was anybody else, dear. But a cloud hangs over the house and over our lives, and my father has something to do with our wretchedness. At one time Angela was as happy as I am. Her future promised to be blissful, but you know what happened. What had she done that her life should be blighted in that way? Why was she to blame? My father could have stopped the trouble had he liked. I overheard part of a conversation between my mother and him. There was something to do with money and blood and tears at the bottom of it. Cecil, you won't mind? If there is anything wrong you won't hurt me in that way?"

The tears were drenching the roses of her cheeks; her eyes were passionate and pleading. Cecil caught her to him hard and kissed her fondly, and a sunny smile broke through the tears.

"I expected you would say that," she whispered. "Cecil, let this be our secret for a little longer. I don't want even my mother to know of the engagement yet, I don't want her to cry and weep over me and prophesy evil; I don't want to flaunt my happiness before Angela. Let the secret remain."

"It shall remain as long as you like, dear," said Cecil. "I'll try to be patient. Meanwhile, we'll go on furnishing the Dower House as if we were doing it for its own sake."

Lugard sat and thought it out long after the family had retired and the house was still. He was not in the least inclined for bed. He preferred to sit up in the library, where he had been provided with cigars and cigarettes, and the other creature comforts men like. Many matters he wanted to ponder in peace and quiet.

Everything seemed to be going his way. He was rich and prosperous, had good health, and the heart of the dearest girl in the world was his. All he had asked Providence for had been granted. Yet there was something strange here, some deep-seated sorrow he had to fathom. Whatever it was, he could not see how it could possibly touch the girls. Even if the father were a convicted thief, they were none the worse. It was not like Jack Barr to throw a girl over for the sins of another, even if that other were her father. Nevertheless, Cecil felt uncomfortable as he thought of it.

He came out of the sea of speculation with a shock. Surely, he heard somebody moving about in the hall. He had promised to fasten one of the drawing-room windows, and had forgotten to do it. If there were a midnight marauder in the hall he had entered the house by that means. Cecil slipped off his shoes and crept into the hall. As he did so a figure loomed out of the darkness and gripped him by the throat. It was so quick, so utterly unexpected, that Cecil staggered back. He had some difficulty in keeping on his feet. Then his nerve returned to him, and he fought grimly and silently for the mastery. A little later the intruder was dragged into the library and flung to the floor.

"If you stir an inch," Lugard said sternly. "I'll break your neck. Try that again and I shall hand you over to the police. What are you?—Good God, it's Jack Barr!"

The man rose slowly from the floor, furious of look, white of face, dirty, dishevelled, with clothes that were little better than rags.

"Yes," he said heavily, "all that is left of your old friend, Jack Barr!"

CHAPTER V

A HUMAN DOCUMENT

As he stood in the blinding blaze of the electric light, the derelict glanced almost defiantly at Lugard. He strangled a sob in his throat. Cecil could see that his chest was heaving under the stress of powers and emotion, but there was no longer any passion in his eyes. For a minute or two the men stared at one another.

"We are safe from interruption?" the intruder asked.

"So far as I know, yes," Cecil responded. "I am more or less a stranger here, but I believe that everybody has gone to bed. But, for God's sake, Barr, be calm and don't look so forlorn. Do you suppose I am going to hand you over to justice?'"

The man shrugged his shoulders. He appeared to be utterly indifferent on that score.

"It doesn't matter," he said. "It would perhaps be doing me a kindness. What a queer, merciless world it is! Fancy meeting you here, of all people!"

"You know something of the house, then?"

"Of course, I do. I had the run of it at one time. I was by way of being an honored guest, Cecil. How easily the old name slips out. All the same, I beg your pardon. I have forfeited all right to speak to you in that familiar way."

A great wave of pity swept over Cecil Lugard.

"Why not?" he asked. "We were Damon and Pythias at one time. You were my greatest chum at school. I should never have got in the first class had it not been for you. At Oxford I shone in your reflected glory. I had the run of your cheque-book—"

"And you saved my life," Barr interrupted. "Those were brave days, Cecil."

"Ah, they were," Lugard said hurriedly. "But time is precious and the past has fled. What are you doing here at this time of night? Why have you come? Why are you dressed like a tramp?"

"Because I am a tramp," Barr said bitterly. "Because I have lost everything. The last time I saw you I said that I was going West. It was not true. I had had a terrible disappointment; I had ruined my life; I wanted to drop my old acquaintances. There was a task I had to do, and I set out to accomplish it. At the end of the year I was ruined. The scoundrel I meant to break was too cunning for me. He broke me instead. To keep up my courage I took to drink, and gradually became what I am. Drink was bad enough, but there was worse to come! Drugs! There are times when I am absolutely mad. Then I am dangerous. That is why the fellow is afraid of me. If he had been here to-night I should have killed him."

There was a brooding light in Barr's eyes as he spoke. He seemed to be communing more with himself than talking to Lugard. The latter started as a light dawned upon him.

"You expected to meet the man here."

Barr looked up as if he failed to catch the drift of the question.

"Whom else?" he asked. "It would have been too dangerous a job for London."

Lugard saw quite clearly now. The madman was after John Sairson. There was no longer room for any possible doubt. Here was another tangle in the mystery that had wrapped itself about the Grange. What had John Sairson done to arouse the bitter hatred in Barr's breast? What abominable crime had he committed? Cecil was conscious of impending evil. What the evil was Mrs. Sairson seemed to know, and perhaps Angela knew as well. The only one at the Grange actually in the dark was Nest. Well, if Cecil could help it, she was not going to suffer.

"What wrong has John Sairson done you?" he asked pointedly.

A smile trembled on Barr's lips. He was quick to see that he might go too far and give himself away. He knew nothing of Lugard's present movements and his presence was wholly unexpected.

"I am not aware that I mentioned Sairson's name," he said. "Anyway it is no business of yours."

"I am not so sure of that," Cecil retaliated. "Clearly it is my duty to detain you and hand you over to the police. From a strictly legal standpoint, friendship should not count. Tacitly you admit that you have come here in the dead of night to do the master of the house a mischief. That he is not here makes very little difference to the fact. As a guest—"

"Which I don't quite understand," Barr interrupted. "What are you doing at Marlton Grange?"

"I am John Sairson's guest. I came to look at the Dower House. Perhaps you—"

"Precisely; I intended to buy it at once, and had practically made all arrangements to do so. I, too, had my dreams of happiness at one time. Strange that you, of all people in the world, should build up your foundation on the ruin of my life. Will history repeat itself? Has that pretty child Nest grown up as sweet and beautiful as her sister Angela? As I see she has!"

For Cecil had flushed and started. Barr's face softened strangely.

"You can tell me if you like," he said. "There was a time when we had no secrets from each other. We used to discuss our youthful follies together. There was the girl in the fur toque—the one with the humming-bird in the front of it—and the girl who quoted Browning!"

"I hope to marry Nest Sairson," Cecil said with some dignity. "I met her some time ago at Berne. I could not ask her then because I had no money. When I came into my fortune I began to look for a comfortable house. My idea was to settle down in the neighborhood where my mother's people came from. By the merest accident I heard of the Dower House. You can imagine my astonishment when I got here."

"Nest always promised to be a beautiful woman," Barr said thoughtfully.

"She is beautiful," Cecil replied. "But that is only one of her charms. She is the most delightful girl in the world, and her manner is absolutely charming; in short, she in unspotted from the world. We hope to take up our residence at the Dower House."

"And you regard yourself as the most fortunate of men," said Barr gravely. "So I deemed myself at one time. There was no girl in the world like Angela. When I found that she cared for me I asked Fate for nothing better. I had money, a good position, a clean record, and, though I say it myself, was the husband that a good mother asks God for on her knees for her child. Ah! and she is a good mother, Cecil. When I told her, it might have been a dagger that I had plunged in her heart instead. Angela might have been a lamb led for the sacrifice. It was a house of sighs and tears, and I was puzzled and bewildered. My first idea was that there was insanity in the family—but it was worse than that."

The last words fell from Barr's lips in a hoarse whisper, and struck a cold chill in Cecil's heart.

"You are not alluding to consumption or cancer?"

"My dear fellow, I am not alluding to any physical or mental affliction at all," Barr said. "There are worse troubles than those, my friend, as you will discover in time."

"An illegal marriage? Or no marriage at all?"

"So far as I know, the Sairsons are man and wife. If it were otherwise I cannot imagine how Mrs. Sairson can remain under the roof. You will find that out for yourself."

"Then you will tell me nothing?"

"Not a word. When you discover everything, you will act for yourself. You love that little girl, and she loves you; it is not for a third person to interfere. You may be so infatuated that nothing matters. And I may kill John Sairson. That's what I came here to do to-night."

In spite of his noted courage, Lugard shuddered. The calmly-spoken words were full of menace. It was clear that Barr meant every word that he uttered. The sense of wrong was deep-seated. It was matter for congratulation that John Sairson was far away.

"Have you any money?"

"Only a few coppers," Barr answered. "I have not even my return ticket to London. When I started on my mission, it did not seem to me to be needed. If you will ask Sairson to come this way—"

"But he is not in the house. He is in London, and has telegraphed that he has been detained over the weekend. For your sake, as well as his, I am glad. I want to help you if I can, Jack; I want to set you on your legs again. Let me give you some money. Go to some respectable hotel and stay there for a day or two. I'll come and see you on Monday if you will send me your address. What do you say?"

Barr said nothing. He stood smiling dreamily, the ferocious gleam no longer in his eye. He seemed like a man utterly overpowered with a desire to sleep. He staggered to and fro as if physically exhausted, but with an effort pulled himself together.

"Perhaps you are right," he said. "I have had no sleep for nights. I shall be able to find a shake-down not far off. I know the neighborhood well. The happiest months of my life were spent here. You wouldn't think it to look at the wreck who stands before you, Cecil."

Lugard took some gold coins from his sovereign purse and passed them to Barr. He dropped them into his pocket without so much as a word of thanks. He turned from the elegance and luxury, the pictures and the gleaming lights, and strolled by Cecil's side to the solitude and darkness of the garden. The fresh air revived him instantly, and he walked with the ease of a man who knew where he was and what he was doing. Pausing presently, he drew a deep breath as he looked up at the silent powder of stars overhead.

"You're a good fellow, Cecil," he said, "and you deserve a better fate. It isn't for me to interfere, and I'm not going to; but if you consulted your own happiness, and the happiness of that little girl, you would leave the house with me now, and never come back. To let them think the worst of you would, in the long run, be the greatest kindness. I don't suppose I shall take the same view in the morning, but that is my opinion now while the glamor of the morphia is upon me. I'll let you know my address, and you can call and see me. Good-night!"

Without waiting for another word, Barr strode off down the drive and vanished in the darkness. For a long time Lugard stood looking after him. It was easier to think with the cool breath of the night breeze on his temples. He felt that the atmosphere of the house was almost stifling and confined. The house of all these mysteries oppressed him. Barr knew the secret and yet he had declined to reveal it. What could be worse than the things he had mentioned? Yet how could they possibly affect Nest and himself?

"But why should I care?" he concluded. "If disgrace or dishonor attach to the family of Sairson, it is the poor girl's misfortune, not her fault. Let all the world know if it likes—I shall love her all the more for that. And when the time comes—"

Cecil paused, and the distant humming of a car struck his ear. Far down the drive he could see the cold blue flash of a pair of lamps, growing gradually larger as they neared the house. Who could it be at this time of night? Perhaps Sairson had managed to get away late and had come down from town in his motor. As the car came along the gleam of the lamp picked out the occupant, as limelight illuminates an actor on the stage. Barr saw him as the car passed, and a queer dry chuckle rattled in his throat.

"Sairson!" he said hoarsely. "Sairson has arrived, after all. There's luck in store yet!"

He turned back suddenly and began to run eagerly in the direction of the house.

CHAPTER VI

THE MONEY GOD

John Sairson sat brooding in his club for the best part of an hour after the receipt of Gosway's message. All his life he had been accustomed to his own way. He had fought for it as a child; he had schemed for it in his early manhood. Now he was strong enough to take it ruthlessly and unfalteringly without regard to the feelings of others. He laughed to himself as he saw the trouble and misery he left behind him.

The man was a bully to the finger-tips, he boasted of his strength and courage. Yet in his heart of hearts he was a coward—and he knew it. He was afraid—physically afraid—and the consciousness of it galled him. He was afraid of a poor broken-down wretch on the verge of starvation. He told himself a score of times he would not stand any more of this nonsense—he would go down to Marlton Grange as if nothing had happened. Yet he lingered in his easy-chair, speaking to nobody, and hiding his gloomy face behind an evening paper.

Gosway came to him presently with an urgent message. He was in the waiting-room; he had not sent in his own name, but one that he always used in emergencies. Sairson strode into the waiting-room, sulky and angry. Here was something to vent his ill-humor on.

"What did you mean by coming here?" he asked. "Running the risk of being recognised, and—"

"As you please," said Gosway. "I wasn't particularly anxious to come. I knew I should find you here."

"How did you know that? I said I was going to Marlton."

"Yes, you said so. But I was sure you wouldn't after my message."

Sairson choked a savage expletive and demanded Gosway's business curtly.

"Well, its about Lord Laurisdale," the latter explained. "He owes John Blaydon and Co. over ten thousand pounds. This you are already aware of. As you probably expected, it is impossible for his lordship to meet these bills. He called and told me as much. He wants them renewed. I said, of course, that such a thing was out of the question. As agreed, I recommended him to see you in person and try to negotiate a loan. He consented, but returned to learn where he could find you without the slightest delay. You know his impatient way?"

"You asked him what you had to do with it?"

"Oh! I played the solemn farce in the usual way. But I promised to find out and let him know at the theatre. If the money is not forthcoming to-morrow, the theatre must close. You had better go down to the Cosmos and see his lordship."

A peculiar smile passed over Sairson's face. Something evidently had pleased him. But that cold evil smile boded little good to anybody else.

"Excellent, Gosway, excellent!" he said. "You have done very well indeed. Upon my word, I have a great mind to see his lordship. As a near neighbor of mine at Marlton it would look well. Lady Laurisdale has never called upon any people."

Gosway broke into a chuckle, and then coughed discreetly. The dull red flashed into Sairson's face. He caught his lip with his strong yellow teeth.

"Never called upon us," he went on doggedly: "but, they shall. 'Phone to Laurisdale at the Cosmos and say you have found me. Tell him I shall be passing the theatre within an hour or so, and that I will look in."

Sairson turned on his heel abruptly and made his way back to the smoking-room. He dined early, and immediately afterwards called a taxi and drove to the Cosmos. The production of his card opened the manager's room to him at once. He found a tall young man awaiting him—a young man with shining hair parted in the middle, with a weak, wilful, effeminate face, and of languid manner. A glass screwed in the left eye added to the supercilious air that Lord Laurisdale effected. He looked exactly what he was-a spoilt, handsome youth who had been allowed to have his own way all his life and was now suffering from the consequences. But despite his air of ease and assurance, Sairson could see that the hand holding the Egyptian cigarette shook, and the thin lips were none too steady.

"Upon my word this is awfully good of you," Laurisdale said. "Really friendly, what? Can't for the life of me remember who the Johnnie was who suggested that I should come to you."

Sairson bowed and smiled. He could have told Lord Laurisdale perfectly well had he chosen to do so.

"Does it in the least matter?" he asked. "If we are to do business together, my lord, it will pay you to be quite candid with me. Understand, we are not money-lenders, though our business is largely financial. Do I understand that Blaydon is pressing you for money?"

"The beast is persecuting my life out," Laurisdale cried. "Ten thousand pounds due on Tuesday, and not a bob to pay it with. Fellow won't renew, either. Awful fix for me, what? And the beastly theatre to be kept going as well! If you care to take up those bills.. .."

Laurisdale looked almost timidly at Sairson. The latter appeared to be deep in calculation.

"This is not a matter we can settle in ten minutes," he said. "I take it you would not be out of the wood unless you could persuade Blaydon to renew your bills. If he does, he would certainly need, say, a couple of thousand on account and make it a stipulation that you renew for fifteen thousand. And I daresay you want a thousand or two for the theatre."

"Four at the very least," his lordship said drearily. "Now, look here, Sairson, would you find me ten thousand and take over Blaydon's bills?"

"My dear Lord Laurisdale, the thing is impossible!" Sairson exclaimed. "We are not money-lenders, as I told you, but financial agents. Nor is Blaydon by any means the rich man you take him to be. I happen to know that. One gets to hear these things in the city. Blaydon has had losses. He is cramped for money in connection with a speculation that involves intricate law business. It's all bound to come right in the end, but meanwhile it keeps him short. Between ourselves I have helped Blaydon. At the present moment those bills of yours are in my safe at Marlton Grange. Blaydon called there to see me, and I lent him the money on the spot. Now what do you think of that for a coincidence?"

"God bless my soul!" Laurisdale gasped. "Regular dispensation of Providence, what!"

"It does seem like it," Sairson said thoughtfully. "I have no doubt that the matter can be arranged. I daresay I can find you the additional cash. But it can't be done on the spur of the moment. We must go into ways and means and the question of security is important. Why not come down to Marlton Grange this evening? I have a car in town. If we started now we would get to Marlton by half-past 12 or 1."

Laurisdale laughed at the suggestion. It was Friday night, and salaries were due on the morrow at noon, and there was small chance of the money's being forthcoming otherwise.

"Your presence here will make little or no difference," Sairson urged. "By remaining, you will be no better off, no nearer a settlement so far as salaries are concerned. If we come to an arrangement, I can wire my people in the morning to send a thousand pounds to your manager."

Lord Laurisdale gave a sigh of relief. He was thinking of the expensive and wilful beauty, the leading lady, who was ruining him by her waywardness and extravagance. If he failed her now, she would never look upon him again. It was all very well to despise this man Sairson, to look upon him as a vulgar-minded snob, but just now he appeared in the light of Laurisdale's guardian angel. He was giving no heed to the poor, neglected wife eating her heart out in solitude at Laurisdale Castle—the young and beautiful woman whose life had once held such promise of happiness.

"By Jove, I'll come," he exclaimed. "I'll leave a note for Sadie Carton, explaining matters. I daresay you can put me up for the night. I will manage to take a day at the castle somehow to-morrow. Haven't been near the place for a month. Model sort of husband, what?"

Sairson's eyes gleamed strangely.

"It seems a pity," he said. "It's about your property there that I want to come to a deal with you. I expect that is where my security lies. But it must be very lonely for Lady Laurisdale. You had better arrange to stay with me till Monday, seeing that we have so much to talk about, and get her ladyship to come over for the day to-morrow. She can lunch and dine with us. In circumstances like this, there is no need to stand on ceremony."

The glass dropped from Laurisdale's eyes in sheer astonishment. His wife call on these people! He could not imagine himself even suggesting such a thing. Blanche Laurisdale was both charming and good-natured, but she had the pride of her race. The curate's wife and her untidy family were always welcome at the castle, but the Sairsons! Laurisdale was not an imaginative man, but he could conjure up the amused scorn on his wife's face should he venture on the preposterous scheme. Every bit of what was passing through his mind was clear as noonday to Sairson.

"My wife is a lady," he said. "She was a Belham. My daughter takes after her. As a matter of fact, Lady Laurisdale should have called on them long ago. It is all in your hands, my lord. I am not the man to go out of my way to be friendly unless I see some return for my investment. But perhaps you may have another source of capital."

"Oh, I'll do what I can," Laurisdale said between his teeth. "Hadn't you better telephone for your car while I write my note?"

With an intense feeling of triumph in his heart Sairson telephoned for his car. They set off in a few minutes, but it was nearly 1 o'clock in the morning before they pulled up at the portico of Marlton Grange. Laurisdale stood on the step whilst Sairson took the car round to the stables. He was thinking of nothing but the triumph of the evening, of the scheme he had planned so long, so cunningly. So far as he could see, everything was plain sailing. He had forgotten about his own danger. With a light heart he conducted Laurisdale into the dining-room.

As he did so a shadow crossed the hall and stood by the door in a listening attitude. Laurisdale was heard protesting that he needed nothing beyond a whisky and soda. The listening figure crouched lower—

Somebody was coming down the stairs—a figure in white with a mass of hair on her shoulders. The face was deadly pale, the lips trembled. She touched the crouching figure with a shaking hand.

"Don't speak!" she whispered. "Don't speak, but follow me and be silent."

"Angela!" the other murmured. "Angela! This is a night of dreams, a night of dreams!"

CHAPTER VII

THE WHEEL WITHIN THE WHEEL

To John Sairson, Philip Gosway was no more than a useful tool who was badly paid for a more than adequate service. It was necessary to have a man of good address and appearance, and Gosway fulfilled those requirements. He had fallen low in the world, but retained a measure of self-respect, and his clothes were neat if well worn. In some strange way he contrived to throw off the suggestion of the city once he turned his face homeward, in Sairson's presence he was usually humble, not to say meek, and gave no impression of being still something of an athlete. By the time he had crossed London Bridge his shoulders squared and his step became more elastic. Sairson imagined Gosway as the type of broken-down fellow who loiters about saloon bars when funds permitted. As a matter of fact it was years since Gosway had tasted intoxicants. The great tragedy of his life had come that way, and there had been a time when Philip Gosway swore he would never touch the dread poison again.

Of his inner life John Sairson knew nothing. He had never heard of the quaint cottage tucked away in the quadrangle behind St. Cedric's Church on the other side of the water. He could not have imagined Gosway fresh and gleaming from his bath, and the subsequent vigorous dumb-bell exercise, as he came whistling gaily down to breakfast on the same Saturday morning on which the trap was baited for Lord Laurisdale. The little sitting-room with the mullioned windows and fine stained glass had once formed part of a monk's refectory, the old oak furniture of the later Middle Ages still remained. Outside was a grass forecourt with a pair of lime trees, where the pigeons came for food from Sybil Gosway's own hand. Here was the secret of Philip Gosway's tardy repentance, the restraining force that had prevented him at the crisis of his life from going headlong to perdition.

Sybil made a pretty figure as she stood there in her white cotton dress, while grey and brown wings fluttered about the shining masses of her hair. She was dainty and sweet enough to have come out of one of Marcus Stone's pictures, the typical daughter of the squire. There was no hint of meanness about her, though she lived amongst poor folk and helped to get her own living with her typewriter. Friends in the common acceptance of the term she had none; she was happy in her daily toil and the company of her father and her books and music in the evenings. Who the Gosways were and whence they came she did not know; she accepted the mystery—if any there were—of her position without demur.

Gosway's eyes lighted tenderly as he contemplated the picture through the curved frame of the doorway. The oval table was laid out for breakfast, but the kettle on the open hearth was not boiling yet, and Gosway had a few moments for other matters. By the side of his plate lay one letter—a letter on thick grey paper, with a monogram and coronet on the back. Gosway hesitated just a moment with a glance at Sybil before he picked up the letter and opened it. The printed heading conveyed the fact that the missive came from Laurisdale Castle.

"Dear Phil," the letter ran, "Quite by chance I happened to see Sybil in Bond-street last week. I couldn't stop because I was motoring with Patricia. It struck me that the child looked pale and run down—in need of a change, in fact. Send her to me directly you get this, and on the off chance I'll meet the 3.40 at Sheringham. Don't say 'No,' Phil; you can't imagine how lonely I am. Let me have Sybil for a fortnight, at any rate. We shall have the place to ourselves as Laurisdale is not here. Don't trouble to wire, but send Sybil on here.

'Yours affectionately,

"Blanche Laurisdale."

Very thoughtfully Gosway tore the letter into strips and tossed them on the fire. He would be terribly lonely without Sybil but, on the other hand, the child would be the better for the change. These occasional visits to Laurisdale Castle were the one bright spot in her life. She was puzzled to know how they had come about; possibly the Gosways might have been friends of the castle people in the past— but as to this Sybil asked no questions. She had an instinctive feeling that they would be wasted.

She emptied the last scrap from the basket and came cheerfully into the house. Bidding her father a cheerful good-morning she set about making the tea. A little maid-of-all-work would come in presently and tidy up. Meanwhile the toast was made, the eggs were boiled, and breakfast stood confessed.

"Are you going to leave at 1 o'clock to-day, daddy?" Sybil asked.

"I'm afraid not," Gosway said. "The company is very busy just now. My services are wanted."

Gosway always spoke of his employer as the "company." In a way they were supposed to be connected with shipping. Sybil's sunny face cleared; she had planned a long Saturday afternoon in the country. It was not difficult for Gosway to read what was passing in the girl's mind.

"I'm rather glad," he said. "We are so busy now that I shall be late every night for the next fortnight or so. It means a good deal of extra money, of course, which is a consideration. But, seeing that you will not be here, I shall welcome the overtime."

"What do you mean by that cryptic remark?"

"Oh! didn't I tell you? How careless of me! But you saw the letter from Blanche this morning—and—and—"

Sybil pretended not to hear. It was by no means the first time that her father had incautiously spoken of Lady Laurisdale as Blanche. All this only added piquancy to the mystery.

"I saw that you had a letter from Lady Laurisdale," the girl said demurely.

"Yes, yes, to be sure. She is alone at Laurisdale, and wants you to stay with her for a fortnight. She will meet the 3.40 at Sheringham if you can get away in time. You can easily manage that, or course. This has fallen out very conveniently, as I may have to sleep at the office one or two nights."

Sybil kissed her father lovingly. There was a perfect understanding between the two. Her father would miss her greatly, but she loved him all the more that he should speak so cheerfully. And the prospect was tempting. Laurisdale Castle would be lovely in this beautiful weather, and she drew in a deep breath of delight as she thought of the wide blue of the sea and the sunshine on the woods. Lady Laurisdale was something of a goddess in her eyes. If it could only be managed!

"You surprise me," she said. "Oh, dad! I should like to go! I have saved up a pound or two on the off-chance that we could go away together before long."

"Oh! the money is all right," Gosway said, with a careless gesture. "At any rate you can have four pounds. I shall have more before long. Now get your traps together whilst I write a letter or two."

Sybil lingered, woman-like, to ask a few questions. She would have liked to know what was the connection between her father and the mistress of Laurisdale Castle.

"How did you first meet Lady Laurisdale?"

"Haven't I told you?" Gosway asked innocently. "She came to me on business. There is a slight connection between the Gosways and her family; not the kind of thing one talks about, of course, because in our position it would be snobbish. You see, when I was in the service—good gracious! it's 9 o'clock. Run away and pack. With a bit of luck I may be able to come as far as Liverpool-street and see you off."

Sybil went her way smilingly. Times out of number her father had passed her questions in this way. Still, there was a certain flavor of romance about it that was delightful. It was nice to think that there was some real connection with the good people.

With a certain pleasure Gosway took out sovereigns from the little hoard that he kept locked in a despatch-box and threw them carelessly over to Sybil. How handsome and upright she looked!

How fond the company must be of him! Sybil thought, as she watched him out of sight. Perhaps they would take him into partnership some day and make things easier for him. Her heart was very bright and joyous as she packed her trunk, placing in it the one precious evening dress she wore when her father suggested a night at the theatre. There were times when tickets came to Gosway—permits from needy actors seeking assistance, or from quondam acquaintances, who tossed them to him contemptuously. But he pocketed his pride for Sybil's sake and the pleasure these treats gave her.

"I wonder what she would say if she knew," Gosway asked himself as he turned cityward. "Some day or another she will have to know. Well, I'll keep the truth from her as long as possible. It's good for a man's self-respect to know one person in the world who believes in him. Blanche will look after the little girl if anything happens to me—provided Laurisdale has not got through everything first. I wonder what Sairson would say if he knew! What a strange world it is!"

Gosway saw Sybil off, all smiles and laughter, and returned to his drudgery. It was a bad day for him, a day of degradation, and his very soul recoiled from it before the work was done. He was sick and tired of the trickery and deceit. Juggle with his conscience as he might, he could not absolutely disassociate himself from it. But for Sybil he would have thrown it up long ago.

He was finished with Sairson's business at last, and he was at liberty to turn his face homewards. It would be lonely enough without Sybil but he had his books and the quietness of the tiny cottage was reposeful. It seemed to him that he had managed to avert the danger so far as Sairson was concerned, and at any rate he would be free till Monday morning. A long tramp in the country on the morrow would do him good.

As he turned to cross London Bridge, a figure accosted him. A tall, hungry-looking man with a ragged moustache and beard barred his way. Despite the man's shabby and gaunt appearance and air of dissipation, there was something about him that spoke of better days.

"Well, what is it, Molliss?" Gosway asked. "Won't it keep till Monday? I've had a day that has sickened me of the whole dirty business. Who is the victim this time?"

"Oh! it's not the Captain," the man called Molliss said huskily. "It's about Barr."

"Barr has gone home. There is no occasion for Mr.—, well, for anybody to fear poor Barr for the present. I happen to know that he has only a few pence in his pocket. But for that Vanburg I might have been compelled to take other steps. If you get any kitchen gossip, for heaven's sake postpone it till Monday morning."

A queer, unsteady laugh came from the lips of the other man.

"Fancy you and me talking like this!" he said. "Do you remember the last night at Sandhurst, and how we talked of what we were going to do? And, my God, what we have done? Look at me and think of me as I used to be! You've managed to hold on to the skirt of respectability, but as for me! Lend me a shilling, Phil; I've not had a meal to-day."

"What is it you really want?" Gosway asked, as he passed over the coin.

"Well, as to that Barr," the other proceeded. "Please forget what I said just now, Mr. Gosway. I was not myself for a moment. It's men like Blaydon who make us what we are. Well, to go on, I made a mistake about Barr. He got money from somewhere. I was at Liverpool-street shadowing that Russian Count you told me to keep my eye on, and I saw Barr take a ticket for Cromer by the express. I didn't like the look of him at all. I was going to drop you a postcard."

A minute or two later and Gosway retraced his footsteps. Mentally he was counting up his money. He had just enough to procure what his humble wants called for.

"I'll go down by the last train," he said. "I must. If I don't, murder will be done. What a world it is! oh, what a strange world it is!"

CHAPTER VIII

A STATELY HOME OF ENGLAND

For centuries past the watch-towers of Laurisdale Castle had been a beacon light for the fishermen far out at sea. It was one of the family traditions that the lights should always be kept burning, and they flame to this day. The castle had figured largely in history; in every great event from the time of the Roses a Laurisdale had taken part. There had been a period when the estate extended for miles along the coast and people had spoken of its lord with bated breath and whispering humbleness. The grand old castle still stood in all its beauty and majesty of outline; here were the hanging wood and the fine old garden, the glass-houses and the park, where the deer rambled knee-deep in the bracken.

But the estate was sadly curtailed now, and the coverts were empty, for two generations of Laurisdale had been busy in an attempt to dissipate a magnificent property. The present head of the family hardly ever came there—he was too absorbed in the allurements of London and the delights of a theatre of his own. For a year or so after his marriage the tenants saw a good deal of him, but of late he had absented himself entirely, though Lady Laurisdale seemed devoted to the place. She seemed to care nothing for the London season, but, as a matter of fact, was hard to it to keep matters going. The idea of a house in town was out of the question.

Blanche Laurisdale's marriage had been a sad disappointment to her. There had been signs at one time that her husband might settle down and become a useful member of society. He was not then the effeminate creature he had since become. There was no quarrel, merely a drifting apart until the separation was more or less complete. To one of Lady Laurisdale's proud, sensitive, nature, the disappointment was very keen. Not that she showed the slightest trace of it to the outer world. She even spoke of his lordship's follies and extravagances with a smile, and then a shrug of the shoulders. Notwithstanding, it was painful to realise that the meretricious attractions of Sadie Carton counted for more than her own mental and other qualities. Perhaps to a certain extent the fault had been her own, but the result was none the less keen.

Lady Laurisdale paid no calls and received none. With all her reserve she was popular with the tenants and the smallest child on the estate was not afraid of her. When she liked to remove the mask and show her real self she could win the love of anybody and, as we have seen, to Sybil Gosway she was little less than a goddess. But then Sybil possessed the gift of sympathy, that innate feeling that conveys rather than speaks of its sincerity.

Sybil stepped lightly from the carriage and indicated to a porter who touched his hat respectfully which were her belongings. Outside the station gates Lady Laurisdale was holding a pair of greys in a firm grip. The fair, haughty face broke into a smile, and the blue eyes grew tender.

"My dear child, I am delighted to see you," she said. "I got so tired of my own company that I wrote to Phil—I mean your father—last night, and asked him to despatch you here instanter. You are not to thank me, as I see you are about to do. It was sheer selfishness on my part."

Sybil kissed her hostess affectionately.

"It was lovely of you," she whispered. "I was hoping that you would write. Only this morning when feeding the pigeons I wished you would write. It was such a lovely morning, and dad said he didn't mind me being out of the way, as he would be so busy for a fortnight. When I went to bed last night I never even dreamt of this! I was envying you the woods and the sea. I was indeed, Lady Laurisdale."

A smile flickered over Lady Laurisdale's face, but Sybil could know nothing of the bitterness that underlay it.

"We are given to that kind of thing," she said. "I wonder how many people would change places with me? And how many of them would be glad to change back again? No. I am not going to let you drive the greys—at least not till you have been here a few days. I wish I could persuade your father to let me have you altogether—at least, as long as it lasts."

The last words were spoken in a fierce whisper, but Sybil's quick ear caught them. She laid her hand on Blanche Laurisdale's arm.

"If there were no daddy, I should love it," she said, "perhaps some day you will tell me why you are so kind to me, and what is the connection between us and a good lady like the Countess of Laurisdale. Oh! you need to be stuffed up in London for months to appreciate the beauty of the country. Fancy! it is two years since I was last here."

"Is that a reproach to me?" Lady Laurisdale inquired with a smile.

"As if I should dare to! I am sure the fault was not yours. Who has been trimming the shrubbery in front of Marlton Grange? Anyway, it is a great experiment; but I thought the place has been empty since Sir George Lugard died. Has somebody bought the estate?"

Blanche Laurisdale's face grew somewhat cold and haughty.

"Some people called Sairson!" she exclaimed. "They bought the place as it stood, and I'm told they have had the good taste to leave everything as they found it. It is a point in their favor."

Sybil listened, drawing her own conclusions. Evidently the people were not friends of Lady Laurisdale.

"You don't like them, then?"

"My dear child, I really have no feeling either way. Mr. Sairson is a London business man. He is a horrid-looking creature, with a great red face and a manner that suggests the foreman of a gang of navvies. They say he makes his money in all kinds of queer ways—that he ruined poor Sir George. I am bound to say that Mrs. Sairson looks quite different. If she were not the wife of that man I should take her to be a lady. And the girls look quite presentable. I'm really sorry for Angela and Nest Sairson."

"Nest Sairson!" Sybil cried. "Lady Laurisdale, I'm absolutely certain I was at school with her at Lucerne. It is impossible that any other girl could love a man like that. Oh! I am sorry! I am sorry!"

"Sorry you were at school with her?" Lady Laurisdale asked with a laugh.

"I don't mean that," Sybil said with a flush of color in her cheek. "Sorry that you don't like them, I mean. I—I thought, perhaps you might have called."

"My dear child, such a thought never entered my head. They are impossible. If you only saw the man you would have no further doubts on the subject. I am the last person in the world to listen to evil gossip, but one can't close one's ears altogether. Of course, I can't tell you anything definite."

Sybil changed the subject. But she sat pondering the matter during the drive to the castle. Throughout the three years she had been at Lucerne, Nest Sairson had been her great friend. Afterwards they had exchanged a few letters, but gradually the correspondence had dropped. It was very strange that they should come together again in these remarkable circumstances. Sybil had rather helped Nest in the old days, but now the position was reversed. All the same, she would very much like to see Nest again, though she couldn't tell whether there was any possibility of her doing so.

There was the grand old castle at length, the great oaks along the avenue and the carved gateway with the arms of the family and the moss-grown motto beneath. It was strange how Sybil seemed to fit into the picture, to feel that she was born to this kind of thing. There were low ceilings in the dim hall where old armor hung, and dead and gone Laurisdales looked down from the tapestried walls. Dinner was served presently in the cosy, cedar-panelled morning-room, and, for dessert, a profusion of the peaches and grapes for which Laurisdale Castle was famous. By and bye Sybil retired and sank with a contented sigh into comfortable bed, where she lay dreamily wondering.

"What does all this mean?" she murmured. "Who am I, and what sort of folks were my people? Did daddy quarrel with them, or had he done anything—but no! that is impossible. Daddy wouldn't do anything wrong. I wonder if that dear old vicar is still here, and that lovely old organ! I'll go and see to-morrow."

It was very pleasant and peaceful as Sybil made her way across the park to the old Norman Church at the back of Dower House.

Lady Laurisdale had pleaded letters as an excuse for not accompanying Sybil. She had a slight headache, but would take a stroll in the park before luncheon. Indeed it looked so inviting under the trees that she hastened her departure. Very quiet and lonely she thought it, but for that trespasser who was making his way to the back of the house. There was something about him oddly familiar to Blanche Laurisdale.

"Phil!" she cried. "Phillip Gosway! What are you doing here? What has happened?"

Gosway looked round with the ghost of a smile on his lips. His mind had gone back a long way. The haunted look passed from his eyes.

"I am trying to realise what I have lost," he said. "I had to come, Blanche. There was something very serious afoot, but I fancy I have settled that. Sybil has gone to church? She was looking forward to it. In that case she need not know that I have been here—in fact, I would rather she didn't. There is a train back to London this afternoon. I thought I'd have one peep at the house. I should like to see the place where I once passed so many happy hours. If Laurisdale is here—"

"Oh, he isn't," Lady Laurisdale said scornfully. "He has superior attractions elsewhere Phil."

"You mean to say that he did not come home last night?"

Lady Laurisdale answered the question by turning away and walking in the direction of the house. Gosway followed with a strange fear at his heart. He saw the great hall dimly, the dead and gone ancestors seemed to frown at him from the walls. He came out of a kind of dream to the discussion of everyday matters.

"Everything seems just the same," he said. "I can see nothing different."

"Not outwardly, perhaps," Lady Laurisdale answered. "But it is a whited sepulchre, Phil. Nearly everything has gone—all lavished on London and the theatre. I have had to borrow money again and again because I was ashamed to look the local tradesmen in the face."

"You mean that you have been to the Jews!" Phil exclaimed.

"Why not? There was no other way. A few hundreds at first and more later. Now I owe one man over four thousand. Goodness knows how he makes it out. He was so civil at first, but it is a very different story now. Phil, you are in business in London, and understand these things. Have you ever heard of a bloodsucker called John Blaydon?"

Phillip Gosway started. It was like a luminous flash of lightning to a man on the edge of a chasm. A score of things were revealed to him in that moment. He hoped Lady Laurisdale had not noticed the expression of his face. A footman with a note on a salver came in and Blanche Laurisdale was reading it. Her eyes flashed with angry scorn.

"Oh, this is unpardonable," she cried. "Laurisdale is down here. He spent the night, it appears, talking business with that man Sairson, whose people I have carefully avoided. He asks me—commands me, I may say—to sink the social difference, and go over to lunch with these people. Me! He must be mad to suggest such a thing! The most atrocious man, Phil."

Gosway's face glowed a deep red. He was thinking rapidly in that brief space.

"I know the man by name and sight," he said. "I wish that I could speak more freely. I know, too, that Mrs. Sairson was a Belham. I can see the hand of Providence in this thing. Blanche, you once promised me that if I asked you a favor you would grant it."

"Phillip! You will not ask me to do this, to outrage all the proprieties, to be compelled to go to a house the people in which know my feelings. Oh! you wouldn't, you couldn't."

Gosway's face had grown very stern and hard. Yet he was trembling like a man laboring under some great stress of emotion. He laid his hand on Lady Laurisdale's arm.

"The time has come to ask the favor," he said. "Blanche, you will have to go."

"Phillip!" Lady Laurisdale spoke almost piteously. "Phillip, this is cruel!"

"Call it what you like," Gosway replied. "Call it what you like, my dear, for God's sake, go!"

CHAPTER IX

A GENTLEMAN AT HOME

By the time Marlton Grange was reached, Sairson had cast off his gloomy forebodings. After all, what was there to be afraid of? He was not the first man whose life had been threatened by a needy desperado full of imaginary wrongs. Usually people put an end to these worries through the medium of the police, but there were urgent reasons why Sairson could not resort to that method. At any rate, there was nothing to be afraid of for the present. He had a distinct feeling that he was taking a big stride forward. The county might turn their backs on him in contempt, but they would not be less ready to do so when they saw friendly relations established between the Grange and Laurisdale Castle. Laurisdale might be next door to an idiot but socially he was still a power in the land.

It was a source of irritation that his wife and daughters had not managed this long ago. He was absolutely incapable of understanding why they shrank from publicity. Why did they not push themselves as other women did? They had plenty of money to spend and a good house in which to entertain their friends. For their sakes he was taking a hand in the game, and it seemed to him that his wife and daughters should be grateful for his efforts. It would cost him a pretty penny, too. By and bye they would get as far as Cumberledge Royal, where the Duchess of Rochdale held sway, and after that it should be plain sailing.

Therefore Sairson swaggered into the dining-room with a flush of triumph on his coarse red face. The big voice rang out stridently. He was profuse in his offers of hospitality. Would his guest have anything? There was everything that a man could need on the sideboard. Lord Laurisdale had only to give it a name. This was liberty hall, and Laurisdale should do as he liked.

"Help yourself, old fellow!" Sairson cried. "Glad to see you. Here's luck!"'

Laurisdale responded with what heartiness he could. His thin cheeks flushed faintly at the clumsy assumption of familiarity. With endless follies to his account, Laurisdale had his pride, and winced under Sairson's heavy hand. With the glass to his lips and a smile on his face, he was regretting the necessity for this visit. He wondered vaguely whether Sairson realised what a horrible bounder he was. He looked strangely out of place against that background of taste and refinement, a horrible, jarring modern note singularly out of tune.

"You are very good," Laurisdale muttered. "Pleased to be your guest, I'm sure."

"Don't mention it," Sairson replied, as he beamed at the roof. "Pleasure is mine. Only sorry I have not had it before. You need a friend of my sort, my boy. You came to me for advice, and, by God, you shall have it. Why, I could save you thousands. Look at the way they take advantage of you and rob you at the theatre. Oh! I know all about it. Many is the speculation of that kind I have financed, and a precious good thing I have—"

"Sort of Blaydon and Co. yourself, eh?" Laurisdale suggested.

Sairson pulled himself up suddenly.

"Nothing of the sort, my boy, nothing of the sort," he protested. "I am a financier, pure and simple. No bloodsucking of that kind for John Sairson. All the cards on the table, face upwards. If I were a man of that type, do you suppose I'd go out of my way to help you? Perhaps I shall be able to give Lady Laurisdale a leg up, too."

Some old sporting instinct stirred in Laurisdale's heart. It occurred to him that Sairson's fat, red face offered a tempting mark for a clenched fist.

"Hadn't we better leave my wife out of it?" he suggested quietly.

Sairson laughed, as he chewed the end of his cigar.

"As you like it," he said. "But the ladies are terribly extravagant sometimes. At any rate, that is what the little birds whisper in these parts. Even local tradesmen need money at times—can't live on the castle patronage, my boy. When you sink all your cash in the Cosmos, others have to wait, eh? Oh! I know something of the ways of the aristocracy. I'm an honest man, Laurisdale, and—"

The blustering boaster suddenly paused and rose in a listening attitude. He could hear sounds of shuffling feet in the hall, and a whispered tearful protest followed by a mocking laugh. Before he could take a step forward to ascertain the cause of the commotion, the dining-room door was flung suddenly open, and two figures entered. Laurisdale gasped with astonishment. In spite of his familiarity with the stage and its many striking effects, he had never seen anything like this.

A clock on the mantelpiece chimed the hour alike the signal for the rising of the curtain, and here was melodrama palpitating with life. The fine old setting to the scene left nothing to be desired. Here was the actor too—a wild-looking man with a mass of hair hanging on his forehead, a man possessed of a consuming rage that gleamed in his eyes and told of something that seemed to spell murder. His clothes were shabby and untended, his boots trodden down at the heel. Pitifully he saw what trouble and despair had made him.

Here was melodrama hot and strong before Laurisdale's astonished eyes, but there was something still more startling to follow. Pressing closely behind the man was the slim figure of a girl clad in a long white wrap, a mass of shining hair draping her shoulders. The beautiful face was contorted with terror, the dark eyes were full of tears. It was a lovely face, as Laurisdale could not fail to see, a face dainty and refined, and stamped with innate breeding that spoke for itself. What on earth was she doing here? Laurisdale wondered.

He saw Sairson stagger back, white to the lips. It was only for an instant, but that was long enough even to Laurisdale's limited intelligence. Whoever that unsavoury nomad was, Sairson was horribly afraid of him. A moment later and the bully was himself again.

"Angela," he said, "what is the meaning of this? Has all the house suddenly gone mad? Why aren't you in bed at this time of night?"

"I—I came down for something, father," Angela said, "and I found—I found—"

She broke off abruptly and turned her face aside. Father! Laurisdale caught himself repeating the word. Could that beautiful girl of refined features and the stamp of culture be the daughter of John Sairson? The mere suggestion was preposterous. Such things could not happen outside the covers of a novel. And what was so dainty a creature doing with this intruder? Obviously she know him, obviously she was afraid of him. Even Laurisdale could see that Angela was on the stranger's side.

He noticed the red veins in Sairson's forehead knit and tighten, and saw the blazing anger in his bloodshot eyes. Clearly Sairson was aching to seize the intruder by the throat, but just as clearly some sense of fear or of prudence was holding him back.

"Some tramp, I suppose," Sairson said hoarsely, "some blackguard seeking a night's lodging. Angela, go to the telephone and call up the police."

The derelict laughed scathingly.

"The very thing," he said. "That is an excellent suggestion, Mr. Sairson. Angela, summon the police at once. That is very kind of you, Mr. Sairson. You can tell the police my story, and afterwards I will tell them mine. But you dare not do it!"

The last words came with a snarl of contempt. Sairson stood astounded.

"I—I am sorry for you," he stammered. "After all, you were a gentleman once. You may go."

"Oh! may I? That is kindness itself. And I was a gentleman once! What praise from so discriminating a judge as Mr. John Sairson! A gentleman once! Precisely: an officer and a gentleman. Let me introduce Captain Jack Barr, late of the Northern Rifles, to your notice."

Laurisdale started with an involuntary exclamation. Verily, this was a night of surprises. So that battered wretch standing there under the searching rays of the electric light was Jack Barr! One of the best! A fine shot and cricketer, a handy fellow with his fists, and the best long-distance runner of his day at Eton. What was he doing in this amazing household? And why was Sairson afraid of him? Why was that beautiful girl with the shining hair and dewy eyes regarding him so tenderly?

At the sound that came from Laurisdale, Barr turned sharply upon him.

"Oh! I know you," he said. "I'm not so mad that I didn't recognise you directly I came into the room. A dramatic meeting, Laurisdale. Shall I tell you what I came here for to-night? I came to kill that great red rat yonder. Look at him standing there, pretending not to be afraid of me! Why, he'd give ten thousand pounds of his beloved money to know that I was dead to-morrow. Ay, and I should have killed him to-night had not this dear girl interfered. When I saw her again my heart melted. I shall feel all the impulse again when she is not near me. This time I come to save you, Laurisdale. Have nothing to do with that man. Take nothing from him even as a gift. Oh! I know him—few men know him so well as I do. A money—"

Angela came forward and laid a hand timidly on the speaker's arm.

"For my sake," she said, "for mother's sake, say no more. Oh! can't you see how deeply you are distressing and humiliating me before Lord Laurisdale? If there is any of the old love left—"

Barr bowed and smiled. The anger died from his eyes; he fumbled his way to the door like one who is blind. There was a sudden click and the dining-room was plunged into darkness. A hoarse moan came from the side of the room where Sairson was standing. Imaginary fingers were pressing on his throat. It seemed to him that he could hear the sound of scuffling in the hall, then the banging of a door. He did not know that a pair of strong arms had grasped Barr from behind and carried him to the hall door. Before he could recover from the surprise, Barr was in the darkness of the garden.

"You fool!" a voice hissed in his ear. "Do you want to spoil everything? If you had an ounce of manhood left, you would play the game. To think that that poor child still cares for a battered hulk like you."

Barr ceased to stagger. The words had an instantly soberising effect upon him.

"That you, Gosway?" he asked feebly. "I—I don't think I really meant to kill him; and when I saw Angela I was sure I didn't. I should have gone when she asked me, if I hadn't caught sight of Laurisdale. He was not a bad sort, and did me many a good turn. That's why I wanted to repay him. I'm so tired, I think I could sleep for a week."

"Come on, then!" Gosway said sternly. "I've got a lodging for you. I followed you from London. Bad as you are, and low as you have fallen, you are too good to hang for a man like John Sairson."

"It was Angela who felt her trembling way to the switch. When the light flared up again, Sairson perceived that Barr had vanished. He drew a long sigh of relief. The florid color slowly returned to his cheeks, and he began to laugh and bluster.

"So the fellow has gone," he said. "Angela—oh, the girl has gone, too! Most astounding scene, Laurisdale. You used to know Barr, I see."

"One of the best fellows that ever stepped," Laurisdale said positively.

"Was he, really? Then, see what drink will do for a man. He was engaged to my girl at one time, but I had to forbid it for her sake. He owes me money to this day. Yet he tells people I robbed him. What do you say to turning in, old fellow?"

CHAPTER X

THE LORD AND MASTER

Mrs. Sairson came timidly into her husband's dressing-room. All the same, there was a tinge of pink in the delicate color of her checks, and her eyes were steadfast. Sairson, struggling into a Norfolk jacket, gave her a surly nod. He looked a grotesque character in the rough Harris tweeds he affected when in the country.

If there were any choice, as Nest said candidly, she preferred her father in frock coat and silk hat, even if he were striding along a country lane.

"There is something I want to say to you, John," Mrs. Sairson began.

"Well, say it," Sairson responded gruffly. "You're entitled to your own opinion, I suppose."

"Would you be so good as to tell me why you asked Lord Laurisdale here?"

"Well, upon my soul, there is no reason in you women. Here you are with all that money can give you. Here am I, slaving from morning till night, so that you can live in luxury. All the return I get is a complaint that the place is too dull for words. You shut yourselves up as if you were royal princesses, and grumble because nobody calls on you. And now that I have managed—"

"You know that nobody calls on us," Mrs. Sairson protested quickly. "Nobody knows the truth, perhaps, but sooner or later these things always leak out. You do not appreciate the finer feelings, so I will ask you to remember that I do. Lord Laurisdale's presence in the house is an insult to me."

Sairson stared at his wife with undisguised astonishment.

"What in the name of fortune do you mean?" he asked. "An insult! Why?"

"Because Lady Laurisdale has never called upon me. On the contrary, she has pointedly avoided us. Not that I mind, not that I should act in any other way if the positions were reversed. If Laurisdale Castle were at a distance and Lord Laurisdale were here on a matter of consequence, it would be a different thing. But seeing that he lives only across the road, so to speak—"

"Upon my word, you women are enough to drive a man distracted. Why not say the same about young Cecil Lugard, who, I understand, is my guest at the present moment?"

A spasm of pain quivered on Mrs. Sairson's lips.

"That is a different matter altogether," she went on. "Mr. Lugard is a bachelor, with no home of his own for the present. He really is here on business. But it would have been easy for Lord Laurisdale to go to his own home, seeing that the castle is so close."

"He couldn't do it, because we had a lot of important business to discuss last night. Besides, he's all right. If he lived here the Countess would have called long ago—he told me so."

"Did he really! And you believe him? I am not so simple as you seem to think, John. I have been a loyal wife to you and a loyal mother to your children; but that does not blind me to the truth. I know as well as if I could read your very mind that you have drawn Lord Laurisdale into your net, and that you are going to ruin him as you have ruined scores before him. You mean to take advantage of his reckless generosity, and at the same time compel him to recognise me. You intend to make him coerce his wife to call here."

Sairson exploded angrily. He prided himself upon his diplomacy; it was hateful to have it exposed in this way. It was unendurable to feel that his diplomacy was both futile and obvious. For if his wife could see as much, then all the world, too, would read between the lines.

"You are a fool," he said sulkily. "A child in these matters. If I refused to help Laurisdale, somebody else would. Moreover, look at the advantages of it. You and the girls will make a powerful friend. Don't imagine Lady Laurisdale is such a fool as to turn her back on ready money. Besides, she's coming here to lunch to-day, and there's an end of it."

"To lunch, John! Without being asked? Without even the formality of a call?"

"Oh curse your calls and formalities!" Sairson roared. "I tell you her ladyship is coming. She's as deep in the mire as her noodle of a husband. A certain money-lender I know of could sell her up to-morrow. She's proud and haughty, but her nose will come to the grindstone at the prospect of the bailiffs sprawling in the yellow drawing-room. That's why her ladyship will come to-day, and deuced glad of the chance. Well, what do you want?"

The question was flung at Angela, who stood pale and slender in the doorway. She flushed under the words, and a defiant flush of color crept into her cheeks.

"I could not help hearing what you said, father," Angela replied. "Mother is right. She is always right in these matters. Surely, we have had enough humiliation without this great indignity being thrust upon us. When I think of what I have suffered, I am astonished that I remained in the house."

"Only do so for the sake of your mother and sister, I suppose?" Sairson sneered.

"But, father, I would not remain another moment," Angela replied passionately; "I would rather starve. I would prefer to be a barmaid—even a barmaid can retain her self-respect. Yet I was happy enough at one time. I had everything that a girl could need. I had the love of a good man then—"

"Tossed you aside like an old glove and took to drink," Sairson laughed.

"He did nothing of the kind," Angela protested. "He found out the truth before it was too late. When I saw that he hesitated, I refused to marry him. You can say that he refused to marry me—it is all the same. If you had been a convict, it would have made no difference. Convicts expiate their crimes and they reform sometimes. But they do not pursue a path of successful cold-bloodedness; they do not parade their vices and take pride in them. And Jack Barr offended you in the altercation."

"He presumed to dictate to me, curse him!" Sairson muttered.

"Well, call it that if you like. You refused, and we were parted—Jack and I. You swore you would ruin him, would bring him to his knees and make him ask for me like a pauper asking for a piece of bread."

"Yes, and I kept my word," Sairson said doggedly.

"You did, at the cost of my happiness. You ruined Jack Barr, but you did not bring him to his knees. You broke his spirit, and drove him the way men go sometimes. Last night he would have killed you had I not been near to restrain him."

"Your presence saved his life, Angela."

"It is a falsehood!" Angela cried. "You were mortally afraid of him. One had only to look at your face to see that. Now a similar cruelty will be perpetrated on Nest."

"What! Is she going to make a fool of herself, too?" Sairson bellowed.

"What I have dreaded for years has happened," Mrs. Sairson said. "Nest has found a lover. We met Mr. Cecil Lugard some time ago; he was Mr. Franklin then, but he has come into his money and taken his mother's name. They have fallen in love with one another; indeed, Nest has confessed as much to me."

For the first time Sairson looked uneasy. His swaggering manner vanished.

"Funny that Nest should pair off with a Lugard," he muttered, "a nephew of the man who once owned this place. I hope he won't he such a fool as Barr."

"He has a high sense of honor," Mrs. Sairson remarked. "He says that General Lugard was robbed of the place by a money lender called Blaydon. He declares that certain papers have fallen into his hands, and that in time he hopes to prove it was usury, and land Blaydon in gaol. He means it, and he says he is bound to succeed. It was a pretty story, John, a very pretty story to come from the lips of the man who wants to marry Nest."

Sairson strode downstairs moodily. All the light had gone out of him for the time. He had an uneasy feeling that his womankind had got the better of him. If was long past the usual hour for breakfast, and Nest and Lugard had already gone to church. Laurisdale, pale and puffy, was making some pretence at despatching, a poached egg and tea.

"Nice morning," he said. "'Pon my word, it's a pity to be cooped up in the house on a day like this. I sent a line to my wife as soon as I rose, and she's sent to say that she will be delighted to come to lunch at 2 o'clock."

Sairson made some suitable reply. There was a suggestion of triumph in his eyes as he sat down to the table.

"Very glad to hear it," he said; "nothing like being neighborly. Shall I send the car over?"

"No occasion for that," Laurisdale replied. "It's only a mile or so, and I promised to meet her at the avenue. Quite Darby and Joan, what?"

Sairson smiled grimly to himself. He had a fair idea of the reception Laurisdale was likely to meet with. The smile was more pronounced as Sairson watched his guest swagger down the drive on his errand.

"You won't mind it so much when you get used to it, my lady," he soliloquised. "I'll give you a taste of John Sairson's real quality and see how you like it. When you find how Blaydon's clutches pinch, you will be glad to come and black John Sairson's boots."

Lady Laurisdale, a tall figure in grey, stood at the end of the avenue. There was something in the carriage of her head and the set of her face that caused Laurisdale to stammer as he spoke.

"Mornin', Blanche," he said. "Rum go this, what? Not the kind of thing I should like for you; but, really, the women are not half bad. Mother a Belham, I'm told; though where she picked up Sairson is one of the things a fellow can't understand."

"Adversity makes us acquainted with a strange bedfellows," Lady Laurisdale said, with a bitterness that caused her husband to wince. "I suppose you have got into such a mess with your affairs in London that you were forced to make up to these people? Well, I have been taken in to dinner at the house of a duchess by a little Jew with dirty nails, so I suppose I can put up with the wife of a money-lender."

Laurisdale relief was almost too transparent.

"You are a good sort, Blanche," he said. "As for my conduct, I am sorry I have neglected you so much. I'll turn over a new leaf as soon as the theatre takes a change for the better."

Lady Laurisdale laughed as if something amused her.

"To be frank, I was not thinking of you at all," she said. "As you spend everything at the Cosmos, the debts here naturally accumulate. You haven't to face that, but I have, and I am just as deep in the mud as you are in the mire. We are a nice pair, Laurisdale. Some day I shall take to keeping paying guests and accepting money for getting them presented at Court. Lead the way, please."

Laurisdale lighted a cigarette with an assumption of carelessness, but he was feeling ashamed of himself. A few minutes later Mrs. Sairson came into the drawing-room, pale and silent, and determined to be on her guard. Lady Laurisdale held out her hand with a frank smile.

"We are all more or less slaves to circumstances," she said. "I make no apology for not calling before. I can nee you are a Belham at a glance. Do you know that my mother was connected with the family?"

CHAPTER XI

"AN ENEMY HATH DONE THIS THING."

Mrs. Sairson smiled slightly. Her long, thin hands were a trifle unsteady, and there was just a tinge of color in her cheeks. Still, she made a brave enough figure.

"I quite understand," she said quietly. "It is always the women who have to suffer."

A crimson wave stained Blanche Laurisdale's face. The rebuke was so dignified, so quiet, and yet in such perfect taste, that she felt ashamed of herself. She had been brought here against her will; she resented the indignity of it. She had expected to be dragged in triumph as a captive at the chariot of Mammon, and had come prepared to take toll with her bitter tongue. But, this, notwithstanding, there was a vast depth of feeling in Blanche Laurisdale.

"I am very sorry," she said. "Mrs. Sairson, will you forgive me for my rudeness. One cannot always help one's temper, you see. I—I don't exactly know how to explain."

"Then let me explain to you," Mrs. Sairson smiled. "You are annoyed that you have been compelled to come here. I suppose there was some urgent reason—business, perhaps. Of all the hateful things in the world the most hateful is money—or the love of it, rather. On the contrary, my husband thinks there is nothing else worth a thought. He says money can do anything. No doubt there is a sense in which he is right. But you can't buy friends with it. Not that my daughters and myself have sought any friends; but my husband was angry that people had not called on us. He—he manages these things in his own way. You cannot imagine how disturbed I was when I knew you were coming to-day. Oh, I do hope you will try to understand my feelings! This is a most annoying encounter—"

"Quite like a scene in a problem novel," Lady Laurisdale said, in a voice that was not under perfect control. "Dear Mrs. Sairson, I appreciate the position. We are both of the same time—the same blood, I may say. I am sorry I did not call before. We are both unhappy women, and I am sure shall do one another good."

Moved by a sweet and generous impulse, Lady Laurisdale stooped and kissed her companion. It was so spontaneous that it brought tears into Mrs. Sairson's eyes.

"Now I understand," she whispered. "Please let us say no more about it. I am sure this is not the last time I shall see you here."

"May I come when I like," Lady Laurisdale asked. "I don't mind confessing that I admire your girls. I liked to look after them, and yet I resented them. It seemed to me that they ought not to be quite what they are. But, of course, I had not seen you."

"Oh, my dear! I am past the age of compliments," Mrs. Sairson laughed. "I am sure you will get on with the girls."

Lady Laurisdale felt easy on that score. Angela and Nest came into the drawing-room presently, cold and distant and on edge to resent the faintest sign of patronage, but the gleam of battle faded from their eyes as Lady Laurisdale rose with a smile.

"You are going to be very angry with me," she said. "You would have been furious had you heard what I said to your mother when I first came. She made me feel like a housemaid. My dear girls, don't be annoyed with me because I have not called to see you before."

"Have we any right to be annoyed?" Angela asked gently.

"Of course you have. Are you not people of importance here? Don't you possess one of the loveliest old houses in the country? Does not your mother contribute handsomely to every charity? The old vicar has sung your praises repeatedly. And if—"

"And if I had been in your place, Lady Laurisdale, I should have behaved in exactly the same way," Nest said in her candid fashion. "It is very awkward, and—and—"

Nest broke down, stammering and crimson. She formed a pretty picture, with the sunshine falling on her masses of dark hair, and the lovely face with its fleeting anger and rebellious red lips. Lady Laurisdale stretched out her hand impulsively. There was something in the mute appeal in her face—a suggestion of loneliness—that touched Nest to the heart.

"What does it matter so long as I am here?" she asked. "I want you girls to lunch with me on Tuesday and fight it out. Come, please show me your orchids."

It seemed very strange, but here was the haughty and distant Lady Laurisdale talking to the Sairson girls as if she had known them all their lives. Nest's face wore a funny smile, and there was the suspicion of malice in her dark eyes. By the time the orchids had been inspected, John Sairson had found his way to the drawing-room.

There was no mistaking the insolent triumph on his face. He had the air of a man who had played for a big stake and won it. Obviously he was going to act the magnanimous, to let this proud woman, in spite of her blue blood, see that he was the dominating force in the situation. She would know, if need were, that she had been constrained to come here, she would have to recognise that money conquers all things. He was noisy and assertive, and assumed the bluff heartiness of the old school, yet looked so completely out of place in that exquisite room that one wondered how on earth he came to be there.

So this great coarse vulgarian, with the cruel face and mouth like a rat-trap, was the father of these two refined and beautiful girls who listened to him with eyes cast down and faces tinged with red. Lady Laurisdale forgot her humiliation in their vexation. Verily, this was the most amazing household she had ever come in contact with. None but a novelist could do it proper justice. It only needed the touch of romance to make the 'curtain' perfect. Even the touch of romance was supplied presently with the entrance of Cecil Lugard. Lady Laurisdale ought to have been surprised, but she was not in the least. She almost felt as if she had expected this. She saw the look that passed between Lugard and Nest, and her understanding was complete. Then Lugard looked at her and elevated his eyebrows.

He crossed over and shook hands, Sairson was expatiating loudly on the folly of allowing so many trees to stand when they could be more profitably used as timber. Laurisdale was protesting in his way, and Nest was taking his part.

"What are you doing in this gallery?" Lugard murmured.

"A few moments ago I might have asked you the same question," Lady Laurisdale said, "had I met you casually. Since you entered I have solved the problem for myself. When I look at the girl I am not surprised."

Lugard laughed awkwardly.

"I met the Sairsons abroad," he explained. "I did not know anything about them; indeed, there was no need to ask. You see for yourself that they are the kind of people you would take for granted. I was a poor man then, with no prospects, so I said nothing. Months afterwards I came here to look at the Dower House, which Sairson had to sell. I had no idea that John Sairson—"

"No," Lady Laurisdale smiled, "you wouldn't."

"It was a staggering surprise to me. Still, it didn't matter. I'm going to marry Nest. Whatever the family skeleton is, I don't mind."

"Your sincerity is beyond question," Lady Laurisdale admitted. "A love that will swallow a father-in-law like Mr. John Sairson will last to the confines of the grave. What does it mean, Cecil? How could a lady—a Belham—like our hostess marry such a man? Look at him! He is not only a bounder, but has rascal written large all over him. I did not realise it till to-day, but we are all in his toils, all being dragged after the chariot of Mammon. Laurisdale is in his power. He obliged me to come here. I thought I was an unhappy woman, but there sits a woman whose misery is greater than mine. What will become of us all before the play is over?"

Lugard shook his head as if in doubt.

"I don't know," he said. "I had a shock last night that caused me a good deal of concern. I won't tell you about it now, but I'd like to drop in to tea some evening for a chat over things. I mean to call upon you, anyhow. You can give me certain information about the poor old General Lugard. I will not rest till the scoundrel who hounded him to his death is exposed. The Dower House is very charming, but I wanted this place. Yes, and but for roguery it would have been mine, and I could have set the family up again. I'm going to find out how Sairson got it. I'm—"

The announcement of luncheon put an end to further discussion. Sairson came forward with obtrusive politeness and offered his am. Lady Laurisdale took it demurely. She admired the arrangements of the flowers on the table and the service of old silver and glass. Everything was in the best of taste, and the setting perfect. The one hideous note was John Sairson—loud, self-assertive, boisterous. His strident tones dominated the luncheon party.

"I'm going to build when I have time," he exclaimed. "A big ballroom on the east side, and a winter garden as well. Make the old place something like—"

"And spoil it," Lugard said quietly. "It would be a sin to add to the house. The very idea ought to turn poor Sir George in the grave."

"Pooh!" Sairson sneered. "Who cares what he might have thought?"

"Well, I care," Lugard said in a quiet voice. "It's possible you may not have the chance of carrying out your improvements, Mr. Sairson. You know what my contentions are. I have always felt, and some day will prove, that my uncle was robbed of the property by Blaydon. I am only short of one or two little facts to prove it, and when they come my way, heaven help John Blaydon, for he will get no mercy from me! I will not rest till that scoundrel is exposed and stands in the dock, which is his proper place. Of all the precious rascals and bloodsuckers who degrade the name of man, he is the greatest and most contemptible."

Lady Laurisdale glanced up quickly. The name was quite familiar to her, and she could have told the company that her information had been gained at first hand. She could see that Mrs. Sairson and the girls had gone strangely quiet, that Angela's face was pale and set. Sairson had dropped his dominating manner and his florid features had grown to a leaden hue. His big, coarse hands were shaking as he trifled with the fruit on his plate. Lady Laurisdale had half expected some furious outburst on his part. In that moment illumination had come to her mind, and a half-startled expression was strangled on her lips.

"A twinge of neuralgia," she explained. "How ferocious you are Cecil! To hear you talk, one would think that the wicked ogre Blaydon was actually present. Do you happen to know anything about him, Mr. Sairson?"

Sairson swallowed a glass of wine hastily.

"I've heard of him," he said; "well-known money-lender. He belongs to a class that is damned out of all proportion to its vices. Still, Lugard may be right. But he forgets the old saying that a fool and his money are soon parted."

CHAPTER XII

A GAME OF "GHOSTS."

Lady Laurisdale shrugged her shoulders carelessly. Her lightness and gaiety had returned.

"Not a very amusing topic of conversation, is it?" she asked. "Fancy talking about revenge on a day like this! Cecil, you ought to be ashamed of yourself. Mr. Sairson, will you do a 'ghost' for me to paste in my album? Your signature ought to make a very apparent and robust apparition."

"I daresay it would," Sairson answered, "only I don't happen to know what you mean."

"Oh, everybody's doing it! You take a sheet of paper and fold it lengthwise, then write your signature along the crease, and, whilst the ink is wet, press the two folds together. When this is opened again it leaves an impression which some call the skeleton, others the ghost, of the signature. Some of these are most weird. And the better the signature the more effective the 'ghost' is."

"My signature is bold enough for anything," Sairson said in his breezy way.

"That is exactly what I expected," Lady Laurisdale said sweetly. "You financiers generally write boldly; that is why I asked for yours. I should like everybody's, for the matter of that. Mrs. Sairson, may we have some paper and pen and ink? We can do it here!"

Sairson entered into the spirit of the game, his coarse, red face shining genially.

"Here, by all means," he agreed. "Letchmere bring in the liqueur and the cigars and cigarettes. I don't suppose the ladies will mind our smoking at the table. Everybody seems to have finished. Glover, fetch me a quill from the library. I always use a quill, Lady Laurisdale. For a man with a fist like mine there is nothing in the world like a quill."

"How interesting!" Lady Laurisdale said, gently. "I wonder whether John Blaydon uses one, too!"

It was a risky remark, but she determined to hazard it.

Sairson turned a sullen, challenging face on the speaker. For a moment his eyes were sombre and malignant. Then he forced a laugh—a strident, mocking laugh—from his lips.

"You must have your joke," he grunted. "I'll ask Blaydon when I meet him. Here comes the pens and the ink. I'll get you to fold the paper to your liking, and then you must tell me exactly what to do."

Lady Laurisdale folded the paper carefully, after which she proceeded to smooth it out flat on the table. She took care though, to make a slight crease where the signature was to come. Sairson signed his name with a series of flourishes—a very bold and characteristic signature, indeed. Lady Laurisdale expressed her admiration. She held it up to the light so that she could see it more plainly. As she did so, it fluttered from her grasp to the floor. She made a grab at it and flattened it on her dress.

"There!" she ejaculated. "I declare I have spoiled it. The signature is all smudged. It is partly your fault for using so much ink, Mr. Sairson. Might I trouble you for another?"

Sairson was willing to oblige. Meanwhile Lady Laurisdale glanced at the paper on her lap. She held it concealed there until the ink was dry, then quietly folded up the paper and slipped it into her pocket. The smile in her eyes was not one of amusement.

"Now, isn't that like a skeleton?" she asked as she passed the second signature round the table after the rest of the company had signed. "On the whole, that will be the best in my book, Mr. Sairson. Let me have the others, please. Cecil, your ghost is a good one, too. This is quite a haul for me."

She gathered the papers and placed them with somewhat demonstrative carelessness in her pocket. Sairson grinned with the air of a man who has distinguished himself.

He expatiated loudly on the virtues of his school of caligraphy, and again usurped the whole of the conversation. With a sigh of relief Lady Laurisdale rose from the table at a sign from Mrs. Sairson.

She felt she needed the fresh air of the garden; she wanted time to think. She fancied she had discovered the secret of the sinister influence hanging over Marlton Grange. Did Mrs. Sairson know it, too, or did the only guess at it? That would come out in due course.

Blanche Laurisdale stepped from the hall into the garden. As a keen gardener she could not but admire what she saw around her. There were flowers and plants that Laurisdale Castle could not boast. Everything was on the most perfect scale, and yet with an utter absence of anything like ostentation. Probably Mrs. Sairson had seen to that. Lady Laurisdale was bending over an exquisite hybrid when Nest joined her. There was a look of frank friendship in the girl's eyes.

"Do you know I am glad you came," she said. "I was furious when I heard of it at first. I felt sure it was a piece of good nature on Lord Laurisdale's part to please my father for business reasons. I don't know why I should have been afraid of you."

"Neither do I," Lady Laurisdale laughed. "I daresay you thought me horrid. We live in a very funny world of our own, but I am glad I came. I am a very lonely woman, and I wish to be friends with you and your sister. You must come to lunch with me on Tuesday. We must remove that sad look from your sister's face if we can."

"I doubt it," Nest sighed. "Angela is always like that. She had a terrible disappointment three years ago, and has never been the same girl since. Perhaps I ought not to have told you—"

"Oh, well, it's a compliment to me, anyway!" Lady Laurisdale smiled. "I am glad you mentioned it, for it shows you trust me. What blackguards men sometimes are where women are concerned!"

Nest fell into the trap at once.

"He was nothing of the kind," she protested. "It was no fault of his, and it was no fault of Angela's. Something came out—some horrid reason why the marriage could not take place. I was supposed to be too young at the time to understand. If you had known Jack Barr you would have pitied instead of blamed him."

"Did you say Jack Barr?" Lady Laurisdale asked. "Of the Northern Rifles?"

"Yes. Do you know him?"

Lady Laurisdale was silent. She was reflecting on the smallness of the world. Twenty-four hours ago Marlton Grange and its inhabitants had been no more than a subject of contemptuous curiosity to her; and here she was, a central figure, an actor on the stage where a melodrama was in progress. She heard the question with a start.

"I know Jack Barr intimately," she said at last. "He was a great friend of mine. I was told by some acquaintance that he was going to be married, and after that I lost sight of him. The next thing I heard was that he had lost his money and was—was—"

"Drinking himself to death," Nest said sadly. "I heard that, too. Perhaps Angela will tell you her story some day. I can't get much out of her. Isn't ours a most extraordinary household?"

There was a distinct challenge in Nest's voice, and in the directness of her eyes.

"We all have our troubles," Lady Laurisdale said caressingly. "If you think that I am any better off you are entirely mistaken. Let us hope your romance will turn out happier."

The color flamed into Nest's face.

"Who told you anything about that?"

"Oh! nobody told me; I could see it in your face. Well, Cecil Lugard is a splendid fellow, and you are a lucky girl."

"Now that is really nice of you!" Nest cried. "You are the first who has said a kind word to me about it. My poor dear mother looked as if I had struck her when she heard, and Angela seemed a shade more melancholy than ever. I have been imagining all sorts of horrible things, wondering, even, whether there is insanity in the family, or a hereditary tendency to drink."

"Perhaps there was that in Jack Barr's case," Lady Laurisdale opined. "Maybe that was why he was not permitted to marry your sister."

Nest shook her pretty head thoughtfully. She could not accept that selfish idea. Whatever the dread taint, it was on her family's side of the proposed alliance. Perhaps she could persuade her mother to tell her so that Cecil should be left to decide. So far as Cecil was concerned she cared nothing what black and bitter disgrace might be behind him. Both her mother and sister had, almost passionately, protested against attaching any blame to Jack Barr, but deep down in her heart Nest had a vague contempt for that unhappy man. The mere notion that Cecil might act from a similar motive was not worth a moment's consideration.

Laurisdale came out of the house presently, accompanied by Lugard. Blanche Laurisdale detached herself tactfully from Nest and joined her husband. He regarded her somewhat anxiously. Clearly he was afraid of a scolding.

"Rum sort of a household, what?" he asked. "Womankind good enough for anything. Thoroughbreds, I should say. 'Pon my word, Blanche, I believe you have enjoyed it!"

"Well, I won't thank you for that," Lady Laurisdale retorted. "I've solved the problem, Dick, and the whole mystery is plain to me. Take my advice, and have nothing whatever to do with Mr. Sairson. Get out of his clutches as soon as you can, for—"

"My dear girl, I ain't in his clutches," Laurisdale protested. "On the contrary, he's going out of his way to settle one or two awkward pieces of business for me."

"Exactly. You have been borrowing money from Blaydon and Co., professional usurers, and they are giving you an anxious time of it. You can't repay the money and Mr. Sairson has offered to do it for you. At any rate, he will advise Blaydon and Co. to renew your paper, as you call it."

Laurisdale regarded his wife with positive amazement.

"Now, how the deuce did you find that out?" he asked. "Sairson told you anything?"

"You don't tell me a good many things, I but I find them out all the same, Dick," Lady Laurisdale said, somewhat sadly. "Left alone here as I am, I have plenty of time to think. I came here greatly against my wish, but I am glad now that I came."

Lady Laurisdale turned away without further explanation. She desired to be alone, to think this strange matter out. She wandered into one of the long conservatories where the orchids were staged. She was lost in admiration of the brilliant and astounding mass of color. The place was an exquisite dream of delight.

Lady Laurisdale was not aware that her host stood by her side and had addressed her more than once.

"I beg your pardon," she said; "I had forgotten the outside world in my admiration of your orchids. Those white ones with the gold edgings are superb. Like a cloud of flies! What do you call them?"

Sairson did not know. They represented heaps of money, he said, and very few other people possessed them. From that point of view he was thoroughly satisfied.

"Would you like a specimen?" he asked. "Let me give you a spray."

Lady Laurisdale protested; it seemed a sacrilege to break off a spray of those exquisite blooms. Sairson moved behind one of the stages to reach the flower. He was half-hidden by the feathery foliage, when he slipped and fell with a crash to the floor. A long, deep sigh escaped him, and something that sounded like a groan passed from his lips.

"I hope you are not hurt!" Lady Laurisdale exclaimed.

The words froze on her lips. For Sairson lay white and still with a dark circular blue hole on the side of his head whence the blood was flowing freely. His grey hair was horribly stained with red. With a wild cry for help Lady Laurisdale fled headlong into the garden.

CHAPTER XIII

SOMETHING MISSING

The whole thing had happened so unexpectedly that at the moment Blanche Laurisdale was powerless to act. It was impossible that that strong man could be lying dead amongst the flowers; it was impossible to associate him with death. In the sunshine everything looked so calm and refined and peaceful. A lamb was bleating in a distant meadow, and a bright-eyed robin with his head on one side looked at Lady Laurisdale as if asking a question. Somebody hidden behind a pergola of roses was laughing softly. Presently Laurisdale crossed a lawn with his hands in his pockets.

"What's the matter?" he asked. "Seen a ghost, what?"

Lady Laurisdale gripped him by the arm, and dragged him towards the conservatory. Pushing the mass of waving foliage and blazing blossom aside, she pointed to the figure lying motionless on the floor.

"That's what I've seen," she whispered. "I was with him at the time. He was showing me a wonderful new orchid. He stepped to the back of the stage to pick a spray for me and he slipped—at least I thought that he slipped. As he did not rise I went to see what was wrong. I found him lying just as he is—dead."

Laurisdale's face was as white as that of his wife. He was shaking with agitation as he bent over the still figure but he kept his nerve. On the whole, he behaved far better than Lady Laurisdale expected. He did not lack a certain courage and coolness.

"Looks like foul play," he said. "That mark was made by a bullet. Did you see anybody?"

"Mr. Sairson and myself were alone here."

"Um! Very strange! It would be difficult for anybody to have hidden here, especially after you were alarmed by the report of a pistol or revolver."

"But there was no pistol or revolver, Dick. I am positive of that."

"Makes it all the more mysterious. A ghastly business, Blanche. I'm afraid the poor chap is dazed. I must raise an alarm. Stay in the garden till I can look up Lugard. He knows these people much better than I do. I won't be long."

There was something alert and practical in the way that Laurisdale spoke. He was showing qualities that brought a vague comfort to his wife. She stood there waiting, her nerves unstrung. She heard Nest laugh close by, and the deeper tone of Lugard's voice. It seemed an eternity before Lugard came, grave and solemn of face. He listened quietly to what Lady Laurisdale had to say.

"Murder!" he said curtly. "I'll tell Mrs. Sairson. Go and telephone for a doctor, Laurisdale. This is a most ghastly affair!"

The task was easier than Lugard had anticipated. Mrs. Sairson dropped her knitting in her lap and looked at him. She could see the story of tragedy in his eyes.

"Something very dreadful has happened," she said. "Don't say it is one of my girls!"

"The girls are all right," Lugard hastened to say. "So are your guests, for the matter of that. I am sorry to say that Mr. Sairson has met with an accident—at least it looks like—"

Mrs. Sairson rose calmly from her seat.

"Will you take me to him?" she said. "I have been expecting this for some time."

"Expecting it?" Lugard stammered. "Expecting somebody to make an attempt on his life?"

But Mrs. Sairson did not appear to be listening. She was strangely collected, as if some long-dreaded catastrophe had fallen at last. By this time, as if by magic, the whole household knew, so rapidly does news of disaster spread. Already two of the menservants had carried their stricken master to his room. Ten minutes later the teut-teut of the doctor's motor was heard in the drive.

After 30 minutes' suspense, the doctor came down to the drawing-room. He looked as grave as the rest, but there was a fighting gleam in his eyes.

"It is well to be candid," he said. "Mr. Sairson is still alive. He has a fine constitution, and has just a fighting chance. If we can extract the bullet he may live. We shall have to get Atterley down at once with the X-ray people. I'll telephone to the County Hospital for a couple of nurses. How did it happen—an accident, I presume?"

"It was no accident, Dr. Paley," Lady Laurisdale replied. "I was with Mr. Sairson at the time. The whole thing was done in the twinkling of an eye. The strange part is that I heard no shot fired. There was no report at all!"

"Very remarkable!" the doctor said. "Yet Mr. Sairson was shot with a revolver bullet beyond all shadow of a doubt. Perhaps you had better telephone for the police."

"Oh, what is the good of that until you are perfectly certain!" Angela burst out passionately. "We are acting merely on surmise. Did you not hear Lady Laurisdale say she was positive no shot was fired? Surely, there is no need to make a scandal of it!"

Angela's face was white and set, and her eyes gleamed like frosty stars. She was unconscious that every glance was turned in her direction. She might have been pleading for her own life.

"Let us wait," she said. "Give my father a chance to speak. He may have accidentally injured himself. I implore you to wait."

A strange household; truly, a very strange household! Lady Laurisdale was trying to grasp the mystery of it all as she sat listening. Angela was concerned for somebody; she was concealing something. Could the girl have cleared up everything had she liked?

"I understand Miss Angela's feelings," Paley said. "She has my sympathy. But all the same, my duty is plain. I should be severely blamed if I neglected it in any respect. You will see my point, Mrs. Sairson!"

Mrs. Sairson bowed. Nest glanced from Angela's white face to the stern look of that of her lover. What had Cecil to trouble him? The singular thing was that nobody was grieved, there was neither sorrow nor distress; nothing but a grave sense of responsibility.

The group in the drawing-room began to break up presently. Angela drew Nest to her side. Her face was still deadly pale, her dark eyes were staring.

"I am convinced I am right," she said. "I am going to ask Cecil Lugard to help me, Nest. He is the only one we have to look to now. Please send him out into the garden to me."

Nest gave the desired promise. It struck her as odd that Lugard jumped at the opportunity.

"Be tender to her," Nest whispered. "She is in great trouble—a trouble caused by others—"

"Have no fear on that score," Lugard smiled. "I think I understand, dear. I am glad of the chance to have a talk with Angela."

Angela paced up and down in the shade of the pergola—waiting. There was a look in her eyes half of relief, half of fear, as Lugard approached.

"You guessed why I asked you to come."

"Well, I think so," Lugard said guardedly. "You believe you have ascertained the truth. You intend to say something about Jack Barr."

"Did you know he had been here?"

Lugard hesitated for an instant.

"Nest told you that Jack Barr was once a great friend of mine?" she asked presently.

"Yes; and I was glad to hear it. It is strange how the world narrows sometimes. When I parted from Jack Barr I never expected to see him again. Something came between us, and my dream was over. He is not to be blamed, remember because—"

"I am not so sure of that," Lugard said severely. "He might have played the man. He need not have wasted his life as he has done."

"Ah!" Angela said eagerly. "Then I was right! You have seen him lately! Please be candid with me."

"I mean to be candid with you," Lugard rejoined. "All the more so, because I see that the same hideous suspicion is in both of our minds. You have seen him, too?"

"Yes, last night, after you had gone to bed. My father came back late and brought Lord Laurisdale with him. I heard sounds, and went down to the drawing-room, and found Jack standing in the hall. It was a frightful shock, but don't ask me to say what his changed appearance implied. Cecil, he was mad. He was there to kill my father. I tried to reason with him, but it was useless. He went into the room, and there was a dreadful scene. Then the light suddenly went out, and when it was switched on again, Jack had vanished. Somebody had carried him away bodily. Was that you?"

"God bless my soul, no!" Lugard exclaimed. "My dear Angela, you have my solemn assurance I had no hand in it. Nevertheless I had seen Barr. He burgled the house, and I caught him red-handed. He came here intent on—well, let us call it mischief. He was, as you say, quite mad. I fear drugs, more than drink, were responsible for his condition. The poor fellow not only lost you, but his fortune and his friends. He was foolish, perhaps—"

"Not so far as the fortune was concerned," Angela said sadly. "He was deliberately robbed of that; and the man who robbed him was my father."

"Indeed!" Lugard said gravely. "We will go into that some other time. You think that in consequence of this—"

"Cecil, I am absolutely certain of it, Jack had found out everything. He had brooded over his misfortunes and was bent on killing my father. But what happened when you saw him?"

"Oh, nothing very much! I persuaded him to go away. I gave him money, and he solemnly promised he would not come back again, and I let him go. He did come back, you think?"

"Oh, I dare not put my thoughts into words," Angela cried. "But knowing what we know, cannot you see how horribly appearances are against the poor fellow? Can't you understand why I am so anxious to keep the police out of this business? Oh, what a house of terror ours is! People envy us the place, admire our grounds and gardens, and all the rest of it. They think how fine it is to have plenty of money. Money! It is the curse of our family—the greed of gold, the lust for possession, particularly of other people's property. If my father had nearly all the money in the world, and some poor wretch had only a few pounds to keep him from starvation, he would scheme till he got that. That is why I call this place the House of Mammon."

"I'll help you out, dear," Lugard said gently. "Perhaps we have made a mistake; but you must not expect to keep this affair from the police. It is possible your father has enemies as bitter as, but less honest, than poor Jack Barr. You want me to find him, to discover whether there is anything in your dreadful surmise?"

Angela nodded; her heart was too full for words. She turned towards the house, avoiding Lady Laurisdale by stepping through the conservatory into the drawing-room. Lady Laurisdale proceeded to the scene of the catastrophe. As she did so, her attention was immediately arrested. Something was wanting; there was a blank somewhere.

"That wonderful white orchid!" she said. "Where is it? It was here half-an-hour ago!"

But it was there no longer. For the wonderful bloom—the unique white orchid—had vanished.

CHAPTER XIV

A CHILD OF NATURE

By-and-by Lady Laurisdale returned slowly to the house. She was debating a good many questions with herself. She had made a discovery, but was considering whether or not she was justified in keeping it to herself. She knew the missing orchid was unique, for Sairson had boasted to her about it at luncheon. He had also stated that he got it cheap. But Sairson had been struck down in that mysterious manner at the very moment that he was breaking a sprig off the orchid. Then in broad daylight, with plenty of people and servants about the house, the orchid had vanished. It was a clue of sorts, and it fascinated Lady Laurisdale to the exclusion of all other matters.

"You won't think it unkind if we run away now!" she said to Mrs. Sairson. "We ought not to have stayed so long. May I come and see you when I have time? You had better let the girls come over on Tuesday. They can do no good here, and perhaps will be better out of the way."

"It is very good of you," Mrs Sairson said. "I think we have gained a friend to-day."

Lady Laurisdale was very quiet and thoughtful as she walked home. For once her husband's small talk was exhausted. He said little or nothing on the way to the castle.

After tea in the hall he lighted a cigarette and began to discuss the events of the day.

"A ghastly business, what?" he observed. "Bit of a shock for you, Blanche. What do you make of it? Didn't you see anything to arouse your suspicions?"

"My dear Dick, so far as that is concerned, I'm as much in the dark as yourself. But I'm glad I went, because I have found out one or two things that may be useful later. For one thing, I am sure that John Sairson was an unmitigated scoundrel."

"Didn't much like the look of him myself," Laurisdale admitted amiably.

"You never are quite such a fool as you look, Dick. Most of the idiotic things you do are done against your better judgement. Yet, with that feeling you were still prepared to put yourself into Sairson's hands. I suppose he promised you all sorts of fine things."

"Well not exactly that, Blanche. You see, Sairson was a business man. Lived for it in fact. He didn't lend money himself but could influence people who did. Odd thing that Lugard should have spoken as he did at lunch about a chap called John Blaydon. Bit scathingly, too."

"Go on, Dick! You are so deliciously transparent. Why didn't you tell me at once that you are in the clutches of John Blaydon, the money-lender! How much do you owe him?"

"Ten thousand pounds," Laurisdale blurted out. "Every penny of it sunk in that beastly theatre. Blaydon says he can't renew those bills. Says he wants the money."

"Really? The same old story! What are you doing about it?"

"Well I went to Sairson. A chap told me he was just the man I needed. And I fancy it's true that Blaydon is hard up, because he borrowed a lot of cash from Sairson and deposited my paper as security. Blaydon seems to have been badly hit in the city lately."

Lady Laurisdale's eyes sparkled. There was the ghost of a smile on her lips.

"So Sairson had your bills? In that case you were his debtor. And he was to make things easy for you. Now let me make a confession. I also am in the hands of John Blaydon. I owe him over £1000."

"I say, Blanche, you have been going it, what?"

"Not at all, my dear boy. You haven't paid a single account here for months. Everything goes into your theatre. To all intents and purposes the mistress of the house is Sadie Carton. Now, I have a natural objection to having servants whose wages are not paid, and I don't like fleecing tradesmen. It may sound quaint and old-fashioned, but the fact remains. I had a circular from Mr. Blaydon, and so I borrowed the money of him, and now he is pressing for payment. An execution in Laurisdale Castle would be a novelty, but I can assure you that it is within measurable distance."

Laurisdale whistled blankly. His slumbering pride was aroused. Trouble in London at the theatre was all very well, but trouble of that kind at the castle was quite another thing.

"I didn't know it was as bad as that," he stammered. "I'll chuck the theatre, Blanche. I might get Willis to take it on and release me from everything. But for the accident to Sairson I should have been all right."

Even now Lady Laurisdale's eyes twinkled with contemptuous mirth.

"You may find that the accident, as you call it, is a blessing in disguise," she said. "Now, I have made an important discovery to-day. I am not going to say anything about it yet, if only out of respect for Mrs. Sairson and the girls. I like them, and we are to be friends. I was furious when I got your note this morning, and if I had acted on first impressions, I should have ignored it."

"Thought better of it at the last moment, what?"

"No, I didn't, I went to Marlton Grange because Philip Gosway asked me to. By the way, I didn't tell you that Sybil Gosway is staying here. Gosway came last night, and I saw him this morning."

"Great Scott! I thought he had gone under years ago. What's he doing?"

"Well, he's getting an honest living, at any rate. He has done his duty by the girl, and she thinks there is nobody in the world like him. Ring the bell, Dick."

A man-servant gave the information that Miss Gosway had gone for a walk. She had gone out with the gentleman who had met her ladyship in the avenue after breakfast.

"Thank you very much, Lushford," Lady Laurisdale said. "Sybil is out with her father. He did not want her to know that he was here, but apparently he has changed his mind. In that case he will probably come back here before he returns to London. I want to see him particularly."

"Then I'll go off and have a look at the stables," Laurisdale said. "Upon my word, I have neglected the place shamefully, Blanche, as well as you. I think I'll stay for a week or two and ask Willis to come down. Philip can arrange matters here."

Laurisdale strolled off nonchalantly, feeling he had said and done the right thing. Blanche Laurisdale stood gazing out thoughtfully across the park. Two figures came along the avenue presently—Sybil Gosway, accompanied by her father. They had parted below the sunk fence, and Sybil came in the direction of the house. It was easy, by means of a short cut through the shrubbery, to intercept Gosway.

"So you changed your mind, after all?" Lady Laurisdale asked.

"Well, yes," Gosway admitted. "It was such a lovely day that I could not resist the temptation of a long walk with Sybil this afternoon. I waylaid her as she came back from church. I didn't tell her I had met you, and I had rather she did not know it. She thinks I came down here on the spur of the moment."

"I am glad I have had a chance to speak to you again," Lady Laurisdale said. "Here is Cecil Lugard! That's fortunate; I had an idea he would come over this evening."

"But he must not see me," Gosway protested.

Lady Laurisdale laid a detaining hand on his arm.

"It is absolutely necessary," she said quietly. "Something has happened that renders concealment no longer possible. Sairson was attacked in one of his glass-houses this afternoon, and, for aught I know, may be dead by this time. I was present at the time. It was most mysterious."

Gosway made no further attempt to get away. He was looking anxious and weary.

"Very well," he said, "I'll see Lugard. Perhaps I can help you in the matter. Hullo, Lugard!"

He spoke more or less defiantly. Lugard, frankly astonished, held out his hand.

"Glad to see you again," he said. "Truly this is a day of surprises. Gosway, did you happen by any chance to be at Marlton Grange last night?"

"Most assuredly," Gosway answered quietly. "I was actually on the premises, I know the house well. I knew also that you had gone to bed, and that Sairson was in the house with Lord Laurisdale."

"Let us be frank. You came to prevent trouble between Barr and Sairson?"

"I admit that freely. I travelled from London especially to prevent mischief. When I saw there was likely to be trouble, I switched off the lights and conveyed Barr away."

"I knew somebody had done so, because Miss Angela Sairson told me," Lugard replied. "Very strange it should have been you, of all people in the world. What happened afterwards?"

"I induced Barr to go. I soothed him and offered him money. He said he had plenty of money; what he most needed was a shelter for the night. I got him that, too. He is staying at Oates's Farm."

"I know it—a queer, tumble-down place with an old market garden attached. Mrs. Oates's people have been there for centuries. She used to have a lodger, a funny old Italian, who raised early salads for a living."

"The very same," Gosway replied. "Nothing is changed, not even the lodger. I put up Barr for the night, and he promised to go back to London with me this evening."

"I'm glad to get this information," Lugard cut in. "I hope to hear that Barr had nothing to do with the outrage on Sairson, but I'm very much afraid he had."

Gosway remained ominously silent; had he taken all the trouble for nothing?

"I should like to hear Blanch Laurisdale's story," he said presently.

Lady Laurisdale repeated her statement as succinctly as she could. It was interesting, in its way, but conveyed nothing that was really practical to the present issue. The more they thought it over, the more mysterious it became. They did not attach much importance to the strange disappearance of the white orchid; still it was a feature in the case and would need due consideration.

"Well, we shan't gain anything by standing chattering here," Lugard exclaimed. "Gosway, if you have got an hour or two to spare, I'd like you to go as far as Oates's Farm with me."

"And do come back and let me know the result," Lady Laurisdale pleaded.

The two men set off together in silence.

"Look here, Lugard," Gosway said by-and-bye, "many things have happened since we met last—many things have come to light. I know all about Barr, and why he has sunk so low. I also know that the man who lies yonder was one of the most loathsome scoundrels that ever breathed. If Barr has killed him he has done a great service to humanity. The secret is more or less ours, and if you like to keep it I am agreeable. If Barr has done this thing, it would be the best to smuggle him out of the country."

"In other words, you suggest that we should compound a felony!"

"Call it what you like," said Gosway with grim contempt. "I couldn't see a man hanged for killing a reptile like John Sairson. What are you going to do?"

They came to the old farm at length, but there was no news to be gleaned. Barr had had his breakfast and had left early, with an intimation that he would not be back. A little old man who was pottering over some dilapidated garden frames gave them the same information in broken English. He had spoken to the gentleman before he had gone on his way. They had been discussing early vegetables together.

"It's just as Paul Givanni says," Mrs. Oates remarked. "Paul never makes mistakes."

The Italian beamed and went on with his work. In moody silence Lugard and Gosway returned to the castle. They had little to tell Lady Laurisdale.

"Where did you get the flower you have in your buttonhole?" she asked Gosway.

"I picked it up by the back door of the farm-house," Gosway explained. "Very pretty, isn't it? I'm no botanist, but I should like to know what it is."

"I will tell you," Lady Laurisdale said. "It's a bloom from the missing white orchid."

CHAPTER XV

ON THE BORDER

John Sairson's wonderful constitution was standing him in good stead. A specialist from London, along with a number of assistants, had, after a deal of trouble and anxiety, extracted a bullet from the wounded man's head. This had passed into the hands of the police, who were satisfied that it afforded a good clue.

But whatever the constables might think, Inspector Skidmore admitted to Lugard that it would not help them. In the whole course of his experience, he said, he had never seen a missile like it before. It was nothing but the thinnest shell of lead, capped with tin. The thing had curled up like a threadpaper; indeed, how it had penetrated Sairson's skull at all was in itself a mystery.

"I've been to Hythe with this, sir," he explained. "They know every firearm in the world, but are as much puzzled as I am. They've never even heard of such a makeshift. They say a chunk of lead must have been rammed into some old muzzle-loading pistol—the sort of weapon that boys are fond of. That is all the information I can get."

"It is quite wrong, then," Lugard retorted. "The sort of pistol you describe makes considerable noise. Now, we know perfectly well, from Lady Laurisdale's statement, that there was no noise at all. She practically saw Mr. Sairson fall, she was within a yard or two of him all the while, and she is positive she heard nothing. I'm afraid that Hythe will not help you in the matter, Inspector."

Inspector Skidmore confessed that he agreed with much of what Lugard had said. He would have been considerably astonished had he known how much more Lugard could have told him. Other people, too, could have enlightened him, but they kept the matter to themselves; they did not even speak of it to one another.

Lugard believed he could have named the actual culprit. Gosway knew as much, to say nothing of Lord Laurisdale. But Lady Laurisdale had warned the latter to be silent.

"It is no business of yours," she said. "The police are paid to find out these things. I'm sure you don't wish any harm to Jack Barr."

"One of the best, he used to be," Laurisdale replied. "Seems almost inconceivable that he should have fallen so low. Poor chap's as mad as a hatter, what! Got some grudge against Sairson."

"And probably attempted his life," Lady Laurisdale supplemented.

"Eh, what? Then you feel pretty sure that Barr did!"

"Dick, I am certain of it," Lady Laurisdale replied. "I have the clearest evidence of the fact. I could convict Barr if I chose, and have him sentenced to a long term of penal servitude. But it would be one of the lasting regrets of my life to see him in the dock. You are not to say a word, Dick, you are not to discuss the matter with anybody. Goodness knows what will come out if you do. I want to be Jack Barr's friend, to try to make a man of him again—if only for the sake of the poor girl who loves him so sincerely."

"What poor girl? Oh, I see! Angela Sairson, what!"

"Precisely. Really you are getting quite brilliant, Dick. You have gone to the heart of the tragedy. Angela knows everything; she is as sure as we are whose hand it was that struck down her father."

"Yes, I suppose she does," said Laurisdale. "She was present at that most extraordinary scene. Never saw anything so striking even on the stage. Well, I'll promise not to say anything about it. Only this business of Sairson's is a dashed nuisance. I don't want to be hard and selfish, but it upsets my plans confoundedly. Goes a long way toward ruining me, what!"

"It will go a long way towards saving you," Lady Laurisdale said fiercely. "I see you don't understand, and I won't enlighten you for the moment. Think of that poor girl!"

All this time Sairson lay unconscious, grimly fighting for life. The grand old house lay peacefully basking in the summer sunshine, as if there were no such things as tragedy and sorrow in the world. There was not much sign of the tragedy, either. The sick-room was given over entirely to the doctor and the nurses, and the family was kept out of the way as far as possible. Mrs. Sairson busied herself over her knitting, and Nest was in and out of the house much as if nothing had happened. She was quieter and sadder, perhaps, but the shadow lay on her shoulders lightly.

In his own household nobody cared whether John Sairson lived or died. Notwithstanding his enormous wealth, it may be doubted whether even the dogs would miss him. Mrs. Sairson sat sedately with her shining needles in her hand, and heard the report of the doctor and the nurse without a tremor. She had done her duty by the wounded man all these years; there was no reproach on her conscience. That some mortal enemy had done this thing she felt certain; in her heart of hearts she wondered why the blow had not fallen before.

But one thing did trouble her—the strange change that had come over Angela. The girl was no longer merely sad and melancholy. She had developed a singular unnatural fear. She appeared to be haunted with some overpowering dread. She started at the slightest noise, her eyes filled with tears at the ringing of a bell, or the sound of a footstep on the gravel.

Nest noticed this condition of nervous fear. There was a deep and abiding affection between the two girls, and the changed demeanor troubled Nest. She discussed it as she stood ready dressed to go out. She had looked forward to the lunch party at Laurisdale Castle, but, at the last moment Angela had declined to go.

"I'm really not up to it," she pleaded. "I hope that will not spoil your pleasure. I believe you will get along all right, and besides, you will have your old schoolfellow, Sybil Gosway, to talk to."

"But, my dear, it will do you good," Nest urged. "You never go anywhere; you stay at home till you are getting old-fashioned. You really ought to make an effort."

Angela smiled frankly. If Nest only knew! If Mrs. Sairson only knew! Nest contested the point no longer, but sadly, half-angrily complained to her mother.

"You should remonstrate with Angela," she said. "The way she is moping is dreadful. Anybody would think that she was the guilty party, or, at any rate, that she was in the conspiracy."

Mrs. Sairson started. These few chance words had set her thinking. She watched Nest until she was out of sight, then went to Angela's room. She found the girl stretched on the bed, her whole frame shaking with tearless sobs. The cool touch of the mother's fingers soothed her.

"You must get up and tell me all about it," Mrs. Sairson said, with wonted sympathy. "I have a right to know, dear."

"You must believe, mother, that I am not worrying over a trifle," Angela forced herself to say.

"My dear, I know that. I have not studied you all these years for nothing. There is something here far worse than the sorrow that has spoilt your life. Nest sees it—it must be more or less plain to the household. Won't you tell me?"

For some time Angela cried on her mother's shoulder, and the pain at her heart grew easier.

"I am glad you came in," she said. "I am glad you found me like this. Have you learned anything, mother? Have you any idea, at all what is troubling me?"

"I fancy so, dear. You think you know who attacked your father. Possibly you do know."

"Mother, others know, too. I am certain of my facts. Lord Laurisdale and Cecil Lugard know, and Lady Laurisdale knows by this time as well. Yet see how loyal they are. For they were all friends of Jack's once."

"There is a curse upon the house," Mrs. Sairson sighed. "Yet how could it be otherwise when every brick and stone of it has been baptised in blood and tears! Then it was Jack Barr?"

"Yes, mother. I heard an unusual noise and came downstairs on Saturday night. Jack was standing outside talking to father and Lord Laurisdale. It seemed like some hideous dream. It was Jack himself, and yet Jack changed beyond imagination. You know what he used to be—so handsome and upright, and so particular about his personal appearance. Imagine him a broken-down tramp if you can—his hair so long and untidy, his face unshaven and dressed as a beggar might be."

Angela paused and Mrs. Sairson's arms tightened about her.

"You can imagine what a shock it was to me, mother," the girl went on. "But I did not faint, nor call out. I stole up to him and caught him by the arm. Then when he turned to me and I caught the expression in his eyes I knew what he had come for. I could see that life had become a worthless possession to him that he did not value it at all. That was perhaps one of the reasons why he had come down to kill my father."

"Did you find out how he gained access to the house?" Mrs. Sairson asked.

"There was no time to ask questions, mother. He was perfectly mad. It was not the heedless impulsiveness of the drunkard, for he spoke clearly and coherently, but there was a blaze in his eye that showed his brain was afire. There were words between him and father, whom he defied to send for the police, and I knew from father's manner that Jack spoke simple truth. Then the lights went out, and by the time they were switched on again, Jack had vanished. Someone had come in and carried him off by main force. There was no more after that, but I knew, mother, I knew who it was that had tried to kill my father."

Mrs. Sairson was silent for some time. It was very difficult to know quite what to say. Deep down in her heart she knew that Angela's suspicions were well founded, and she was constrained to believe that others also shared her opinion. Moreover, she could not conceal from herself the fact that they were all ready and willing to shield Jack Barr from the consequences of his criminal act. They were all against John Sairson.

"What do you think about it, mother?" Angela asked.

"What can I say, my dear?" Mrs. Sairson sighed. "Our duty is plain—the duty of the others is plain. We owe a duty to society, if not to your father. And yet I couldn't do it dear—I could not, indeed. It is possible too that we may be in error—that we may be blaming the wrong man. I recognise that appearances are against the poor fellow, but it may be a hideous mistake all the same."

Angela shook her head sadly. The tears were running down her cheeks. "It is very good of you to talk like that," she said. "But there is no doubt in my mind. It is more for Nest's sake than for mine that I grieve. My life is finished; it has been wrecked by the one man in the world whom I should honor and respect— my father. In the circumstances you need not be surprised that the word conveys nothing to me. But the trouble will come to Nest as well; the great happiness of her life will be changed to the greatest curse. The very thought of it makes me miserable."

Somebody tapped at the door, and a nurse entered. She looked grave and anxious, and desired to speak to Mrs. Sairson. Mrs. Sairson stepped quietly from the room. Angela lay hardly conscious that she was alone.

"What a house!" she moaned. "What a house of sorrow and tears—the House of Mammon!"

CHAPTER XVI

A LOVER OF NATURE

Nest went to Laurisdale Castle with a certain thankfulness that Fate had provided her with something in the nature of occupation. She ought to have been anxious and uneasy about her father, but she recognised that she had no feeling of the kind. She had never cherished the slightest affection for him, and, on his part, he had shown her none, as far back as she could remember. It had always been a source of bitter disappointment to John Sairson that a boy had never been given to him. Ah! and as he lay between life and death, nobody shed a tear for him, and Nest could not help thinking that her father was himself to blame.

The weight of the trouble seemed to lie on the shoulders of everybody; even Cecil Lugard—whom she met on the road—was moody and thoughtful. He made no attempt to be cheerful, and nothing Nest could say seemed to rouse him. He said he could not stay any longer at Marlton Grange, alleging that unless he could be of service he must only be in the way. He had taken rooms in the village where he thought he would be comfortable. Meanwhile he pleaded that he had pressing business to attend to.

"Then I shall not be back before dinnertime," Nest said dolefully. "What is wrong, Cecil? Why, you might have had a hand in the outrage yourself!"

Lugard avoided a direct reply. He made no attempt to detain Nest. There really was urgent work clamoring for his attention, he said. He would walk as far as the Castle with her, and perhaps fetch her back. With that Nest was forced to be content.

What a grand place it was, to be sure! Everything was much as it had been for the last five hundred years. Small wonder Lady Laurisdale had looked down on the Sairsons from a distance. Nest tried to picture her father in the venerable castle, but in the meantime she was conscious that the footman was looking at her with undoubted interest. No doubt the attack on her father had been detailed and discussed in the servants' hall. The scene was changed when Lady Laurisdale came down the great stone staircase and kissed her quite affectionately.

"It is very good of you to come, dear," she said; "and now that you have the freedom of the house I hope you will call whenever you are so disposed. You are a true Belham, Nest. As you stand there, with the sun on your face, I see the wonderful family likeness."

"Well, that's a comfort, anyhow," Nest laughed contentedly. "But have I mistaken the day? You are dressed to go out!"

"I'm obliged to," Lady Laurisdale confessed. "A duty visit to some people at Cromer, whom I couldn't put off. Very likely I shall have to stay to lunch. But I wish you to feel quite at home here, and I don't want to disappoint Sybil Gosway. You'll find her on the terrace."

In an angle of the long stone terrace Sybil sat reading a book. She dropped the volume with a cry of pleasure when she saw Nest.

"Well, this is a delightful surprise," she exclaimed. "Fancy seeing you again like this! I thought we had parted for ever."

"I ought to have written to you more regularly," Nest said. "I have no excuse to make. My father says that it is only the idlers who can never find time for anything—the industrious man always can. I'm afraid there is a good deal of truth in that as far as I am concerned. I might have asked you to come, dear."

"But I should not have been able to," Sybil smiled. "I have to earn my living. My father always told me I should have to look to myself, and my education was all that he could give me. I am afraid he had to pinch and plan even for that."

"You were always very clever," Nest said.

"Yes, that was the general impression," Sybil laughed. "But the world is full of clever people. I found that out as soon as I came in contact with it. My word, it was different from school. I was to be a governess with a hundred a year, and people should compete for my services. As matter of fact, nobody would look at me. That is why I learnt typewriting and shorthand and stayed at home with dad. And, on the whole, I am not dissatisfied. I do get my pleasures sometimes, and this is one of them."

"Isn't it lovely?" Nest cried. "Isn't it strange that until last Sunday I had never spoken to Lady Laurisdale. I thought she must be horrible and patronising and beastly. She was absolutely delightful, Sybil. But, of course, I must not talk of that. Is she any relation to you?"

"My dear, I can't tell," Sybil admitted. "There seems to be a tacit understanding that I am not to ask questions. My father speaks of Lady Laurisdale as 'Blanche' in his unguarded moments—and I know she thinks of dad as 'Phil.' I have not been here for two years, since you took Marlton, anyway. But sit down and let us have a long, cosy chat. We have the place to ourselves, and I am to act as your hostess. After lunch I propose we should have a ramble along the cliffs as far as the Dale. Then we can come back here to tea. What do you think of the programme?"

Nest promptly confessed that she did not think it could be improved upon. They sat on the long terrace in the sunshine, forgetting the world and its troubles. Then they lunched in a room that looked across the cliffs towards the sea. Two footmen waited on them, somewhat to Nest's embarrassment. It seemed such a waste of tissue and labor.

"Oh, dear! I am so glad those men have gone," she exclaimed when at length the fruit was on the table. "Now we can talk without being polite to each other. I detest a lot of servants about me at mealtime." After they had had a long interchange of sentiments and experiences they set out for their walk.

They rambled along the cliffs and thence into the valley called the Dale. They found it hot and tiring, and Nest's wish for a cooling drink seemed but to increase their thirst.

"A glass of fresh milk would be delicious," said Sybil.

"But, where shall we get it?" Nest asked.

"Nest, you ought to be ashamed of yourself," Sybil answered teasingly. "You don't deserve to live in this lovely spot. You ought to know every foot of it by this time. But, you know, the shoemaker's children are the worst shod. Fancy not knowing Mrs. Oates of Oates's farm! A charming old lady. I have not had a chance of calling on her since I came, but you'll see how glad she is to see me!"

Sybil did not exaggerate. Mrs. Oates expressed her pleasure freely. She brought a couple of chairs from the sacred recesses of the parlor and dusted them, spotless as they were, with her apron. She poured out the foaming new milk in a pair of quaint glasses.

"Well, I am main glad to see you, miss!" she said. "And who may this young lady be?"

Sybil proceeded to explain. At the mention of the name of Sairson Mrs. Gates drew back coldly. There was no mistaking the expression on her ingenuous face. It disappeared in a moment, but Nest colored slightly.

"I am sure you are most kindly welcome, miss," the old woman said. "Dear, dear, how things change! It only seems yesterday the poor old general was alive and well."

Nest understood, and the color surged into her face again. Perhaps Sybil saw something of the awkwardness of the situation, for she sprang to her feet and declared that it was a shame to keep Mrs. Oates from her work.

"Besides, I want to show my friend the garden," she explained. "The most delightful old garden in the world, Nest. There are no strawberries like Mrs. Oates's. I'm looking forward to a talk with Givanni. I hope he is still here, Mrs. Oates!"

"Ay, and likely to be," the old woman laughed, "as kind and gentle and just as ever. Give him his flowers and his bit of food and he's happy, though he do talk like one of those bloodthirsty Socialists."

At the bottom of the rambling garden Givanni was pottering about his frames. Most of them were covered over with matting, and had a kind of rude stage underneath. The suspicious look in the dark eyes cleared—the Italian smiled and raised his hat.

In spite of his shabby clothes and long untidy hair, he was quite a gentleman, Nest thought. He was old, bent, and worn with toil, but the dark eyes still had the fire of youth, still had the touch of passion that told of power to resent wrong and to repay injury. He took Sybil's hand and raised it to his lips with a grand air. His eyes flashed as they rested on Nest's face.

"I know who you are, young lady," he said. "Miss Sybil may call you Sairson, but you are a Belham. God bless the name! I have good cause to. How or why does not matter, for it is an old story now. But I never forget. That is why I thank God you are a Belham and not a Sairson."

Certainly a little mad, Nest imagined. A moment later the old man was talking of his beloved flowers. He showed one frame after another filled with the most exquisite blooms. There were scores which Nest had never seen before. The old man's enthusiasm was infectious.

"They are mostly hybrids," he explained. "I have discovered the art of cross-fertilisation. When these blooms are perfect I shall startle the world. In the meantime I almost deprive myself of food for them. It is all done by electricity. In that shed yonder is a battery, and from it wires are connected with the frames. I have great successes already, but nothing to what I am going to win some day. You see there the fruit of ten years' labor. I should have reached perfection two years ago but for a terrible frost one night. Only one of my choicest orchids survived, and I had to make money by it to start again."

"You might make thousands out of them," Nest suggested.

Givanni looked up thoughtfully from one of his frames.

"I might, little lady, I might," he said; "but, your true artist hates to give the world anything but his best work. My one perfect orchid I lost—or parted with. Ah! that was a bloom for you! Never was anything like it since the first flower bloomed in the Garden of Eden. And I had to part with it, for times were hard and I needed money for food. These terrible temptations always come at the worst time. I showed the bloom to a man and he wanted to buy it. He offered me a price that made me dizzy. He must have seen his way to get his money back, or he would not have made such an offer. I refused."

"He did not get the flower, then?" Nest asked.

"Ah, I did not say that, little miss," the Italian went on. "When a man is clever and unscrupulous he finds a means of gaining the end of his ambition. There is the thing you call advancing money, what you say, mortgage? You give me so much and I give you security. If I pay you back, well and good. If I not pay you back, then you keep the security. So it was with my flower."

"What a shame!" Nest cried. "Did you lose it, then? Couldn't you pay the money?"

"The money was not what you call forthcoming. There was one misfortune after another, as always happens when one borrows gold. One night my furnace fires they go out. It was a cold night, and the flowers suffer terribly. Why the fires go out is a mystery to this day. You may say I forgot to pull out the dampers, I say that every damper was pulled out—as if I would forget such a thing! And in the morning every damper was pushed in close. Oh! I have my suspicions. Some day I find out, and when I do, it will be a bad day for the man who did that unkind thing."

Givanni was speaking almost to himself; he appeared to have forgotten the presence of the girls. The dark eyes flashed and the wrinkled face twitched convulsively.

"I hope the scoundrel will be properly punished," Nest said hotly.

Givanni's face changed. The pleasant smile came back to his lips again.

"Oh, I think so!" he said, "I think so! You see, it is like a mother being robbed of her only child. And such a lovely, innocent child! Though the child will come back again one of these days, it is— But there are other things I should like to show you. No; not that frame—that is empty. This way, please."

Nest followed wonderingly. For the frame that Givanni spoke of as empty was full of bloom. Nest could see as much through the meshes of the net that covered it.

CHAPTER XVII

MR. RUFUS SEBAG

Lady Laurisdale was awaiting tea in a shady corner of the terrace when the girls returned. She appeared to be deeply interested in the story of the afternoon's proceedings. Her interest in Givanni was almost flattering. She asked a score of questions concerning him.

"Fancy my not having heard of Mr. Givanni before!" she exclaimed. "Really I didn't know I was so ignorant of my neighbors. You must think I take little interest in the people about me. And that is a man that might have saved me many an hour of boredom. You say he has quite new flowers?"

"Well, neither of us had seen them before," Nest explained. "They are what he calls cross-bred flowers. He does not appear to be in the least satisfied with them. He spoke of one perfect bloom that somebody had robbed him of. He seems to miss it very much."

Lady Laurisdale balanced a teaspoon thoughtfully on the edge of her cup. There was an eager gleam in her eyes.

"Ah! I can quite imagine it," she said. "I should feel just like that if I were in his place. He didn't happen to tell you anything more than that, I suppose?"

"No, he was rather reticent about it. He was very angry about something, and yet in a way, glad. He was mysterious, too, he did not wish us to look at one frame, because, he said, it was empty. But I could see between the meshes of the netting that covered it, and it was full of the most beautiful flowers. I believe the man is a genius, Lady Laurisdale."

"I am certain of it," Lady Laurisdale smiled. "It is evident I must cultivate Mr. Givanni's acquaintance. Why did you never mention him, Sybil?"

"But I have done so more than once," Sybil protested. "I remember telling you about Givanni the last time I was here. Probably you did not listen, or you may have been thinking of something else. But I have never seen such flowers before. Givanni, however, on that occasion was only eloquent on the subject of early vegetables."

Nest rose regretfully to her feet. Her conscience was beginning to trouble her. This had been a delightful day on the whole, but from the hour she had left home till now she had not given her father a single thought. Really, it was time she returned to the Grange.

"I don't know when I have enjoyed myself so much," she said. "It is horrible to say so when there is so much trouble at home, but I hope you won't think me heartless, Lady Laurisdale. Perhaps you will let me come again some other day?"

"You are to come whenever you like," Lady Laurisdale said cordially. "I want you to use the castle as if it were your own. Besides, Sybil will be glad to see you as long as she is here."

Nest left her ladyship, feeling somewhat cheered and uplifted. She had it in her heart to be grateful to her father for bringing this thing about, whatever his own motives may have been. Her cheeks tingled as she thought how it had been managed, but she would not pursue the line of her reflections farther. She parted with Sybil at the lodge gates and made her way thoughtfully homewards across the fields. At the bottom of the avenue a little man was talking excitedly to the lodge-keeper.

"I tell you it's no use," the latter was saying. "You can't see him. Reason? He won't be able to see anybody for a long time. Met with an accident, he has."

"But my business is most pressing," the stranger urged.

"Then it will have to keep," was the reply. "Mr. Sairson is unconscious. Injury to the head. Funny you haven't heard about it, seeing that the account was in all the papers. But if you don't believe me, ask this lady. Ain't what I say true, Miss?"

"I regret to say it is," Nest said gravely. "My father can see nobody at present."

The little man regarded Nest with undisguised astonishment.

"I beg your pardon, miss," he gasped. "Did I understand you to say that Mr. Sairson is your father?"

"Precisely. I am Miss Nest Sairson. Can I do anything for you?"

"Accident!" the stranger exclaimed. "It seems about impossible to imagine—There now, what am I saying? I had no idea there was any trouble here. I came this afternoon on business of the utmost importance. Still, it can't be helped. Would you be so good as to take my card, Miss, and give it to your father directly he is in a position to understand things?"

Nest took the card in her fingers. She saw that it announced Mr. Rufus Sebag, and that he was a lawyer with offices in a street off the Strand. Its owner was a dapper little man, very dark and very oily; his nose was long, his lips were thick, and his clothes had a glossy look that suggested newness and a measure of prosperity to which, apparently, the wearer had not been long accustomed. Had Nest but known it, he was the Jew of melodrama to the life. She took the card with a certain indifference, and very faintly acknowledged the flourishing sweep of Mr. Sebag's glistening silk hat.

"I am greatly obliged to you, miss," he said. "You are a witness that I am here, and that I have complied with Mr. Sairson's instructions. I wish you good evening."

Once more the glossy hat glistened in the sun, and Mr. Sebag was gone. The puzzled look remained on his face as he walked along the road. Despite his air of prosperity he produced a packet of vile cigarettes and lighted one with a safety match.

"Well, if that isn't the limit," he muttered. "When that girl told me her name, you could have knocked me down with a feather. A real thoroughbred from top to toe. I haven't been a money-lender's tout all these years without knowing the real thing when I see it. So that's John Sairson's daughter. And he never so much as bragged about her. Out of his line, perhaps. I should like to know what the girl honestly thinks of him. Met with an accident, has he? Somebody gave him a biff on the head, more likely. He was always expecting that sort of thing. Prepared for it, too. That being the case, my course is clear. In the circs, I'll have to see Lady Laurisdale."

The cigarette was finished at length, and Sebag turned his steps in the direction of the Castle. He admired the regality of the park, but though he was impressed, he was not in the least overawed. He rang the bell with a firm hand, and demanded to see Lady Laurisdale at once. The footman eyed him with sleepy insolence. He had reckoned up Mr. Sebag to an ounce. This was some impudent dun, of course.

"Her ladyship is engaged," he said. "What's your business?"

"My business is with Lady Laurisdale," Sebag responded, "and your business is to take this card to her. Are you going to do it yourself, or do you want my help?'"

Sebag walked coolly into the hall, where he proceeded to interest himself in the family portraits. Some of them aroused his professional admiration. He cheerfully hummed an air as he skipped from one canvas to another. The big footman looked at him superciliously for a few seconds, then shrugged his shoulders. Clearly it was useless to try to snub Mr. Sebag. He came back a moment or two later.

"Her ladyship will see you in the library," he said. "Kindly step this way, young man."

Sebag's eyes glittered. He was ushered into the library where Lady Laurisdale was seated at a table in one of the oriel windows. She appeared to be regarding Sebag's card with vague curiosity.

"You wished to see me," she said. "Some charitable request, I presume?"

"Well, no, my lady," Sebag responded. "Matter of business, I assure your ladyship. I've called on behalf of Mr. John Blaydon. You see, as your ladyship takes no notice of our letters—"

"Our letters! Have I had any correspondence with you?"

"Indirectly, your ladyship, quite indirectly. If you could let me have a cheque for the money—"

"Cheque! And failing that? Suppose I say that it is not convenient for the present?"

"That would be very awkward," Sebag murmured. "We have already got what is called a judgment against you at the suit of John Blaydon. Over £1,200 altogether. I am empowered to act for Mr. Blaydon in the matter. Of course, if the money is paid by to-morrow—"

"Let us understand one another," Lady Laurisdale said. "If you don't get the money, I am to understand that unpleasant consequences follow. Is that what you mean?"

"I am merely the agent in the matter," Sebag rejoined. "We shall have to put a man in possession—what is commonly called a bailiff, your ladyship. Very awkward for you."

"But you can't take this step without definite instructions from Mr. Blaydon. I mean written instructions. Do you mean to tell me that you have these instructions?"

Sebag hesitated for a second, and then produced a letter from a pocket book and handed it to Lady Laurisdale. She read it with a gravity befitting the occasion.

"I begin to understand," she announced. "I see this is an official letter emanating from Mr. Blaydon's office. Am I to take it that this is his signature?"

"I desire your ladyship to suppose that such is the case."

Lady Laurisdale smiled. For one in an awkward predicament she was singularly at her ease. In an uneasy way Sebag was conscious that she was making fun of him. He was a new type to her, and she was studying him curiously.

"Now, please, be very careful," she said. "I take it you have not seen Mr. Blaydon lately, and that you are only acting on a general line of policy. This is the kind of letter you get from Blaydon's people periodically, at the times unfortunate clients are to be sold up. Now, Mr. Sebag, I shall be obliged if you will look at me and tell me whether this is Mr. Blaydon's own signature?"

Sebag shuffled in his chair. Lady Laurisdale was exceedingly fair to look upon, but Sebag appeared to find a great difficulty in doing so. His dark eyes traveled restlessly about the room.

"Well," he said in a sudden burst of candor, "to be absolutely correct it isn't. The letter is probably signed by Mr. Blaydon's manager. Still, for my purpose—"

"Quite so; for your purpose it is sufficient. In the ordinary way it would enable you to proceed, it entitles you to go on with your business with the comfortable feeling that you are doing a good thing for your client and yourself. Now, I happen to know that Mr. Blaydon does not wish to press this—at least, not for the time being. If he had been at the office the letter would not have been sent. If you wish to lose one of your most valuable and most esteemed clients, act up to your instructions. But you will be well advised to take the trouble to communicate personally with Mr. Blaydon first."

Sebag said something under his breath. What all this meant he could not for the life of him understand. Yet Lady Laurisdale was so collected and sure of her ground that he hesitated.

"Mr. Blaydon is—is—away," he stammered; "I can't get at him."

"Oh! really? In that case you had better go on with the business. When shall we look for your man in possession? I should like to have a few hours' notice of his visit. I think that will do. Please, ring the bell for me—Letchford, will you show this gentleman out?"

Mr. Sebag departed without further words. Over another of his cheap cigarettes he pondered the situation. He did not know that Lady Laurisdale was watching him from the library window.

"I feel sure of it," she said. "I am absolutely convinced now. What will happen to those two poor girls when the truth comes to be told?"

CHAPTER XVIII

CROSSED SWORDS

Public curiosity had been aroused, naturally enough, by the mysterious attack on John Sairson. It was one of the crimes that instinctively appeals to the popular imagination, and a great deal had been made of it in the press. There was a small army of "special correspondents" in the village with a free hand, and it was necessary, therefore, to keep the excitement going. As was only to be expected, Lady Laurisdale came in for her share of attention at the hands of the reporters. They had all sorts of ingenious excuses for calling at the Castle, until the whole thing began to get on her ladyship's nerves. She wrote to Major Renton, Chief Constable for the county, asking his advice. A day or two later Renton arrived to counsel her in person.

"I thought I'd drop in to see you," he said. "May I beg a mouthful of lunch? I don't know how we are to get to the bottom of the affair till Sairson is in a position to speak for himself."

"And that event may never happen, I suppose?"

"That is an error. Sairson appears to have the constitution of an ox. He was sensible yesterday, and Paley tells me he will be about again at the end of the week. How the man's brain escaped injury is a miracle. There was no particular loss of blood, either. Now are you sure you heard no report? You saw nothing at the time that the outrage was committed?"

"I have already said so a score of times," Lady Laurisdale replied. "There was not the slightest noise, and the orchid house appeared to be empty. I can tell you no more than that."

"It is most mysterious," Major Renton said thoughtfully. "We can get no light from the School of Musketry at Hythe, and Scotland Yard is as much in the dark as I am. The thing must have been done whilst you were looking on."

"I suppose so. What was the bullet like?" Lady Laurisdale asked.

Renton took an envelope from his pocket. From it he extracted a little fragment of bright metal, like a scrap of tinted gold foil from the neck of a champagne bottle. He held it out for Lady Laurisdale's inspection.

"There is the cause of the trouble," he explained. "There is what, for want of a better name, we call the bullet. It is obvious that no man in his senses would load a pistol with a wad of tin foil. Besides, when pistols are discharged, they make a noise. If there had been any noise you could not fail to have heard it.

The doctor took this wad of stuff from the base of Sairson's brain, and his escape from death is a miracle."

Lady Laurisdale looked a little less anxious. She was thinking about Jack Barr. In the face of the fresh evidence it was not easy to connect him with the crime. He had come in his desperate condition with the intention of killing John Sairson, but this very fact would preclude any theory of a cunning plot and the use of something subtle in the way of a destroying agent, something novel even to the authorities.

"Are you sure there is nothing else you can tell me?" Renton said again. "Never mind how small and trivial it may appear to be. There are no such things as trifles in our eyes."

Lady Laurisdale shook her head. There were one or two little things, but she had made up her mind that she would not say anything about them to Renton. She preferred to wait and discuss the matter with Sairson himself. He would be sure to mention it at the first opportunity. And, according to the Major, that opportunity was not very far off.

"I am sorry I cannot help you further," she said. "I have told you everything. Are you going to the dance at Rochdale Royal?"

"I suppose so," Renton replied. "The duchess has asked me to bring a few men for the dancing. Are you making up a party for it?"

"I shall have a few guests, as usual. I have offered to get a few men together for her, and put them up here. The duchess has a passion for actors, and Dick helps me there. I can take as many as I like. Sybil Gosway is going with me this time."

Renton's eyes gleamed.

"Miss Gosway is staying with you, then?" he asked. "I shall be glad to meet her again."

"Well, so you shall," Lady Laurisdale laughed. "Come over and dine to-morrow night. Sybil is somewhere in the grounds with Nest Sairson. Oh, you need not elevate your eyebrows in that fashion, Major! I have called on the Sairsons. Let me tell you there is nothing wrong with the womenkind. Mrs. Sairson was a Belham, and the girls are Belhams, too. There they are!"

The two girls burst into the room at this moment. Renton held Sybil's hand a little longer than was absolutely necessary. His eyes bore a message to her. The two had been great friends during Sybil's last visit and she had not forgotten.

"How is the struggle for existence going on?" he asked. "You remember what you told me, don't you? We must find an opportunity to discuss that question. I hope you are making a long stay. How many dances will you give me at Rochdale Royal?"

"I am actually going," Sybil smiled shyly. "I shall wake up presently and find that I have been dreaming. But dad has let me prolong my holiday. Fancy the City Cinderella at Rochdale Royal! What would the duchess say if she knew!"

"She would be delighted," Lady Laurisdale assured her. "Mary Rochdale is one of the most cosmopolitan hostesses in England. You meet all kinds of people there."

Nest stood listening rather enviously.

"This dance is one of the great events of the year, is it not?" she asked.

"So far as we are concerned, it is," Lady Laurisdale replied. "Rochdale Royal in itself is worth a visit. Everything is done on the most magnificent scale. Those people are so rich that they don't know what to do with their money. I wonder whether—"

Blanche Laurisdale pulled herself up suddenly. With her eyes fixed on Nest Sairson's wistful face, she was going to make a suggestion. She was wondering whether it was altogether impossible to include Nest in the party. But her Grace of Rochdale could draw the line; she had systematically refused to be conscious of the existence of the Sairsons.

Nest began to talk eagerly of something else. With quick, sensitive instinct, she had guessed what was passing through her hostess's mind. She pondered it as she walked homewards. Cecil Lugard would be asked, of course, and probably he would think it his duty to go. What would her position be when she was married? She did not see how these exclusive people could leave her out of the charmed circle then. Would they draw the line between her and her mother and Angela? Nest clenched her teeth firmly as she thought of it.

How dreadfully dull it was at home! Cecil was away on business in London, whither he had gone with Lord Laurisdale. A crisis was impending at the Cosmos Theatre, and Lugard was taking a hand. Mrs. Sairson was with her husband, who had demanded to see her. As Nest sat outside she could hear her father's voice as it boomed through the open window. Angela, pale and thoughtful as usual, came out of the house with a book in her hand.

"I hope you have been enjoying yourself," she said, in her gentle way.

"Pretty well," Nest admitted. "I'm going to the Castle for the whole of Friday. They were talking about the Rochdale Royal dance. I should love to go."

"I daresay you would, dear. But that is out of the question."

"I don't see why," Nest said rebelliously. "Lady Laurisdale was on the point of suggesting it. Major Renton is going. You know the man I mean?"

Angela nodded dreamily. She knew everybody by name; it was impossible to live amongst these people and not take some interest in their movements. But there were so many other things to occupy her attention, so many other causes to detach her thoughts.

"I fear you are preparing yourself for a disappointment," she said. "Come, my dear Nest, you don't seriously expect an invitation to this dance. I understood that there was nobody in the whole country more exclusive than the duchess."

"Well, she is and she isn't," Nest persisted. "Lady Laurisdale says she's cosmopolitan."

"Oh! really? What may that mean? Liberal statesmen are popularly supposed to be like that. But one does not expect to find the butcher and baker dining with his lordship at his family seat. It means that the Duchess graciously stoops to patronise certain actors and artists and the like. That kind of thing always looks so well in the newspapers."

"Why, Angela, you are growing cynical."

"My dear girl, it is as well you should realise these things. It is only lately that you have begun to build up such hopes. A little time ago you were content—"

"I wasn't!" Nest protested vigorously. "I never have been content. Ask mother if you don't believe me. Why should we suffer? Why should mother be pushed aside like that. On mother's side, at any rate, we are as good as anybody in the country."

Angela shook her head sadly. She was quite sorry for Nest.

"We are the daughters of Sairson," she said. "We are the Sairson girls. I have no doubt but that is exactly what the county calls us. Oh! what is the good of harping on the fact that mother is a lady? We are ladies as far as that goes. All our instincts are Belham instincts. I daresay it is very nice to go to Lady Laurisdale's house; I am rather inclined to fancy that you have a good friend in her. But you may not find others so anxious to follow Lady Laurisdale's example. Take my advice and make the best of things as they are."

Nest did not pursue the subject further. She ought, perhaps, to have been satisfied with the beauty and luxury of her surroundings. After all, she had a great deal to be thankful for. And it was possible that things might go her way yet. She was grateful to Lady Laurisdale for all she had done and, as youth always is, was anxious for more. Nor was she satisfied that Angela was as perfectly contented as she pretended to be.

"Well, I shall go on as I have begun," she said. "I don't mind a few snubs. Anything will be better than the dreary monotony of this house. I hate all this mystery and underhandedness. And I don't believe you are as contented as you profess to be."

Angela started slightly. A little color crept into her pale cheeks.

"You have no right to say that."

"That's why I said it," Nest retorted coolly. "You and I are made of different clay, my dear. It is not in my nature to sit down and accept what looks like the inevitable. Are you contented?"

"It depends on what you mean by contented."

Nest paced restlessly up and down the room.

"I won't force your confidence," she said. "But I am truly sorry for you."

CHAPTER XIX

TRYING THE SCREW

It takes a good deal to alarm certain people, and Sairson was one of them. He did not suffer from any terrors of imagination, for it was a quality in which he was utterly lacking. He was puzzled and amazed and suspicious and anxious to get even with things, but he was not easily frightened.

Meanwhile, many matters called for immediate attention. He could not go to town, but there was much he could "handle" at the Grange. He was looking forward to the time when he should have the people in these parts under his thumb, when he could compel them, not only to recognise his family, but, as it were, to bow down before them. It never occurred to him that if he had from the first kept himself in the background his wife might have done all this for him. But it was always his way to believe he could do everything far better than anybody else. Therefore, as soon as he found himself able to attend to business again, he wrote to Lady Laurisdale saying that he proposed to call and see her.

To this letter he received no answer. He was not yet aware that Lady Laurisdale had gone far out of her way to show Nest various kindnesses, nor did he know that at the very time when he proposed to call on her ladyship, Nest was sitting outside on the terrace of Laurisdale Castle waiting for Sybil. Sairson called in due course, but could not guess that Nest was so near at hand. He was ready for the fray and not the less inclined to be loud and hectoring because Lady Laurisdale had admitted him at once. It was only when Lady Laurisdale entered the drawing-room and addressed Sairson by name that Nest discovered the personality of the visitor.

She started violently at the sound of her father's voice. Half involuntarily she rose from her seat, but, on second thoughts, resumed it. It was by no means her intention to play the eavesdropper. At the same time, why should she not learn something, why should she be kept in the dark? She had to wait for Sybil in any case. Yes, she would remain.

She heard every word from the drawing-room distinctly.

"This is an unexpected pleasure, Mr. Sairson," Lady Laurisdale said. "I trust you will not suffer any inconvenience from your exertion in coming here. What may I do for you?"

"You can do a great deal if you like," Sairson answered. "Of course, what I propose to say may sound strange in your ears—but I have my way of doing things. It is all very well for you people to sneer at Sairson, but I fancy there's a good deal of envy in it. My wife and girls—"

"They have my sympathy, Mr. Sairson."

"Ah! but don't talk to me like that," Sairson objected. "Knowing what we do know, I am surprised you should take up that tone. They are as good as you, my lady."

"I am not concerned to deny it, Mr. Sairson. Since you force me to speak plainly, there is no doubt but that they are gentlewomen, but unfortunately, your daughters are—your daughters. You understand?"

"Yes, and I'll make you understand, too," Sairson broke out. "None of that nonsense for me, my lady. I've waited pretty patiently, but the time's come for action. We'll make a bargain if you like. You take up my wife and girls, give them your hand, and the thing is done. Get Nest invited to the Duchess's dance. Do that, and I'll keep my mouth shut about certain things I could speak of that your husband wouldn't like. Don't let's quarrel. Let's shake hands on it. But no nonsense, mind!"

"Are you threatening me?" Lady Laurisdale asked quietly. "Is this an ultimatum?"

"As you like it. The thing has to be done."

"And if I refuse? If I order you out of the house? I will make no bargains—I will do as I please; and be good enough to remember that, this is my last word!"

"Oh, is it!" Sairson cried. "We shall see about that, my lady. It's one thing to talk big—"

"Pardon me, Mr. Sairson, I am not talking big. I am merely stating a fact. You have managed to get my husband in your hands; you pretend you are doing him a favor by standing between him and the creature who is known as John Blaydon. The first thing you stipulated for was the recognition of your people. My good man, I could have 'recognised' them in such a way as would have caused them never to want to see me again. You are not capable of appreciating these subtle distinctions, but your wife and daughters are. You think you have done a fine thing, that you have compelled me to respect your wishes. That is why you come in this insolent manner and demand the entree to Rochdale Royal for Nest. There are limits, and you have reached them. I decline to do this thing. This is the point where you threaten me. I say, do your worst, and when you do it, the whole world shall learn that you are John Blaydon. It would then be better for you if I declared you were the common hangman. My proofs are ready."

It was strange that Sairson stood and listened quietly to this tirade. At home he would never hear arguments; he always rode roughshod over his womankind. By sheer strength of will and character Lady Laurisdale impressed him. He wished he could be certain that this was only so much brag and bluff on her part, that she meant nothing by it. But he cared not to look into her beautiful eye and haughty face and believe that.

"Have you anything else to say?" Sairson asked.

"I don't think so. You can please yourself as to what you will do next. You can avail yourself of your chance to ruin Lord Laurisdale and myself. If you decide on that course, you must take the consequences. In the meanwhile, I will do nothing and say nothing. I am very fond of your little daughter; she has wormed herself into my heart. For her sake I will remain silent as long as possible. I won't set Cecil Lugard at your throat unless I am obliged to."

Sairson started violently. On the terrace Nest stood quivering from the stab. She had forgotten that side of the matter. What would Cecil Lugard say when he knew? He had sworn to track John Blaydon down and bring him to justice—he had said as much to John Blaydon's face. This was misery deeper and more tragic than the trouble that Angela was suffering from.

It was impossible to hear more. Nest must go away and hide herself somewhere. If she remained much longer, Sybil would return and read things in her face and ask questions. If she did so, the truth must be told. She understood now what Angela meant when she declared that her life was finished. Her own existence had seemed to perish in the last few minutes. She must release Cecil; but what could she say? She would only tell him she had changed her mind and that they could be no more than friends in the future. He would press for her reasons, and she would not be able to disclose them.

It was clear the hideous secret was not to be violated. Lady Laurisdale had beaten her father all along the line, and he was going to accept defeat lying down. The very tone of his voice told her so much. Lady Laurisdale had found the one thing even he was ashamed of. In other respects he would be as hard and unrepentant as before, would pursue his schemes of robbery and plunder, but he was mortally afraid lest the world should hear of his dual personality.

One crumb of consolation was left. Lady Laurisdale knew her father's real character, probably had known it for some time past, and yet, she had treated Nest and the others with the greatest kindness. Clearly she was giving them her sympathy and support. She had not objected that Nest was the daughter of one of the most pernicious rascals in England. She could not take her to Rochdale Royal, of course, but that was only a small consideration. If only Cecil Lugard—

Nest turned away and walked across the terrace to the rose garden and thence to the fields. She could not face Sybil just then. Perhaps to-morrow she would feel stronger. What she wanted now was the seclusion of her own room and the kind relief of tears. But peace of mind was not so easily won. Physically, she suffered from a hot, aching head; mentally, there was a sense of rebellion against fate. She was angry with the world, angry with Angela, who could take things so quietly. Angela, already dressed for dinner, was reading in her room. The expression of her face changed as Nest came in.

"My dear child, what on earth is the matter?" she asked. "You look as if you had seen a ghost, but your cheeks are on flame. Let me send for—"

"Send for nothing," Nest cried. "No doctor can do me any good. Not poppy, nor mandragora, nor all the drowsy syrups of the world. I have seen a ghost—the ghost of my departed happiness. I heard him speak, and his voice was the voice of John Blaydon."

Angela laid her book aside. The smile faded from her face. She put her arm about Nest's shoulders and gently drew her to a seat.

"You poor dear child!" she whispered. "Poor little Nest. So the knowledge has come to you at last. I had thought the secret was safely locked up."

"It is no secret," Nest said. "Lady Laurisdale knows it. She must have known it before she came to the house, so you see how splendidly she has behaved to mother and us! Everybody probably knew it but myself. I overheard my father and Lady Laurisdale talking a little while ago. He went to the Castle, ill as he is, trying to force Lady Laurisdale to take me to the Rochdale Royal dance. You can imagine her contemptuous amusement. Rochdale Royal and the daughter of Blaydon, the money-lender!"

"She did not order him out of the Castle?"

"No, Angela; she was wonderful! Her cool contempt cut him like a whiplash. He had them all in his power, and she knew it. Yet she never showed the slightest trace of fear. She told him what she had found out, and what she meant to do, and how he would be exposed. He never even denied that he was

John Blaydon. How strange it seems! I am the daughter of John Blaydon, the money-lender. He is the man that Truth loves to castigate. I have read the things they wrote about him! So that is our father, and we are dependent upon him for our bread and butter!"

"Try not to take it too deep, dear!" Angela whispered.

"Oh! I am trying to realise it—to comprehend that the hideous dream is a reality. I am trying not to wish that that accident had ended the career of a man who takes the bread out of the mouths of the widow and the fatherless. I am wondering whether I can continue leading a life of luxury with these facts staring me in the face. How long have you known?"

"Three years, Nest. Jack Barr discovered it. He told me and I released him. After that I did not seem to take any interest in anything. We kept the facts from you so that you should have all the pleasure you could get before the inevitable happened. When I speak of the inevitable, I mean Cecil Lugard. But perhaps—"

"No! no!" Nest cried. "Pray do not count on that! It may not be possible to keep the thing secret, but Cecil need not learn it from me. I may see it my duty to tell him, but at present I simply could not do so. I shall send him about his business, and there will be an end to it. But I refuse to stay here; I would rather go behind a bar and sell beer. No, you need not pity me. There's the gong!"

Nest came to dinner presently, astonishingly calm and collected. She was late, and Sairson stared at her; he seemed to be in one of his worst moods. The others sat with downcast eyes.

"I am sorry," Nest said. "It shall not occur again. You are frightening my mother. If she took a leaf out of Lady Laurisdale's book it would be the better for her."

"What do you mean?" Sairson asked gruffly.

"What I say," Nest replied. "I was on the terrace when you called at the Castle to-day, and heard all you had to say. I should like to know what you intend to do about it!"

CHAPTER XX

IN THE OPEN

John Sairson's coarse face grew dark. No member of his family had ever ventured to address him like this before. Indeed few people would dare do so. The big veins on his forehead stood out like whipcord. He glanced round the room, his angry gaze taking in the beauty and elegance of it all. And all belonged to him—every picture and every work of art. In sheer money the house and its contents would fetch a hundred thousand pounds. Men whose opinions he valued had praised his old prints and his furniture. It was all his—he had made it himself. He had climbed out of the gutter, and men took off their hats to him. He had known what it was to starve, and he boasted of it. He knew of the cruelty and inhumanity of the world, and had modelled his life accordingly.

He was not going to be spoken to like this. He waited, though impatiently, till the decanters and cigarettes were placed on the table, and the servants left the room. He would put Nest in her place. His glance swept from the pale agitation of his wife's face to the pallid humility of Angela's downward glance. He looked for some kind of shrinking on Nest's part. With a certain uneasiness he noticed no sign of fear. Nest was as pale as the others, but her eyes were steadfastly blazing.

He burst out furiously, bringing his fist down upon the table till the glasses jingled. What on earth did she mean by it? What did she expect to gain by speaking to her father like that! But all this roaring, red-faced anger was wasted on Nest.

"You are forgetting my mother and sister," she said. "There is no occasion to be vulgar. I ask you a plain question and I should like a plain answer. Are you John Blaydon?"

Sairson hesitated to reply. It was one of his boasts that he was afraid of nothing. He professed to pooh-pooh the attempt on his life. And yet he equivocated. Lady Laurisdale was quite right—there was one thing that he was afraid of, and that was the truth about his other self.

"What difference can it make if I am?" he demanded,

"We will come to that presently," Nest went on. She was astonished at her own audacity. "I want to know whether Lady Laurisdale's accusation was correct."

"Accusation!" Sairson snarled. "Anybody might suppose you are speaking of a criminal."

"John Blaydon is a criminal," Nest said sternly. "There may be no punishment in the courts for such as him, but he is a criminal for all that. He is worse than the wretches who conspire to put up the price of meat and bread. Look what the papers have said about him! They say he does not scruple to take fees from poor people without the faintest intention of lending the money. They scrape a few shillings together which John Blaydon pockets and smiles. 'Truth' openly declares that he ought to be put in gaol. And you—you are John Blaydon!"

Sairson said nothing. The bitter words seemed to fascinate him. It was almost impossible to believe that they proceeded from the lips of this while-faced girl. He had an uncomfortable admiration for her pluck. Still, the words rankled none the less because they were true.

"You don't know what you are talking about," he replied. "Nobody believes what the papers say. Besides, they hit wildly at anybody in these cases. I know how to keep Lady Laurisdale's mouth shut."

"Ah! I daresay you do," Nest said calmly. "I gathered as much. If I remember rightly, she promised to keep the shameful thing secret for my sake. But there are others whom you cannot silence."

"I should like to know where they are, then!" Sairson sneered.

"Mine!" she said. "Mine! Unless you kill me, you can't keep me silent. My duty is too plain. A day or two ago I was the happiest girl in the world. I had given my heart to a good man; I was secure in his love. I am speaking of Cecil—"

"Was there ever such a fool!" Sairson blazed out. "What has Lugard to do with it? Why tell him at all? It is no business of his."

"That is exactly what I expected you to say," Nest retorted. "But on that score I prefer to have the opinion of my mother and Angela. I know what they will say, and that I shall agree with them. Cecil Lugard has a task before him. He means to track down and expose John Blaydon, the man who stole the property from General Lugard, and is responsible to God for the poor old man's death. You heard Cecil say so, he told you as much to your face. We are living in Cecil's ancestral home—the home you robbed the Lugards of. Cecil thinks you bought the property from Blaydon. What will he say when he knows the truth?"

"The girl's mad," Sairson said hoarsely, "stark, staring mad."

"You may think so. But your code is different to mine—to ours. Do you suppose I could marry Cecil Lugard in the circumstances? Could I become the wife of the man who has sworn he will not rest till he has sent my own father to prison?"

"And you actually mean to tell him everything?" Sairson gasped.

"Tell him! Why should I tell him? He is bound to know. Ask mother and Angela what they think!"

Sairson scowled round on his family. There was no occasion to ask any questions. He saw at a glance that wife and daughter both sided with Nest. A wild impulse to fly out at them, to lay violent hands on them, possessed him. If this publicity happened, then the work of the last ten years was undone. With all his bluster he was really ashamed of his connection with John Blaydon; with all his bulldog tenacity he feared the contempt of his fellow-men. He was full of the gospel according to Mammon, he clung to the tenet that money could do anything. He had made up his mind to get in with "the county;" sooner or later he would be a welcome guest everywhere. Already he had compelled Lady Laurisdale to be friendly with the family. The conquest of Rochdale Royal was only a matter of time.

Now this infernal thing had come to light. Lady Laurisdale was aware of facts that were unknown even in the City of London. How on earth had she found it out? What ill luck that Nest should have overheard that compromising accusation! If she spoke, the whole family must clear out of Marlton Grange. No servant would stay with them, and the very village children would call after them in the street. And this silly, white-faced girl had this tremendous power in her hands. The like danger had occurred three years before, but it had been easier then. The circumstances had changed since then, and the peril was far closer. Cecil Lugard was made of different clay from Jack Barr.

Perhaps Nest might think better of it. She was hurt and angry, but was talking wildly. No doubt she would see things otherwise in the morning. She was fond of the house, and would not be in the least anxious to be pointed at as the daughter of John Blaydon. She would think of the scandal as Angela had done. Angela had burst into a torrent of tears and rage and despair, but had thought better of it in the end. Perhaps he had exaggerated the danger.

"Go to bed!" he said harshly, "and don't discuss matters you don't understand."

He flung himself from the room and withdrew to the library. Nest followed her mother and Angela into the drawing-room. Her eyes were still dry and hard and tears were far away yet. She turned impatiently from her mother's caressing hand.

"Not yet," she said; "not yet, mother. Let us sit down and talk this over. How long have you known?"

"I have known it for some years," Mrs. Sairson said timidly. "Not at first, of course, but when Angela was a little girl. You can imagine what a shock it was to me!"

Nest hurried over to her mother and kissed her impulsively.

"I'm a selfish beast," she cried. "Thinking about myself all the time. Oh, I know how you must have suffered. But why did you stay?"

"My dear, few of us have the strength and courage to get away from our environment. There were painful reasons then why I should stay. After you were born and Angela grew older, I decided to make the best of my wrecked life for your sakes. You will understand some day what a mother's feelings are."

"Never!" Nest said. "My life is finished, just as yours and Angela's. There, talking about myself again. Did Jack Barr go away because of this dreadful thing?"

"In a measure," Angela explained. "I did not tell him. I merely explained there was a reason why I could not become his wife. He found out the truth for himself. My father thought he had deserted me, and set to work to ruin Jack, swearing he should come back on his knees asking for terms. I don't want to talk about it. Oh, I had hoped you might never know. It was only when Cecil Lugard came on the scene that I saw the story must be told."

Nest lapsed into silence. She was trying to grasp the hideousness of it all. The gracious space and peace of the drawing-room oppressed her. The pictures, the flowers, the shaded lights seemed so remote from the ghastly truth. Everything was so refined, in such good taste, and her mother and Angela were such perfect dears. It was almost impossible to believe that John Blaydon was brooding and sulking close at hand in the library. What had the money-lender to do with a scene like this? How could such a person be her father?

"I will go to bed," she said wearily; "not to sleep, but to lie awake in the dark and work this out. I daresay I shall get over it in time. I must not be less brave than you two poor darlings; but you can imagine how I feel to-night!"

Angela would have followed had her mother not detained her.

"Better leave her to herself," she declared. "The child is a Belham, and will get over it in time, as we have done."

Nest made her way wearily across the hall. At the sound of her footsteps Sairson came out. There was something like the parody of a smile on his face. Evidently he was disposed to be friendly.

"Come into the study for a minute," he said. "I want to speak to you. Now, look here, my girl, I daresay this has given you a shock and that sort of thing. I've been trying to make allowances for your feelings.

Your mother has brought you up in this way, and perhaps she has been right. But her ideas about honor and integrity are played out. Money is everything nowadays. I have it, and don't know how rich I am. If you want money—"

"Money!" Nest retorted scornfully. "What is money to me? I hate the very name of it. But for money you might have had a claim on me to-day. Money is the cause of nearly all the crime in the world. The love of it poisons friendship."

"Would you like to have £10,000?" Sairson asked doggedly.

Nest smiled serenely. Her father was actually attempting to bribe her to keep silent about everything.

"Ten thousand pounds!" he repeated.

"But when you see Lugard again, I want you to—"

A man servant stood suddenly in the doorway, and Sairson paused.

"Mr. Lugard would like a few words with you, sir!"

CHAPTER XXI

CROSS QUESTIONS

That knowledge is power was an axiom in which Mr. Rufus Sebag firmly believed. Not that he regarded it from a lofty intellectual level; on the contrary, his knowledge was more or less personal. He liked to know about people and their ways—to hear their little secrets. He had risen from the gutter by such methods; by means of a cunningly concocted story he had compelled his late employer to give him his articles and thus had become a distinguished ornament of the law. That he would go far and make money was now certain. It had been a good day for him when John Blaydon's dirty work came his way. It was a glorious opportunity for finding out things. But, curiously enough, he had never seen John Blaydon.

Everything had been done by correspondence, and all accounts were settled with one of Blaydon's clerks. Sebag bided his time, knowing that it would come some day. Certainly he must have pleased Blaydon, or the delicate matter of Lady Laurisdale's debt had never been placed in his hands.

He had come down to Cromer full of importance. It was a puzzle why he had been instructed by letter from Blaydon's manager to go and see Mr. Sairson. He knew something of Sairson by reputation, possibly he and Blaydon did business together. Perhaps Sairson had bought Lady Laurisdale's debt. Before Sebag had reached the Castle his astute mind had grasped the truth. Sairson was desirous of making his way into society. He had a daughter, a very pretty one, too, Sebag thought. The Grange and the Castle should know each other.

But Lady Laurisdale's reception of him had been on different lines from what he anticipated. It had been a staggerer to find her so cool about his threats. She behaved as if she were mistress of the situation.

Why had she questioned Blaydon's signature? This sorely upset him as he made his way back to the village.

A few discreet questions, however, might throw light on the matter. He had smoked one or two more of the cheap cigarettes before it dawned upon him. He chuckled gleefully. Of course, that was the explanation.

"Why didn't I think of that before?" he asked himself. "It's as plain as the nose on my face, and there's nothing much plainer than that. What a joke! If I were in John Sairson's place I should enjoy a joke like that. That's the way I get the best of these swells. After all, they can't get on without money. Bring their aristocratic noses to the grindstone! Threaten to sell 'em up! Sairson then gets into the best set if he cares to. John Sairson and John Blaydon are the same man. If this doesn't put money into my pocket I'm not Rufus Sebag. He's ashamed of the fact, that's what's the matter with him. And her ladyship knows it. She spotted the difference between their signatures like a shot. There's a woman for you. Fancy Laurisdale pottering about a painted old woman like Sadie Carton when he has a wife like her ladyship. I think I'll stay here a day or two and see how matters shape. It'll be worth my while."

It was no very difficult matter to procure quarters at the Laurisdale Arms. There was a general store in the village, where Sebag obtained such things as he could not get at a hotel. One or two men lounged about the bar of the old-fashioned inn with the obvious mark of London upon them. Sebag wondered what they were doing there. He had forgotten the mysterious accident to Mr. Sairson for the moment. With his new knowledge he followed the conversation eagerly.

"No sort of a clue, I suppose?" he asked.

"There's no clue, and there never will be," the landlord said significantly. "I tell the gentlemen they are wasting their time here. Not but what I'm glad of their custom."

One of the journalists lighted a cigarette thoughtfully. He hesitated before he accepted Sebag's hospitable offer of liquid refreshment.

"I'm not so sure of that, landlord," he said. "Anyhow, it's an interesting story. My people don't think I have been wasting my time. They've given me a free hand till Monday. I've no objection to a holiday. It's a first-rate story."

"I understood it was an accident," Sebag said. "Funny I'd heard nothing about it, though I was sent here to see Mr. Sairson on business."

"Accident be hanged!" the pressman exclaimed. "I've been at the game too long to be taken in with a theory like that. Her ladyship could tell a tale if she liked."

Sebag pricked up his ears. Evidently he should hear something.

"I wish you'd tell me about it, sir," he asked. "There's nobody can tell a story as well as you gentlemen of the press. What lady do you allude to?"

"Why, Lady Laurisdale, of course," the reporter explained. "She was with Sairson at the time. But perhaps I had better begin at the beginning. Here is the thing in the nutshell. Lady Laurisdale is having luncheon on Sunday at Marlton Grange. As far as I can make out, it was the first time she had ever been in the house. Rather looked down upon the Sairsons, it seems. On the contrary, Lord Laurisdale was staying in the house, which is rather queer. But we need not go into that. Anyway, her ladyship arrives to lunch. Afterwards she goes into one of the orchid houses with Sairson to look at the blooms. The place is quiet, no servants or gardeners about and, of course, everything is quite clear in the sunshine. I've been in that orchid house. It is full of flowers, but the foliage amounts to nothing; plenty of feathery bloom, and all that, but you can see through them easily. It would be impossible for a cat to get into the place without being spotted. Mr. Sairson steps behind one of the stages to pick off a spray of blossom for Lady Laurisdale. She sees him stagger and fall, and thinks he has met with an accident. Nothing of the kind, sir. Sairson has been shot. A fraction of an inch lower, and he would have been a dead man."

"Was the door of the orchid house open?" Sebag asked.

"That's a shrewd question, sir!" the reporter said. "'Pon my word, you should be one of us. As a matter of fact the door of the orchid house was carefully closed. You take no risks with these expensive orchids. Sairson lay there—"

"Pardon me," Sebag interrupted, "Lady Laurisdale saw nothing, you say. Did she hear anything? I mean did she hear anything like a shot?"

"She heard nothing," the journalist said emphatically. "On that point she is absolutely clear. I asked her myself. You see how important it is. If there is one thing certain it is that Mr. Sairson's life was attempted by means of a shot. The missile used was an extraordinary one, but it came from the barrel of a firearm of some kind. Now, so far as I know, there is no firearm the world that does not make a noise, but Lady Laurisdale heard nothing. It was a still and peaceful afternoon, and nobody was about. If there had been a report it would have been impossible to mistake it. Oh, it's a stunning mystery!"

Sebag pondered the matter in silence. He was asking himself several questions. His experience of life taught him to doubt everybody and everything. He had a profound impression that honesty was only a word, and meant nothing. There might be honorable people about, but he had never met them. Duplicity and crime were only a matter of degree. For instance, Lady Laurisdale might scorn to pick a pocket, but she would have no trouble in wiping out her indebtedness to John Blaydon. Sebag was sure she had discovered that Sairson and Blaydon were one and the same. Probably she had used the secret to tie Sairson's hands and he had defied her to do her worst. It was possible she was at the bottom of the whole tragedy. The theory seemed rather far-fetched, but one never could tell. At any rate, if she had had no hand in the crime, she knew who the guilty party was. To say she had heard no explosion was absurd. That was where she was overdoing the thing. It would have been far better had she admitted the explosion. It would be worthwhile to keep an eye on Lady Laurisdale.

"Have you any theory advance," Sebag asked.

The journalist closed his left eye knowingly. No specialist cares to acknowledge defeat, and he was no exception to the rule.

"My boy," he said solemnly. "I've been fed upon this sort of thing all my life. You say you know it, but I am the man who got to the bottom of the Redsands Mystery. I dare say you recollect the sensation it made in the 'Record' ten years ago. Now that was a pure piece of deduction. Sherlock Homes might have been proud of it. I don't say I have found out anything definite, and I don't say I haven't; but at any rate I have satisfied my chief that I'm not wasting my time here."

Sebag offered the due meed of admiration. All the same it was plain that this braggart knew nothing. The journalist cleared off presently and gave Sebag the opportunity of addressing a few questions to the landlord.

"It isn't for me to say," the latter said. "I'm his lordship's tenant. He's all right if he would only stay at home and look after the estate, and not waste his money on those actresses in London. Her ladyship? Oh, she's proud and haughty—regular aristocrat, in fact, but kind-hearted to a degree. Do anything for any of us. Children all love her."

"Very friendly with the Sairsons, I suppose?"

"Well, not till quite lately. Never went there, in fact, till the other day. But she seems to have taken up with the Grange young ladies sudden-like."

"Very pretty ladylike girls, they are."

"Oh, the girls are all right! Real good bred 'uns they are, and so is the mother. How Mrs. Sairson could ever have married that man is a mystery."

"He doesn't seem to be popular here."

"Popular!" the landlord snorted. "A common chap like him! He may have heaps of money, but he's as common as dirt. Look at him! Like a monkey in his best clothes! Look at his coarse red face, and listen to his bullying swagger! Why, I'm a gentleman compared to him. They do say he made his money in a scoundrelly sort of way. Nothing will ever convince the people about here that he did not swindle poor old General Lugard out of his property, though I've heard it said that the estate was bought and paid for."

"Then you don't know anything definite?"

"No, and don't want to. Well, what can I do for you?"

The question was addressed to a man who swaggered into the bar. He stood facing the landlord, and, as he did so, jingled some coins in his pocket.

"Too early for champagne," he said. "Alas! for liqueurs! Whisky and soda interfere with the finest work of the brain or genius. Draw me a glass of beer."

CHAPTER XXII

"A POOR PLAYER."

At the sound of the stranger's voice, Sebag started. It was a sonorous voice, clear and yet truculent, the rolling of the r's suggested long contact with the stage. The man was tall and stout, dressed in sufficiently loud tweeds, the pattern of which only seemed to emphasise his amazing assurance. The boots had at one time been patent leather, now they were mere shells held together by shreds and patches.

The greasy hair hung down under the brim of a white bowler that was tipped to an extraordinary angle over the left ear. The fat, impudent, sultry face was clean-shaven, the bulging eyes were filled with tiny red veins. In short he was one of the type that Paul May loved to draw—the thoughtless broken-down comedian, blaming the whole world for his failure, excepting, always the one person most responsible for his misfortunes namely, himself.

"Ah, bright ale thou art, my darling!" he hummed cheerfully. "O, my faith, landlord, a pleasant beverage. I would fain have another. I would also pass the night here, between your sheets scented with lavender, lulled to sleep by the sweet silence of the night."

"A deposit of five shillings will put that right," the landlord returned distantly.

"Ah! that is where the difficulty comes in, landlord," the stranger smiled. "It seems an odd thing for Dudley Beaumont to say—you have heard of Dudley Beaumont, of course?"

"Never heard the name in my life," the landlord said stolidly.

"Really! You surprise me! And this—as a great statesman once observed—is fame! Rack your brains my gentle host. Think! Dudley Beaumont, the actor, the actor! The man who more than once has played at Sadringham by command of his Majesty. Look at that ring. Take it in your hand. The King himself gave it to me—from that day to this it has never been off my finger. It would not have been off my finger now, but for the fact that my manager at Cromer decamped yesterday with the treasury and left a star company absolutely stranded. For a moment I was stunned. I trusted that man—he had been with me from his earliest childhood. I was stunned, I say. There was nothing for it but to walk over here and beg a temporary loan from my old friend, Lord Laurisdale."

"Lord Laurisdale is up a tree," the landlord said.

Mr. Beaumont was greatly concerned. He clutched his head and staggered back. It was a blow that he had not deserved at the hand of fate. Speechless with emotion he held out his glass to the landlord.

"No good," the the landlord said. "Can't be done at any price below twopence. If the King gave you this ring the jeweller grossly deceived his Majesty, for it ain't worth a shilling. I wasn't valet to the late Lord Laurisdale without learning something of those matters."

Dudley Beaumont finished the fresh drink without a word. He dropped into a chair with the air of a man who is beyond the reach of fate. The landlord left the bar in response to a call from outside, and Sebag spoke for the first time.

"What wind blows you here, Mr. Beaumont?" he asked. "Can I be of any assistance?"

The actor turned his eyes as if in mute gratitude to Heaven.

"Now this is a manifestation," he said. "In the darkest hour before the dawn—"

"Cut it short," Sebag said. "If a sovereign is any use to you—"

"My dear sir, my very dear sir!" Beaumont wept. "How can I sufficiently thank you? Do not despise these tears; do not say they are unmanly. There are times when even nerves of iron collapse before the one touch of nature."

"Oh, stow it," Sebag said. "The landlord will be back soon. Is a sovereign any good? What are you doing here? Of course, we can dismiss all that pretty story of the star company."

"A playful fancy," Beaumont smiled, as he clutched the gold coin. "For the time being I'm broke. I lost a shop at Norwich last week, because of the persistent—-"

"Because you wouldn't keep sober. Oh, do drop it, Mr. Beaumont! I may be able to help you a little if you will only be rational."

Beaumont ceased to caress his dome-like brow, as he would have called it. He tossed the sovereign on the counter with a lordly air and demanded a brandy and soda of the landlord who had resumed his place at the bar.

"And take your five shillings out of that, my good fellow," Beaumont said. "It pleased my humor to have a little sport at your expense, but there are many other fellows where that paltry one came from. Fact is," Beaumont went on in lower tones, meant only for his patron, "I did come here to see Laurisdale. A little secret in your ear, Sebag. You've done me one or two good turns, but I've money in thy purse—I mean in thy way. But I think it never occurred to me to tell you that Sadie Carton is my wife."

"Bless my soul!" Sebag exclaimed.

"Oh, its true!" Beaumont said with glowing pride. "When I married her I was in a very different position from what I am in now. Then I had money to spend. To look at me you wouldn't believe that I was at Clare College, Oxford, but I was. I always had a weakness for the stage, and should have got on well but for the—"

He lifted the big glass of brandy and soda significantly.

"I should have made a name for myself as a comedian. Plenty of folk prophesied it, and Irving was one of them. When I met my wife first she was in the second row of the chorus. She was wonderfully fascinating in those days—not clever, you know, but she had a way with her. I spent no end of money on her when we were first married; I used all the influence I had, and she began to get on. She never could act, and she never will; but she managed to get round people. I suppose she cared for me as far as it was in her nature to care for anybody. But she was always greedy and grasping, and ready to take presents from her admirers. Now see where she has got to, drawing her hundreds a week, piles of money and jewels—and I am starving. For years she has refused to see me; she won't reply to my letters, and declines to send me a farthing."

Beaumont hid his face in his hands, and shed a few maudlin tears. From under heavy eyelids the black eyes of Sebag watched him curiously. This business was very well in its way, but the little Jew felt he was getting no farther. His quick instinct told him that Beaumont was there for some desperate purpose, and he must find out what it was. Half intoxicated, as he was, Beaumont managed to parry the most dexterous of his questions.

"But you did not tell me why you came here?"

"Yes, I did," Beaumont remonstrated. "I came to see Laurisdale. I wanted to put my unfortunate case before him. When he hears that I am the husband of his leading lady, he must help me. If he doesn't do that, he may put in a good word for me with Sadie."

"He's got no money," Sebag said. "He's as poor as you are—in Blaydon's hands my boy."

The news did appear to distress the comedian. He chuckled amiably.

"Is that so?" he asked. "Well, it might be worse. It might be a great deal worse. I can put Blaydon in his proper place when the time comes. Like Sairson."

"Oh, really!" Sebag said. "Then you know something of Sairson?"

"My dear boy, I know all about him. There is nothing connected with the amiable Sairson that is not known to me. For instance, let me tell you—"

Sebag leant forward eagerly, his dark eyes twinkling.

"Go on," he whispered, "I'm listening Mr. Beaumont. You were saving that—"

"No, I wasn't," Beaumont said doggedly. "I was saying nothing of the sort. You are too prying, Sebag. You are too fond of poking your nose into other people's business. Mr. Sairson is a man of the highest reputation and is connected with me by certain ties that I am not going to mention. In certain circumstances he may be good for a loan of substantial amount. If I can see him I may get a large cheque from Mr. Sairson. It's possible I shall do so."

"Not at present," Sebag replied. "Sairson is ill. He met with an astounding accident—had the narrowest escape of losing his life. He's getting about, it is true, but he does not see anybody. In fact, I am here on his business."

Beaumont showed no violent emotion on hearing this, he did not appear half so distressed as he did when Sebag informed him casually that Lord Laurisdale was in London. On the contrary, he chuckled to himself, to Sebag's great annoyance.

"That's all right, my boy," he said. "You must rise very early in the morning to get the better of Dudley Beaumont. I have a project on hand, but it needs £2,500. The money will be found. I'm going to take a troupe round the halls on the cleverest entertainment you ever saw. Full of mystery, on the same lines as Maskelyne and Devant's turns. I'll show you how to kill a man without hurting him. I could kill you as you sit in your chair with the landlord looking on, and nobody any the wiser. There are Anarchists in London who would give thousands for the secret."

Sebag diligently studied the floor. He was particularly anxious that Beaumont should not see the expression in his eyes.

"Sounds very interesting," he said indifferently. "Does it require a large company?"

"No, it doesn't," Beaumont said. "Only five all told. If I had £2,500—"

"Well, perhaps I could find it for you. I've been very lucky lately. I daresay—"

But Beaumont was asleep. His head was sunk on his breast, and he snored profoundly. He remained for a long time in that attitude, till, in fact, Sebag had had his supper and night had fallen. He woke up cross and irritable and demanded food. When he had partaken of this he lounged out of the house with a furtive glance about him. Evidently he had some definite object in view, and had no desire that anybody should follow him. Sebag had been watching his movements unobtrusively from the smoking-room. He stepped out into the darkness presently and followed Beaumont. He was not surprised when the latter passed through the lodge gates of Marlton Grange, and went towards the house, with the manner of a man who knows what he is doing and where he is going.

Beaumont stood before the house as if considering what he should do next. The long line of windows presented a brilliant blaze of light. One of the windows on the first floor opened and somebody looked out. A low snigger came from Beaumont's lips. Sebag could just catch a few muttered words before Beaumont went round to the side of the house and entered a conservatory which, so Sebag judged, would open on the morning-room. This room was so dark that the Jew followed cautiously and hid behind a mass of ferns by the door. By and by there was a click, and the place was filled with soft shaded light.

Peering from his hiding-place, Sebag saw a tall, elderly woman in evening dress. Her white sad face was crowned with white hair, and her eyes were red with weeping. Sebag concluded that Mrs. Sairson stood before him.

"Kate!" Beaumont said. "Kate ain't you glad to see me?"

"Why do you come here?" Mrs. Sairson asked passionately. "Why do you come here? Surely, I have enough sorrow without this!"

CHAPTER XXIII

A BLOOD RELATION

Mrs. Sairson's words fell on deaf ears. Beaumont was gazing around him with an air of critical approval. With all his faults he was a keen admirer of the beautiful; indeed, his love for the beautiful—and costly—was largely responsible for his downfall. He admired the artistic arrangement of the light, the dainty beauty of the flowers, the feathery droop of the palms and ferns. He could see through an open door into the hall beyond with its gleam of painted canvas and glow of polished oak. Here and there was the glint of armor. The whole was set in an atmosphere of great refinement.

"Upon my word, Kate?" Beaumont exclaimed, "you are a lucky woman."

Mrs. Sairson's eyes filled with tears, but in a moment her face grew hard again.

"How difficult it is for others to gauge," she said. "You call me lucky. There is not a maid in my kitchen with whom I would not gladly change places."

"Didn't you say something of the sort the last time we met."

"I daresay I did, and it was as true then as it is now. You were proud enough of your family at one time. What would your feelings have been had I come to you and said that I wanted to marry John Sairson?"

"But, Kate, I don't think you have done so badly for yourself."

"Really!" Mrs. Sairson said bitterly. "What do you know about it? What do you care? When did you care about anything but your own selfish pleasure? It is hard to see ourselves as others see us. I wonder whether I have changed as much as yourself."

"A little older, a little greyer," Beaumont said jauntily. "Nothing more. If you look at me—"

"I don't wish to look at you. I am sorry you came. To think that a Belham should have sunk so low. Oh, the pity of it, the pity of it!"

Beaumont flushed uncomfortably. Something penetrated his drink-sodden hide and stung him.

"I have had my misfortunes."

"Your misfortunes," Mrs. Sairson echoed scornfully. "Did you ever bear one of them? The misfortunes were those of the people who came in contact with you. You had health, good looks, a fascinating manner. You had the command of money. You might have been respected and prosperous, if you had possessed anything like a conscience. You spent your own money and that of your friends. You fell into the clutches of John Sairson, whom you robbed, and he would have prosecuted you had I not gone to see him. He was pleased to fall in love with me, and my consent to marry him was the price of your freedom. I did not know then that he was Blaydon, the most notorious money-lender in England—that humiliation was to come later. My friends thought me mad, and turned their backs on me. My mother and father refused to attend my wedding. God help me, they thought that I wanted to marry John Sairson. All this bitter trouble and humiliation I went through to save you. Then I discovered the truth. I was married to a bloodsucking blackguard, who was ambitious for social advancement. Things improved when my girls came. When they were young I lived in them and for them. As they grew older, the haunting fears came back, because I realised that they must discover the truth. It is one of my few consolations that I never had a boy. He might have been like his father—I could not have expected all three to be Belhams."

"You've got a lovely place," Beaumont remarked.

Mrs. Sairson's eyes dwelt scornfully on the picture.

"A lovely place, indeed," she said. "The House of Mammon, the house of blood and tears. My husband swindled Sir George Lugard out of it, and the poor victim committed suicide. Everybody here knows that John Blaydon robbed Sir George of his home. John Sairson is supposed to have bought the house from Blaydon. Do you suppose that the knowledge is not always before me? I have to live here with the ghost of my own past, and the ghost of the Lugards. There is a Lugard here now—one of the finest specimens of his race—and he wishes to marry my daughter Nest. At any other time I would thank God on my knees for a son like that, but not now, not when he tells me at my own table that he will bring that crime home to John Blaydon and get that rascal the punishment he so richly deserves. My husband heard that, and Nest sat listening by. Oh, yes, Dudley, I have a deal to be thankful for!"

"What a situation for a play!" Beaumont muttered. "If I were a younger man—"

Mrs. Sairson laughed harshly. In the midst of her trouble and humiliation, there was something in her brother's ingrained selfishness that moved her.

"A situation for a play, indeed," she said. "Since your mind is bent on that, I will give you another situation for your drama. The young man does not know that the girl he loves is the daughter of the scoundrel whom he is tracking down. She has given him her heart, and has since found out everything. At present she is in the library with her father and the man who loves her. Possibly, by this time the whole story has been told. And you are responsible for it all."

"Oh, come!" Beaumont protested feebly. "I didn't marry John Sairson."

"No, but I did, to save you from the consequences of your folly, and to spare the mother who was so passionately devoted to you. Since then you have had the grace to keep out of my way. Why do you come here at this particular time?"

"I've had my misfortunes, too," Beaumont declared. "When I wrote you that letter yesterday I hoped you would be in a position to help me. I'm desperate, Kate."

Mrs. Sairson's gaze wandered over the speaker from head to foot. It seemed almost impossible to believe that this dilapidated wreck could be her brother.

"It is out of the question," she said. "I have no money—I never have had any money. My husband does not believe in wasting his substance in jewellery. He pays all the accounts by cheques. Never since I have been married have I had a five-pound note to call my own. As for ready cash, my housekeeper is better off than I am."

For the first time Beaumont appeared to be deeply moved.

"Now that's too bad," he exclaimed. "It's really too bad, and that man rolling in money. You should have made a better bargain than that, Kate. You should have had settlements. I've got the chance of my lifetime, and I must have a hundred pounds at any cost. I'd better see Sairson. I have some information he will be glad to get. I hear he's met with an accident."

"Nothing of the kind. An attempt was made on his life."

"Well, that comes to the same thing. They tell me the police are puzzled over the affair. I daresay you'd laugh if I told you I could solve it in ten minutes."

"You always talked like that, Dudley."

"I used to be a conceited young man, I know. But I'm in dead earnest, Kate. A guinea to a gooseberry I could tell you how the whole thing was faked."

"Is this a ruse for obtaining money?"

"Kate, you have my word of honor," Beaumont said solemnly. "I swear to you that I am telling you nothing but the truth. An attempt was made on John Sairson's life; it failed by a fraction of an inch. The police are baffled. Yet the wanderer now before you has the solution in the hollow of his hand. For Sairson's sake, this thing must not be allowed to remain where it is. The miscreant, emboldened by his success, is certain to make the attempt again. I should be worse than a criminal if I remained silent."

The intruder behind the clump of ferns cocked his ear. This was something far beyond his wildest expectation. There was no doubt but that Beaumont was telling the truth. He was no longer the swaggering strolling-player, but a man in deadly earnest. The information might or might not prove valuable, but Sebag was going to hear it.

"Won't you tell me?"

"Well, I don't know," Beaumont said with an engaging air of frankness. "Anxious as I am to help you, I have myself to think of. By making this thing common knowledge there is a serious chance of spoiling a really splendid prospect. I have a fortune in my grip. By making the story public I shall lose that fortune. What I want is to see Sairson and make a bargain with him. If I write he will refuse to see me; if I force myself into his presence he will order me out. It is your positive duty as a wife and mother, Kate, to act as the go-between in the matter. Tell Sairson all I have said, and let him know that I am in a position to prevent any further attempt upon his life. I am approaching him at a great pecuniary sacrifice, and I shall need to be compensated."

"And if he refuses to believe this, Dudley?"

"He will not refuse to believe. With all his threatening, bullying swagger, he is an arrant coward at heart, and will jump at the chance of getting on the safe side of the hedge. Tell him I can prove everything I say up to the hilt, and, if necessary, will show him the ingenious engine of destruction that came so near to ending his career. Only I require at least a thousand pounds for my trouble."

"Then you will not give me any further information, Dudley?"

Once more Sebag stirred uneasily. Was fortune really on his side, or was he to be baffled at the very last?

"I think not," Beaumont said. "You see, the story is too long to be told at a hurried interview like this. Try to get me a chance of meeting Sairson to-night, and then—"

He broke off sharply as a figure fluttered into the hall. It was the young and graceful figure of a girl, with a handkerchief pressed to her eyes. She stood in the full blaze of the light, a prey to overmastering grief. She pressed her handkerchief convulsively to her head and dashed the tears from her eyes.

"Mother!" she cried. "Mother, where are you?"

"It's Nest—my child," Mrs. Sairson whispered. "I must go, Dudley. Something dreadful must have happened. I must go to her at once. Come again to-morrow night at the same time."

"I'll wait," Beaumont replied. "No time like the present. I shall be safe here."

With a passionate gesture Mrs. Sairson turned away.

Beaumont heard low, angry voices in the darkness, followed by the banging of the door.

"I think I'll wait," Beaumont said. "They'll come to their senses presently."

CHAPTER XXIV

A HALF TOLD STORY

Meanwhile events were moving in the library at Marlton. Nest had spoken brave words, and she meant what she said when she declared to her father that Cecil Lugard should know everything. Only a few hours since she had thought she could not bring herself to do this, but her opinion had been modified and she would, if necessary, tell the whole sordid story at the first opportunity. She was fully impressed with the idea that such was her plain duty, but, as the servant stood in the doorway with the announcement that Mr. Lugard desired to see her master, Nest's heart failed her. Her face turned from red to white, and something seemed to rise in her throat and choke her.

Nor was Sairson much less moved. He was perturbed by Nest's apparent determination. He could not forsee what she would say in the excitement of the moment. It might not be too late to induce a change of mind.

"Tell Mr. Lugard to wait in the drawing-room a few minutes," Sairson said. "When I ring the bell, bring Mr. Lugard here.. .. Well, Nest, what do you intend to do. Have you considered it carefully?"

Sairson's manner had changed, and his voice was no longer harsh and strident. "Here is the opportunity you were wishing for. Pshaw! you are nothing but a child!"

"I was yesterday," Nest replied, "but not to-day. Oh, you don't understand—you never could understand. It would be comparatively easy to keep silent to deceive Cecil, to let things take their course. But do you suppose that he is blind? He would notice the change in me at once; he could not fail to see how unhappy I am. He must be told."

Sairson rang the bell passionately. He would test these fine words; he had a feeling that Nest's courage would fail her at the last moment. At any rate, the onus should be on her. She should tell the story, and he would not help her in the least. He was looking subtle and dogged as usual, as Lugard came smiling into the library.

"I hope you will pardon this late visit," the latter said. "I have just come back from London with Laurisdale. Well, Nest, what is the matter? How white you are child!"

Nest murmured something. It was getting to be very hard after all. The mere presence of her lover set her nerves trembling like harp strings. Could she tell him the truth? Could she really part with her life's happiness in this fashion? She would get used to it in time; no doubt as Angela had done. She wondered whether Cecil had any idea of what was passing through her mind. There was a grain of suspicion in his eyes—a certain distrust.

But Lugard had guessed nothing. If he suspected anything it was that Sairson had been bullying the poor girl. Lugard had no illusions about his prospective father-in-law. He disliked the man exceedingly, did not trust him—and there were others who shared his views.

"You look as if a good night's sleep would do you good," he said tenderly. "I beg you to leave me alone with your father, as I have something important to say to him."

"But, I also have something to say," Nest gasped, "and most important."

Lugard placed an arm about her and almost carried her to the door.

"Not to-night," he whispered, "not to-night, Nest. Meet me in the morning on the cliffs, at the usual time. Sweetheart, how tired you look."

How hard he was making it for her, Nest thought. The touch of his hand and the sound of his voice seemed to take all the strength out of her. Her resolution turned to water at a glance from his eyes. She made one more struggle to preserve her independence.

"I must see you presently, Cecil. I'll wait for you in the hall. I shall be in the alcove by the big fireplace. I must speak to you before I sleep to-night."

The warm light faded from Lugard's face as he closed the library door, and a queer look filled his eyes as he turned to Sairson.

"It isn't anything pleasant that I have to say," he remarked. "As you are aware I have been to London with Laurisdale. At his request I have been looking into his affairs. It required no great business head to see that he had got into a terrible mess. He seems to have been foolish enough to borrow money from that notorious scamp, John Blaydon. He also tells me that Blaydon's bills have passed into your possession. Is that so, Mr. Sairson?"

"Better not interfere with what does not concern you," Sairson growled. "You're not a business man—I am; and there is no sentiment where business is concerned. Blaydon may be all that you say he is, and more, but that will not prevent me from doing business with him if I can see my way to make money out of it. It is all very well for you to be sentimental—I can't."

"I suppose not," Lugard said coolly. "I am going to ask you to do me a favor."

"If possible," Sairson said. "I dare say I can manage that for you. What is it?"

"I want you to bring me face to face with Blaydon. I know that that rascal robbed my uncle of this very house; I know the infamous robbery drove the poor old man to suicide. Some day I shall prove it and then there will be an end of John Blaydon. But he is not to know this yet—I won't show my hand till the time comes. Meanwhile, I want to see him about those bills of Laurisdale's. As far as I can judge, he has been robbed in the most cold-blooded fashion. Now, I am prepared to take up those bills, and pay for the—"

"The deuce you are," Sairson said blankly. "Why?"

"Mainly to help Laurisdale. If he will drop the theatre and come back quietly here I fancy I can save the situation yet. But I must meet Blaydon to do it."

"There are many difficulties in the way of that," Sairson said. "Blaydon is a queer chap. Then he has a physical infirmity that he is very sensitive about."

"Really! I am glad he is sensitive on some point. Pray go on."

"Well, he is shy of strangers. A confidential clerk sees his clients. Nobody seems to know anything about him. I'm sure he will not see you."

Lugard smiled grimly.

"I expected something of this kind," he said. "I daresay I shall be able to manage without bothering you further in the matter. I will take up those bills, and pay what is due on them up to half their true value. The thing is a swindle, and if Laurisdale is pressed for payment, we shall take this matter into court. I shall see Blaydon then, you know. He will have to come forward in support of his claim and give evidence. I don't suppose he will look forward with any pleasure to a cross-examination by the Attorney-General."

Sairson appeared as if about to say something then suddenly changed his mind. The veins in his forehead bulged out like knotted rope, and the bleary eyes started from his head. This was a situation which he had not foreseen. And Laurisdale was slipping through his fingers when he seemed most secure. Besides, Lady Laurisdale knew the truth. Nest, too, knew the truth which she vowed she would declare to Lugard. Sairson tried to picture to himself what would happen when Lugard knew everything.

"Blaydon will fight you," he blurted out.

"I wish I could think so," Lugard said grimly. "I am afraid he will do nothing of the kind. I begin to suspect you have good reasons for keeping us apart."

Sairson burst out explosively. Lugard was forcing a new role upon him, and the bully was resenting it. Usually he issued his commands, and men obeyed him timidly.

"You must drop that tone," he cried. "I'm in my own house, Mr. Lugard. If you think I am to be spoken to like this with impunity, you're mistaken. I may be tough, but I'm honest. You'll be saying next that I am in partnership with Blaydon."

Sairson thrust out his coarse underlip with his face close to that of Lugard. The latter clenched his fist threateningly. Some instinct prompted him to smash that red face between the eyes, to pick up Sairson and pound him to a jelly. He had never so hated a man before. He bitterly resented the fact that this great, coarse brute was Nest's father. With an effort, however, he had himself in hand again, though he was still tingling to the tips of his fingers.

"You are getting offensive," he said quietly. "Please do not come so close. You have taken the words out of my mouth. You are in partnership with Blaydon, or next door to it. I have found that out during the last few days."

"What do you mean by next door to it?" Sairson asked uneasily.

He seemed to think there was a double meaning to the words. Had Lugard by any chance discovered the secret of the two sets of offices that communicated with each other. The conversation was taking a personal turn that Sairson did not care for. There was only one way of it—to pick a quarrel with Lugard and get rid of him. It would be easy to patch up a truce afterwards. But in the interval he would have time to think out a plan of campaign.

"Do you suppose I mean to be insulted like that in my own house?" he replied. "Who are you to come here giving yourself these airs? Do you suppose it is an honor you are conferring on my daughter by asking her to marry you? Apologise this minute, and get out."

"When I have anything to apologise for I shall gladly do it," Lugard said, white to the lips.

"Apologise!" Sairson roared. "Apologise, you hound! Do you hear me? Apologise, and get out!"

The words rang through the house as Sairson flung open the door violently. Nest heard them and rose shaking from head to foot. She had heard her father in these violent moods before. The red blood of shame chased the pallor from her cheeks. She stood angrily dabbing the tears in her eyes, and calling aloud for her mother. As Mrs. Sairson came hurrying from the conservatory into the hall the study door closed with a bang and Lugard came out.

His face was set, his eyes flaming with anger. He did not appear to notice Nest, and the girl shrank back to let him pass. Clearly this was no time for explanations, and she would see him in the morning. Mrs. Sairson laid an arm about Nest's shoulders.

"Let him go," she whispered. "Don't stop him my dear. I suppose there has been some terrible quarrel. No good man could ever be with your father for long without one."

Lugard strode forward almost blindly by way of the conservatory into the garden, closing the inner door behind him. Sebag was in hiding in the greenery between this door and the one leading into the garden. As he passed, Lugard thought he saw a pair of dark eyes looking at him curiously. Was it a burglar studying the house, or a poacher concealed there until all was quiet. Instinctively Lugard made a dash forward and gripped the trespasser by the arm.

"Give an an account of yourself," he said. "What are you doing here? Ah, it is of no use to struggle. If you try that game it will be the worse for you. Who are you?"

"For heaven's sake, don't make a noise, Mr. Lugard," Sebag whispered. "Don't give me away. I have something to sell you, and I'll sell it cheap."

CHAPTER XXV

THE MIDNIGHT MESSAGE

Lugard relaxed his grip on Sebag's collar. Verily, this was a night of surprises. But the little Jew made no effort to escape. For one thing, he had nothing to gain by such a course. He had betrayed himself to Lugard, and the latter would be sure to seek an explanation later. Sebag was no coward, either, especially where his own interests were concerned.

"Don't make a fuss, Mr. Lugard," he said confidentially. "If you think I am up to any harm you are mistaken. I'm not after the plate. I'm a respectable solicitor—a gentleman, by Act of Parliament."

"An Act of Parliament seems to have been necessary," Lugard said grimly.

Sebag grinned. He had no longer any fear of personal violence. Moreover, he had something to sell, for which he expected a fair price.

"You will have your little joke," he said. "Anyhow, I want you to know that I am not a thief, sir. I am a man of good position. Before long I shall have a large business and a staff of clerks. I shouldn't wonder if I got into the House of Commons some day."

"That would not surprise me," Lugard said in the same grim way.

"Ah, well, sir, it takes all sorts of sheep to make up a flock. What I need for the development of my ideas is capital. When you don't possess any, it's foolish to be scrupulous about the means of acquiring it. That's why I am here. I've done work for you—"

"Stop!" Lugard said curtly. "I wanted certain things done and I was recommended to employ you. The gentleman who recommended you was not complimentary. He had no illusions as to your moral worth. He told me you were prepared to do anything for money. So far I have found the statement absolutely correct. You have been well paid for a deal of nasty work, and to do you justice, I have every reason to be satisfied with my outlay. But I don't want you here, and that is a fact."

Sebag's eyes gleamed. Lugard's scathing sarcasm was not lost on him.

"I'm not complaining, sir," he said. "Only too pleased to be of service to so liberal a gentleman as yourself. Believe me, I am here on your business."

Lugard had not expected a reply like this. It filled him with uneasiness and vague fears. Long stifled suspicions drifted across his mind again.

"I thought you were on the track of John Blaydon?" he suggested.

"So I am, sir; so I am. That's what brings me here."

"So there is some connection between Blaydon and Mr. Sairson, eh?"

Sebag came very near to blurting out the truth. But there was a big thing on its way—quite the biggest thing he had discovered as yet—and it represented big money. Lugard was not going to get it without adequate payment.

"I shouldn't like to go as far as that, sir," he said. "I prefer to be sure of my ground. Give me a day or two longer. I assure you, sir, the work is not congenial to me. My only consolation is that I am not wasting my time. Don't let Mr. Sairson know you saw me here. Because, you see I do work for him as well as you."

Lugard smiled at this ingenuous confidence.

"Upon my word, you are a candid rascal," he said. "I suppose I must trust you. Somebody is coming this way. I think you had better go."

Sebag was emphatically of the same opinion. There was a chance that Lugard might fix him with an awkward question or two when it was least desirable to answer them. He pulled off his hat with a flourish and disappeared into the darkness.

At the same moment a shadow darkened the door of the conservatory, and, looking back, Lugard saw that Nest stood there. She seemed to be challenging someone in a voice that was none to steady.

Lugard turned back. Was it fancy, or could he hear somebody moving furtively in the bushes? It was as if the place was full of spies. What was wrong with this household. Whence came it that Sairson had all these enemies. The man was a private, probably a professional broker of companies, but there were scores of men in the city like him, and theirs were more or less recognised methods. There was nothing secret or melodramatic about them. A new idea flashed into Lugard's mind—an idea so wild as to bring a smile to his lips. Surely, Sairson was doing nothing to bring him within reach of the strong arm of the law? He could not be a forger or a maker of counterfeit coins? Lugard had read such things in the Sunday papers.

Still, it was impossible to associate Marlton Grange with such an idea. As he looked into the house through the conservatory door, he saw its well-ordered peace. Then he heard Nest speak again. He did not ask himself what she was doing there, but stepped into the light.

"I was quite frightened," Nest said. "I felt sure that somebody was in here, but I'm glad to know that it was you."

Lugard was content to let it go at that.

There was no occasion for Nest to know anything about Sebag and such vermin.

"What are you doing outside at this time of night?" he asked.

"I have already told you," Nest said. "I had a stupid idea that somebody was trying to get into the house. My mother and father are in the library. He is in one of his moods to-night. I hope he was not very rude to you, Cecil."

"Oh, we had little dispute, that's all," Lugard said carelessly. "You see, we regard things from a different standpoint, Nest. I daresay I should have seen eye to eye with him had I been educated to the ways of the city. As it is, I don't like their methods at all."

"You never could," Nest smiled sadly. "Of that I am certain. It will always be a consolation to me to feel that the man I loved once—"

"The man you loved once!" Lugard colored. "Nest, what do you mean? Why do you speak like that? You are not the least like yourself to-night. When I came into the house an hour ago you were as pale as death. You looked dreadful. I am sure that something has happened. Tell me what it is, darling. Confide in me. If I cared for you less than I do—"

Nest stopped him with an imploring gesture.

"Please don't," she whispered. "Don't make it any harder for me than it is, Cecil, I am not strong enough, to-night. I will meet you in the morning as you suggested, and if I have to tell you that I no longer care for you—"

"I should not believe you if you did, dear."

Nest laughed forlornly. With the best intentions in the world Lugard was going to make her task very, very difficult. He would not believe her, and in an inconsequent way the knowledge was full of comfort to her. She put up a hand to keep him off, but he was not to be denied.

"Nest, you are shielding somebody," he said.

She made a feeble protest. She could see the lovelight in his eyes, and she cared for him more than for all the world. She was very young to a lover's happiness. He took her in his arms and kissed her fondly. All her strength and courage left her at the touch of his lips. These were her last few blissful minutes in the world, and she must enjoy them. She would tell him everything on the morrow, but to-night she would drain her cup of pleasure. He saw the white misery fade from her face and the rosy smile that took its place. The egotism of the lover blinded him to everything else. The whole of the sweet-scented world seemed to be their own.

"I knew that I could comfort you," Lugard whispered. "When the morning comes you will have forgotten all your troubles. I am older than you, darling, and I know. And if I don't happen to hit it off just as I should with your father, what does it matter?"

Nest replied that she could not tell. At that moment, she did not know or care. She was intoxicated with the night and the pure pleasure of the hour. And the morning seemed a long way off. She would tell him then, of course. But not now, not now.. ..

Her mother's voice was calling her from somewhere, and she came to herself with a start. Very quietly she withdrew from Lugard's close embrace.

"I must go," she said. "Mother will wonder what has become of me. I will meet you on the cliffs at 11 o'clock. Good-night, Cecil."

She closed the conservatory door behind her. As she secured the lock she saw a white envelope on the floor. With a vague curiosity she took it up and turned it over in her hands. It was of thin, foreign paper, strong and crackling, and on the front of it in pencil, her own name had been hurriedly scratched. How had it come, and who had placed it there? With her finger under the flap Nest hesitated.

"Where have you been, child?" Mrs. Sairson asked.

She was standing in the doorway looking towards the girl. With a secret impulse, of which she was half ashamed, Nest thrust the envelope into her pocket.

"I thought I heard somebody prowling about outside, mother," she said. "I went out to see, and found Cecil. Was there a quarrel to-night?"

"I have been trying to find out, dear," Mrs. Sairson answered. "I fear there is not much love lost between your father and Cecil Lugard."

"It would be strange if it were otherwise," Nest said coldly. "I am ashamed to ask Cecil very much about it. He told me they had had some difference of opinion on business matters."

"Connected with Lord Laurisdale, my dear. I found out that much. Your father says that Cecil has been interfering in matters that don't concern him. He is very angry indeed. Did—did you tell Cecil as to—"

"Mother, I hadn't the courage," Nest replied with self-scorn. "I was such a coward that I put it off till to-morrow. When he looks at me as he can do, and speaks to me in his caressing voice, I feel helpless. If you only knew how he loves me!"

Mrs. Sairson wiped the tears from her eyes.

"I know dear," she said. "I had my own romance years ago. I had to tell him that it was a mistake, and that I wanted to marry John Sairson. He didn't believe me—he told me that I was selling myself for money. The sting of it was its truth. Let us go to bed, dear child. It is useless opening old wounds."

Nest kissed her mother, and hastily retired to her room. After she had switched on the light and locked the door she recollected the envelope in her pocket.

There were only a few words inside in pencil, evidently written in a great hurry.

"Do nothing yet," it was written. "Tell him nothing. As you value your happiness wait. The time is coming when you will thank me for this golden advice."

CHAPTER XXVI

THE GENTLE EXILE

Sybil Gosway sat on the terrace at Laurisdale Castle debating in her mind what she should do that beautiful afternoon. She was disappointed that Nest was not coming over. Nest had written a note pleading a bad headache, nor had she suggested that Sybil might come as far as Marlton Grange. Lady Laurisdale had important letters to write that sufficiently occupied her mind to the exclusion of everything else, for she sat grave and preoccupied at luncheon with hardly a word for her companion. An air of depression that troubled Sybil hung over the house and she was glad to escape into the sunshine with a book in her hand.

But it was far too lovely an afternoon to waste over a book, however exciting. The cliff and the blue sea were calling to Sybil, and she could not resist their cry. The book was flung aside, and she set out across the park. She rambled along the cliffs into the valley beyond until she came almost by a kind of instinct, to Oates's farm. It seemed to her that she had made up her mind to come here. She wanted to have a further talk with Givanni about his wonderful flowers.

The struggling old farm-house was shut up, and repeated knocking on the stout oak door elicited no response. Obviously Mrs. Oates and her one stalwart man had gone to market. Givanni might be in the garden for he was never very far from his beloved blossoms. Sybil found him bending over a shallow frame filled with a mass of glorious scarlet and gold blooms.

He looked up quickly, with a scowl upon his face, but the frown cleared away almost instantly.

"I am sorry if I am in the way," Sybil said. "But I am so fond of flowers, and there is none like yours, Signor Givanni! I'll go away if you like—"

Givanni smiled gently, and became at once a different man. A dreamy enthusiasm filled his eyes; the shadow of discontent had fallen from his shoulders.

"Ah that, is a bond of sympathy between us," he said. "In all the world there is nothing like flowers. What I should have done without them I cannot tell. There are people—friends of my youth—who would laugh if they could see me now. Mazzini and Garibaldi, but I talk nonsense."

Sybil's face flushed eagerly.

"Did you know those great men?" she asked. "Modern history is my favorite study. But surely, you could not—"

Givanni knew what the girl intended to say.

"I am older than you imagine—over 70. You are surprised. It is because I lead an outdoor life that I look so young. After all, we speak of things barely half a century old. Yes, I played my part in the stirring times—and since. There were reasons why Italy was no longer safe for me, and I came here. Only you are not to speak of these things, little lady. I don't know why I tell you, except that you have your mother's eyes."

"Signor Givanni!" Sybil exclaimed, "what are you talking about?"

"I grow old and foolish," Givanni said sadly. "I ramble; it is just as well at my age that I keep myself to myself. But you have your mother's eyes. If you ask me if I knew her, I reply that I did."

"Then you can tell me who she was?" Sybil asked.

"I could do that," Givanni said coolly, "but as it is apparent your father has not done so, the business is none of mine, dear child. The age of romance is not yet dead, cara mia. Your father would tell you that much."

"Signor Givanni," Sybil laughed, "you are a fascinating mystery."

"A mystery, no doubt," Givanni agreed, "and it is not for you to ask more questions. Lady Laurisdale could enlighten you if she chooses. Now come and look at these blossoms. You will never guess what they are. Two years ago they were common, and therefore valueless, as are the red poppies of the field. That wonderful result I and the bees have achieved between us."

"Do you mean that the honey-bees helped you?"

"Certainly, they are my best friends. I can almost make them do what I tell them. I have accomplished some things by means of a camel's-hair brush, but the delicate touch of the bees is far better. Look at this dainty pink bloom like a loose rose. A year ago it was a common daisy. I could show you many others were it discreet to do so. But I have enemies who do not scruple to try to get the best of me. There is one in the neighborhood now."

The ugly look crept into Givanni's eyes again; he was the conspirator once more. Sybil remembered the hints he had dropped the last time she was here.

"Somebody had put your fires out," she suggested timidly.

"I know it," Givanni whispered fiercely. "I am sure of it. Under shadow of night the rascal pushed the dampers of my furnace in, and next morning many of my pretty children were dead. That is not the greatest wrong he has done me. But I got even with him for that; oh, yes! I got even with him for that."

The last words were spoken hissingly under Givanni's breath. He appeared to forget he had a companion. Then his eyes caught the questioning glance in Sybil's face and he laughed. "I am trying to frighten you," he said. "You will take me for one of the villains of melodrama. But I am only a poor old man earning a frugal living by his flowers. Indeed, they are my sole means of support, cara mia. All these things I tell you, because, when I glance at your face, I see you have your mother's eyes."

He bent down and picked off one of the glorious scarlet blossoms abstractedly. Once more his thoughts were far away. A telegraph boy walked smartly up the path with an orange-colored envelope in his hand.

"Do you seek anybody here?" the Italian asked.

"Party of the name of Givanni," the boy replied. "Care of Oates's Farm. Are you him?"

Givanni nodded as he took the envelope. He read the four words contained in it and his eyes gleamed. There was a tender smile on his lips.

"No answer," he said. "Stop a minute! Do you want to earn a shilling? But, of course, you do. I wish this letter to be sent express to Cromer. See that it goes off at once.. .. Now little lady, I must get you to excuse me. That telegram gives me plenty to do. Come again and I will show you some orchids the like of which you have never seen before."

He took off his hat with a grand flourish which, despite its exaggeration, had something of the grand seigneur about it. But when he was alone he went on with his gardening, as if he had nothing else to occupy his attention. He did not move till the creaking of the farm cart told him that Mrs. Oates had returned.

"Ain't you ready for your tea, Signor?" Mrs. Oates said.

Givanni fastened his glass and closed his frames carefully. Not until he had satisfied himself that everything was in order did he make a move toward the house.

"I will have a cup of tea, if you please," he said in his best manner, "and some of your cake. Mrs. Oates a friend is coming to dine with me this evening. Dinner I have already arranged for. May I beg of you the best parlor for the occasion. You will perhaps wait on us yourself! I can trust your discretion, as usual, eh!"

Mrs Oates gave the desired assurance. In her simple way she had a shrewd suspicion that Givanni was something more than the simple grower of flowers he pretended to be. In her heart of hearts she was certain that he was some foreign nobleman in disguise. It was at such time that he particularly impressed her. There was a quiet dignity in his manner, as if he were a feudal lord giving his orders to a trusted retainer. And this man only paid her a few shillings a week.

"You can have the parlor with pleasure," she said, "and the fine linen I had from her late ladyship when I married Oates. I've real silver, too, though I don't brag of it. As to the flowers, Signor, I reckon you'll want to look after them yourself."

A couple of hours later Givanni surveyed the table with pleased satisfaction. The linen was fine, the silver good, and the glass most of it antique. There were wax candles in branches, and a feathery arrangement of flowers. With the antique furniture of the parlor and the panelled oak walls the room was one of taste and refinement. Givanni, in evening dress, nodded his satisfaction. He appeared a different man altogether; he looked like one to the manor born.

From a cupboard in his own room he procured a bottle or two of rare and curious wine which he proceeded to decant with loving care.

"Behold a transformation!" he said to himself. "Behold a dining chamber in a baronial hall! The veritable atmosphere of the 17th century. There are vulgar rich people in London who would give their ears for the furniture in this room. Mascani will be surprised, he will be pleased. He will say that I am a greater enigma than ever."

Mrs. Oates bustled into the room with an air of some importance. In her best black silk and similar apron she was the true model of the old family servant. Her manner to Givanni had undergone a subtle change. He was no longer the familiar lodger; she spoke to him as if he were an honored guest at the Castle in the days when she was in service there.

"The gentleman has arrived sir," she said. "He is at present in the hall, taking off his coat. Shall I show him in, sir?"

Givanni signified his assent. A moment later Mrs. Oates came bustling back, followed by a tall man in evening dress. In age he had the advantage of Givanni by twenty years or more, but his dark hair and clean-shaven face made him look considerably younger. There was an air of distinction about him that was not lost upon Mrs. Oates.

"Signor Mascani, sir," she said. "Shall I serve dinner, please?"

As the door closed behind her, Signor Mascani lost his reserved manner. He advanced to Givanni with both hands outstretched.

"My dear old friend!" he exclaimed. "My dear old friend and benefactor. I am rejoiced to see you again. If there is anything I can do for you, pray command my services. You cannot tell how pleased I was to see your writing once more. If you are in any trouble—"

Givanni waved the suggestion aside.

"We will come to that presently," he said. "And that shall be deferred till the coffee and cigars. My housekeeper is an excellent cook, as you shall see for yourself. My dear fellow, pray be seated. I have here some Chianti that is fit for a king. A little soup to start with?"

The dinner was despatched at length, and, with a contented sigh, Mascani inhaled a cigarette and sipped his coffee. He was waiting for his host to get to the point. An hour passed in general conversation and then Givanni produced some papers from his pocket.

"Now I want you to look at these, my dear Tito," he said. "If you think—Well, what is it, Mrs. Oates? A gentleman to see me? Does he give his name?"

"Mr. Dudley Beaumont, sir," Mrs. Oates said. "Am I to ask him in?"

A flash of lightning gleamed in Givanni's eyes, but he spoke quietly enough.

"If you please," he said. "Ask the gentleman to come this way, Mrs. Oates. You will observe, my dear Tito, that the eagles are beginning to gather together!"

CHAPTER XXVII

A "STAR" TURN

Dudley Beaumont came swaggering into the room with the aspect of a man who feels sure of his welcome. He looked singularly out of place, his loud and flashy seediness being in sorry contrast with the simple dignity of the parlor. He strode in with his hat on one side of his head, and smiled as he saw the decanters and cigars. Evidently he had come at a most favorable time. Mascani regarded him gravely with the quiet, searching glance of the scientist trying to place some interesting specimen. Givanni, his hands behind him, ignored Beaumont's outstretched fingers. The latter hummed, and said gaily, "I have run you to earth. The old fox has been found. Confess that you did not expect to see me!"

"Consider the confession as made," Givanni said gravely. "I did not. And now, sir?"

The stinging contempt of his manner moved Beaumont slightly. He laughed as he took up a cigar and bit off the end of it between his yellow teeth.

"I'll have a liqueur of brandy as well, if you don't mind," he said. "I don't usually drink brandy at this time of night, but—"

"Your habits are improved for the better, then?" Givanni asked.

The cold, bitter smile was still on his face. He was not the least like the absent-minded old gardener now. He stood erect and alert, every sense on the stretch, his eyes steadfast and clear. Beaumont had anticipated to see him sullen and uneasy. This contemptuous confidence worried him.

"I'd drop the high and mighty, if I were you," he blustered. "My idea of calling here is friendly, but you can have it the other way if you prefer. If I could have a few minutes alone with you?"

Mascani flashed a questioning glance at his host. The latter shook his head.

"I can conceive nothing that will warrant a private interview," he said. "My dear Tito, I beg of you to sit down. The gentleman will state his business before you."

"I'll be hanged if I do," Beaumont protested.

"Then in that case it will not be told at all," Givanni said. "This is my friend Signor Tito Mascani. This is Mr. Dudley Beaumont, the eminent comedian. He would have been still more eminent had not the fates conspired against him. Jealousy of his amazing talents on the part of lesser but more prosperous men has kept him down. Malignant enemies declare that he is a dissolute drunken rascal, but on that point I leave you to judge for yourself."

Beaumont gulped the brandy and refilled the glass.

"You must have your joke," he retorted. "For some reason you are annoyed with me. I suppose you did not want to be discovered. Everything comes to the man who knows how to wait. My lucky star is in the ascendant to-night."

"Which accounts for your being here, I presume?" Givanni asked. "How did you find me out?"

"Oh, nobody told me," Beaumont grinned. "My powers of deduction are amazing. Anyone in the profession will tell you that. I was paying a visit to a friend this evening. There is no occasion to mention the lady's name. In the conservatory—"

"Ah!" Givanni exclaimed. His eyes flashed like livid lightning. "Ah! Before you proceed further allow me to do a little deduction. It was Mrs. Sairson you went to see. You didn't meet her; on the contrary, she gave you an assignation in the conservatory. Very probably she would be ashamed to have you in the house."

"You insult me," Beaumont protested. "You take advantage of your age."

"I take advantage of nothing," Givanni went on. "What I say is true. You came here to try to extort money from Mrs. Sairson. She granted you an interview in the conservatory. My dear Tito, you may find it difficult to believe, but this man is a Belham. He is a brother to that most unfortunate of women, Kate Belham."

"God bless my soul!" Mascani exclaimed. "You don't say so."

Beaumont's red face grew redder still. There was no mistaking the expression of Mascani's words. He screwed a single glass in his eye and examined Beaumont with marked curiosity.

"Very interesting," he murmured. "As a psychological study, most fascinating! It only shows what a rapid thing degeneration is when once it sets in. Drink, I suppose?"

"That and congenial and congenital blackguardism. Go on, Mr. Beaumont."

"Oh, I am going on right enough," Beaumont said truculently. "Since it is your pleasure to blurt out these things, you may as well say that I was in one of the conservatories at Marlton Grange with my sister. It matters little what we were talking about. Your name was not mentioned. I can't tell whether or not Kate knows you are living here."

"She doesn't," Givanni hissed. "She is absolutely ignorant of the fact that I have been her near neighbor for three years. See you don't mention it."

"Oh, I won't," Beaumont smiled, "I'll keep your secret if—if—you understand."

"If I make it worth your while. In other words, you begin to see a wide and extensive field of blackmail opening up before your eyes. You will get nothing out of me for more reasons than one. In the first place, I have no money."

Beaumont laughed and waved his arms towards the oak round table.

"Looks like it don't it?" he sneered. "All this is enough for a duke. Let's discuss this problem at some more fitting time, I knew you were here by certain flowers I saw in Sairson's conservatory. I knew they could only come from one man, and that man yourself. I didn't waste any time in discussing the matter with my sister—I didn't suppose she would be able to tell me. I made a few inquiries when I got back to the inn where I am staying. They told me about an eccentric Italian called Givanni who grew flowers— they gave me your address. That is why I have pleasure of meeting you to-night."

"The pleasure is mutual," Givanni said gravely. "Go on."

"Well, I came to renew our old acquaintance. I expected to find you eking out a precarious livelihood by the sale of your flowers. Instead, I find you surrounded by every of wealth and luxury. Yet you tell you are poor."

"I have barely sufficient to pay my modest way," Givanni said.

"Well, we will let that pass for the moment. I have a proposal to make to you presently, which will, I hope, prove to our mutual advantage. A paltry hundred pounds as your share, my dear sir, will place a fortune in your pockets. This is the great opportunity of my lifetime. I have a show the like of which the world has never seen before. The most amazing mystery the stage has ever witnessed. I might call it 'Who tried to kill John Sairson?' Do you follow?"

Givanni's lips were moving, but no sound escaped them. His face was ghastly white against the blackness of his hair. He was moved to the depths of his soul, a prey to some terrible agitation, and yet Beaumont, watching him calmly, could not flatter himself that it was fear.

"Why do you make that suggestion?" the Italian asked.

"It is the same thing," Beaumont went on. "My show would account for the murderous outrage on John Sairson, my esteemed brother-in-law. Look at this!"

He took from his pocket a shabby, old, printed theatrical bill in colors. It was one of the long shop bills usually employed with travelling companies. On it were not displayed the names of leading actors and actresses who had performed before the crowned heads of Europe, but the whole was devoted to a single artist, called La Veni, who was to appear at a certain place for six nights only in her marvellous feats of magic. La Veni was the only person in the world possessed of the secret of taking life without the aid of a weapon. She had it in her power, so to speak, to slay at a glance. She had only to raise her hands and clouds of birds fluttering about the stage dropped dead at her feet. Rabbits and other such animals were subjected to the same marvellous power. A ferocious dog had attacked a little child in the street of Rothesham and La Veni happened to be passing at the time. She merely extended her hand and the dog lay dead at the feet of the uninjured child.

"What do you think of that?" Beaumont demanded triumphantly, as Givanni laid the bill on the table. "Now there is positively no deception. You shall come to Cramer to see for yourself. The news of this famous exhibition has not as yet travelled far because of a lamentable lack of funds. When the money is put up, it will be the talk of Europe. And you, my friend, are the man to advance the money."

"Why?" Givanni asked. "Why should you fix on me?"

"Why? Because of your old friendship with my family. Because in your own defence, you wish to retrieve your shattered fortunes. Because Sairson was attacked in a similar way. Because—well, because you are not a fool, and can undertake the role. Of course, it may be no more than a mere coincidence, but it is a strange thing that Sairson was attacked and nearly killed by much the same methods as La Veni used. It can't have been done by the same hand, because it can be proved that La Veni was far enough away at the time."

Beaumont helped himself to a further glass of brandy and another cigar with the air of a man who had made his point and confounded his enemies. There was something sinister, almost threatening, in the way he smiled at Givanni. The latter stood by the table drumming moodily with his fingers on the polished oak. He seemed undecided what to do next.

"What nationality is your talented young friend?" he asked.

"Now for so talented a man as yourself, that is an exceedingly foolish question," Beaumont answered. "Is it possible that you are actually trying to deceive me—me! La Veni is young and timid, but she will get over that, in time. She is nice-looking and an Italian. Farther than that, I have not troubled myself, but I can ascertain if you like."

"Where is she to be found at the present moment?"

"I can only say that she is at Cromer. My dear friend, let us play the game. There are those with La Veni who understand her value. They will do nothing till the money is put up. They had those bills printed as a speculation. If you will give me—"

But Givanni was no longer listening. He moved over to a desk in the corner of the room and hastily wrote what looked like a letter. This he handed to Mascani.

"I will ask you to retire," he said. "There are reasons why Mr. Beaumont and I should have a few words together, Tito. Dine with me here at the same time to-morrow night. I will leave you to find your way out. You have a lovely evening for your walk."

Mascani took up the envelope and vanished. The envelope was addressed to himself. When alone he tore open the flap and read the words inside eagerly:—

"Go to the address here given," the letter ran. "Go to-night, late as it is. Show no surprise at anything you see, but above all things be discreet and silent."

CHAPTER XXVIII

LA VENI

Nest woke with the consciousness that her troubles lay heavily upon her. Had she lived her life and was the end of her happiness at hand? The grey years were terribly long and dreary to contemplate. Yet it was difficult to imagine such things. Marlton Grange was no setting for a gruesome and sordid tragedy. Here was a perfect morning with a world bathed in a flood of glorious sunshine, and silvery dew bedecking the geraniums and roses in the garden. A gardener was whistling blithely at his work. A Persian kitten was playing with a ball of wool. Everything was so peaceful, so refined and far removed from all that was mean and squalid.

It was absurd to believe that this was the home of so notorious a rascal as John Blaydon! Why, a man of that type could never have felt comfortable here! He would have needed something far more flashy. The well-trained servants moved quietly about the house, and the old breakfast gong sounded presently with its drowsy murmur. Yet here lived the man who was responsible for all her misery—the man whom Cecil Lugard had sworn to haul into gaol.

How could she tell Lugard all the story? And what would he do when he heard it? He might stay his hand for the sake of the girl he loved, but, he would never marry her. After the story was told he could not. Other people, too, were on the track of John Blaydon. Somebody else had found him out, or that murderous attack in the conservatory would not have taken place. People were beginning to forget it, but Scotland Yard had not forgotten, and an arrest might be made at any moment. If this were the case, the whole world would know of the connection between Sairson and Blaydon.

If that attack had succeeded! Nest turned pale at the mere thought that she had let such an idea take hold of her. Still, had Sairson died, the whole situation might have been saved. She ran downstairs to the breakfast-room, where she found her father alone. He was worrying his food in a savage, suspicious way, as if he half feared it. His manner was loud and flurried as well, and he was bullying the footman because the toast was too thick. Nest wondered how long a servant would remain in the house were it not for her mother.

"Where are the others?" she asked.

"Gone out—at least Angela has," Sairson answered. "Your mother has a headache and is taking her breakfast in bed. Well, what are you going to do?"

The question was a direct challenge, and Nest took it up.

"I have seen no reason to change my mind," she said, "and, after all, it does not very much matter what I do. Mr. Lugard will have to be told."

"In the name of common sense, why should he be told?"

"I suppose it is impossible for you to see things in a proper light," Nest said. "Do you suppose I could marry Cecil Lugard and conceal from him the fact that I am the daughter of John Blaydon, the money-lender?"

"There's nothing to be ashamed of in the fact that one is a money-lender."

"Then why are you ashamed of it?" Nest retorted. "Why do you trade in an assumed name? Why do you take most extraordinary precautions to disguise the truth? Oh! There are money-lenders and money-lenders, I know. Some are fair and honest enough; but there are others. All our property is built up on a foundation of blood and tears. How many ruined households have gone to the making of it? How many men have gone to their graves after you have sucked the life and manhood out of them? I have read letters in the papers written by your victims. There have been cases where the money has been paid three times over, and yet the home has been broken up so that you could divide the cash with some villainous lawyer tool of yours. I felt I could kill a man who did such a thing as that. When I realised that it was my own father—"

"You are a fool," Sairson said harshly, "a silly, sentimental fool. All this comes of your mother's training—the training of a Belham, forsooth. You would not talk like that if you had not been brought up in the lap of luxury. Thousands of those who despise me would be glad to come in and share my money, all the same. You've never learnt the value money—I have. But you shall do so if you persist in this folly. I'll turn you out of the house, by Gad, and send you to London into an office at a pound a week."

Sairson bent over the girl, scowling and muttering. It was clear he meant all he said. He was quite capable of it, as Nest was perfectly well aware. She met his gaze defiantly.

"I am not to be bullied," she said. "I shall do what I feel to be right. If the shameful story is to be told—and I don't see any way out of it—I shall quit your house. Far better to work for one's bread than live in splendid deceit and misery like this. I may be able to do without you at all."

She pushed her plate away, and rose from her chair, leaving Sairson with an irritated sense of defeat. It seemed odd that he should be defied like this in his own home and by this slender slip of a girl. She was plucky enough, and that was a quality that Sairson could admire. Well she could try it; if she liked she could attempt life in London on a pound a week and a bed sitting-room in a Bloomsbury attic. If that did not bring her to her senses nothing would. Nevertheless, he was not feeling easy in his mind. Once the story was out the mischief would be done. But would she have the necessary courage to tell Lugard? If she were really fond of him, she would not risk her life's happiness in that reckless way.

Nest went across the garden in the glorious sunshine. She glanced back at the grey front of the old house, so bright and peaceful, sitting so perfectly into the picture. It would be a hard wrench to give this up for a sordid London street, and the slavery of an office. Yet if the worst came to the worst, Nest would take her father at his word. She would not linger on in splendid misery as Angela had done. She would go out into the world and see things for herself. Perhaps, on the whole she would not tell Cecil that morning. It was such a lovely day and all the world was bright and beautiful. A day or two would not matter. She was very young to part with her life's happiness, and she felt justified in clinging to it a little longer.

Moreover, she had not forgotten the mysterious message of the night before. Some good friend was watching and shaping the way for her. It seemed a pity, almost a breach of faith, to fly in the face of that kindly warning. By the time Nest had breasted that hill and stood with the fresh breath of the sea on her face she had almost made up her mind.

At any rate she would have the glorious morning to herself. Afterwards she might screw up the necessary courage to tell Cecil everything. He had not arrived yet, so that she still had time to shape a definite course. A lark sang in the blue over her head, a pair of lovers, happy and gay, passed her, hand-in-hand, a little way along the cliffs. From the bottom of her heart she envied the simple rustic pair. Possibly if they had given her a thought, they might have envied her. Ah! there was Cecil sauntering along with a cigarette in his mouth. He seemed to have put the unpleasantness of the previous night behind him, for he waved his hand joyfully. Nest saw the smile on his lips before he came up to her.

"Do you know," he smiled. "I was troubled with the idea you would not come this morning."

He took her in his arms and kissed her. There was a new light of possession in his eyes, and his tenderness thrilled Nest to the core. It was going to be harder, harder than ever she had expected.

"What gave you that impression?"

"Oh, if you are going to ask me for an explanation!" Lugard laughed. "Well, you looked so anxious and restless last night. And I had had rather a unpleasant scene with your father. I am afraid that he and I regard things from quite a different standpoint, perhaps because I don't understand what is called business. But now that I have got you, darling, I won't waste the precious minutes talking of those things. Shall we go further, or stay here?"

Nest simply couldn't tell her story—how could she with her head on his shoulder and his arm about her waist?—so full was she of the future and all that should happen when they were settled in their new home. Perhaps it would be better to write a letter to him—to put it all on paper. Yet she felt like a traitor as she sat listening dreamily to all that Lugard was saying. What would he have thought had he known!

"I suppose your father can't object?" he asked.

"To you?" Nest said, coming out of her reverie. "I—I don't think so. Isn't it rather the other way about, dear? Isn't it that you rather object to him?"

"Well, anyhow he's your father," Lugard said ingenuously. It was a generous speech, and its very generosity touched Nest to the quick. "Besides, you are you."

"You mean it would make no difference what my father was?"

"My dearest girl, what a question! Why should it? If he were a chimney-sweep or a returned ticket-of-leave man it would be all the same to me. Even if he were a—a—"

"John Blaydon?" Nest whispered. "What would you think then?"

Lugard's face clouded and his eyes grew sombre. Nest had touched a sensitive nerve. She held her breath waiting for the reply. It seemed as if her whole happiness depended upon it.

"The idea is unthinkable," Lugard said curtly. "We won't discuss that, little girl. John Blaydon, the cur, is the red rag to the bull. I don't know what I should do. There are limits. But let us talk of something else. The lovely morning won't last for ever."

"Well, it pretty nearly gone," Nest sighed. "It's nearly one o'clock, and I must return. I feel horribly guilty—because I came away without seeing my mother, whose headache kept her in bed. Well, another ten minutes, if you like."

They parted presently, Lugard turning back along the cliff. Two men came hurriedly up the slope, eager-eyed and panting, as if looking for something. One of them flung Nest a question as he passed, and she answered vaguely. As she walked through a clump of gorse, where a sheep track made a short cut home, she nearly stumbled over something in the path. After the first startled moment, she made out the figure of a girl lying there—young, dark, and pretty, with a pair of black, frightened eyes that appealed to her. Under a ragged cloak Nest saw a tawdry, white satin dress covered with gold fringe as tarnished as the frock. As Nest drew back the girl caught her by the knees.

"Don't call out!" she whispered. "Don't let those men know that I'm here! You look kind and generous—as you are young and happy yourself, have pity on me!"

"You need not be afraid," Nest said. "Who are you, and what are you doing here?"

The girl brushed the tears from her eyes.

"I am keeping out of their way," she said. "I'll tell you everything presently. You may have heard of me—I am on the stage and they call me La Veni."

CHAPTER XXIX

LADY LAURISDALE TAKES A HAND

Here was something, at any rate, calculated to take Nest out of herself. There was something in the pleading depths of those dark eyes that moved her to the deepest pity. She could read in them abject misery and unhappiness far deeper than her own. The men she had seen a few minutes before were disappearing along the cliffs in the direction of Cromer.

"I don't think there is anything to be afraid of for the moment," Nest said. "Those two men—"

"Have they gone?" the girl asked eagerly. "Are you sure of that?"

"Quite," Nest smiled reassuringly. "But why are you afraid of them? Have you done anything—anything—"

Nest hesitated to finish the question. It seemed almost absurd to accuse this pretty child of doing anything wrong or desperate. The stranger flushed angrily.

"Oh! you need not be afraid," she said coldly. "I have done nothing wrong. Neither am I a thief. I have taken nothing belonging to anybody, and alas! I have no dear ones whose duty it would be to see that I did nothing foolish. I have not a single friend in the world—not one relative whose name I know in England. There is one old friend of my family, but I cannot find him. I am an actress, and those men make money out of me."

"Do you mean that they take your money?"

"Ah! they could not well do that; but it comes to the same thing. I am under what you call a contract. I signed a paper binding myself. At that time I was starving. If I break my word they can put me in prison—they have told me so often. But I can go on no longer, it is so cruel."

"Do you mean that these men are cruel to you?"

"It would be not fair, perhaps, to say that. I speak of the performance. I hate to see those innocent little birds lying dead on the stage. It is not always necessary to kill them, but I am anxious not to fail, and then I go too far. So I ran away."

"I see," said Nest, thoughtfully. "And you have no idea what you are going to do?"

"Practically none," the girl said sadly. "If I could only find the old friend of my family—Givanni; but it is as if the whole world were his hiding place."

For the time the name conveyed nothing to Nest. She was profoundly sorry for the little waif with the large, black eyes and engaging manner. She spoke with the slow hesitation of the foreigner who is not sure of the proper words, but her accent was refined, her manner perfect. She might have been no more than a little strolling player, but she had never been brought up to a life like that. She seemed to gather what was passing in Nest's mind.

"You will help me and be my friend?" she pleaded.

"You may be certain of that!" Nest replied. "It will be no fault of mine if the persecution does not cease. But we shall have to be careful. I will tell my mother and sister about you. You must come up to the house and have some luncheon. What shall I call you?"

"Call me Anita," the girl said. "That is my Christian name. I promised my mother before she died that I would never speak of her real name. And yours?"

"My name is Sairson," Nest said. "Nest Sairson of Marlton Grange."

Anita repeated the words with a pale face and lips that trembled. She could not have been more disturbed had Nest dealt her a blow.

"Impossible!" she said with a hissing indrawing of her breath. "It is impossible but I am frightened of shadows. Impossible with a face like yours. Sairson is a common name?"

The question was flung at Nest impetuously.

"There is a good many Sairsons in England," Nest smiled. "Why do you ask?"

"I was upset for the moment," Anita stammered. "Trouble like mine makes one foolish at times. It makes you imagine all kinds of things. With a face like yours it is impossible.. .. I do not know that I have the right to trouble you in this way. If you would lend me a shilling or two."

"I will do nothing of the kind," Nest said firmly. "You shall not go until I have seen that you are being looked after. My dear child, you could not come to the house in that extraordinary attire. I will bring you a cloak and hat, so that I can take you past the servants into my bedroom and give you some of my own clothing. We are both small and slender, and about the same size. My mother and sister will be sorry for you."

"If they are like you, I am certain of it," Anita said, with tears in her eyes. "Oh, this is the friend that I have been praying for. What can I do—"

"Well, in the first place, you can stay here till I come back," Nest smiled. "I must fly, for lunch must be nearly ready by this time. Wait here till I return."

Without, another word Nest dashed across the fields towards the house. She came back presently with a big cloak, a pair of shoes, and a hat and veil. Anita, slipped her feet into the shoes and took off her tawdry satin slippers, and looked quite presentable as she walked along by Nest's side. In a dreamy way she allowed herself to be led through the hall of Marlton Grange and up the wide, shallow stairs to Nest's room. The splendor and spaciousness of the house seemed to overawe her, the elegance and luxury of it all fascinated her.

"What a lovely old place," she murmured. "How fortunate and how happy you must be!"

Nest smiled quietly. If this little waif on the sea of life only knew everything! She busied herself over Anita's wardrobe.

"It is so very lovely," Anita went on. "These beautiful rooms with the pictures and flowers. It is good to be a young English lady of position. To think that your ancestors have been here for generations. I can remember something like it when I was a tiny child, only that was a palazo in Venice, when my mother was rich and famous all over Europe—but I promised to say nothing of that."

Then Nest's first impression had been right after all—the wandering player had been born in a sphere as exalted as her own. She had found a romance in the most attractive form. Certainly, there was nothing in the appearance of the poor child to belie it. She looked the part, too, even though dressed only in a frock of blue serge with white collars and cuffs.

"You look lovely," Nest whispered. "My mother and sister will be very glad to see you. I have already given them a few hurried particulars. Come to the drawing-room now, for the gong has gone. I am particularly anxious the servants shall know nothing."

In the drawing-room Mr. Sairson and Angela were waiting. Anita crept into the room timidly, her heart beating fast. But the kindly expression of Mrs. Sairson's face put her at her ease at once. It was so soothing to be petted and made much of by these wonderful strangers.

"I can't find words to thank you," Anita said. "You're daughter told me that—but you are not well?"

Mrs. Sairson dropped back in her chair with her hand to her heart. A ray of light had fallen on the strange girl's face and picked out the features strongly and distinctly. It was as if Mrs. Sairson had seen a ghost in that pretty dark face.

"I am quite well," she gasped. "I—I feel the heat sometimes. You are very like a girl I used to know, Anita. What did you say other name was?"

"I—I would rather not say," Anita stammered. "Do you think me ungrateful if I refuse. Do not imagine that I am concealing something dreadful."

Mrs. Sairson appeared to be content to let it pass. Only Nest was disturbed and anxious. What was there about the stranger to cause this agitation on her mother's part? Why had Anita herself been so moved at the mention of the name of Sairson? For a passing moment she was sorry she had brought the girl there, then she put the suggestion aside. It was impossible to look in Anita's face and feel that she was concealing anything of a dubious past. Her innocent talk proved that. She was open and candid enough about her life during the four years that had elapsed since her mother died, and the pretty little home at Richmond had been disposed of, and she had learned the bitter truth that she hadn't a penny in the world.

"My mother was robbed and deceived," she said with flashing eyes. "There were reasons why her family should not know where she was. But there was no lack of money. She knew a business man who professed to be her friend—she left everything to him. When my dear mother died I was penniless. But my mother found out that she was being plundered, and she warned me against that man. How she ever came to trust him is a mystery. Young as I was I already hated and distrusted him. He had so terrible a face. And I was quite alone in the world—because we have no friends in England."

"But how did you drift on to the stage?" Nest asked.

"I can't tell you," Anita said softly. "They always said I had gifts that way. My mother taught me a certain secret. My father had told it to her years before. He was a man of adventure who played a great part in the secret history of Europe at one time; in fact, he lost his life that way. He had obtained a marvellous recipe from a client—an old anarchist of his acquaintance. My father was a fanatic, you understand; good and kind and gentle to the weak, but a fanatic. And so this secret became mine. I practised it till I was perfect. A little time ago the men who had the travelling show that I was attached to found out my gift, and they used it for money. I joined the travelling by answering an advertisement in a paper. It was a cruel swindle, but the experience was worth something, for I desired to get on, and some day be a famous artist. If you only knew what I have gone through you would not wonder that I ran away from these men. If I had stayed with them I should have done something desperate. So I am all alone in the world."

"Don't be anxious about that, my dear," Mrs. Sairson said. "Come to the dining-room. I daresay we shall be able to devise something for you."

The windows of the long dining-room were open to the lawn, and sunshine flooded the room. Anita drew a deep breath of admiration and delight as she looked around her. She wandered from one point to another with an astute eye for the beautiful. She came presently to a table covered with photographs in silver frames. At the sight of one of them she slipped back with blazing eyes, and clenched hands. The expression that swept across the pretty dark face was almost murderous.

"Who is that man?" she asked, between her teeth. "Is he a friend of yours?"

"My father," Nest replied coldly. "You cannot have met him before."

Anita made no response, and further question was checked for the time by the entrance of Lady Laurisdale. She came forward in her best manner, but the words died on her lips as she looked at Anita. Her lips opened as if for some pungent utterance, but she changed her mind. For some half an hour or more she sat talking eagerly with Mrs. Sairson. She rose to go at length, and came to speak to Anita.

"I have been hearing something of your story," she said. "I am deeply interested. I fancy that I know something of your mother. Would you like to stay a day or two with me, dear? It is possible that you would be safer at Laurisdale Castle than here, though it may seem rather boastful to say so."

Anita grasped Lady Laurisdale's hand fervently. She spoke in a gentle whisper.

"Oh! you are too kind," she said. "Everybody is too kind. But I cannot stay here, there is a reason why I cannot remain in this house. Take me out of it, and I shall be your grateful slave for ever."

CHAPTER XXX

A Ray Of Light

Lady Laurisdale laid her hand almost affectionately on the girl's arm. She could feel the child trembling from head to foot.

"I should like to take you home with me," she said. "I have a girl staying with me and I believe you would get on with her very well indeed."

"Sybil!" Nest cried. "How strange I never thought of it before! Do you not see a great likeness between them—between Anita and Sybil, Lady Laurisdale!"

"I have been thinking the same thing," Lady Laurisdale said casually. "Yes, perhaps you are right. One is fair and the other dark, but the features are similar, and the expression is the same. But one is always discovering chance likenesses."

Lady Laurisdale spoke with a carelessness that she was far from feeling. But she was more disturbed in her mind than she would have liked to confess. In a blind sort of way she was groping towards the light—it seemed to her that she was on the verge of a great discovery, and this pretty child was an instrument in her hands. Yet Lady Laurisdale talked in her easy, graceful fashion as if her mind were free from care. She rose presently, and made a move towards the door.

"I really must be going," she said. "I came over in the car on my way to Cromer shopping. I will take Anita with me, and take such steps this afternoon as will free the poor child from any more persecutions. She will be safe at the Castle."

Anita murmured her thanks. She was too bewildered really to grasp what was happening. She allowed Nest and Angela to fuss over her as Mrs. Sairson and Lady Laurisdale led the way to the car. The latter's face grew graver.

"You recognised the likeness?" she asked. "As a Belham, you would. Now, what do you think of it? What does it all mean? What is to done?"

Mrs. Sairson shook her head hopelessly.

"I implore you not to ask me," she said. "Already I have more troubles of my own than I can bear. I have an uneasy impression that you know what they are. Why everything should be happening just now I don't understand.. .. Of course, I recognised the likeness. Anita is her mother again. I am afraid that we are the cause of all the trouble. If you only—"

"Not another word, please," Lady Laurisdale answered. "We are all under the shadow of the same trouble, and goodness knows where it will end. It is our own fault because we have shirked our responsibilities. But whatever happens you have a friend in me."

Mrs. Sairson responded that she was sure of it. Her face was grave, and even cold as she turned away from the car, and moved towards the house.

For some time, Lady Laurisdale was silent, but it was with satisfaction that she contemplated the slender figure by by her side.

"Do you know what I am going to do with you?" she asked.

"Only what is good and kind, I am sure," Anita murmured.

"Oh! that, of course. Well, I mean to keep you with me for a time. I will get you some clothes at Cromer this afternoon. We will return to the Castle with your luggage as if we had fetched it from the station. You are my protege, Miss Anita Hampson, who is going to stay with me. You come from Paris, you understand. It is necessary to take these precautions if only to keep the servants from gossiping."

"What have I done," Anita asked, "that you should be so very, very—"

"My dear child, you mustn't talk like that. Something more than good fortune guided your footsteps here. Was your mother a famous singer?"

"Did you happen to know her?" Anita exclaimed.

"My dear, I knew her very well indeed at one time. I have stayed in the house where you were born. I knew your mother's family intimately, and so did Mrs. Sairson. She must have recognised the likeness. But how you came to know Mr. Sairson is a mystery."

"I have not said that I do know him," Anita said, guardedly.

"My child, you are very transparent," Lady Laurisdale smiled. "It is loyalty to the good friends at Marlton Grange that keeps you silent. But it was a great shock to you to recognise Mr. Sairson's photograph in the drawing-room, and to find that he was Nest's father. Now you are going to tell me all about it, and about your life during the last 10 years. Believe me, I am not asking out of idle curiosity. Your whole happiness depends upon your trusting me."

Anita hesitated no longer. Tears gathered in her eyes as she slipped her hand in that of her companion, and she spoke quite frankly and freely. It was impossible to do otherwise with Lady Laurisdale once her sympathy was aroused. She listened with a smile on her lips, but there was hot anger in her heart all the same. Well, she would know what to say and what to do when the time came. She would be able to lift the black shadow from Marlton Grange and the Castle later. And this innocent child was the great weapon ready to her hand.

"It is a strange story," she said. "Here you are wandering about the country like this when you should be in the enjoyment of a great fortune. But I must not tell you more about that at present. And this romance is going on almost under my eyes. Givanni close by, too! You don't happen to know where he is to be found, do you?"

Anita shook her head.

"I don't," she confessed. "My mother meant to tell me, but she always put it off. He is not far away from here. He is poor, and grows wonderful flowers—orchids."

Lady Laurisdale suppressed the sudden exclamation that rose to her lips. She was rather silent for the rest of the way to Cromer, and only when Anita's wardrobe came under discussion became herself again. She stopped at the post office and despatched a long telegram; after that she was ready for the business of the afternoon.

"Now we will go home to tea," she said gaily, when the work was done. "Remember what your name is and where you come from. You can tell Sybil Gosway what you like. She is one of the nicest and most delightful of girls, and she will keep your secret. You will be great friends."

Lady Laurisdale's prophecy proved correct, for the girls seemed to take to each other at once. Her ladyship watched them with quiet pleasure. By dinner time they might have known each other all their lives. The lights were turned on presently, and the blinds were drawn.

"Now go into the drawing-room and amuse yourselves," Lady Laurisdale said. "I have a lot of letters to write in the library, and I am on no account to be disturbed."

It was getting late before a footman announced that a gentleman had come to see her ladyship by appointment. He came into the library, apologising for the hour of his call. Directly the footman closed the door behind him, the visitor's manner became more familiar and eager.

"What is the meaning of this, Blanche? Why that urgent telegram? I could not have come, only Sairson has had to go unexpectedly to Paris."

"I make no apologies, Philip," Lady Laurisdale smiled, as she held out her hand. "I had to see you without delay. Sybil does not know that you are here, and I would rather she did not know. Guess who is under this roof?"

Gosway shook his head. He waited curiously for Lady Laurisdale to speak.

"Anita Givanni's girl. Oh, you needn't look so startled! She came here by the merest accident. A strolling player kicked from pillar to post and badly treated by a set of rascals who were exhibiting her for her abilities. Did you know that Givanni lived close by?"

"Yes," Gosway appeared to admit reluctantly. "I did. But I didn't tell you because—"

"Oh never mind your reasons. We will come to them presently. The fact that Givanni is in the locality explains a mystery that has baffled everybody. I am talking about that strange attack on Mr. Sairson. Already the papers are saying that no solution will ever be found. They are wrong, for Anita could tell them in a few words."

"Blanche! Do you mean to say that that child could—"

"I do. Mind you, she has not the least idea that she holds so tremendous a secret. She would be distressed beyond measure to learn how closely tragedy has been treading on her heels. But if she stood for a few minutes in the witness-box the whole world would know the means by which John Sairson was brought to death's door. Fancy that baby with such a secret—and not knowing it, either!"

"Then you think that Givanni—"

"No, I don't. I don't know what to think. I don't know what to do for the best. I want to protect everybody, myself included, and I want to help the Sairsons. Whatever has happened or will happen to John Sairson he has only himself to blame. The police are still looking for Jack Barr, and when they lay hands upon him they will move heaven and earth to convict him of the crime. Every day I dread to hear that he has been arrested. If you can tell me that he is safe—"

"Barr is quite safe. I could prove that to you in a minute. When I got your telegram—"

"Well, thank goodness for that," Lady Laurisdale interrupted. "As I was saying just now, Sairson has brought all this on himself. I have found out something about him, and I have proved what only a few dimly suspect. You have been in his employ for years. Do you know his secret?"

A sullen red stained Gosway's face.

"I could not help myself," he said. "I have to live. I had to atone for the follies of my youth and God knows, I have paid for them in sackcloth and ashes. I have lived in dread and fear ever since. I have lived a good and sober life for the sake of my little girl, who suspects nothing. For some time I was on the verge of starvation. For Sybil's sake I had to take what I could get."

"I don't blame you, Philip," Lady Laurisdale said gently. "I know how you have wiped out the past during the last few years. But did you know that Sairson and Blaydon were one and the same man?"

"I did," Gosway confessed. "I have done his dirty work for years. Why?"

Lady Laurisdale crossed over and laid her on Gosway's arm.

"You poor man!" she said. "Oh, I can guess what you have suffered. I know the dreadful secret now, and it explains many things. And the Sairsons know. Nest last found out during the past few days. Oh! I am so sorry for them, Phil, and Jack Barr, too. If I could only see him—"

"You can," Gosway said, "he came here with me. I thought it best to bring him after getting your telegram. He is waiting for me outside at this moment."

"And the police on his track! How rash!"

"Shall I bring him in?"

CHAPTER XXXI

THE CAGEBIRDS

Whether guided by prudence, or owing to pure forgetfulness in the distraction of the moment, Anita had said nothing about the events preceding her romantic appearance on the cliffs where Nest found her. Signor Tito Mascani had been the instrument of her deliverance, but the hand of Fate had directed the matter from the time that Mascani quitted Oates's farm, at Givanni's instigation, and turned his face towards Cromer.

Mascani had obeyed the written word without the least hesitation. He was content to leave Givanni to deal with the swaggering, blustering Dudley Beaumont. He smiled grimly to himself as he thought how enraged the comedian would be. Besides, there was a touch of adventure about the thing, and adventure had not come his way lately. A soldier of fortune and a lover of intrigue, Mascani welcomed the opportunity. That he had no idea what he was to do made little difference. Givanni trusted him implicitly, and the reflection was bracing to the nerves. If there were danger so much the better. Even prosaic England offered scope for adventure sometimes. As to this last, he should wait and see.

He went coolly on his way, smoking his cigarette and thinking the matter over. At the end of an hour the lights of the town began to gleam below him. He should obtain such information as he needed from the next wayfarer. A belated visitor in flannels, strolling in the direction of the open country gave him the chance. Mascani inquired where he would find the address that Givanni had given him.

"You are close to it now," the stranger said. "They call it a street, but in reality is it an open road. The Romans called the roads 'streets,' didn't they?"

"I believe they did," Mascani said gravely. "Watling-street is a case in point. Very interesting; so I am practically on the spot, sir?"

The stranger intimated that he was. Something more than a mile and a half lay between the place where Mascani had pulled up and the town itself. It was a deep road, with high banks on either side, and beyond the bank substantial houses standing in their own grounds. Every house had a wicket gate at the foot of the bank, and on this gate was a number. Mascani could make this out by the light of a match. Presently he found the number he was looking for.

He gave a grunt of satisfaction, for the adventure was certainly not going to be a sordid one. It was a good house, surrounded by apparently well-arranged land of some three or four acres, and as Mascani mounted the flight of steps he detected the scent of roses. It was a disappointment therefore on reaching the garden proper to find an agent's board at a drunken angle setting forth that the house was to be let furnished, and that applicants were to apply to Sutton and Co., Cromer, or the caretaker on the premises.

Clearly the house, though furnished, was empty. It seemed hardly possible to believe that Givanni had made a mistake. Mascani had enjoyed the close confidence of Givanni for many years, and had never known him do such a thing before. But, on the other hand, had Givanni made a mistake? The mere fact that the house was in the hands of a caretaker might indicate that the adventure was of a sinister description. Caretakers are usually poor, and open to the temptation of the purse.

Mascani decided to make further inquiry before proceeding. He would have a word or two with the policeman on the beat. It only meant waiting in the road for him. Presently the heavy tread of the constable's boot smote the silent air, and Mascani threw open his coat. He knew the value of an immaculate evening suit assisted by a cigarette of the best brand.

"I am rather in a quandary my friend," he said. "This house here—"

The officer saluted. He flattered himself he knew when he was speaking to a gentleman.

"Captain Hickman, sir," he said. "Gone to the Canary Isles, sir, I understand."

"The captain did not tell me that," Mascani said calmly, "Most absent-minded man I ever met. He had a reputation for it in India. I particularly wanted to see him before I returned to the East. Knowing he was a late man I delayed calling until this hour of night. I suppose if I write a message and put it in the letter box the caretaker will have the sense to forward it."

"I'll see to that, sir, if you like," the policeman answered. "I did hear that one of the young ladies was ordered abroad sudden-like. Consumption they say."

"Ah! that would be poor little Margery," Mascani said feelingly. "She was always delicate. I am much obliged to you, officer. I'll just drop my card in the letter-box."

Something metallic clinked in the policeman's hand. No, he did not know the name of the caretaker. He was under the impression the man was an old servant sent by Captain Hickman from his London house. The whole thing had been settled in a hurry. The officer's instructions were to keep an eye on the place, but nothing more.

Mascani walked up the path with the comfortable assurance that he had won the confidence of the law, and that he was in a position to do as he liked. So far as he could see, the house was in total darkness, probably the caretaker had retired to bed. It was difficult to associate such a mansion as this with mystery and crime. Nevertheless, Mascani had every reason to believe that such was the case, or Givanni would not have sent him here. True, his instructions had been less than vague, but that was due to the fact that Dudley Beaumont had put in an unexpected appearance on the scene. If there was something wrong here, Mascani was expected to get to the bottom of it. For all he knew to the contrary, his mission might be a dangerous one, but he was ready to take his chance of that. Danger and difficulty were things he revelled in, though of late years he had not had much experience of either.

He was not so young as he used to be, but his muscles were of steel and his limbs agile. To some men intrigue and diplomacy are as the breath of life, and Mascani was one of them. He had not the least idea what he was required to do or how he was to set about it. That was in the lap of the future—the first thing to do was to find the adventure.

Very quietly Mascani crossed the lawn and stood in the shadow of a cedar tree regarding the house. Not a sound save the bleating of a distant sheep broke the silence. So far as Mascani could see, the windows were shuttered, for the house was an old one with that kind of protection. Along the whole front there ran a balcony covered with creepers on to which the principal bedrooms opened. Mascani smiled as he noted this.

"What a strange thing is custom," he muttered, "or, perhaps, I had better call it fortune. Every window on the ground floor has shutters to keep out the midnight marauder, but not to be unduly suspicious and inhospitable, the builder thoughtfully provided that balcony so that the least athletic of burglars might climb up and enter the bedrooms. The old creepers that have been planted there render access easier still. At my time of life I should be grateful."

With great care and caution Mascani proceeded to ascend the balcony. He realised that he could no longer depend on the protection of the law. The gullible policeman himself might have his suspicions roused by the sight of a man—even in evening dress—climbing up a balcony at midnight.

Mascani smiled as he thought of this. He had taken the first step, had no intention of retreating. If necessary, he would not hesitate to enter the house, but it was long odds he would find a window left open for ventilation. He proceeded to move slowly along the balcony looking for what, in his cynical way, he called the line of least resistance.

Then suddenly, without warning, a window in front of him blazed into light and the figure of a woman was outlined on the blind. She seemed to stand waving her hands as if to ward off something—a number of small, quick-moving objects fluttering about her head, as if a score of people were pelting her with stones. In a few seconds the light vanished as quickly as it had come, and all was dark again.

"They've got electric light in the house, anyway," Mascani remarked. "The place is not as old-fashioned as it looks. What the dickens was that woman doing and what was she afraid of? I'd give a heap to know what those little objects were. I wonder if she's gone!"

The time had come for taking risks, and Mascani took them promptly. His curiosity was roused. He must learn what he could about that woman and what was happening to her. As he advanced towards the window a light flashed in a room close by. The light was so strong against the darkness that Mascani could see tiny points of flame between the meshes of the coarse blind. He was on the same level with the window, so that it was possible to look in. He had to move his head quickly to and fro so as to get some sort of picture of what was taking place inside. The picture was not too distinct seen as it was through half a dozen different pinholes but it sufficed.

The room was half boudoir, half bedroom, very tastefully furnished, with electric lights in silver fittings on the walls. In the centre was a tall, forbidding-looking woman in a black wrap of some kind. Her dark features were stern and harsh, and she appeared to be speaking angrily to someone. Huddled up in a big armchair in one corner was a young and slender girl in white. Her head hung down and her hands were raised to her cheeks, so that Mascani could not see her face. She suggested youth and grace and elegance, despite the fact that her dress was flashily theatrical. Whether her mood was one of sullen passion or abject despair Mascani could not guess. Anyhow she seemed to be taking little or no interest in what the dark woman was saying. For a minute or two she sat motionless. As if stung to fury by this apathy, the woman crossed over to the armchair, and, taking the girl's shoulders in her hands, shook her silently backwards and forwards.

For the first time the girl looked up. She sprang to her feet and pushed the woman backwards. Mascani saw that her face was white and set with tears. But the eyes were sparkling with passion. It was a very dark and beautiful face, and Mascani staggered as he saw it.

"Merciful Heaven!" he said to himself, "am I dreaming or have I gone back thirty years of my life. Was there ever such a likeness! Did Givanni know or did he guess when he sent me here. I'll get to the bottom of this if I stay here a week. I must hear as well as see."

He turned from the window and crept along the balcony, feeling at the catches of the sashes as he went. The very next one he came to afforded him grave satisfaction. It was the room where he had seen the first flash of light. Almost as he touched it the latch yielded and the sash opened slightly. A second later and Mascani was in the room.

"So far so good," he murmured. "If there is anything—What, was that?"

The whole room was a mass of something soft and rustling, fingers seemed to touch his face. There was rushing in the air around him. He would never forget the thrill of it.

"Birds!" he exclaimed. "Birds! The room is full of them! I must run the risk of it and strike a match."

CHAPTER XXXII

THE ONE WAY OUT

While fumbling in his pockets for his safety match box, Mascani felt the wings licking against his face and dipping over his head. His presence had alarmed the little creatures; perhaps the opening of the window had had something to do with it. He was growing used to the situation, though puzzled as to what he should do next. Box in hand, he ruminated for a few seconds; to do nothing was a mere waste of time, to light a match was hazardous. But the risk had to be taken, especially in view of the discovery he had already made. He could accomplish nothing by remaining where he was, so he took a match from the box and struck it, carefully shielding the light in the hollow of his hand. Almost instantly the rustle of wings ceased and the birds fluttered back to cages that lined the walls. The place was a mass of loose cages, arranged one on top of the other; as to the birds, they were the ordinary denizens of wood and hedgerow. Mascani was conscious that a hundred pairs of beady eyes were turned upon him curiously.

No doubt this would explain itself presently, but meanwhile more important work had to be done. The intruder crossed over to the door and turned the handle. A moment later he was in long dim corridor with a night-light in a saucer for its only illuminant. So far this was satisfactory, seeing that the corridor was filled with furniture and pictures in piles, behind which it would be easy to hide if necessary. In an adjoining room the girl and the woman were situated. The door was not closed, and he could readily hear what was going on.

"I'll teach you to hit me like that," the woman said.

"Very well," the girl replied. "Do as you like. As to myself, there is an end of it. I will never appear again before the public—never. You can kill me if you choose."

"Little fool," the woman hissed. "Have I not explained a hundred times to whose advantage it will be in the long run? These men imagine they are going to exploit you for their own ends. They expect to live on your talent for years. You are afraid to leave them, because you are poor and dependent upon them for the food you eat. And how long will it be like that? You think, perhaps, for always! But you are wrong. The performance will be talked about, and create a great sensation from one end of England to the other. La Veni will be a queen in her way—as famous as a great comedy actress. Newspaper men will run after you, and your photograph will be in the papers. When this time comes these men cannot touch you—if you are wise you will be beyond their reach. You will be able to kiss the tips of your fingers to them and say adieu. Make use of them, my child; make use of them!"

"I tell you, no," the girl said wearily. "I do not trust you; I do not trust any of them. You are false to one another. You all come and whisper the same story to me in turn."

The woman was taken aback at this statement.

"A precious set of snakes they are," she said bitterly. "So that's the game, is it? You think to get better terms by playing one off against the other!"

"I have not given it a thought," the girl went on in the same weary tone.

"What do I care for your petty intrigues? Of what use would the money be to me? I loathe the whole thing from the bottom of my heart. The horrible cruelty of it fills me with misery. It is loathsome to destroy those poor little birds. I will do it no more."

"Then you defy me, girl?"

"Call it that if you like. It is all one to me. You dare not beat or flog or starve me. All you can do is to keep me a prisoner here."

"A prisoner, indeed! In a lovely house like this?"

"But this is not your house," the girl exclaimed. "You only obtained it by a trick. You may have to leave it at any moment. I heard the men talking about it last night. Say what you like, I am a prisoner here, with no means of escape. If I walk about in the garden, I know my every movement is watched. If I ran away I have nowhere to go, and no shelter for my head. My mother's friends are a long way off, and I cannot find them. But I will appear in public no more. I have said the last word as far as that goes."

The woman murmured something that Mascani could not follow. She appeared to be changing her tactics. When she spoke again her voice had dropped to a whisper.

"But suppose I show you another way?" she asked. "Suppose you could make plenty of money and at the same time leave your work and the stage for ever? What would you say to that? Did you ever hear the name of John Sairson?"

The listener started. He was not to waste his time after all.

"Have I not?" the girl answered bitterly. "Was it not the worst day of my poor mother's life when she met that man? He pretended to be our friend, and to look after our interests. He was to make my mother's money more, and she was grateful. He robbed us of everything, and when my mother died I hadn't a penny. Do not speak to me of that man!"

"Nor speak to me in that tone, child. I want to be your friend."

"I want no friends. But for so-called friends I should have been happy and prosperous now."

"Fool! I am not speaking of false friends. I want to make your future happy and prosperous if I can. Now listen, Mr. Sairson lives near here. He has a fine house and a fine family. They have not been here long, but Sairson's great ambition is to be a man of social position. With his money he will manage it in time. But he has enemies—bitter and malignant enemies. Only a few days ago one of them made an attempt on his life."

"The attempt failed! What a pity!"

"Little spitfire! Some people say the thing was a mystery accident. The papers have been full of it. Mr. Sairson was showing some of his very choicest orchids to Lady Laurisdale."

"I have heard my mother mention that name. Go on!"

"Suddenly he slipped and fell. Lady Laurisdale thought he had hurt himself. Then she noticed he was bleeding from a wound in his head. Though the orchid house was closed, the thing had been done. Lady Laurisdale heard no sound whatever, and yet a shot must have been fired, for they took some lead from Mr. Sairson's head. It looked like a piece of crumpled up tinfoil. Am I interesting you, child?"

An exclamation of horror crossed the girl's lips.

"Is it possible?" she cried. "Then someone else knows the awful secret! Somebody tried to murder Mr. Sairson as I kill the— But you know what I mean!"

"I know what you mean, child. The whole thing is a mystery to most people, but what a light you could throw on it. Sairson may suspect nothing, but he is never safe. I tell you he has been attacked even in his own house. And all the time his assailant feels secure. Sairson is a doomed man, unless he can learn the truth. With all his bounce and swagger he is a cur at heart, but he fond of his money, and fonder still of his bloated body. How many of his thousands would he not give to know the truth, eh? Do you follow?"

"Oh, I am listening!" the girl said impatiently. "Why do you keep me up when I am longing to be in bed? If that man wants to see me again to-night—"

"Dudley Beaumont? I daresay he will. Patience, child; patience! How stupid you are in business matters! If you go to Mr. Sairson—"

"If I go to Mr. Sairson! Why should I go to that scoundrel? He would laugh in my face and would offer me a shilling for an insult, and put me out of his house."

"Little idiot! Not if you told him part of the truth—enough to whet his interest and his sense of self-preservation. You could make any terms you chose. Promise to tell him how his 'accident' had happened and that you could shield him from any accident in the future, and he would listen to you as eagerly as a condemned man in the cell to a word of hope from his gaoler. Let me come along with you—let me state the case!"

"Go alone and state your own case," the girl said contemptuously.

"What is the use of that? The secret is your own entirely, and you have never revealed it to anybody. I daresay if one tried—"

"Oh, you have tried! You have all done your best to get the secret. But, you will have to kill me first, and then you'll not have succeeded. Go to this man yourself and make the best bargain you can. It will be what you call a task congenial."

Mascani stepped back as he heard the woman move. She laughed and spoke loudly.

"Come, think it over," she said. "Don't reject my suggestion in that way. I have shown you how to coin money, and if you don't like it you are a greater fool than I took you for. Good-night; I don't suppose Mr. Beaumont will be back till morning. I'll lock you in, as usual."

The last words were uttered with a sneer. The girl returned no answer, the door was locked, and the key turned on the outside. Mascani stood against the wall as the woman passed him, and, taking up the night-light, disappeared at the end of the corridor. Mascani pondered in the darkness what he should do next. He must have speech of the prisoner in the bedroom before he left, and the sooner he acted the better. She might retire at any moment, in which case an entrance would be unsuitable. He turned the key in the door and waited.

"Who is there?" the girl asked.

"A friend!" Mascani whispered. "I have come here to see you. I was sent by one Givanni."

"Come in," the girl said curiously. "It doesn't matter who you are. In any case you could not be more unwelcome than Dudley Beaumont and his friends. Please enter."

As Mascani stepped into the room there came a tremendous knocking, and the sound of much noisy speech downstairs, followed by a heavy thud. "I don't care," a hoarse voice cried, "I mean to see her now. Get out of the way."

The girl's face turned a shade paler.

"Mr. Beaumont!" she whispered; "and not too sober. If he finds you here—"

Mascani took the key from the door and locked it from the inside.

"He's coming upstairs," he said. "Keep him in talk so that I may have a few minutes to think the matter out. The situation grows exciting."

Alone with Givanni, Dudley Beaumont appeared to regard himself as master of the situation. Being a man of considerable imagination, he began to see comfortable pictures in his mind's eye. Givanni was sure to surrender at discretion and find the money Beaumont so urgently needed. Of course, the old man was lying when he declared his poverty. Poor men did not sit down to dinner in evening dress in a room of fine old furniture, and dine off the fat of the land, to the accompaniment of choice wines and cigars of the best. As a connoisseur in such matters, Beaumont had not failed to note the quality of the brandy. Anything so exquisite had not crossed his lips for a long time. Ah! and he possessed the means to unlock Givanni's money-bags.

He was in the swaggering, blustering mood, born of opportunity and old brandy, and felt more than equal to the task before him. In his eyes the abrupt departure of Mascani was a confession of weakness on the part of Givanni. He glanced round the beautiful room with a smile of approval. The decanter was close to his elbow, and, as he helped himself again, he dropped into a chair and pulled luxuriously at his cigarette.

"That is what I call being sensible," he said. "No use kicking against the pricks, is it? Glad you've got rid of that picturesque old pirate. Have I met him before?"

"Does it matter?" Givanni asked. "He knows you. Please go on."

Givanni's long yellow fingers toyed nervously with the handle of the fruit knife on the dessert plate, and the hard, metallic glitter in his eyes was lost on Beaumont. Apparently surrender was the last thing he contemplated.

"Want me to speak plainer?" Beaumont asked.

"It would be as well," Givanni responded. "Candor is always refreshing. To a lofty mind like yours the truth must always be clear. Without wishing to violate the dictates of hospitality, let me remind you that I am a poor man, and that my brandy is of the year 1820. Something more potent, perhaps? I am sorry the fiery whisky more congenial to your comrades is not accessible."

Beaumont relinquished the decanter somewhat sulkily.

"Oh, hang your satire," he said. "What's the use of playing the grand seigneur to me? I'm past all that sort of thing. What I want is money—"

"I have already told you I have no money."

"Nonsense! Look at this room! It may only be in a farmhouse, but look at it. A pretty penny it cost you. And dinner fit for a king, by Gad. Regardless of expense. Topped off by 1820 brandy and cigarettes grand Khedive. No money! You make me tired!"

"Nevertheless I have no money," Givanni repeated quietly.

"Well, perhaps not so much as you have been accustomed to," Beaumont conceded. "Let us say a thousand a year. At 5 per cent, that represents a capital of twenty thousand pounds. If you give one of these thousands I shall be letting you down lightly."

"You threaten me, sir?"

"Why put it in that way? Say that I am in need of money to finance a theatrical enterprise—that I see my way to a fortune by means of one of the most talented girls that ever trod the boards. Mind you, I could do without the money, if necessary, because the girl is so valuable an asset. But if I could get the money, I could take her out of the country till, well, till the mysterious attempt on the life of John Sairson is forgotten."

"Really? I must beg a little of that candor you spoke of just now. Something in your manner does not commend itself to me. Why am I to be blackmailed to get the girl away? What has her performance to do with me?"

"You had better come and see it," Beaumont said significantly. "Bring the police with you. There will be no occasion to point out to them the similarity between her performance and the manner in which Sairson met with his singular accident. They will see that for themselves. I need not add that the police are fond of asking questions. They want open replies. Do you follow me?"

Givanni nodded gravely. He did not appear to be in the least alarmed. The light of battle in his eyes narrowed down to tiny pin-points of flame. About him was a certain suggestion of sleepy alertness, as of a well-fed cat that has a mouse within reach of her claws.

"I follow you perfectly," he said. "My good Beaumont, pray proceed."

"Oh, hang it! Why pretend not to understand?" Beaumont blustered. "You know all about it. The police will start on a new track and before long it will lead them this way. They will ask to see your orchids. It is known that you grow that fashionable flower. Simultaneously with Sairson's accident a very rare orchid was removed from his greenhouse. If it is found here—"

"Let one admit that it will be found here. What then?"

Beaumont shrugged his shoulders. Things were not progressing as he had expected.

"It might be very awkward for you," he said.

"Granted. I should be asked to explain certain matters. There would be something in the nature of a scandal. Unless I find you money you will stir up trouble!"

"You won't permit anything of the kind, old friend," Beaumont said. "You are going to part."

"I other words I am to pay you this money you demand. You understand that this is blackmail of the worst and most despicable kind?"

"Call it what you will, so long as you hand over the cash, old man."

Givanni rose to his feet and paced up and down in the shadow beyond the light cast by the candles. It was well, perhaps, for Beaumont, that he could not see the expression of his host's face.

"You will get no money out of me," he said. "I would not part with a shilling to save you from the hell to which you are travelling headlong. You hint that I had something to do with the attack on Sairson, that I have discovered some novel method of committing murder. Well, I have a safe way of getting rid of any man who stands in my path."

"Now you are beginning to talk sense," Beaumont said.

"Then let me continue to do so. Mine is supposed to be the hand that struck Sairson down. I did it so that I could get possession of a certain orchid he had in his house. That orchid was mine, and Sairson robbed me of it as truly as if he had come here and stolen it. He would take as much trouble to rob a child of a doll's house if he needed it. After Sairson was picked up it was found the orchid had vanished. You surmise that I know where it is?"

"Of course you do," Beaumont muttered. "Take me for a fool?"

"Not unless a man can be both a knave and a fool. Now, we'll admit, for the sake of argument, that the orchid is in one of my forcing houses at the present time. What then?"

"What then? What a question! You are the man who tried to kill John Sairson."

"Nothing of the kind. The one admission does not necessarily imply the other."

"The police might form a contrary opinion. If I went to them and said—"

"What you propose to say unless you obtain the money which you ask for?"

"How disagreeable to state one's intention in that way!" Beaumont protested. "I don't wish to be unpleasant, you know."

"No, but you need the money, and you will be revenged on me if I don't supply it. Oh, what a subtle knave it is! How he plays with the poor Italian whose sole claim to consideration is that he was the friend of Mascani in the old days that are dead and gone! The drunken, swaggering, strolling player is more than a match for one of the men who built up the kingdom of Italy! Dolt, pig, idiot! You have not obtained the value of a farthing from me, and you have to-night given me information worth a king's ransom. Take your precious story to the police and let them make the best of it!"

Beaumont stared stupidly at the speaker. The words fell from Givanni's lips with a hiss like water when it touches fire. In the bemuddled brain of the actor an uneasy conviction was growing that he had said or done something inconceivably foolish. He wriggled in his chair.

"If you think you can bluff me," he began, "you will find—"

"Bluff!" Givanni cried. "In the school of diplomacy where I was trained we had no such word. I invite you to do your worst. As an object-lesson—"

"I thank thee, Jew, for teaching me that word!" Beaumont quoted. "An object lesson! Well, the object lesson shall be played out before the public with the girl as a medium. The first time you see her in public you will come to me for peace on my own terms."

A grim laugh broke from the other's lips.

"I will make a compact with you," he said. "Go back to the pig-stye whence you came and leave me in peace. Make what arrangements you like. If the girl appears in public, send me a card for the performance and I'll come and see it. Should it take place I'll give you a present of anything that I have in the world down to the last blossom in my greenhouse. I am a man of my word, as you know, and I make this solemn promise well knowing what I am doing. Does that satisfy you?"

It would have satisfied the average man, but carried no comfort to Beaumont. He turned a pair of fishy eyes on Givanni's face as if trying to read his thoughts.

"I'll take you!" he said. "But no tricks, mind."

"Tricks! You talk to me of tricks—a shabby hound like you! Never was a great and noble family cursed with such a son before. To think that, for your sake, the best and most beautiful woman in the world was sacrificed to John Sairson. To think what she gave up and what I lost to save you from prison. It would have been far better for everybody had you gone there. I am an old man now, but I was only 40 at the time of your rascality, and your sister was only 20. But she loved me, and I loved her, and all the world was before us. She little dreams that her lover is so near her; indeed, I don't suppose she'd recognise me if we met. Does she know?"

"Not from me!" Beaumont stammered.

"That is well so far. Remember, if you betray me, I'll kill you like a dog. I ought to have done so years ago, but I spared you for her sweet sake. Be off, you ranter!"

There was a finality about the last words that brought Beaumont to his feet.

"Oh! very well," he said sulkily, "very well. But you have made me a promise, and I'll see that you stick to your bargain. When this girl appears—"

"The girl will not appear. You will never see her again. Fool, get out!"

Beaumont went off, muttering uncomfortably. He turned his face towards Cromer and walked rapidly forward, full of vague imaginings. He would have been still more nervy had he known that Givanni was dogging his footsteps.

"What's the old fox after?" the actor asked himself wearily. "By Gad, I don't like it a bit—I don't, indeed!"

CHAPTER XXXIV

INTO THE DARKNESS

Beaumont pushed his way along, still muttering discontentedly to himself. Despite his cheap egotism and vaporing conceit, he was conscious he had suffered humiliation at the hands of his elderly foe. The ease of defeat was rank in his nostrils, and the loss of the prospective money was by no means his only regret. To get the better of others by mean and shady ways afforded him more satisfaction than the most remunerative but honest transactions would have done. He felt very bitter against Givanni just then, and thought of the dreadful revenge he would take, knowing full well that that revenge was remoter than ever.

He came at length to his destination—the house which Mascani had entered an hour before. He let himself in with a latch-key, and Givanni followed so closely that he nearly stumbled against two men standing in the shadow of some cedars on the lawn. It was a very near thing, and the wily Italian pulled himself up only just in time.

"Surely there were two of them?" a voice exclaimed excitedly.

"Well, I thought so," the other voice said. "Must have been a mistake on our part, sir. Anyhow I am prepared to swear that only one entered the house."

Givanni drew a long, deep breath as he hastily concealed himself in some bushes. The voice of the first speaker was perfectly familiar. He had heard it too often to be mistaken. A lurid gleam shone in his eyes. He had blundered on something of the deepest interest and importance. He crept close to one side of the cedars and listened.

"You have not made a fool of me, Sebag?" the first voice asked.

"Would I do such a thing, Mr. Sairson?" the little Jew attorney asked in an aggrieved voice. "Just as if I should dream of such a thing, sir. When I sent that message to your London club I knew what I was doing, sir. You came here quietly?"

"I did; my people think I am in Paris. Well?"

"I want to help you, sir; you've been a good friend to me, sir, and so has Mr. Blaydon. Do you understand what I mean? Then play the game!"

The last words had a note of alarm in them. Sebag was losing his temper.

"If you speak in parables to me, I'll break your neck," Sairson threatened.

"No you won't, sir; indeed, you won't. Two can play at that, Mr. Sairson, sir. If you don't care to listen to what I have to say, there are others who will be glad to. Mr. Lugard, for one, and the Countess of Laurisdale for another. Oh, I know what I'm talking about."

"You're a slimy rascal," Sairson muttered. "Come out with it! What connection can there be between me and John Blaydon?"

"You might be one and the same person," Sebag said slyly. "No, drop it! If you lay a hand on me again I'll not speak another word. You've paid me a lot of money from time to time, but I've earned it. I was bound to discover the truth sooner or later, Mr. Sairson. Not that I want to blab. I can hold my tongue where a client like you is concerned. The point is this! Other people have discovered your secret as well as myself."

"Really? What makes you think that?"

"Matters or obvious deduction, sir," Sebag retorted. "The person who tried to take your life the other day knows it. That's why the attempt was made."

"Bless my soul!" Sairson said in a startled tone. "You may be right. I never thought of that. Go on, Sebag, I see you have a good deal more to say."

"When the proper time comes," Sebag responded. "I've made a discovery, sir. The discovery is that you and Blaydon are the same man. But that is not what I was going to say. Lady Laurisdale knows the truth as well as I do."

"Go on," Sairson said grimly. "Let's have the whole brutal truth. On behalf of John Blaydon you went to see her ladyship. You told her what she had to expect?"

"I did, sir. That was part of my unpleasant task. I advised her to plead for time. She would do nothing of the kind—she laughed in my face. She let me know that she was aware how matters stood, then rang the bell and had me shown out of the Castle. Then I began to ask myself questions."

"With a view to turning the discovery to the best financial advantage," Sairson sneered.

"Why, certainly, sir. Luck was on my side from the first. In a very short time I had a pretty fair idea how the attack on you was done. Astonishing how luck favors you when once it starts going your way. I met the man who has just gone into that house."

"Another pawn in the game, by any chance?"

"He is, sir. He happens to be your own brother-in-law, though he calls himself Dudley Beaumont. I didn't know that till recently but I know it now. Note that house he's just entered, for it contains the clue to the mystery. Did you ever hear of Anita Givanni?"

"You are the most amazing little devil I ever came across," Sairson cried. "Tell me what you know of the woman who was once famous as Anita Givanni."

"You forget, sir, that you have employed me in connection with certain business relating to that unfortunate lady's estate. You pretended to be her friend, and would help her out of the clutches of John Blaydon, into which she had somehow fallen. I was acting for Blaydon—in other words, I was acting for you, while Sairson was professing to do everything he could for Madame Givanni. You will not have forgotten that there was something mysterious about Madame Givanni's husband. He had a daughter, and to that daughter was confided a certain secret. If that secret were set in motion against you, your life would be in peril. Now do you see what I am driving at?"

A startled exclamation came from Sairson's lips.

"Go on!" he said heavily. "The plot thickens with a vengeance. By gad, you are right, Sebag; the man or woman who knows the secret possesses a terrible power. But a mere child like that—"

"I wasn't thinking particularly about the child," said Sebag. "All the same I have reason to believe she is in that house, where she is kept prisoner by Dudley Beaumont, and another man, who are proposing to make a pile of money out of the girl's gift. If you could get hold of her, it would be of enormous advantage to you, sir. I can fit in the other details as they are required."

"And that you are prepared to do?"

"Certainly—at a price. I hold the game in my own hands, sir."

"A pretty figure you'll ask, I expect. Well, I suppose I can refuse it if I like."

"I don't think you will," Sebag said softly. "I don't think you will. After all's said and done a live Sairson is worth a dead Blaydon any day. Not all your money can save you unless you place yourself entirely in my hands. My price is ten thousand pounds. Oh, you need not laugh, I am a man with an ambition. I'm not fond of this dirty pettifogging work. In five years I could make the name of Sebag one of the most respected in London had I the necessary capital. For that money I am prepared to save your life and make you safe. If you refuse, take the consequences. You'll be a dead man in a month, and what good will your money be to you then, my boy?"

Sairson allowed the familiarity to pass. He appeared to be deep in thought.

"What do you suggest I should do?" he asked.

"See Dudley Beaumont the first thing," Sebag answered. "Only keep me out of it—don't let him know that I am anywhere near, or the game will be spoilt. Bluff him over Anita Givanni. Tell him you are the guardian of the girl and that you insist upon her being handed over to you at once. Mind, I am not absolutely certain that the girl is in the house, though I would stake my last shilling on it. When she is in your hands you can smile at danger for the future."

"You don't suggest that she had any part in the outrage in my orchid house the other—"

"Bless my soul, no!" Sebag exclaimed, with contempt. "She is only what you call a pawn in the game. Get her, and I'll show you how she can be used. Go and do it now. I don't suppose you are afraid of such a blustering blackleg as Dudley Beaumont."

"I should be a coward if I were," Sairson retorted. "I haven't seen him for years. The last time he attempted to blackmail me I threatened him with gaol. He would not dare to come within a mile of my house."

Sebag chuckled. He knew better than that. He could have told much that was interesting about an interview between Mrs. Sairson and her scamp of a brother and how much he had learned on that occasion unknown to either or any part. But this was not part of the game, as he saw it at present.

"Well, see him now," he suggested. "How these people obtained possession of a house like this puzzles me. However, that does not matter in the least. Go and see him!"

Sairson was suspicious of everything and everybody. Even now, when all looked to be plain sailing, he was wondering whether this was not some plot on Sebag's part. Was there not some conspiracy to lure him into this strange house and murder him? It was impossible to see what Sebag could benefit by being party to such violence as that, but one never could tell. On the contrary, the Jew attorney appeared to have everything to lose by disloyalty to his employer.

"I think I'll risk it," Sairson said presently. "Only mind, if you play me false—"

"Oh, drop it!" Sebag said, with some asperity. "How could I gain by that? I want ten thousand pounds, and it's your money I want, so why should I not go straight? Do you suppose that Beaumont and his lot could find a hundredth part of that sum? If I had wanted to betray you I should not have done it in this open fashion. Go and get it over, and I'll wait till you come back."

Once more Sairson allowed the easy assumption of familiarity to pass. Though his nerves were still slack, as the result of his accident, he would go far to fathom the mystery of the attempt on his life, and most assuredly he had little or nothing to fear from his brother-in-law, Beaumont. He strode up to the door and knocked loudly. By and bye a woman appeared and demanded his business. As the light fell on her face, Givanni, from his hiding-place, smiled grimly.

"My name is Sairson," the intruder said truculently. "I am a relation of Mr. Dudley Beaumont. Tell him I want to see him at once."

The door closed behind him, and the darkness fell again. Givanni could not stir, for his slightest movement would reach the Jew's ears. He waited patiently for the best part of half an hour; he saw lights flash out at different windows of the house, and heard a commotion as if some violent quarrel were in progress. Then he beheld a window open, and something white move to the edge of the balcony and stand still. A moment later and the white figure dropped from the balcony to the ground and sped away into the darkness of the night. Givanni heard the crash of shrubs and undergrowth as the figure vanished in the distance. He strangled the curse that rose to his lips and controlled himself with an effort.

"That was the child herself," he soliloquised. "I can't follow her without raising the suspicions of this little devil here. I can only wait till I see Mascani. If it is possible—"

The door of the house opened again, and Sairson stood in the light.

"Sebag!" he called. "Sebag! come this way! You are wanted!"

"It's too late," Sebag retorted, "the bird has flown."

CHAPTER XXXV

Mascani turned to the girl with a smile that tended to calm her fears. She had been through too many bitter troubles and humiliations to care much what happened now. There was something about Mascani that won her confidence. To begin with he looked so different from the men she had recently been in contact with—he looked a gentleman. Anita recognised that at a glance. The man's style and manner, the way he carried his evening dress, appealed to her. She smiled faintly in return.

"I am not afraid of you," she said. "But why do you lock the door?"

"To keep that drunken ruffian out," Mascani said. "Believe me, I am your friend. I am here solely to help you, my child. You are the daughter of the late Madame Givanni? Your likeness to her is too strong for doubt."

Anita nodded wonderingly. Here was a man who had known her mother, and who was, doubtless, a compatriot of that celebrated singer.

"Yes, I felt sure I was not mistaken," Mascani went on. "Yet people say that the age of romance has gone! Behold the man who in happier circumstances might have been your father. Only your mother preferred Signor Givanni to me. You must understand that your father and I were none the worse friends for that, for our rivalry was open and honorable. Did you ever hear of Paul Givanni?"

"Mr uncle?" Anita asked. "But I thought he was dead?"

"Dear me, no! He was very much alive when I saw him an hour ago. He sent for me, and I went. I begin to see now why he wanted me, though circumstances prevented him from telling me anything. We were interrupted by an actor, the most distinguished, who calls himself Dudley Beaumont. Do you happen to know the man?"

Anita shuddered violently. The look of loathing on her face told its own tale.

"Oh! I know him," she whispered. "The drunken man outside. He is one of my gaolers. These dreadful men brought me here. Though they had no money, yet a beautiful house like this was at their disposal. But I feel that they fear the police. Mr. Beaumont wants me to go round the provinces with him giving a certain performance. They say it is a wonderful feat."

"So it is," Mascani said, coolly. "Oh! you need not look so surprised. I have not seen your performance, but I can guess what it is. The secret was confided to you by your father before he died. Is that not so, little one?"

"Indeed it is," Anita confessed. "But how you could tell—"

"I could tell because the invention was partly mine. At any rate I gave certain hints in connection with it. So did Paul Givanni for that matter. Ah! our blood was hot in those days, when we meant to alter the political map of Europe. Kings were to tremble before us and thrones to rock. The grand secret, with its stupendous power, was to compel the attention of monarchs to the requirements of the multitude. What fools we were! But I can see what a performance it would make at a circus. But cruel, cruel!"

"That is why I shrank from it," Anita said eagerly. "Those poor little birds! How could anyone kill them who has heard them sing? If I were free—-"

The girl broke off sharply as a knock came at the door.

"Come out at once!" the female gaoler demanded. "What mischief are you up to? How did you get the key inside of the room? Mr. Beaumont wants you."

"Refuse to see him," Mascani said in a whisper. "Dare her!"

"It is too late," Anita said. "I will see nobody to-night. I will explain about the key in the morning."

"That's not good enough for me," the woman said shrilly. "Open the door at once. Do you hear?"

The silence on Anita's part was followed by a tempestuous assault on the door. The house echoed to the noise. Down below a man was heard roaring angrily.

"Drop it, you fool," Beaumont, yelled. "What does it matter? The girl will come to her senses in the morning. Do you want to bring the police about our ears? There! What did I tell you? Somebody is ringing the bell. Come and answer it at once. I'll see the girl if I want to."

"That is Mr. Beaumont talking," Anita said.

Mascani nodded. His brows were knotted and his eyes glittered. In the hall he heard a confused noise as if the people were engaged in an angry altercation. After a moment's hesitation he softly opened the door.

"I am not going away," he told Anita. "When you fight scoundrels it is wise to make use of their own weapons. In plain English, I mean to listen."

So saying Mascani crept to the top of the stairs. The electric light had been turned on in the hall, and he saw without difficulty what was taking place below. Opposite to Beaumont stood a man, the sight of whom made him quiver from head to foot with palpitating surprise.

"No you don't," Beaumont cried. "If you've got anything to say I prefer you to say it here. This is my home, and I do as I like in it."

"Always a liar and always a braggart," Sairson smiled. "Did you ever tell the truth except by accident? Your house! How did you get it? What did you pay for it? If I asked the police the question I dare say they could answer it."

"Why don't you get to the point?" Beaumont demanded.

"Oh! I am coming to the point fast enough," Sairson went on. "If you suppose I came here at this time of night for the mere pleasure of your society you are vastly mistaken. I have not long known that you were in the locality. If you had looked me up—"

"Don't worry about that, Sairson; I was going to look you up."

"I don't doubt it," Sairson continued, with the same bitter sneer in his tone. "Temporarily under a cloud—a little misfortune with some promising financial scheme. If I lend you a hundred till Monday you will repay it with a thousand per cent. interest."

"Nothing of the kind, Sairson. I was coming to save your life."

"Really? What have I to be specially afraid of?"

"Well, you are afraid," Beaumont retorted. "You are afraid to call your soul your own. You are frightened into violent perspiration by your own shadow. You haven't the smallest idea where the blow is coming from, or when it will fall, and you'd pay half your fortune to know. That's where I come in, honest John. That is where I can save you, my boy."

"I was practically sure of the fact," Sairson said coolly, "and that is why I am here. Fetch Anita Givanni downstairs and let me see her."

Beaumont gurgled queerly at the back of his throat. His jaw dropped, and his face looked long and glum. If Sairson had struck him suddenly in the face he could not have been more astounded. He stood gasping noisily.

"What—what are you talking about?" he stammered. "What girl do you mean?"

"I've already told you," Sairson retorted. "Fetch her down at once. Come, no nonsense!"

All the bluster had left Beaumont. How had this cunning devil got at the truth, he asked himself, and what had become of all his dreams of wealth? He moved uneasily as he saw the brilliant prospect fade away. There was a cruel and vindictive gleam in Sairson's eyes as he rammed his advantage home.

"Fetch her down!" he cried. "Let me see the child who holds the key of the situation. Perhaps we shall learn the truth from her, unless she has been too long in your hands. Did you think to beat me, you fool? A broken-down scion of a noble house, a besotted thief whose scanty brains have long been sapped by drink, at your time of life, you were coming here to pit your wits against those of John Sairson."

"Why not call yourself John Blaydon?" Beaumont replied sullenly.

"So you know that, too. Everybody seems to know it. Well, it doesn't very much matter. John Sairson or John Blaydon—it's all the same as long as they have the money between them. These poor aristocrats will come fast enough so long as they can get something at Marlton Grange. I'll buy up the lot of them, I'll pay their debts, I'll keep them out of bankruptcy. Now go and fetch the girl."

Beaumont moved heavily towards the stairs. He was cudgelling his muddled brains for a way out of the impasse. If he brought Anita face to face with John Sairson his power was gone. He could not use the girl as a lever for obtaining money.

Mascani had listened with good-humored contempt. The danger was getting close, and his duty was to avert it. Come what might, he had no intention of allowing the child to meet Sairson. It was not easy to see how this was to be avoided, but difficulties and dangers were the things which the soul of Mascani loved. He darted back into the room.

"There is danger," he said, "but you must be guided by me. Don't be afraid."

"I am afraid of nothing as long as I have a friend by my side," Anita answered.

"Good child! Spoken like your own mother's own girl. There never yet was a coward in her family. A man downstairs insists upon seeing you."

"You are speaking of Mr. Sairson," Anita said quietly. "Yes, I heard his voice."

"Ah, yes. You seem to know more than I had expected. He demands to see you. That is the last thing in the world I desire. You must not be here when the fellow comes. I will drop you over the balcony. Put on a wrap and do as I tell you. Directly you are free of the garden go into the road and wait for me. I don't know what I will do with you yet, but I can devise a plan, never fear. Will you trust me?"

"Oh, yes, yes!" Anita exclaimed. "I feel I can do so. I thank God for your friendship to-night."

Mascani wrapped a mantle around Anita and, without another word, pushed open the window and led her to the edge of the balcony. Raising her in his arms, he lifted her over and held her until her feet were near the ground. He saw her drop lightly into some bushes and dart across the lawn. Then he returned to the bedroom to hear Beaumont hammering vigorously on the door.

"Come out," the latter cried. "Don't you hear me, come out! If you don't—"

"Stand aside!" Sairson rasped out hoarsely. "You are wasting time. If she don't come out to us we shall go in to her. I will force the door."

He flung his full weight at the door, the latch gave way, and he staggered into the room. Mascani was calmly standing with his back to the fireplace smoking a cigarette.

"Good evening, Mr. Sairson," he said quietly.

"My God!" Sairson cried, huskily. "It's—it's Tito Mascani."

CHAPTER XXXVI

PLAIN SPEAKING

As he confronted the Italian it appeared as if the mask had fallen from Sairson's face. His dark, heavy features grew moist and flabby, and his forehead was studded with beads of perspiration. He had had several unpleasant shocks lately, but none was quite like this. Mascani closed the door and stood with his back to it, smiling gently. There was nothing sinister or threatening in his aspect, but Sairson was none the easier in his mind on that account.

"You are right, my friend," the Italian purred. "So you recognised me at a glance. Such a meeting would delight the heart of the dramatist. How long since we met last, Sairson?"

"What's the good of asking me?" Sairson responded, sulkily. "How do I know?"

"My good man, you know perfectly well. You could name me the day and the very hour if you wished. One of the great regrets of my life is that I did not kill you when I had the opportunity. A common acquaintance—still living—afterwards pointed out to me that such a glorious chance might never occur again. But you see he was wrong."

"None of that nonsense," Sairson blustered.

"Oh, you need not be afraid, Sairson. I shall run no risk by ridding the world of you. Besides, the job has been taken out of my hands, it seems."

Once more the pasty white spread over the red of Sairson's face.

"I might have guessed," he cried. "So Jack Barr is the man that—"

"Really! You suspect Jack Barr—Captain Jack Barr? Well, he had every justification. You ruined him lock, stock and barrel—you drove him to despair. But Jack Barr had no hand in the assault in the conservatory. Upon my word, I am greatly obliged to you for mentioning the matter. It explains one or two points that puzzled me. As a student of the daily papers I was deeply interested in that conservatory business. Barr was a fool to come to your house and make a scene. The police were equally foolish to regard Barr as a criminal on the strength of his folly. It was very awkward for you, because you could not properly explain matters—at least not without revealing the fact that you and Blaydon are one and the same man."

Sairson suppressed a groan. Had the whole world suddenly stumbled upon his shameful secret? He looked round the room for some means of escape. But Mascani stood calm and smiling with his back to the door, looking, as in plain truth he was, master of the situation.

"I won't detain you long," Mascani went on. "It must have been a shock to find me instead of the poor, defenceless girl you meant to bully and terrify. So far as she is concerned, you had better abandon any hope of getting to the bottom of the mystery. It was not her hand that struck you down."

"No, but she could tell me something," Sairson muttered.

"I doubt it. Others know that secret—Maldini for one."

Once again Sairson started.

"Maldini has been dead for years," he said hoarsely.

"You think so. I thought so, too, but I have seen reason to change my opinion. But I am delaying you—there is nothing here I do not know, nor do I care. Doubtless the police will investigate that later on. Your scoundrelly brother-in-law could throw some light on the matter. Will you be so good as to tell him, with my compliments, that he is not likely to see the girl he calls La Veni again? The child has ceased to be a pawn in the game."

"I haven't the remotest idea what you are talking about," Sairson said sulkily.

"Come, cease fooling," Mascani retorted. "You are here now to see the girl—at Dudley Beaumont's instigation. You are up to your neck in trouble and danger; you walk in fear of your life. Once you affected to be the friend of the cause we all had at heart, but even then you were betraying us for money. With the money you obtained you set out on your present successful career. Yet when you grew rich you could not be honest. You robbed the widow of the man who gave you your first start in life, you robbed Anita Givanni of her patrimony. You robbed Captain Barr of his, and incidentally did your best to break your daughter's heart. But you have come to the end of your tether, John Blaydon. Make the most of your time."

Without waiting for a reply, Mascani opened the door and strode down the stairs. He would not have been surprised had his departure been challenged, but the house was still, and no sign of occupation was visible. Mascani walked along the drive until he reached the road. There he paused as if uncertain what he should do next, for he could not see Anita anywhere. Finally he retraced his steps to Oates's farm, smoking thoughtfully as he went.

He must see Givanni again before he slept. He was, of course, ignorant that his friend was only half a mile in front of him. As a matter of fact, Givanni had accepted the inevitable. Things had not gone as well as the wily Italian had anticipated, and he was sorry he had not been more explicit with Mascani. But the unexpected appearance of Dudley Beaumont had diverted his attention, and his policy had had to be decided upon the spur of the moment.

At any rate the girl had got clean away—of that Givanni was satisfied. He had been denied the opportunity of following her; the presence of the rascally Sebag had prevented that. There was nothing for it, therefore, but to hope for the best and pray that Anita might fall into good hands. It might be possible to do something in the morning.

Givanni accordingly retraced his steps homewards. Mascani would give him all the details in good time. He lingered to smoke a final cigarette and drink a glass of Chianti. His hand was on the screw of the lamp when he heard a cautions tap on the window. Givanni pushed it carefully open and looked out.

"Who goes there?"

"Who but myself?" Mascani replied. "Upon my word, old friend, you have paid me a very pretty compliment. Most people would declare that I was far too old for this kind of sport. Knowing my record, you thought otherwise!"

"It was very good of you to come back so soon," Givanni said. "Wait a moment, and I will open the front door for you."

By way of reply, Mascani vaulted through the window into the room.

"What do you think of that for sixty?" he asked. "Ah, but there is life in the old dog yet. I have had a pretty adventure, comrade."

"I know it," Givanni replied. "I followed you as soon as possible. I ought to have sent for you much earlier in the day, but my plan was not ready. When that fellow Beaumont turned up this evening there was no time to lose. It was necessary to help that poor child at once. You were very successful."

"How can you know that?"

"Because I was at your heels," said Givanni coolly. "I followed Beaumont, as a matter of fact. Unfortunately, I could not keep on the track of the girl for the simple reason that there were spies about. What did you make of John Sairson?"

Mascani smiled as he reached for the cigarette box.

"What I made of him years ago," he said. "That scoundrel has shot his bolt. Within a day or two we shall have him thrown to the vultures. Now, my friend, I want you to be more candid with me—to tell me why you sent for me. Have you any fear for your personal safety?"

"My safety!" Givanni echoed. "What possible danger do I stand in?"

"Then you have not realised the position? Well, you were never a coward, my dear Paul. Now, let us see exactly how the thing works out. You pose here as a poor man called Givanni—"

"Givanni being my proper name."

"Precisely. But nobody dreams that you are the Givanni who played so brilliant a part in the freeing of Italy from the Papal yoke. You are a poor man who lives by selling flowers. They are wonderful flowers, which is an important item in the story. You are too proud to apply to people who are under the deepest obligations to you, but you are not too proud to go to a money-lender called Blaydon. It matters not that you do not know that Blaydon and John Sairson—who married your first and only love—are one and the same person. To Blaydon you mortgage everything, even to the wonderful orchid upon the rearing of which depends your future welfare. You intend to repay the money, but at the appointed date you have no money to pay. Then Blaydon forecloses and your orchid goes to Marlton Grange. Is that not so?"

"Correctly stated," Givanni answered, "and that is the point where I made the discovery that Blaydon and John Sairson were identical. It was an obvious deduction. I discovered that when I discovered the new home of my beloved orchid."

"An admission to that effect in a court of law would procure you ten years for the attempted murder of John Sairson. Your motive? To recover your orchid. You got your orchid back, and probably it is in one of your frames at the present moment."

Givanni flicked the long grey ash from his cigarette.

"I won't deny it, my friend," he said. "The orchid was the one thing I could not part with. Blaydon had more than enough security for the money without it. But the orchid was restored without any action on my part."

"Then Lady Laurisdale's statement goes for nothing? You remember what she told the police—that the flower she actually admired was missing, and the missing orchid is now in your possession! You cannot deny that you know the means by which Sairson's life was attempted!"

"Have it so," Givanni agreed.

"Very well, then. Oh, what a lawyer I should have made! The attempt lies between you and Captain Barr. About the same time Jack Barr called to see Sairson and was expelled the house. At present the police are looking for Barr. Sairson saw to that. But they will not catch Barr!"

"You know that he is safe?"

"I do, for the simple reason that he has been with me for some time. I found him a secure hiding place. Philip Gosway placed him in my charge. For a fortnight or more I have been his gaoler. I see that he gets no liquor or drugs! I am making a man of him. At least I was so engaged until yesterday, when he disappeared."

"Can he have fallen into the hands of the police?"

"I don't think so. Nor do I think that he had a hand in that attack on Sairson. I am sure you hadn't a hand in it, either."

"Then whom do you suppose—?"

"My dear friend," Mascani said softly, "have you not thought of Maldini?"

"No," Givanni whispered after a long pause. "I had not thought of Maldini. The man—the very man!"

CHAPTER XXXVII

LIKE ONE FROM THE DEAD

The stars seemed to stagger in the sky as Sairson returned home. He shuffled in his walk like a man weary of the struggle and ready to fall by the wayside. For the first time in his life he was experiencing what nerves meant. Hitherto he had had a fine contempt for them; they were all very well for a parcel of women who had nothing to do and nothing to think about but themselves and their imaginary ailments. A fine constitution, a perfect digestion, and the utter absence of conscience had been his assets in the battle of life. He had "got on" wonderfully, had amassed money, and most men he met were afraid of him.

Now everything seemed to be different. All at once everything had gone wrong. It was as if he were walking beneath a veritable avenue of Damocles' swords. Whence had his enemies arisen? Whence came their astonishing knowledge of his past? Some of these people he had forgotten years ago; he had come to regard them as dead and buried. There was Mascani. How many years was it since they had met last? Surely, it must have been twenty. That had been in London just before the political troubles that had threatened disaster to Italy. Sairson had made money out of Mascani and other hot-headed Italian patriots who had squandered fortunes to support the cause they had so closely at heart. A set of wild, visionary fools, Sairson had labelled them in his contemptuous way. Any business man would have adopted his methods. And they had never found him out. They regarded him as a friend of Italy, too. They did not know that he was plundering their funds right and left, under the guise of a financial agent acting on behalf of "John Blaydon." Mascani had been suspicious, and had not hesitated to say things— and prove them, too—but Mascani had suddenly disappeared, and Sairson had concluded that he was dead long ago. Sairson had smiled at the time. It was his usual luck. Luck and he went hand in hand in those days.

Those high-souled patriots had been a perfect gold mine to Sairson. They were so simple, so confiding, and never asked awkward questions. They had jewels to pledge, and fine old furniture to dispose of; they signed accounts in a manner that made Sairson smile. He robbed them without fear and without shame. So long as Mascani was out of the way all was well. This had been going on with relatives of the same old families for years. Perhaps the greatest haul Sairson had ever had was the administration of the affairs of the great singer, Givanni. She had been the last of the old Corsican connection.

Now Mascani had turned up again after all these years, and at the worst possible time. Sairson wondered nervously how much he knew of the prima donna's affairs. It was sinister that he should be here protecting the woman's daughter at this particular moment. His manner had been that of a man who trod on very firm ground. Possibly Mascani had been secretly watching him for years. Well, something would have to be done, Sairson told himself as he plodded homewards. He kept on thinking the same thing as he sat in his study brooding over the matter, without coming to a satisfactory solution. He sat there till the sun rose from the haze of the sea and the chill world was flooded with the light of a glorious summer day. The lawn and flower beds lay drenched in silver dew, and blackbirds were heralding the morn. Sairson refreshed himself with a cold bath and passed out into the garden. He stood admiring the house with a dissatisfied pride.

The place was his—anyhow he had bought and paid for it. The Sairsons should be very important people one of these days. It had always been one of his grievances that his wife had borne to him no son. He had longed for a boy after his own heart. The girls were very well, but they were girls after all. They would marry in the course of time into good county families and Sairson would be able to boast of his sons-in-law. The grand old place was his, and a host of servants hastened to his call.

It was wonderfully peaceful, so tranquil, that Sairson wondered why he had not cultivated the habit of early rising. It was just the same next morning, when he came down again after a restless night following a worrying day in town. As John Blaydon he had had an annoying letter from a firm of lawyers, asking pertinent questions regarding the estate of the late Signora Givanni. Sairson could trace the hand of Mascani here. They were very awkward questions, and it would tax all his cunning to answer them satisfactorily. He was glad to be out of town, drinking in the freshness of the morning. It was so quiet that he started to see a figure in black emerge from the house.

One of the servants, Sairson decided, and up to no good. He hastened to cross the grass and intercept the girl before she passed into the shrubbery. With a vague feeling of uneasiness which it would have been hard to account for, Sairson found himself face to face with Nest.

"Where are you going to at this time of the morning?" he asked.

Nest colored. Her face was drawn and pale, and there were dark rings under her eyes. Yet she looked at her father fully and squarely as she replied.

"I am going away," she said. "I am taking you at your word."

"You sentimental idiot," Sairson exclaimed. "What do you mean?"

"I thought my words were quite plain," Nest said coldly. "The understanding between us was complete. If I did certain things you would turn me out of the house to earn my own living. If I told Cecil Lugard the truth I was no longer to regard myself as a child of yours."

"I did say something of the sort."

"Something of the sort! Your words were brutally plain. Nothing could have been plainer. But my duty is equally plain."

"Was ever a man plagued with such a child!" Sairson cried. "Why go out of your way to make trouble? Lugard has family and money; he is very fond of you, and you could twist him round your little finger as you pleased. You will have money, too, some day—lots of it. Let him find out for himself if he likes. When you are his wife—"

"Not under false pretences," Nest cried. "Cecil is looking for John Blaydon. The very idea of the meeting sets me trembling. Heaven knows what the consequences may be. Do you suppose that Cecil, with all his love for me, would consciously marry John Blaydon's child? Never! And, since I know the truth, it is my duty to tell it to him."

"Then you are bent on doing so?"

"I mean to do so. Cecil is coming here to-day to try to induce me to fix the date of our wedding. I cannot, I dare not, meet him. That is why I am playing the coward and running away. I have left a letter for Cecil, and this he will get when he calls. If you only knew what the writing of that letter cost me; if you could only realise—"

"It will cost you more than you bargain, my girl," Sairson said angrily.

"Oh! I know what you mean—that I shall gave to struggle for myself in the future, that I shall be at the beck and call of hard folk who will look upon me as a white slave. Well, there are worse fates than that, and to stay eating one's heart out here is one of them. I cannot meet Cecil; it is impossible, and that is why I am going."

"Have you any money?"

"I have a few pounds to keep me till I get work to do."

Sairson burst into a peal of laughter.

"You work!" he roared. "You arrant little fool! How long will your money last? A month! And what will you do afterwards? You have not a single thing at your finger ends by which you can earn so much as a crust of bread. Now, don't look to me for anything. If you starve, you will never get a single farthing from me. I have said it."

Sairson strode away to the house, feeling satisfied with the effect of his words. He had seen Nest blanch and noted the pain and terror in her eyes. He had only to be firm and she would never carry this wild scheme into effect. She would probably return before she reached the station.

After her father left her, Nest pressed her hand to her eyes to wipe away the scalding tears, for a sense of utter desolation and loneliness possessed her. A footfall coming to her ears, she looked up and uttered a cry of surprise.

"Jack!" she exclaimed. "Jack Barr! What have you been doing? What strange change—"

"I am glad to hear you say that," Barr smiled. "Is the change so marked?"

Nest nodded. She had seen Barr not long since bent and broken, the trembling wreck of his former self. He was pale still, his thin nostrils flickered nervously, but his eyes were clear, and he held his head upright.

"Behold what three weeks have done for me!" he said. "There are times when it seems like a dream. It was a dream, Nest, a hideous dream, and the nightmare was of my own making. I was going headlong to perdition in my own way when a kindly hand stopped me. The hand was a heavy one, but it was cruel only for my own good. The better part of my nature has come back to me in these weeks. Already I have lost the craving for the poison that was spoiling my brain. Only three weeks ago I came here to commit a murder. But for the grace of God I would have done that deed. I am here again, but not for violence, not for crime. Oh, what a fool I have been!"

"I don't understand it," Nest faltered.

"Of course you don't. How could a child like you understand what a rascal is capable of? Why, I did not understand it myself until a friend made the matter plain for me. Nest, I have come here looking for my lost happiness. If Angela will only forgive me and say—"

"Oh, I am sure she will," Nest cried. "She has waited all these years for nothing else. Surely, as she has so much money to look forward to, and you—you—"

"I have so little," Barr smiled. "At present yes; but when I have done with a certain man, no. Then I will be rich, too. I am looking for him now; I mean to compel him to account for certain things. Never mind who the man is."

Nest asked no further questions; she simply was afraid to. She did not need Barr to tell her that he was alluding to her own father. Well, there was a chance that Angela would be happy after all, and that was so much gained. There would be great trouble and tribulation yet, but Barr, she fancied, was going to win through. To see him now in his right mind was little short of a miracle, and if one miracle happened might not another tread on its heels! A reply trembled on Nest's lips, as the bushes parted and Cecil Lugard stood there.

"Barr!" he exclaimed. "I thought I recognised your voice. Why are you here with Nest? What on earth have you been doing to yourself? I never in my life saw such a change in so short a time. If I may be allowed to suggest to you—"

"In good time," Barr smiled. "I have been in the hands of Tito Mascani. It is too long a story to tell at present, Cecil. You shall hear it in good time. But since you ask why I am here, I'll tell you that I am looking for somebody."

"An enemy by the tone of your voice. Who is he?"

"I am looking for John Blaydon," said Barr quietly. He gave a warning glance in Nest's direction, but she saw it, and her limbs trembled. "You know the man I mean?"

"Know him?" Cecil said slowly. "Ay, I do. And I am looking for him, too. Only show me where I can find him, and I shall be your debtor for—"

Barr pointed to all opening in the trees—Sairson might be seen walking on a distant part of the lawn. Nest darted forward and laid her hand on Barr's arm appealingly.

"Not yet!" she said. "Not yet! I beg of you to let me speak before you say another word."

CHAPTER XXXVIII

A PLEA FOR MERCY

"My poor little Nest, what is the matter?" Lugard asked anxiously. "Why are you here so early, and what has Jack Barr said or done to upset you and make you cry?"

Nest lifted her pale face to that of her lover. The pleading look in her eyes moved him strangely.

"He has said and done nothing deliberately," she replied. "He came unexpectedly, and at first I did not recognise him. The last time I saw him—but he will not like me to sneak of that."

"You can if you like," Barr interpolated; "it will only be what I deserve."

"No—no!" Nest exclaimed. "Why should I? You have had your troubles and misfortunes and have paid the price. Did you ever tell Cecil why you parted from Angela?"

"No, I didn't. I told nobody. If you knew the reason you would be sorry for me."

"I do know the reason, Jack. They kept me in ignorance, regarding me as a child. I made the discovery for myself. If I had been in your place I should probably have behaved in a similar way. I know that it was for our family's sake you kept silence."

"You have guessed it correctly," Barr replied. "But I was a fool all the same, and a cruel fool into the bargain. I should have remembered that Angela was a Belham to the finger-tips, and hadn't an atom of Sairson in her. But the shock was too much for me. Had the disgrace been anything else but what it was I should have said nothing. I thought only of my pride and my own family. I took refuge in the bottle! Fool that I was! It was playing your father's game exactly. He even came to visit me and try to bring me to my knees asking for his bounty. When the revulsion came and I saw what I had done, it was too late to show my face to a good and innocent girl. I looked upon myself as lost, and only wanted to drink myself into my grave. Then came madness, the madness that brought me here to kill John Sairson."

"What is all this about?" Lugard asked. "Is all the world mad this morning?"

"Patience, Lugard!" Barr continued. "I came here to kill Sairson, and, but for the goodness of God and Philip Gosway, I should have done so. Gosway put me into the keeping of Mascani for the best part of a month, and he cured me. He is a wonderful doctor. Day by day I got better, day by day I regained strength and nerve. Of all my sufferings the knowledge of my own folly was the worst and most painful. Then I began to ask questions and go into figures. What a consummate ass I had been. I had been robbed in the most shameless fashion. But I shall get it all back and make Angela happy, too, if she will allow me the privilege."

"Oh! I am perfectly certain of that," Nest cried.

"From the bottom of my heart I hope so," Barr went on. "It will be my own fault if I do not make amends for the past. I hope you will intercede for me, Nest."

"There will be no occasion," Nest said tearfully. "Oh! how little you men know of the sacrifices we women are capable of when the heart is given where we truly love! But my father—"

"Your father will do exactly as I say," Barr broke in sternly. "Shall I tell Lugard?"

Nest trembled and averted her head. The blow was about to fall, and it might as well come from Jack Barr's hand as from her own.

"Upon my word, I shall be glad to hear what it is," Lugard said drily. "Your explanations leave me more bewildered than ever. If Sairson has wronged you—"

"He robbed me of all I had," Barr resumed. "He schemed to do it, and ruined me deliberately. His plea was to break my pride and force me to sue for time. I took to drink instead. Shall I tell you why I refused to become his satellite?"

"That is what I wish to hear," Cecil replied.

"Because he was a money-lender. I had found out that John Sairson and John Blaydon were one and the same man."

The words were spoken only a little above a whisper, but they sank deeply into Lugard's mind. In that moment of disclosure he never looked at Nest. He was thinking entirely of himself—his position. He was a Lugard, with all the pride of his race and name. He stood on soil that had belonged to his ancestors for generations. This very mansion had been filched from his people by John Blaydon. Cecil could prove this up to the hilt. He had boasted in Sairson's presence of what he would do when he and Blaydon met face to face and he had been talking to the treacherous dog himself all the while. And he was pledged to marry this man's daughter!

He turned to Nest and held out a hand.

"How long have you known this, little girl?"

"Only a few days," Nest faltered. "I learned it by accident. I longed to tell you at once, but lacked the courage to do so. If you knew what I have suffered—"

She broke down and wept bitterly. It was hard to think of words to comfort her. Lugard turned angrily on Barr, who felt the situation was painful.

"I could almost quarrel with you for telling me this," he said. "Still, it had to be done. So, Sairson and Blaydon are one and the same. I have half-suspected as much more than once, but drove it from my mind as an idle fancy. There will be no violence, Barr?"

"Not as far I am concerned," Barr responded. "I hope I am in a better frame of mind. I have been a selfish fool Lugard and must try to atone for it. But at present I am de trop."

He bowed to Nest and vanished in the bushes. The silence was growing painful, but Lugard spoke at last.

"Come for a walk with me," he said. "Let us go along the cliffs. I cannot speak at ease on soil that rightly belongs to me."

Lugard's words were quiet, but there was a dash of bitterness in them. His face was stern, but the misery in his eyes betrayed the trouble that possessed him. They reached the lovely cliffs presently and sat down together.

"What do you wish me to say?" Lugard asked.

"Is the question fair?" Nest answered. "I wish you to speak the truth—honestly and frankly like the man you are. But I must first give you this."

She drew Lugard's ring from her finger and placed it in his hand. He turned it round and round absently, as if it conveyed no meaning to him.

"This—this is your engagement ring," he said awkwardly.

"It was," Nest replied. "A day or two ago it was my most treasured possession, and now I feel as if I had no right to it. You are free from the money-lender's daughter, Cecil."

"I suppose so," Lugard said thickly. "Nest, we must be fair to one another, but don't let us do anything rash on the spur of the moment. I know what you must have suffered these last few days—no wonder you are pale and worn. Of course, you would have told me—"

"I'm glad you admit that, Cecil!"

"My dear, I could say no less. I may appear to be talking in rather a silly way, but I'm confoundedly upset. It is my plain duty to have this matter out. In common justice to his memory, I must tell how my poor uncle was treated by your father. They say that Sairson is to be made a magistrate. Fancy that man on the bench! I'll put a stop to that at all hazards. How can I marry the girl whose father I'm trying to put into prison?"

Nest wiped the tears furtively from her eyes.

"If you have ceased to care for me—"

"But I haven't," Cecil protested. "I never shall do so. I love you more than ever, and feel like a wretched cad and snob at the same time."

A queer laugh broke from Nest's lips.

"I suppose there is humor in everything if one can only see it," she said. "Perhaps we had better say no more till we have had time to think it over. Meanwhile, you are free, Cecil."

Lugard nodded moodily. He had thought his duty quite plain. He had made a vow and he must carry it through at all costs. But the worst of it was he loved the girl more dearly than ever. He longed to take her in his arms and cover her white set face with kisses, to hold her to his breast and swear that nothing should come between them. Yet at the very same time deep down in his heart was the fixed determination to punish Sairson to the uttermost. A groan burst from his lips.

"You are right," he said. "We had better wait. What a selfish beast I am. If anybody had told me I could treat you thus, I should have resented it. Nest, what will you do?"

Hot words trembled on the girl's lips. She would tell Lugard everything—how she had parted from her people and was not going home again. She would confide in Sybil Gosway, whom she had neglected so much of late. Perhaps when Cecil ascertained what she had decided upon, he might come up to London and—and—

But she put the temptation from her swiftly, and forced a smile to her lips.

"I have not been able to think calmly," she said. "Possibly I may not stay here. Leave me to myself, Cecil; this has been a trying hour for me. On such occasions it is always the woman who pays."

Lugard rose to his feet, and slowly departed. He looked back once or twice before he disappeared round the headland, but Nest's eyes were not turned in his direction. She sat motionless as a statue, gazing out to sea. Her eyes were dry and tearless, and she seemed utterly incapable of any feeling at all. The strings of her life had snapped and there was no more music in her soul.

Of course, this was the end. Cecil Lugard would never come back to her. After what he had said, and in the face of what he had to wipe out this was impossible. Nest sat for two hours, unheeding that the morning was waning and that it was long past the breakfast hour. By-and-by she grew conscious of someone speaking to her, and looked up with a start.

A man stood before her, the skeleton of a man, with dark hair and ruthless, blazing black eyes. From the hollowness of his cheeks and the pallor of his face he was plainly suffering from need of food. He was well-dressed withal, and his clothes gave no hint of the poverty which his face conveyed. He gazed steadily at Nest, his crooked fingers working restlessly. The girl rose with a vague sense of alarm, for the spot was lonely and help far away.

"What do you want?" she asked. "What are you doing here?"

The man laughed and muttered some words in a soft, liquid tongue that was meaningless to Nest.

"I do not understand what you say."

"Then I will speak English," the man said. "You live at that fine house yonder—you are a Sairson. I have sworn to wipe out the whole accursed brood, and you must die. See! I have the weapon. I escaped from the asylum garden and walked miles and miles to get it. For two days I have had no food—but that matters not at all. You are going to die!"

Nest jumped to her feet and yelled for assistance. She flew screaming along the cliff, the lunatic behind her in hot pursuit. She fancied she heard a voice calling to her that help was coming. Then something soft and warm seemed to strike her on the hand, and as it did so she had a fleeting vision of a stone hurtling through the air and striking the man behind her on the forehead. She heard a yell and fell senseless on the soft turf.

"Who is the girl?" Mascani asked.

"Nest Sairson," Givanni answered. "She has only fainted. What of the fellow you knocked down so neatly with that fragment of rock, my friend."

"He will give no trouble for the present," Mascani said grimly. "Can you guess who it is?"

"My God!" Givanni whispered hoarsely. "I know whom you mean. It's Maldini!"

"Maldini it is," was the curt reply.

CHAPTER XXXIX

A MASTER OF SURGERY

Mascani and Givanni glanced at one another significantly. The same thought was evidently passing through the minds of both. Nest lay between them, her pale face turned to the sky. She looked as if she were sleeping peacefully—a locket at her throat rose and fell regularly, and a sigh occasionally crossed her lips. Mascani bent down and laid his long slim fingers on her heart. He was a man familiar with tragedy, and he was thankful to find that there was no trace of it here.

"She has had a narrow escape," he whispered. "She is suffering from shock. It is fortunate women wear corsets. The poor child has to thank hers for her safety. Maldini's aim was less deadly than usual. Look there!"

Nest's dress in the region of the waist was torn as if by a wild animal. The hole was round and ragged, as if sharp teeth had been worrying it. Nest opened her eyes and stared round her in a dazed kind of way.

"What did he do to me?" she asked. "What has become of him?"

"A man attacked you," explained Mascani. "Do you remember it?"

"Oh, yes, I recollect. I was sitting on the cliff and he came up. He appeared to have some grudge against my family. He talked as if he were mad, and I ran away from him. I was conscious of a frightful pain in my side, and I fainted. I feel the pain still."

She closed her eyes and lapsed into semi-consciousness once more.

"Get Maldini out of the way," Mascani commanded. "I hope the poor fellow is not badly hurt. It is as well the girl should not see him. I had better carry her home—it would never do for you to go to Marlton Grange. Heavens, how like that girl is to her mother!"

Givanni nodded sadly. His thoughts were very far away.

"It shall be as you suggest," he said. "Take the girl home and come back to me as soon as possible. I know how to treat Maldini. Then we will convey him back to Landseer's. I should like to have a chat with Dr. Landseer. There are several things I am not satisfied about. See, she is moving again."

Nest opened her eyes and staggered to her feet. Mascani was by her side in a moment. He was anxious that Nest should not see the body lying behind a patch of gorse. He slipped his arm through hers in his most masterful manner.

"I don't think you will be much the worse for the adventure," he said cheerfully. "When you have got over the shock you will be yourself once more. I will see you home."

Nest murmured her thanks. For the present, at any rate, she had abandoned her idea of leaving Marlton Grange. In her then condition a walk even as far as the Castle was out of the question. All she wanted to do was to lie down and rest. In a dim confused way it struck her as rather odd that her protector should be of the same nationality as the man who had attacked her.

"Did you see anything of my assailant?"

"He is quite safe," Mascani explained. "He is a compatriot of mine in whom I take an interest. He has escaped from a private asylum where his friends had placed him. Givanni and I had no idea he was near here."

"Then you are a friend of Givanni?" Nest asked. "I felt sure he was a gentleman."

"That is a very pretty compliment!" Mascani smiled gravely. "Givanni has been my friend and trusted comrade for many years. But, please, don't talk unless you feel inclined to."

Now that the excitement had passed, Nest was feeling faint and giddy. With a sense of relief she crossed the great stone portico and entered the house. Mascani watched her as she went up the stairs. He turned rather reluctantly to go. But Nest was in safe hands, and there was no occasion for him to remain—there were reasons, too, why he should seem indifferent. As he turned to hurry back to the cliffs, a startled cry arrested him. Mrs. Sairson was coming up the portico steps with a bunch of roses in her hand. The dewy, fragrant flowers dropped from her fingers and lay in a crimson and golden mass on the marble steps.

"Allow me Madam," Mascani said gravely. "May I assist you?"

"Tito Mascani!" Mrs. Sairson whispered. "Why did you come? What are you doing here?"

"I have had the good fortune to be of some assistance to your daughter. She has had an adventure on the cliffs. I think you will find she is not much the worse for it."

"Why do you speak to me in that formal manner?" Mrs. Sairson interrupted, in an agitated voice. "Why do you talk as if we were merely strangers, Tito? There was a time—"

Mascani's manner changed. He spoke almost in a whisper.

"They were glorious times, too," he said. "I hope to see them again. I am here by accident, but that I should see you sooner or later was inevitable. My dear old friend, there are troubles in front of you, but if you face them as bravely as I know you will, there will be some happiness left for you yet. In the meantime, I am always yours to command."

Mascani lifted Mrs. Sairson's hand to his lips and vanished without another word. His face was somewhat stern, and his lips were compressed thoughtfully as he made his way along the cliffs to the scene of Nest's encounter with the mad Maldini. He saw Givanni nearly a mile away walking slowly in the direction of Oates's farm. The garden gate had been reached before Mascani caught his friend up. Maldini, staggering like a drunken man, was leaning heavily on Givanni's arm.

"He'll do no more mischief for a day or two," Givanni remarked. "We must put him to bed and keep him there. Mrs. Oates will look after him and not gossip. If I tell her he is a friend who has met with an accident she will not ask any questions. Dr. Paley is discretion itself. We'd better call him in, I think."

"Certainly," Mascani agreed. "Then we will go over and see Landseer. I confess I should like a few words with him. The doctor is greatly to blame for this. Considering how handsomely he is paid to look after Maldini, he has grossly neglected his duty."

Within a couple of hours Mascani and Givanni sought admittance to the residence of Dr. Edward Landseer. They passed through a lodge gate in a high wall protected by spikes, and a surly keeper demanded their business. The house was a long, grey stone structure, with bars before all the upper windows. By-and-by a man servant led them across an untidy hall covered with faded and torn floor-cloth into a room, half study, half surgery. The furniture was good in its way, but faded and shabby like the rest. Presently there entered a stout man with an immense head, utterly devoid of hair. His seedy clothing and nervous air were in keeping with the house. There was little about Dr. Landseer to suggest that, as a nerve and brain specialist, he stood almost alone. That in some way he had made a failure of his life would have been apparent to a child. He changed color as he shook hands with his visitors.

"Where is Maldini?" Mascani asked curtly.

"Maldini?" the doctor stammered. "It is of him that I wish to speak. I was on the point of telegraphing to you, Mr. Mascani. Maldini has—has—"

"Escaped," Mascani said in the same abrupt way. "The mere fact that he is in safe hands again reflects no credit on you. How did he escape?"

Landseer stammered something futile in the nature of an excuse. He had been very busy lately, his patients had taken up a great deal of his time. One or two pressing calls in London had interrupted the discipline of the establishment. He could give every assurance that such a thing should not occur again. For the life of him he could not understand how the thing had happened.

"You see, in a house like mine," he explained, "it is necessary—My dear, don't you see I am engaged?"

The door had opened suddenly, and a woman came in. She was so stout that one would suppose she suffered from disease, so stout that she wheezed as she walked along. Her dress was neglected and untidy to the last degree. Missing buttons had been replaced with safety-pins, and a mass of rusty hair hung over her face and half covered her vacant eyes.

"I don't care," she muttered. "What have you done with my syringe? Why did you take my bottle away? Do you hear what I say? Give it me at once. I don't mind—Give it me."

With a sigh Landseer opened a locked door and took out a leather case, which he handed to the woman. She pounced upon it with an alacrity that was remarkable in one of her amazing bulk, and gloated over it as if it had been a precious treasure. Without a glance she waddled from the room. Something in Landseer's white, despairing face moved Mascani to pity.

"Some unfortunate patient with the drug habit?" he surmised. "Do you allow them to keep—"

"My wife!" Landseer said, with bitter candor. "The whole tragedy of my life is summed up in these two words. If you look at me and my house I need say no more. When I married her she was young and pretty, but had already contracted the habit. I thought I could cure her, but I failed. I gave her up in despair long ago. Some day she will be found dead in her bed and I shall be blamed. She is quiet now, but you should see her when she is roused! But for her I should have a house in Harley-street, and every capital in Europe would be glad to welcome me. I should not have told you this, gentlemen, if it had not been forced upon me. Now you will understand how Maldini escaped."

"My dear follow, I am dreadfully sorry," Mascani murmured. "I had no idea of anything of the kind. It is a dreadful misfortune for a man of your attainments. I have never properly thanked you for the miracle you worked in so short a time on my friend, Captain Barr."

Landseer waved the compliment aside almost contemptuously.

"That is nothing," he said, "unless you count the years I have spent in studying character. In that case I had willing material to work upon. As a rule, my patients don't help me; on entering here they seem to regard me as an enemy. I am greatly distressed about Maldini."

"Never mind about that," Mascani said. "Maldini is in safe hands again. And now, Dr. Landseer, I will ask you a candid question to which I request a candid reply. Has Maldini ever escaped from this house before?"

Landseer appeared to have some trouble at the back of his throat.

"Well, sir, he has," he admitted. "I didn't like to trouble you about it as it was only a matter of some four-and-twenty hours altogether."

"All, quite so," Mascani responded. "Can you remember the date? If not, let me refresh your memory. Was it on Sunday three weeks ago?"

After a brief consideration Landseer inclined to think that it was. Presently he was certain that was the date. Mascani's eyes gleamed. Before he could offer any further remark, a man servant came in with a card on a tray. The owner of the card desired to see Dr. Landseer.

"Signor Paolo Tosca," he read, "of the Italian police in Rome."

Mascani's tongue clicked against his teeth.

"Oh," he exclaimed, "the plot thickens with a vengeance!"

CHAPTER XL

AN ARREST

"Do you happen to know the name of this gentleman?" Landseer asked.

"I know him very well," Mascani said. "In fact, he is well known to both of us. I am afraid that at one time we gave him a deal of trouble. A wonderful man, and a terror to continental scoundrels, despite the fact that he is well over seventy years of age."

"What can he want with me?" Landseer asked.

"I think I could give a pretty shrewd guess," Mascani answered. "He intends to ask a few questions about your patient, Maldini. It is a curious coincidence that we should be here at this particular moment. I shall be greatly obliged, doctor, if you will reply to his questions as frankly as possible. At the same time you will confer a favor by suppressing my name and the fact that we are here to-day. Tell him that Maldini escaped yesterday, and you have found no trace of him as yet."

Landseer left the room, shaking his head in some perplexity, and Givanni turned eagerly to his companion.

"What do you make of this?"

"That Tosca is on the right track," Mascani replied. "Except by a lucky accident the London detectives would never have done so. Tosca must have been sent by the authorities at Rome. They probably saw the account of the accident to Sairson in the papers. Tosca knows. He had a large experience in the ways of the little fraternity that made so much history in Italy forty years ago. You will recollect, my dear friend, that we did things in those days of which we are heartily ashamed now, and we mixed with some very shady company. The 'removal' of tyrants was the policy of one wing of the Brotherhood, though neither of us had any sympathy with that kind of thing. Your brother thought otherwise."

"The poor fellow was always a visionary, Tito."

"Well, the law might have given it another name," Mascani smiled grimly. "Some of us used to strike in a fashion that caused Europe to thrill with uneasiness. The man who had to be removed died in the street, or at the table of some hotel, or in a cab, or anywhere, without a sign. He was dead, and there was an end of it. And nobody knew how the thing was done. The secret has been well kept, but the man who struck Sairson down possessed it. Depend upon it, Tosca meant to get to the bottom of the business. You cannot say that he has been wasting his time!"

"That is apparent on the face of it," Givanni said, gravely. "It may be my turn next!"

"It will!" Mascani said. "You may be certain of that. The whole world shall know the story of that strange attack on Sairson. You may be accused of it. That poor child, Anita, may be accused of it. By the way, I wonder what has become of her?"

Givanni did not appear to be listening. Apparently his mind was occupied by graver matters.

"I wanted to spare the woman I loved," he said presently. "But you are right, the thing has gone too far for further concealment. We can only do what we can. Here is Landseer again."

"The Italian has gone," he explained. "I had some difficulty in convincing him that I was telling the truth, but I managed it at last." The doctor's countenance testified to his relief. "Signor Tosca was, however, seriously disappointed and put out. Can I do anything more for you, gentlemen?"

"Only be discreet," Mascani answered. "We shall probably see you again in a day or two. In the meantime say nothing to anybody."

Landseer gave the desired assurance eagerly.

For some time Mascani and Givanni pursued their way in silence. They had sufficient to occupy their thoughts. It was necessary also to be wary in their movements, lest they should meet with Tosca. To do so would be to give the whole game away. It was late in the afternoon before they reached Oates's farm. Dr. Paley had called again and his report was favorable: Maldini was still affected by the injury he had received and was likely to remain in a dazed condition for a day or two. Meanwhile it was improbable that he would give the slightest trouble—all he required was attention and food at regular intervals. Mascani pulled at one of his eternal cigarettes with an air of satisfaction.

"On the whole, he is doing very well indeed," he said. "Now, obviously the next thing is to discover what has become of Anita. She can't be very far off, and I only hope she has fallen into safe hands. We had better part company and make inquiries."

Givanni readily fell in with his friend's proposal. At the expiration of two hours Mascani had made little progress. In an aimless fashion he had wandered along the cliffs where, early in the morning, he had met Nest Sairson. At one or two of the few scattered cottages it might be possible to pick up a clue. He was heading for one when he caught the flutter of a white dress and heard the sound of voices. As he approached the speakers he recognised Nest who was accompanied by another girl, only less pallid than herself. The likeness between the two was striking.

"My fair damsel and her sister," Mascani told himself. "How like their mother they are, to be sure! The very sight of them carries me back twenty years or more. It is possible—"

Mascani paused and raised his hat, and Nest greeted him with a faint smile.

"I am glad to see you out again," Mascani said. "It tells me that you feel but little the worse for your adventure this morning."

"Many thanks to you," Nest said. "But I am not eager to repeat the experience. May I introduce you to my sister? This is the gentleman who saved my life this morning, Angela. It is stupid, but I don't know the name of my preserver."

"My name is Tito Mascani," the Italian answered. "I am a visitor here, looking for a girl, the daughter of a life-long friend. She is, like you—"

Nest and Angela exchanged glances.

"We may be able to help you," Nest said. "I found a girl who was in great trouble and without any definite idea where to go. If you are really her friend—"

"With one exception, I am the best friend she has in the world," Mascani replied earnestly. "If you can tell me where to find her you will do both of us an inestimable service. Did she happen to call herself Anita?"

"That was her name."

"Good! This is a piece of fortune I had not anticipated. Tell we about it?"

"I found her hereabouts yesterday, early in the morning. Some men were searching for her, and she implored me to assist her to avoid them. In spite of the strange dress she wore, I saw at once that she was a lady, and I helped her. She came to the house with me, and I provided her with a change of clothing."

"She is very charming," Angela murmured.

"Really delightful," Nest went on. "I am sure her story was fine."

"Is she still with you?" Mascani asked.

"No! she did not wish to stay, for some reason. I ought not to say so, but I am sure my mother knew why!"

"Then I may have some trouble to find her?" Mascani asked.

"Not at all. She went away with Lady Laurisdale. Her ladyship was deeply interested in the poor child's story. You will find her at the Castle now."

Mascani asked no further questions; he did not even require to be directed to the Castle. He reached the noble avenue of trees without delay, and speedily inquired for Lady Laurisdale. The footman said that her ladyship was on the west lawn, but if the gentleman would wait—

"No occasion to trouble you, my good man," Mascani said; "I know the way."

He swung round the wing of the Castle as if he were familiar with every foot of the ground. Out of the glare of the sunshine, under a group of cedars, Lady Laurisdale was reading. By her side was a gypsy-table ready set out for tea.

"May I beg a cup at your fair hands, Blanche?" Mascani asked.

Lady Laurisdale rose with a cry of pleasure.

"Tito Mascani, or his ghost!" she ejaculated. "Why, it must be fourteen years since I last saw you—when I was a girl and you used to come to the dear old home. Sit down at once and tell me what you have been doing all this time. How odd you must feel it to have no machinations on hand. Europe has grown comfortable in these days."

"Europe has grown commonplace," Mascani smiled. "Well, it doesn't matter. Besides, my blood isn't so hot as it used to be."

"So you have come all this way to see me? What a compliment!"

"My dear Blanche, truth compels me to say that I do not deserve your approbation. In fact I should not be here at all but for some most unpleasant business. Still, you can render me invaluable assistance. You have a girl—"

"Anita!" Lady Laurisdale cried. "Why did I not guess it at once! It is positively true, Tito, that Anita is here, and I am only too delighted to know that so good and powerful a friend has turned up to help her. She is penniless—has been robbed of her inheritance by a cold-blooded scoundrel named John—"

"Blaydon!" Mascani supplemented. "I know the story. Ah! and you know him too, by the expression of your face. Which means that Laurisdale, too, is in his hands. Well, I fancy John Sairson, alias John Blaydon, has shot his bolt, and will have to disgorge before long. But we can't afford to leave him out of our calculations. Where is Anita?"

"She has gone for a walk with another girl, who is staying with me," Lady Laurisdale explained. "I am expecting them to tea at any moment. Anita is safe with Sybil Gosway."

"Gosway. Any relation to Philip Gosway, whom I used to know?"

"His daughter. How we seem to be flocking together again after all these years! Isn't that the girls yonder?"

"I'll go and meet them," Mascani said.

He rose hastily and strode along the avenue. For he had seen somebody else besides the girls—nothing less than the trim figure and white hair and moustache of Paolo Tosca in the shade of the trees.

"What are you doing here, Tosca?"

The other raised his hand in a military salute.

"I am on business, Signor," he said. "Anyone but me would consider it remarkable to meet you here at this fortunate moment. A certain Anita Givanni—"

"Ah, yes! She is here, as you suggest. What is your business with her?"

"It is a matter of my office, Signor," Tosca said. "I am from Italy on purpose. I have to arrest the young lady on the charge of attempting to murder Mr. Sairson. The warrant is not in my pocket, but an officer in attendance will produce it when necessary."

CHAPTER XLI

TOWARDS THE LIGHT

Mascani's smile was quite pleasant. He did not appear in the least surprised.

"My good Tosca," he said. "The passage of years has dulled your intellect. You must know that Anita Givanni is as innocent as I am!"

"Truly not a very happy comparison, Signor." Tosca said coolly.

"Well, perhaps not. There were days when we gave you a lot of trouble, when we stood a chance of standing with our backs to the wall facing a squad of infantry in the grey of the dawn. But we were honorable foe as you will admit. That being so, why do you bring an abominable charge again this young girl?"

"She may be guilty," Tosca said, in the same calm way. "On the other hand, she may be the gudgeon that will bring the big fish to hook. It is impossible to say. But there is one thing you are bound to grant me, Signor—she could explain the strange attempt on Mr. Sairson's life. I read of the case in a London paper, and asked myself a few questions that had to be answered, and noted the strong resemblance between this thing and the vengeance of the Sicilian Brotherhood in the days gone by. I came to London to make sure. Almost directly I struck on the track of Maldini."

"Maldini has lost his reason, poor fellow. He is under restraint."

"He was," Tosca corrected. "At the present moment they don't know where he is. In so slack a house he may have escaped before. That I shall doubtless be able to clear up in good time. Now consider, Signor! First, I hear of Maldini; then I learn that the daughter of Madame Givanni earns her living by means of a performance, which is most interesting to me; finally, I meet you in the same locality, to say nothing of Signor Givanni!"

"Ah! So you have ran him to earth, too, old fox?" Mascani asked.

"Even so, Signor; all the elements of tragedy and crime."

"I was always against violent methods, Tosca."

"There, Signor, I am with you. Always you were a clean and honorable fighter. At the same time it would be perhaps prudent to arrest the whole of you. After all I am only being, what these English call, cruel, to be kind."

Mascani reviewed the situation hurriedly in his mind. Sooner or later, he felt, the truth would have to be told. It might be a time of trouble and terror for Anita, but in the long run she would come to no harm. She would be beyond the reach of her enemies, at any rate.

"I have made my protest," he said to Tosca, "and there is no more to be done. Let me introduce you to Lady Laurisdale. I see they are having tea."

Lady Laurisdale with Anita and Sybil Gosway sat under the shade of the cedar, talking quietly.

Mascani made the presentation with befitting gravity.

"Signor Tosca, of the Italian police," he said, "an honorable opponent in the old days."

"Won't you have a cup of tea?" Lady Laurisdale inquired.

Tosca regretfully declined. He had pressing business on hand, In the circumstances it would be improper to partake of her ladyship's hospitality. For he had decided that Miss Anita Givanni should accompany him to Cromer. He had to go through the formality of placing her under arrest in connection with the mysterious attack on Mr. Sairson. He put the matter delicately and tactfully, but there was no mistaking the gravity of his words.

"But the charge is ridiculous," Lady Laurisdale cried.

"Precisely, your ladyship," Tosca admitted. "Nevertheless, my duty is plain. One must investigate this affair to the bottom."

Anita listened with some comprehension as to what was going on. In a few words, Mascani made the situation absolutely clear. It was a matter of form. Tosca was merely acting in the interests of justice. In a few days Anita would be free again. There was no occasion for her to be in the least afraid.

"I am not afraid," Anita said quietly. "I will go with the gentleman as soon as I am ready. May I be allowed to pack a few things? I will not run away!"

Tosca was politely assured of it. There was no hurry, no hurry at all. Anita laid a hand on Sybil Gosway's arm, and the two girls went away together.

"I am bewildered," Sybil said. "What does it mean?"

"I think I can guess," Anita answered. "But I am not alarmed. Help me to collect my few belongings. I wish you to do me a favor. I believe that in this neighborhood lives a Mr. Lugard—Cecil Lugard. He is the nephew of the famous soldier who was once a friend of my family. My mother said he would help me if occasion arose. Till this moment I had forgotten about him. Give him this key which I take from my chain, and say that it comes from me. It opens a box which is stored at the address engraved on the key. Do you understand?"

"Oh, yes!" Sybil exclaimed. "Why I know Mr. Lugard. He is engaged to Nest Sairson. My father knows him, too. He is a splendid fellow, and I am sure will be a good friend. But you are not frightened, Anita?"

Anita smiled bravely. It was good to know that she had so many friends. There was a catch in her voice as she parted from Lady Laurisdale.

"No, no!" she protested. "I am going quite alone. I will not give anybody the trouble of accompanying me. I shall be perfectly happy. Signor Tosca, I am ready."

"A carriage?" Tosca asked.

"No carriage is needed," Anita said firmly. "It is only a few miles, and I shall enjoy the walk. You can explain things on the way, Signor Tosca."

Tosca expressed his pleasure. He was loth to take this step, but he could not see how it could be helped. They came at length to the road where the house stood from which Anita had so recently escaped. Tosca regarded her shrewdly.

"Are you acquainted with this part?"

"I have been here before," Anita said. "I was taken to that house by the people who are searching for me. It is a house so different from the lodgings I had been used to that I wondered how they could afford to rent it."

"That may be explained, too," Tosca said drily. "A great many things will be explained during the next few days. All this tallies with my investigations. Do you happen to know that man at the garden gate?"

The expression on Anita's face changed. Her eyes were full of loathing. Tosca observed the shudder that passed over her.

"That is the man who ruined us," the girl said. She spoke as a child would have done, with frank sincerity. "Sairson—Blaydon—it is all the same. He is the father of the dearest girls I have ever met! It seems impossible, Signor Tosca."

Tosca looked grave. His duty was plain, but he ignored it.

"Don't tell anybody else that," he said. "My child, you are convicting yourself out of your own mouth. That is Mr. Sairson, whose life you are supposed to have attempted."

"He is a horrid man, and the cause of all our trouble. See! he is coming this way. Don't let him speak to me."

Tosca gave the requisite assurance, and they walked on. Sairson stared after them till they had vanished round the bend of the road. He turned abruptly to his companion, Sebag.

"That is Anita Givanni," he said. "I knew her mother well. What's she doing here?"

"Odd that you should know her," said Sebag. "Very odd, in the circumstances. That chap is a detective from Italy. He's been hanging round here making inquiries. Fancies he knows all about that trouble of ours. Looks to me as if he had the girl in his charge. She's the very one you want to get hold of."

"What! Not the girl Dudley Beaumont was gassing about?"

"The same, Mr. Sairson. Regular mix up, I call it. At any rate, she's the girl Mascani released. Like to bet on it?"

Sairson cast a suspicious glance at his companion.

"What do you know about Mascani?"

Sebag chuckled; there was a familiarity in his manner that Sairson resented.

"I know a great deal more than you like," he said. "I've made money all my life by getting information. Never can tell when it is going to be useful! Besides, clever as you are, you let out a good bit, yourself! Now, that girl could tell as all about it. She could tell us just how the thing was worked. Beaumont raved about her performance, and a wonderfully clever business it must be. That's why I wanted you to meet her. You'll feel much safer after you've done so."

"I daresay I shall," Sairson growled. "But why so mysterious? Why don't you open your mouth a little wider? I don't trust you, Sebag!"

Sebag politely expressed his regret. He was doing the best for everybody, including himself, only this aspect of the affair he did not enlarge upon. Sairson would have been far less easy in his mind had he only guessed half of what Sebag knew. There would be awkward revelations presently, and Sebag hoped to benefit by them. It was as well, therefore, to be prepared to change sides when the time came. He had been in communication with Lugard. He was not an ally after Lugard's heart, but one could not be nice in the choice of weapons where a man like Sairson was concerned.

"Well, let's get on! You did not ask me to meet you here for nothing?"

"I didn't," Sebag confessed. "I hoped to find the girl back here by this time along with your esteemed brother-in-law, Dudley Beaumont. With a little judicious bribery we could have seen the whole of the performance. The birds—"

"Birds! What birds?" Sairson demanded impatiently. "What have birds to do with it?"

Sebag chuckled again. The sense of his superior knowledge pleased him. At that moment the door leading to the garden of the house was thrown open and two men appeared. To the meanest intellect it was plan that they were connected with the police. They pushed before them a handcart filled with cages containing birds.

"I don't like the look of this," Sebag said blankly.

"Can't you speak plainly?" Sairson grunted. "What are these confounded birds for? How do you connect them with my business?"

But Sairson was no longer interested in birds. He was staring at a newcomer who came briskly along the road in his direction. His jaw dropped uneasily.

"Captain Barr!" he muttered. "Barr or his ghost. Looks another man, too, Sebag, go on ahead and wait for me at the corner of the road."

CHAPTER XLII

FOR THE GIRL'S SAKE

Nest was profoundly shocked to hear the news from Sybil Gosway. It was incredible that Anita had anything to do with the attack on her father. The more Nest thought the matter over the more bewildered she became. Sybil was only a shade less uneasy. She took the first opportunity of laying the matter before Major Renton during one of his frequent visits to the Castle. The chief constable had facilities for obtaining information denied to the general public, and would do much to oblige Sybil.

"I can't make it out at all," he said. "What that fellow Tosca is doing puzzles me. The police applied for a remand for a week to-day, and on the evidence the magistrates shouldn't have granted it. If Miss Givanni had been represented they couldn't have done so. But Tosca and Skidmore tell me it is for the best, and so I say nothing."

Sybil was properly indignant. In her eyes the whole thing was disgraceful. She despatched a hasty note to Marlton Grange asking Nest to come to discuss the matter. Nest resolved to comply, but was detained by Barr at the lodge gate. His face was eager, and there was a look of triumph in his eyes.

"I have just had a long talk with your father," he remarked. "We parted a few minutes ago. I am to call this afternoon and discuss certain business with him. Nest, what a fool I have been!"

"I will not contradict you," Nest said stiffly.

"Now, please don't be severe," Barr implored. "I have had a lot to put up with, and have paid a very heavy price for my lesson. I wish to see Angela, to see her now. You know what you said the last time we met!"

"If it concerns my sister's happiness," she faltered, "perhaps I ought—"

"My dear Nest, her happiness and mine depend upon the interview. Do go and fetch her."

Nest returned in a few minutes, accompanied by Angela. Barr stood behind the bushes until they were close to him. As he stepped out a cry came from Angela's lips. She would have fallen had he not caught her in his arms.

"Jack," she whispered; "Jack! You look as you used to be in the old days!"

She swayed towards him again, and her voice broke. But there was gladness in her eyes, and her manner evinced neither coldness nor resentment. Nest's eyes were wet as she hurried to keep her belated appointment with Sybil. She had not hastened, as she probably knew more of the case than Sybil. So far as Angela was concerned, perhaps she had done a foolish thing—certainly an undignified one—but she felt no regret. What did the rest matter so long as these two had come together again? And why had they parted? Nest asked herself bitterly. Had she been a man, mayhap she would have taken a man's outlook. Yet, after Cecil had had time for cool reflection—

Meanwhile Angela and Barr were seated in a cosy corner overlooking the sea, in blissful oblivion of the world and mundane things.

"It is like a dream," Angela murmured. "Tell me that it's true, Jack!"

"It's true, darling," Jack responded. "I suppose it must be a dream in a way—a kind of delirium on my part. You haven't a single reproach for me."

"But why should I?" Angela asked innocently. "You were right; when you found out this dreadful trouble you were right to give me back my freedom. I never had one drop of bitterness in my heart against you, dear. If I had been a man of honor I should have acted just as you did. Who would marry the daughter of a money-lender?"

"Well, I for one," Jack smiled. "It's wonderful what foolish things one will do in the name of honor."

"But my name is Sairson," Angela pointed out.

"There is no Sairson in your blood," Barr protested. "Thank goodness you don't resemble your father."

"Nest said you had seen him this morning."

"So I have, dear. He took me for a ghost. There is nothing surprising in that, Angela. What a battered wreck I must have seemed the last time we met. That was barely a month ago. I was mad then, for I deliberately tried to spoil my life. When I gave you up I felt there was nothing left. I sank lower and lower, and became the sport of circumstances. And I was the being who was too proud to marry the daughter of John Blaydon, the money-lender. Open-eyed, I allowed your father to carry out his scheme of revenge against me."

"This is the first I have heard of it," Angela said.

"Of course it is. He would not tell you, or anybody else for that matter. His idea was to lay a trap and ruin me. When every penny of my money had passed into his pocket he expected I would come back and sue for mercy. He would restore my money provided I married you and held my tongue about the past. In my sober moments I could see this plan actually accomplishing itself. It is incredible, but I made no effort to stop it. I imagined I could pull myself together whenever I chose and expose the whole conspiracy. But I was weakened by drink and drugs and I knew that I should never do it. Then I swung round to wild notions of revenge, and then came that horrible night. But for you I don't know what I would have done. Philip Gosway, Sybil's father, saved me by handing me over to Tito Mascani, who placed me in the custody of Dr. Landseer, a wonderful man, who cured me. In these three weeks a miracle has happened. After the third day I wished to get well, to live and get my own back, and, above all, I longed for you, dearest. Day by day my mind cleared and my body grew young again. There is no medicine in the world like Landseer's. It is his tragedy that his wife—another drug maniac—is the only patient he has never cured. At the end of a week everything was plain to me. I saw the pitfalls into which I had been lured. Then I determined to take steps to recover my estate. Your father will lend no more money, Angela."

"You told him all this to-day, Jack?"

"And a great deal more, Angela. I proved my case up to the hilt, and offered him two alternatives. He refused them, but he is bound to accept one or other sooner or later. I frightened him—he is not really the strong man most people suppose. I hate to have to tell you this, but it is absolutely necessary. When I have finished I will never refer to it again. All I wish is to see everybody happy."

Angela sighed gently; she was thinking of Nest.

"I hope so," she said. "It is a pity to have wasted these three years, Jack. But I hope there is a good time coming. Poor Nest!"

"Why poor Nest? Hasn't she got Lugard?"

"My dear boy, Lugard is a proud man. He has just learnt the truth, and is behaving as you behaved. It was a great shock to him. Nest goes about like a flower drooping for want of water. Jack, can't you help me to save Nest?"

"Oh! I'll help you," Barr said, between his teeth. "It is unthinkable that Lugard should be as great a fool as I was. What a deplorable business it is."

"If I could only get away from here, Jack! I feel hot with shame when I think of it all. You have a score to settle with my father. Then Cecil proclaims at our own table what he will do when he meets Blaydon. This in my father's hearing! Fancy my mother's feelings when she listens to such talk from Nest's lover. There are scores of others who have suffered in a similar way. Our home is a house of blood and tears;

the money we spend like water has blood on it—every coin of it. But your money is your own, and Cecil Lugard's is his. If you can persuade him, Jack!"

Barr departed, bent upon doing what he could. In a day or two he ran Lugard to earth at Cromer on the morning of the second hearing of the charge against Anita Givanni. Cecil listened to Barr in grim silence.

"You don't know how hard it is," he said at last. "As a Lugard—"

"Try to look at the affair less personally, Cecil," Barr interrupted. "I have a grievance, too. I was robbed by that blackguard as your uncle was, but I see now that I was a fool to throw away my happiness for the sake of an empty pride that only filled me with misery. Between us we ought to be able to drive that rascal out of the country. He shall return Marlton Grange to you, and you shall marry and settle down. The two girls are ladies born and bred—Belhams, both."

Lugard wriggled uneasily in his chair.

"I'll think it over," he said. "I'm not prepared to say anything definite as yet. The business has been a dreadful shock. I loved the little girl, Jack; I loved her—"

"I know, I know," Barr said comprehendingly. "I've been through it, Cecil. It's easy to see you are as fond of Nest as ever."

"More than ever, Jack, if I must speak the truth. But let the matter rest for the time. Come to the court and hear the case in which that poor little Givanni girl is mixed up. Upon my word, it's an infernal shame they should keep her in custody without offering the smallest evidence against her. I must go; I promised to meet Mascani."

The court was crowded to suffocation when Barr and Lugard arrived. They were in time to hear the opening speech of the prosecuting counsel, who wound up by undertaking to prove that the prisoner, if not the actual aggressor, at any rate knew the means by which the crime had been committed. Mascani nodded significantly at the words.

"Can he do so?" Lugard asked.

"Probably," Mascani whispered. "Tosca has taken care of that. It looks as if he were going to give evidence. Yes, he is getting into the box."

As Tosca took the oath, counsel for the prosecution asked permission to make a statement. This was, he said, in some respects a remarkable case. It involved a certain amount of what he could only call dumb evidence, and this he should produce. He made a sign to Skidmore, the chief of police, whereupon a number of officers came into court carrying cages in which little feathered prisoners were hopping about excitedly. The tense silence was broken only by the twittering of the birds.

CHAPTER XLIII

Sairson sat in his study with a mass of correspondence before him. Usually he prided himself upon the summary way he dealt with his letters, but they lay before him neglected and almost forgotten. It was nearly noon, and he had not written a line. His face wore a moody frown, and his hand shook so much that the ash dropped from his cigar on to the table. Something stirred uneasily within him—something that might perhaps be called conscience. Sairson would have scoffed at the suggestion and would preferably have granted that he had been working too hard and needed a holiday. Six months ago the mere idea of a holiday would have called up all his scorn. He had never had a holiday in his life, and look at him! People were too careful of themselves in these days. He did not believe in mollycoddling. A holiday, indeed!

Nevertheless, Sairson was contemplating one now. He wanted a day or two so that he could be alone to think. He would make some excuse for going to the Continent and forget to leave his address. He was up against opposition that could not be so confidently swept aside. Hitherto, if anything unpleasant had cropped up he had trampled it underfoot, or bellowed his way through. But it looked as if these lawyers were banded together for common action. Their letters were studiously polite, but there was no mistaking the meaning of them. It would be necessary to answer these questions, and others would follow.

Sir George Lugard's solicitors raked up things forgotten long ago, while another firm requested ample information relating to transactions with their client, Captain Barr. A firm in Lincoln's Inn Fields seemed to be extremely interested in the estate of Madame Givanni. And in every one of these precious communications the name of John Blaydon was mentioned.

He liked the letter from Lincoln's Inn Fields the least. He knew he should never be able to shake off these people, that their faculty for picking up information was amazing, their resourcefulness abounding. It would be impossible to fool them. Did they identify him with John Blaydon or not? Certain books in his office should have been destroyed long ago—he had been a fool to overlook them. Had anybody been tampering with his clerks?

And who had been coaching Captain Barr? For some years he had looked upon him as a poor besotted fool, as intelligent as a child in business. He had ruined Barr for ceasing his attentions to Angela, and had been proud of it. He had not been scrupulous in his methods, and the law might have taken a stern view of some of them. Now Barr was to the fore again, clothed and in his right mind, and apparently ready for mischief. Barr had spoken very freely an hour ago. He had the audacity to ask for complete restitution and a signed confession of guilt. He had not even stopped at that, for one of his conditions was that Sairson should leave England under compact never to return.

The angry blood flamed into Sairson's face as he thought of it. Lugard, too, was trying a similar game. He was not going to marry Nest—he intended to carry out his threat. The letter from his lawyers proved it.

"I'll see the thing through," Sairson resolved. "I'll teach these fellows a lesson. I'll show them the price of meddling with me. I'll fight them with their own money. If I could only lay hands on the miscreant who tried to murder me.....I wonder whether that girl really knows anything about it. Funny she should be the daughter of Madame Givanni. I've a good mind to go into Cromer and listen to the proceedings."

But he never stirred, but continued to pore over the letters with a gloomy foreboding that there was grave trouble ahead. He locked his desk presently, and shuffled into the garden. He tried to summon up the old pride in the house, but black care was not to be shaken off.

By-and-by he saw Nest coming up the path with a mass of flowers in her arms. She looked pale and sad, and dark rings under her eyes spoke of much weeping. She would have passed on with a cold good morning, but Sairson followed her up.

"What's the matter?" he demanded. "You look as if you had seen a ghost!"

"Perhaps I have," Nest replied. "The ghost of my dead happiness!"

An ugly sneer crossed Sairson's face.

"So that is how the land lies?" he said. "Lugard has backed out? He declines to marry John Sairson's daughter, or John Blaydon's for it is the same thing. Do you understand what that means? It means that everybody will be talking about you. People won't stop talking because they don't regard you as good enough to associate with them. The same thing happened when Barr turned cur."

"He did not turn cur," Nest said. "None of us ever blamed him."

"No, because you are steeped in silly sentiment," Sairson cried. "Your mother has never allowed you to forget that she is a lady by birth and breeding. It's a mania with her and you. A little common sense on her part and Barr would have sung a different tune. It I had had my way he should have been served with a writ for damages, my girl!"

A smile hovered on Nest's lips.

"You refer to what is called a breach of promise?" she asked. "I thought that kind of thing was the prerogative of actresses in need of advertisement, and barmaids eager for a husband. You can scarcely be serious?"

Sairson growled something under his breath. He was always conscious of an uncomfortable sense of inferiority when his girls talked to him like this. It seemed to convey the impression that he was of different clay. While he was fumbling for a retort, Nest passed on and entered the house.

Well, she could go her own way. If she enjoyed being treated in this fashion by Lugard, it was her affair, not his. He had forgotten his threat to drive her from the house if she dared to breathe a word of the truth to Lugard. Obviously Nest had done so, for she spoke as if her engagement had come to an end. In that case Lugard was free to move when and where and how he liked. Nothing could hinder him from carrying out his threat against John Blaydon. It was only when Sairson studied the situation in all its bearings that he realised how greatly he had relied on Nest's engagement to save himself from serious accusations.

Beside the personal issues, there was the dread of another attempt on his life. It was absurd to suppose that Anita Givanni was the actual culprit. She might be able to throw light upon the outrage, but the hand of the would-be assassin was not hers. The police appeared to have blundered in their usual way. Sairson was still turning the matter over in his mind when his wife came out to him.

"I want to say something to you," she remarked.

Sairson turned to her with a scowl. Her face was as white and worried as Nest's, and he resented it as a personal grievance. What had these women to complain of? Why did they continually irritate and annoy him? They were surrounded with every luxury, they lacked nothing that money could buy, and yet they were not satisfied.

"What on earth is wrong with you all?" he thundered. "Why do you creep about as if there were a corpse in the house? Upon my word, this is a pleasant place! If it is about Nest, I don't want to hear it."

"It has nothing to do with Nest," Mrs. Sairson said. "It is about Anita Givanni."

"Oh, hang the girl! I'm sick of her very name. I can't understand what the police are thinking about. What she had—"

"I did not know till yesterday what her name really was," Mrs. Sairson went on. "When she came here she only called herself Anita, and seemed very reticent."

"Oh, she came here!" Sairson exclaimed. "What, in the house?"

"Certainly, John. Nest found her wandering about the cliffs, having escaped from a house where she was being detained against her will, and brought her here."

Sairson was too interested now to keep up his show of ill-temper. It was more than strange that the girl he had been looking for had come here of all places in the world. Why had the information been kept from him?

"It would only have annoyed you," Mrs. Sairson answered. "You would probably have called us fools and ordered us to put her out at once. Not that there was any occasion, for directly she came here she showed a most marked aversion to the house. As a mater of fact, she went away with Lady Laurisdale, with whom she remained till the police trumped up this ridiculous case. You have met her before?"

"Never!" Sairson protested. "The girl is a stranger to me."

"Then how comes it that she knows you? She was quite happy and comfortable in the house until she saw your photograph in the drawing-room. The sight of it made her tremble with sudden fear. Probably that was why she left so readily with Lady Laurisdale. It was only when I learned the poor child's name that I began to see light. Givanni—a friend of mine years ago—lost all his money through some financier. Was that John Blaydon?"

"John Blaydon can't recollect every fool he has dealings with."

"Then I will not ask you any more," Mrs. Sairson said sadly. "Your answer is sufficient. I might have guessed without troubling you so far. It is only another load added to the heavy burden I have to bear."

Blaydon paused in an angry retort, for at that moment a cab drew up by the portico and Sebag jumped out. The little man's manner was excited, and he approached Sairson as if his mission was one of importance. He pulled off his hat with a flourish.

"Sorry to intrude, sir," he said. "I hope you will excuse me, madam; but I have come on the most pressing business."

Mrs. Sairson bowed coldly. Something about the glossy lawyer repelled her. Sairson jerked his thumb towards the house.

"Come in," he said. "We can talk better in the library."

Sebag followed with a glance of admiration at all he saw about him. Some day or other he hoped to have a house of his own like this. He helped himself to a cigarette and lighted it without waiting for Sairson's permission.

"Go on," the latter said violently, "make yourself at home! Ring for the butler and ask him to bring up the champagne. Well, what is it? Where do you come from?"

"Cromer," Sebag said jauntily. "I've been hearing the charge against Anita Givanni. The court has adjourned for a few hours for a witness who had not arrived. The case has taken a curious turn. It will be to your advantage to hear the rest of the evidence. Your name has cropped up, and for your own credit's sake you ought to be there to testify."

"What on earth for? What has it got to do with John Sairson?"

"I didn't say Sairson," Sebag responded drily. "I'm speaking of John Blaydon. As John Blaydon you'd better come and look after yourself."

CHAPTER XLIV

AN UNEXPECTED WITNESS

Undoubtedly something out of the common was going to happen to John Sairson. There had been sensation enough in regard to the mysterious attack on his life, but to find a palpitating romance attached to it set even the nerves of the seasoned pressman quivering. There was an air almost of the occult about it. It was like the first "curtain" of a sensational novel. What connection could there be between these innocent little birds and a serious crime?

The reporters bent over their notebooks, intent to get every word down. The padding had already been done. They had described the court and the magistrates, the kind of day it was, and what the prisoner was wearing. They spoke of her pretty pale face and innocent pathetic eyes which plainly hinted that the police were making a hideous blunder. One or two, better informed than the rest, had ascertained that the prisoner was the daughter of one of the greatest singers of her day, and that Madame Givanni had been connected with the best blood in Italy. They also called attention to the fact that Madame Givanni had died penniless owing to the confidence she had placed in a perfidious friend.

But what had these little birds to do with the case? was the question that everybody was asking. Barring a pigeon or two, they were ordinary birds of the fields, the sort, that a professional bird catcher brings in every day. They twittered in their cages as if quite at home, and one or two broke into song.

The chairman of the bench looked benevolently over his spectacles. From the very first he had been well disposed towards the prisoner. He happened to be a retired solicitor, and was therefore fully vested in the procedure. It was evident, too, that he had not as yet been much impressed by the case put forward by the prosecution.

"Isn't this rather unusual, Mr. Polgate?" he asked. "What connection can there be between the birds and the offence the prisoner is charged with?"

Counsel for the prosecution looked up defiantly.

"I must be allowed to conduct my case in my own way, sir," he said. "It is a most unusual case, and presents many singular features. I am expecting some remarkable testimony from these birds as to the crime in question."

There was a flutter in the audience as the chairman polished his glasses and bowed to Mr. Polgate. Something quite unexpected was about to happen. The interruption was followed by a whispered consultation between the police and their representative—finally, a name was called that was not familiar to anybody in the court.

"Call James Patten."

The witness shuffled along, confusedly conscious that every eye was upon him, and that every detail of his appearance was being examined. He received a flattering amount of attention that was out of all proportion in the story he had to tell.

"I am a bird-catcher," he said. "All kinds of wild birds at the proper season of the year. The birds in the cages yonder were provided by me. I have been providing them for the prisoner for a considerable time—for the last two months, in fact."

"Ordered by herself?" the chairman asked.

"Well, no, your worship," the witness answered. "By a man named Sheppeard. He told me he was managing for a music hall artiste called La Veni—"

"The prisoner's professional name," Mr. Polgate explained.

"I was to be paid for the birds at so much a dozen," the witness proceeded, "but up till now I have not been paid anything. I understood there had been a good bit of trouble one way and another. The birds were for exhibition purposes."

"Much as you supply pigeons for shooting purposes?" Mr. Polgate asked.

"That was what I thought, sir. Kind of mysterious shooting without any powder and shot."

There was a stir in the audience at this. People with more imagination than the rest began to see things, or to fancy they did. Probably the prisoner possessed some secret process for the destruction of life which might account for the mysterious attack on Mr. Sairson. But at the same time it was hard for these imaginative persons to credit this pretty dark-eyed girl with such a crime as premeditated murder.

"Did you see the performance?" Mr. Polgate asked.

"No, sir, I didn't," the witness said. "It was only held one night at Fairstead, where I live, and I couldn't manage to go. Fairstead is an old-fashioned place, and a good many of the ladies belong to all kinds of societies. Never was such a place for societies for preventing people from doing all sorts of things."

A ripple of laughter followed this sally. The witness himself smiled with the air of a man who has said something decidedly clever.

"Those ladies objected to the performance?" Mr. Polgate suggested.

"Yes, sir, they did. Said it was repellent energy or something of that sort. Lady Corriston it was who complained to the police. She sent an officer from the Society of Prevention of Cruelty to Animals, and he saw a private performance. Then the police interfered, and stopped any performance at Fairstead. That's why I didn't get my money. They had to pay for the hall and the printing and other expenses, so there was nothing over."

"There was no prosecution, I suppose?" the chairman asked.

"Not so far as I know, sir," the witness answered. "The show was only stopped."

"Were the birds cruelly treated?"

"Perhaps I had better explain to the bench," Mr. Polgate interrupted. "We don't suggest that there was any cruelty at all. If there had been, it is pretty certain the magistrates would have been bound to dismiss the case. There was no cruelty, for the simple reason that the birds were killed on the spot. The performance is just as legal as pigeon shooting, and perhaps a little more civilised. But at Fairstead one has to bow to popular prejudice. We shall call a witness to prove this. Jasper Cottenham!"

This witness turned out to be an officer of the Society for the Prevention of Cruelty to Animals, and was stationed at Fairstead. He was fully impressed with the importance of his position, and stated his case at some length.

"I had a note from Lady Corriston," he said. "Her ladyship informed me that the performance advertised to take place in Fairstead should be stopped. She was under the impression that gross acts of cruelty to some birds—"

"No, no!" Anita cried. "There was no cruelty. I did not want to do it, because I am fond of birds, but cruelty—never!"

The chairman looked over his glasses at Anita benevolently.

"You must try to control yourself," he said. "Understand we are not prejudiced against you in any way, and we shall help you all we can. We shall judge for ourselves how far the witness is biassed in saying what he does. Go on!"

"After getting that letter from her ladyship my duty was clear. They offered me a private performance."

"You put no pressure on them to do so?" Mr. Polgate asked.

"None whatever, sir. I went by arrangement the following afternoon and saw the performance. So far as I could see there was no cruelty about it, although some people might think different. Still, her ladyship had said the word, and in a place like Fairstead her ladyship commands a deal of respect!"

"Oh, get on!" Polgate said impatiently. "As we have no intention of calling her ladyship, this is beside the question. What was the nature of the performance?"

"It's a kind of play, sir. The lady is supposed to possess supernatural powers. She has the forces of life and death over all about her. The stage is converted into a large cage, and all the birds are turned loose on it. When the performer wants to destroy them she holds up her hand and points at a particular bird. Directly she does so the bird falls dead at her feet. So far as it was possible to judge, she had nothing in her hand. But the bird falls dead, and there is no mark to show how it is done. There seems to be no weapon, there is no report and no sign of shot."

The audience moved uneasily. Many of them began to perceive in which way the case of the prosecution was heading. The prisoner was alleged to possess some secret means of taking life. Nothing like it had ever been done before. It would be possible for her to exercise this mysterious gift anywhere, even in a crowded room or a railway carriage. She could drop her victim at her feet and nobody would suspect her with the crime. A semblance of awe came over the listeners—it might be the turn of any one of them next. It was astounding that such an innocent-looking child could wield such a terrible power. It was, however, hard to see why she should exercise it on a stranger like Sairson, why she should single out him for a victim. Several of the audience were asking themselves why Sairson was not present. This girl was being tried for attempting his life, and he had not even bothered to put in an appearance!

Sairson was not popular; nobody within miles of the place had a good word to say for him. Possibly he had done the child or someone near and dear to her, a terrible injury, and she had made up her mind to take a sure and terrible revenge. They might come to the motive presently.

"All this is very interesting," the chairman said. "As a performance it might be worth seeing. Presumably the prisoner has some secret which, in certain hands, might work horrible mischief. But I fail to see the connection, Mr. Polgate. Nothing has been shown yet to indicate that the attack on Mr. Sairson—"

"We are coming to that, sir," said Mr. Polgate eagerly. "It has been necessary to demonstrate the fact that the prisoner possesses this power—a secret power which nobody would suspect. The risk of detection is practically nil."

"There you will allow me to differ from you," the chairman said. "How did you discover this girl has the power? Why, by her voluntarily performing the trick in public? She went about the country exhibiting her wonderful power; there was no concealment at all. That being so, she took a palpable risk. I hope you see my point."

Mr. Polgate bowed.

"I propose to show the connection," he said. "I propose to show that the prisoner had a grievance against Mr. Sairson. I propose to show this by letters found in the possession of the prisoner—letters written by her mother to Mr. Sairson—and his replies."

"Are you going to call Mr. Sairson?" the chairman asked.

Again Mr. Polgate bowed. Lady Laurisdale turned eagerly to Lugard, who sat beside her twisting a paper nervously in his hand.

"Mr. Sairson had better be called," the chairman said. "I will adjourn the case till 3 o'clock for that purpose, Mr. Polgate."

CHAPTER XLV

THE "GHOST" IN EVIDENCE

What was the matter with himself, Sairson wondered. Why did he feel so nervous and restless about such a trifle? There had been crises when the shadow of the law had been over him, and the fact had not deprived him of an hour's sleep. He had faced the greatest danger without an extra heartbeat. Now he was trembling from head to foot at Sebag's mere suggestion of a journey to Cromer. What had he to be afraid of? He debated the question over and over again in his mind with no satisfactory result. The police had informed him that his presence would not be required to-day, and the knowledge had relieved him. Why? In the ordinary course it was nothing. As a fact he should have been glad—glad in the knowledge that the mystery was on the point of being solved and the danger removed for all time.

"I can see nothing to be gained by going," he said to Sebag.

The little lawyer smiled. Something in the smile irritated Sairson exceedingly.

"You've a very nice place here," Sebag remarked cheerfully, "a very nice place. Many a millionaire would be proud of a place like this. Nothing showy, nothing ostentatious, and yet everything of the best. Pictures and furniture look as if they had been here for generations."

"They have," Sairson said curtly. "What next?"

"I was only thinking that these things are not much use unless you have peace of mind. That's worth everything else."

Sairson glared at the speaker. What was the devil driving at?

"I'll come with you," he said. "On second thoughts I'll follow. I'll not be seen with you, Sebag."

Sebag did not seem to resent the suggestion contained in these words, but promptly disappeared, leaving Sairson to his gloomy thoughts. Half an hour later the latter stopped his car outside the "Golden Lion" in Cromer, whither a goodly number of the audience in court had gravitated for a meal. By joining the throng he might pick up some information. Sairson glanced round the room, seeking a place at one of the smaller tables. He saw that Lady Laurisdale was alone. She might ignore him or not; but at any rate she could not prevent him from sitting down at the same table. And if she were disposed to be friendly, it would be something in the way of a triumph for him.

He nodded defiantly as he took his seat, conscious that many eyes were turned in his direction. Lady Laurisdale smiled in friendly fashion.

"Good morning, Mr. Sairson," she said. "I have been looking for you for a long time. I expected to see you in court to-day."

"Police said I should not be wanted," Sairson answered. "Seem to have changed their minds. Has anything of importance turned up—I mean importance to me?"

"Your name has been mentioned," Lady Laurisdale replied. "It is a most ridiculous case. You must see that for yourself!"

"Are you not prejudiced?" Sairson asked guardedly. "The girl is a friend of yours."

There was a challenge in the question, Lady Laurisdale took up instantly. Her manner was smiling and gay, but there was a hint of battle in her eyes that Sairson did not like.

"I know her somewhat!" Lady Laurisdale said. "By marriage we are connected with the Givannis, who belong to one of the oldest families in Italy. I lost sight of Madame Givanni for a long time; in fact I had not seen her for years before she died. I understand she was robbed of her fortune by that scoundrelly money-lender, John Blaydon."

The words were spoken with a smile, but there was an edge to them that made Sairson writhe in his chair. How much did Lady Laurisdale know?

"You speak as if you had grounds for your statement!"

"Oh, I have! To be candid, we have been in the grip of that man for some time. In business my husband is a perfect child—that unfortunate child who thinks himself clever. It looked at one time as if we were utterly at Blaydon's mercy. Luckily I confided in Mr. Lugard, who really has a business head. From what he tells me, we have grounds for very serious complaint against Blaydon. Mr. Lugard thinks that if we proceed criminally he will 'do time.'"

"Have you seen Lugard lately?" Sairson asked hoarsely.

Lady Laurisdale had not seen Lugard for a day two. Sairson breathed more freely. This was merely a coincidence. Lady Laurisdale was not playing with him. Her next remark, however, set his fear aflame again.

"You seem to have forgotten a great deal," she said. "That blow in the conservatory has affected your memory. Need I remind you that I discovered that John Blaydon and John Sairson are one and the same man? Don't you remember the game of 'Ghosts' we played in your dining-room on that eventful Sunday?"

"When I gave you my signature!" Sairson stammered.

"You gave me two signatures, which you very seldom gave to anybody. Your clerks did all your writing, you know. I pretended that the first signature was smeared and useless, but as a matter of fact I concealed it. It matters little how my suspicions were aroused; anyhow, I wanted to compare the signature of John Blaydon with that of John Sairson. Even a novice in that kind of study could see that the resemblance was most marked. But, we need not pursue that. You know that I know, and doubtless that Jew Sebag told you as much."

"I had forgotten it," Sairson said carelessly.

"That I believe, and make no apology for using my knowledge to set you at defiance. You are going to have a bad time, Mr. Sairson. The truth is bound to come out during the investigation of this charge against Anita Givanni. You know how foolish the charge is, but the police are not as stupid as they seem. They are only trying to force the real culprit into the open."

"They say that the girl did it," Sairson retorted sturdily.

"Absurd!" Lady Laurisdale said. "The child is as innocent as myself. But they intend to prove certain things that will make the case look still blacker before her innocence is established. They are going to prove that the child had a grievance against John Blaydon."

"Oh, are they?" Sairson said thickly. "How is that?"

"I understand they have obtained a lot of letters. There are copies of appeals to Blaydon and Blaydon's replies. This does not imply any case against Mr. Sairson, but if Mr. Sairson can be identified with John Blaydon the complexion of things will be altered altogether. The sensational elements of the case are not yet exhausted."

Sairson listened with uneasiness and anxiety that were reflected on his face. Apparently Lady Laurisdale took a pleasure in teasing him. But the strange gleam in his eyes told her there was something more sinister than this.

"Go on!" he said heavily. "You are not talking to a fool. Speak plainly."

"Is there any occasion to go any farther," Lady Laurisdale asked. "The facts must come out—they must be told in public. The marvel to me is that the secret has been kept so long."

"This is being done for revenge," Sairson protested.

"Not at all! You flatter yourself, Mr. Sairson. So far as you are personally concerned I have no prejudice one way or the other. But noblesse oblige, an axiom you do not understand or appreciate, I fear. It will be the best thing that could happen to your family in the long run. They will get sympathy—the best people will not forget that your wife is a pure and cultured woman. So are your girls, as anybody may see at a glance. You forced a horrible Jew on me once, Mr. Sairson, and this is my revenge for the affront. Besides, Anita Givanni is under my protection. I believe that you, or rather John Blaydon, robbed her of a fortune. I mean to test this, and Mr. Lugard will help me. The first step towards restitution shall take place this very day before the magistrates."

The sneer died away from Sairson's coarse features. For the first time in his life he was afraid, and was forced to admit so much to himself. It was maddening that this impecunious society butterfly, as he had always regarded her, should keep him in a tight corner like this. The very thought of it made him murderous. He had a wild desire to seize her by the throat and strangle her. She proposed to make him the outcast of the county, to remove his mask and expose him for what he was. And only a week or so ago he had flattered himself that he had compelled a friendship between the Castle and Marlton Grange. He felt that everything was slipping away from beneath his feet. The idea of compromise brought the blood to his face, but it had to be done.

He leant forward, speaking in a hoarse whisper.

"Look here," he said; "we had better be frank. You want to make a bargain. Say nothing and I shall be ready to follow your lead. I have certain bills of Laurisdale's, and if I care to make you a present of them, that is no one's business. I'm prepared to wipe the whole thing out, and give Laurisdale a fresh start. If he'll drop the theatre I can show him a way of making the estate pay hand over fist. All I ask in return is that you keep your knowledge to yourself. You can be discreet if you please! You are a clever woman, and I was foolish not to see it before. What do you say to a deal?"

Lady Laurisdale smiled quite pleasantly.

"Oh, I really couldn't be so selfish as all that!" she said. "There are other friends to be considered. Mr. Lugard has a long standing account, and so has Anita Givanni. There is another Givanni, for that matter, Mr. Sairson. What about these good people? Really, I believe that the eagles are beginning to gather."

"I shall have to make terms," Sairson smiled sourly.

"You would be lucky if it rested there," Lady Laurisdale said coolly. "I am afraid it is too late in the day to suggest compromise. There are too many creditors. There is one, for instance!"

She indicated a newcomer who was looking around for a table. With a fluttering at his heart, Sairson recognised the familiar features of Philip Gosway.

"Let me ask him," Lady Laurisdale suggested. "We are old friends."

"What do you want here?" Sairson asked. "Do you wish to see me?"

"I didn't come on purpose," Gosway admitted. "I was sent for by the police. They want me to give evidence in this charge against Anita Givanni."

CHAPTER XLVI

"I AM THE MAN."

Sairson's fighting instincts were aroused, and the queer sensation in the region of his heart vanished. Dimly he began to comprehend that he was the victim of a plot. Someone was utilising this charge against Anita Givanni for the purpose of forcing his hand. A deliberate attempt was being made to oblige him to declare in public that he was John Blaydon. Possibly Lady Laurisdale knew something about it—there was mischief in her eyes. Or, perhaps, Philip Gosway had betrayed him. Sairson turned fiercely upon the man whom he had ruled with a rod of iron so long.

"You have been letting your informed tongue wag," he said fiercely.

"You forget that Lady Laurisdale is here," Gosway said. "You know perfectly well I have said nothing to betray you. For years I have kept your secret faithfully. Besides, you had a hold over me!"

"A hold you would not break?" Laurisdale asked.

"One I could not break," Gosway murmured grimly. "I sank pretty low at one time, so low that I transgressed the law and placed myself in Mr. Sairson's power. He could have procured for me a term of imprisonment had he liked. It suited him to do nothing of the kind, and consequently I have been his slave for years. But I think the servitude is ended now."

"You have betrayed my confidence," Sairson blustered.

"I have done nothing of the kind, and you know it," Gosway went on quietly. "Nobody was more surprised than myself to receive a subpoena to attend the hearing to-day. I did not see how the connection came in at first, but I do now. These people are going to prove that you are John Blaydon, and I, as Blaydon's clerk, have been called to testify to the fact. I don't suppose that this is news to Lady Laurisdale!"

"It isn't," Lady Laurisdale said. "Much has come to light on other points that is not news to me. Had we not better go back to the court?"

Sairson rose sulkily from his chair. He would have liked an hour or two to think matters over. The thing had come upon him like an avalanche. He had an uncanny feeling that the plot had been hatched for his undoing. All at once he realized that he was surrounded by enemies who had been digging a pit for him for a long time past. Many episodes in his past might lead to more than social ruin, and if some of them came out he might find himself in the dock fighting for his life.

The time had come when it would be necessary to confirm that he was John Blaydon. This he did not so very much mind, now that the crisis was reached. With all his money he could very soon compel people to forget that. It was preferable that they should not know, but if they insisted upon the truth, they should have it. But the other matters were different. He wished he had not been so reckless in his dealings with Signora Giovanni, Captain Barr and the rest; that he had been more careful to cover up his tricks.

The court was crowded as he entered. It was characteristic of the man that he contrived to get a good place where he could see and hear everything. Something important was taking place, for the audience swayed with excitement. The chairman called for silence.

"You have a statement to make, Mr. Polgate," he said. "I understand you have had an interview with the prisoner during the adjournment."

"I venture to suggest a certain course, your worship," Mr. Polgate answered. "The prisoner should be represented by counsel."

"I presume it is a question of means," the chairman observed.

"Possibly, your worship. The prisoner has consented to give an example of her skill. It appears to require certain apparatus which we have procured from the house where the prisoner spent a day or two last week. I only desire to do what is fair and proper, but on examining certain belongings of the prisoner's, we have found some letters. They relate to transactions between Madame Givanni, the prisoner's mother, and a money-lender called Blaydon. You may have have heard of him!"

"The name is sufficiently notorious," the chairman said drily. "I don't wish to express an opinion, for the press does that pretty thoroughly out of meagre material. But what has that to do with the case?"

"It will be my duty to show that presently," Mr. Polgate went on. "By means of these letters I will establish a motive for the crime with which the prisoner is charged."

"But there has been no attack on Mr. Blaydon," the chairman pointed out.

"We are by no means so sure of that, your worship," Mr. Polgate said drily. "I wish to be quite fair, but at the same time my duty is clear. I will read some of these letters by and by. Meanwhile, I should like the demonstration to proceed."

Anita nodded her head eagerly. A change had come over her during the interval. Her face was no longer deadly pale, and the hunted look had left her eyes. Her mouth was hard and firm and her hands shook.

"You are ready?" Mr. Polgate asked.

"Oh, yes," Anita responded. "I am ready to carry out my promise. Will you hand me the little box on the table there? I will not be more than a minute."

The audience rocked with excitement; this was something unprecedented, the like of which had never been seen before in a court of law. They were to witness for themselves the method by which John Sairson had been struck down in his own home on that Sunday afternoon. It was marvellous that the solution of the mystery should be in the hands of this slim, pretty girl with the pathetic dark eyes, and pleading manner. Not a soul but watched her with a breathless interest that was not without fear.

If there were an exception it was Sairson. He was puzzled, and he hated to be puzzled. Something was about to happen to his detriment. He comprehended that behind all this parade was something designed to do him harm. As he glanced round the court he met the eye of Paolo Tosca. There was a smile on the dark face of the Italian. Sairson wondered irritably where he had met the man before—why the sight of him conjured up unpleasant memories. The truth burst upon him with staggering force a moment or two later.

"Tosca!" he muttered. "Tosca the policeman who pretended to be the foe of the Brotherhood, the man who knows everything. He knows everything about me! Heavens! If I could only get some idea of the trap they are setting for me. They're all in it, every one of them, Gosway, too. They are bent on my ruin. Well, we shall see!"

Anita stood up presently, with something obviously concealed in the palm of her hand. To those nearest to her it looked like a short, hollow tube—a tube that glistened in the light. She had put aside all her timidity, and stood there, as her mother might have done, fearless and smiling before all the curious eyes glued on her every movement. Her hand shook slightly as she pointed to one of her cages.

"Open the cage," she said. "Make the birds come out. Shake the cage."

The birds fluttered restlessly, beating their wings against the bars. Then the door was opened and the birds struggled out. A moment later and the silent court echoed with the beating of the wings. A grey pigeon wheeled in circles till it hovered for a moment over the head of the girl who was looking upwards steadily. She raised her hand for the fraction of a second—the pigeon stopped in its flight and fell like a stone at Anita's feet.

"The poor bird is dead," she said. "Let the magistrates see for themselves."

One of the policemen handed the dead bird up to the bench. It was passed eagerly from hand to hand and examined carefully. There had not been the slightest sound—no report, no flash, not the least suggestion of smoke, and yet the pigeon had fallen like a plummet at the motion of Anita's hand. There was something uncanny about the whole thing.

"I told you it was cruel," Anita cried. "It is a sin to kill the innocent birds like this. But I continue the exhibition for the last time—never again shall I kill the little birds. See!"

She raised her voice to a shout. Her right hand waved rapidly in all directions, and with every quick and dazzling motion a bird fell to the ground. They dropped one after the other like flies at the time of frost; they lay amongst the spectators; they lay amongst the tables where the solicitors sat, with never so much as the flutter of a feather.

"That is all!" Anita cried. "I have finished!"

She took the glittering thing from the palm of her hand and stamped it underfoot. Lady Laurisdale rose as if to protest, but Tosca touched her arm.

"No matter," he said. "There are other instruments of the kind, and I undertake to produce them at the proper time. Everything is going splendidly, my Lady!"

Lady Laurisdale resumed her seat. The court buzzed with excitement. It required no explanation to see how the mysterious attempt on Sairson's life had been made. The chairman called sternly for silence.

"It is very wonderful, Mr. Polgate," he said. "We have carefully examined several of the birds, and cannot detect a single wound on any of them. But we fail to gather the object of the demonstration. It tells against the prisoner, though it is a point in her favor that she has voluntarily given us this remarkable exhibition of her powers. But you have not connected her with Mr. Sairson in any way. If it were Mr. Blaydon—"

"May I be allowed to interrupt your worship?" Mr. Polgate asked. "Suppose for a moment that we can connect the two persons you mention. Suppose that Mr. Sairson and Mr. Blaydon are one and the same man?"

A sharp exclamation broke from the chairman's lips. He was shrewd enough to see the significance of the whole thing. He glanced at Sairson, who returned the look significantly. People in the vicinity of Sairson began to edge away from him.

"Do you make that suggestion seriously?" The chairman asked.

"I was never more serious in my life," Mr. Polgate said. "I will prove that Mr. Sairson and Mr. Blaydon are one and the same person. In the interests of justice, it is necessary for me to do so. Call Philip Gosway!"

The name echoed in the passage outside, and a moment later Gosway appeared. Nobody, however, regarded him at all; every eye was for Sairson, who stood by himself glaring in every direction. His coarse red face was hard, and his eye was full of contempt.

"No need to say any more," he said. "I've got to thank Mr. Polgate for this. He says that John Sairson and John Blaydon are one and the same man! He says I'm Blaydon! Well, I admit it! What then?"

CHAPTER XLVII

BY THE SAME HAND

There was no sign of flinching about Sairson. The danger had come and he was ready to meet it. He saw pretty clearly the line the prosecution intended to take. They wanted to establish a motive for the attack upon his life, and had made a successful effort. As John Sairson he had not incurred Givanni's enmity, but when he stood confessed as John Blaydon, it was a different thing altogether. For this was the man against whom Anita Givanni had a bitter grievance.

Sairson would have gone a long way to prevent this exposure, but the thing had been done. All the cunning schemes and elaborate precautions of years were swept away. He did not trouble himself to inquire who had betrayed him—he wasted no time on idle speculations. The dramatic suddenness of the exposure gave him fresh courage. He faced black and hostile looks undaunted.

"This is quite irregular," the chairman said. "I must ask you not to interrupt the proceedings, Mr. Sairson."

"Don't want to," Sairson said, sharply. "But I'm a business man, and I hate routine and red tape. You are going to call my man Gosway to prove my connection with Blaydon. I've already told you that I am Blaydon. I'll testify it on oath, if you like."

"Nevertheless, I wish to ask Gosway a few questions," Mr. Polgate said. "A great many letters have come into our possession—letters from the prisoner's mother to John Blaydon. We have evidence, too, that the prisoner has been following up the matter. The bench will appreciate the evidence that tends to prove a motive. It is alleged that John Blaydon robbed Madame Givanni of a large sum of money. The witness Gosway may be able to throw light on that point."

Gosway gripped the rail of the witness box nervously. Sooner or later he had always felt that an experience like this was inevitable. He had paid the price of his early folly over and over again, and he thought this was the crowning humiliation. For an hour or more he sustained the fire of questions from Mr. Polgate. Long before the lawyer had finished, the listeners had learned some of the secrets of the money-lending fraternity. Sairson alone appeared unaffected. The story was out, and the details mattered nothing. There was not an atom of shame about him. But people moved farther and farther away from him as the sinister facts leapt to light.

"The poor child will get her money back," Lady Laurisdale whispered to Lugard. "Do you know I was the first to discover all about the Jekyll and Hyde business."

"I think I heard something about it," Lugard replied moodily. "Didn't you get Sairson's signature under the pretence of making a ghost of it? I had forgotten that you knew Blaydon's signature."

"Most of us do," Lady Laurisdale said drily. "I found it out at the very first."

"But you were still friendly with the family!" Lugard said bitterly.

"Well, why not? It was no fault of theirs, poor dears. Cecil, if you let this come between Nest and yourself you deserve to be whipped!"

Lugard turned away impatiently. He was feeling very sore and wounded. Besides, he had his own bitter grievance against Blaydon.

"Gosway stepped out of the witness-box presently with a sigh of relief. He would have passed out of the court had not Lady Laurisdale detained him. She made room for him by her side. The set whiteness of his face moved her.

"Mr. Sairson will never forgive you for this," she whispered.

"Yes I'm afraid Othello's occupation is gone," Gosway said gravely. "Well, he can't say that I have not served out my sentence to the last day. I think I might have been spared this cruel stroke of fate, for if ever a man paid for his folly I have."

"Nobody will give you a thought," Lady Laurisdale said shrewdly. "Hardly one of the papers will reproduce your statements about yourself. They count for nothing; they are a mere bagatelle compared with the grand disclosure. I have no doubt it is all for the best. I want you to come here and look after the business of the estate for Laurisdale. Cecil Lugard says we shall pull round again with careful management—especially as there will be no more theatrical enterprises."

"If we could only keep it from Sybil," Gosway murmured.

"My dear Philip, Sybil adores you. There is only one man in the world—at least there was only one man till lately, and now I fancy there is another. That is why I have kept Sybil here so long. You are going to lose Sybil very shortly."

"My dear Blanche, she never said a word to me about it."

"Because she doesn't know herself. I dare say that sounds very cryptic, but to an old woman of the world the signs are plain. The girl who marries Major Renton will be lucky, and that lucky girl is Sybil Gosway."

"Oh, so it's Renton? The Rentons used to be friends of mine in the old days."

"Yes, and they will be your friends again. Fate is too strong for you, Philip, as it is too strong for most of us. Yet there are reasons why you should feel thankful. You have been driven out of a horrible groove into an honorable and more congenial occupation. You will have a pleasant outdoor life and be with your friends again, and you will be near your daughter when she is married. Upon my word, Philip, you are a lucky man."

A smile flitted across Gosway's face.

"Upon my word, I believe I am," he said. "I'm very grateful for your offer, Blanche. You can't imagine what a hell my life has been. I had to put up with it for the sake of the girl. I shall be glad to see her married to a good man before I die, though I shall miss her terribly."

The attendance in the court was getting less, for the dramatic interest had gone out of the proceedings during the last half hour. Sairson had vanished with one parting glance at Gosway—a glance full of malignant bitterness. Mr. Polgate whispered something to Tosca and the police officer in charge of the case, then he turned to the bench again.

"There has been an extraordinary development in this matter," he said. "Further particulars have only just come to my knowledge. I shall have to apply for an adjournment till Saturday. I view of what I have just learnt I shall make no opposition if your worship admits the prisoner to bail."

"This is a serious charge, Mr. Polgate," the chairman said.

"It is, sir," Mr. Polgate replied. "At the same time it is possible that the police have made a mistake. In the interest of justice it is policy sometimes to make them."

The chairman smiled. The bench would be guided entirely by the police. A little later Anita walked across to the hotel to tea, the centre of a group of people bent upon making much of her.

"This charge ought never to have been brought," Lady Laurisdale exclaimed. "Ah, there is Major Renton. I will ask him to have tea with us, and find out everything he knows. I presume these proceedings have been put off as a blind to give the real culprit a false sense of security."

But Major Renton declined to be drawn. Perhaps the police had made a mistake, but they had been actuated by the best intentions. They had received trustworthy information from Signor Paolo Tosca, and were justified in acting on it. A further arrest might be made in the course of a few hours. At any rate, certain most important facts had come light, and, in the end, this apparent mistake might turn out to Miss Givanni's advantage.

"Mr. Gosway may help us," Lady Laurisdale said a little maliciously. "This is Mr. Gosway, Major Renton— the father of Miss Sybil Gosway."

Gosway bowed coldly, watching Renton's face narrowly. But if he expected to see any change in it he was disappointed. Renton held out his hand.

"I am very glad to meet you," he said suavely. "Your family and mine are very old friends. I am sorry we had to trouble you to-day, but you will recognise the necessity before very long. It may not be discreet to say it, but Mr. Sairson occupies an awkward position. Investigations are bound to follow now, and the truth will have to be told."

"The truth is only known to Sairson himself," Gosway said. "One can suspect, but Sairson is a man of ingenious methods and keeps certain of his books himself. He will lose no time in making his situation secure, especially as I am out of the way. He has been my employer for more years than I care to count. It has not been easy to keep the truth from Sybil. It was only for her sake—"

"I understand," Renton said hastily. "I have a very high regard for your daughter, Mr. Gosway, as you will learn presently. At my suggestion Lady Laurisdale kept her away to-day, because I knew you were to give evidence. The reporters have promised to cut down your evidence to what was strictly relevant to the case, and to suppress all reference to your own career. Lady Laurisdale, am I not dining with you to-night!"

"So also is Mr. Gosway," Lady Laurisdale answered. "He is coming to talk business with me. He has undertaken to look after the property in future."

The room was filling with people eager for tea. The Duchess of Rochdale bustled in with a large party of her guests, and then there entered Nest and Angela Sairson. Nest drew back as she saw Lugard, and dropped into a chair at the table behind him. The Duchess was seated a little way off, and her shrill voice rang through out the room.

"I seem to have missed all the fun, Blanche," she said. "They told me it was better than a play. So our neighbor, Sairson, turns out to be Blaydon, the money-lender! Oh! what? I beg your pardon, Miss Sairson, I did not know you were so close."

Nest's face grew crimson. She felt all eyes were turned upon her, and rose and moved towards the door. Lugard rose from his seat, too, his heart flaming with love and pity and indignation. He laid a detaining hand on the girl's arm.

"Come and sit at our table," he said. "The Duchess meant no harm. Lady Laurisdale, will you make room for these two girls? Duchess, you don't know Miss Nest Sairson, I think. Let me introduce her to you—as my future wife."

CHAPTER XLVIII

THE CHOSEN INSTRUMENT

Nest caught her lips between her teeth in an attempt to stifle the cry that seemed to force itself from her heart. Whatever happened she must be brave and steady, the observed of all observers. She felt the reassuring touch of Lugard's hand on her arm, the loving pressure of his fingers. He had done a fine and noble thing, and done it in a fine and noble way. For a second it flashed across her that Cecil might be acting out of pity, but the gaze in his eye and the smile on his face banished that thought. He stood with a look of possession—with the air of a man who feels that the world is well with him.

The great lady held out her hand in the frankest possible way to Nest. She had said a thing she regretted, but there was no suggestion of apology about her. The Duchess of Rochdale could do and say anything, and she was by no means blind to the fact.

Now she had been asked publicly to acknowledge the children of John Blaydon, the notorious money-lender. There was something, too, in the dainty and refined beauty of the girl that appealed to her. She was going to be Cecil Lugard's wife, and the Lugards had been people of importance in the county before the ducal house of Rochdale had been heard of. She drew Nest towards her and kissed her frankly.

"I am very pleased to meet you my dear," she said breezily. "This is your sister, I suppose. Really, I ought to be ashamed for not calling at Marlton Grange before. I suppose you know that the Belhams are connections of mine, and you are both Belhams! The fact is, people spoil me, and let me do as I like, and that makes me careless. I don't mean to be rude my dear! Now, sit down here, and make yourself comfortable."

Nest had recovered herself by this time. A few minutes ago she was reviling fate for this crowning indignity. She would have given everything she possessed in the world to be removed from the cruelty of this exposure. Now she was in the seventh heaven of delight, her lover by her side, smiling into her eyes as if there were no such thing as trouble in the world at all.

"Really, the place is most uncomfortably crowded," Lady Laurisdale remarked, "and quite insufferably hot. I am going home in the car. Philip, you will come with me? No; I will take no refusal. I want you all to come and dine with me to-night, and talk matters over. Laurisdale is away, but he will fall in with anything I suggest. Let it be informal—no evening dress—then we can dine on the terrace. I want you all to come!"

"I think we ought to go home, Nest," Angela suggested.

"Positively, I will take no refusal," Lady Laurisdale persisted. "I have set my heart on this scheme. Where is Jack Barr? It is essential he should be one of the party. We can telephone to Marlton Grange from the Castle, and let them know that you have taken pity on my loneliness. Please don't say no."

Lugard pressed Nest's fingers under the table, and she relented. They ought to have gone home; it was their duty to return and tell their mother what had happened, but the temptation was too great. She would have a quiet hour or so alone with Cecil, a delicious clearing up of all misunderstandings. Nest was looking forward to it with mingled dread and delight.

"So that is settled," Lady Laurisdale cried. "It will be most enjoyable. I wonder whether I can induce the Duchess to join us."

The Duchess shook her head regretfully.

"I should be delighted," she said, "only I have some very dull people to dinner. If I could get out of it I would. Give my love to your mother, my dear girls, and say that if she will let me, I'd like to call some day next week."

It was good to leave the town behind and enjoy the cliffs in the glorious sunshine. Barr and Angela had gone on ahead, and Nest and Lugard were together. There was not a soul in sight, and they seemed to have the whole world of sea and land and sunshine to themselves. For a while they walked on in a blissful silence.

"Are you sure," Nest asked timidly, "quite certain Cecil, that—"

"Of course I am," Lugard smiled. "My dearest girl. I know what you are going to say. It's in the style of the most approved novels. Do you think I spoke as I did because I was in honor bound, or from a sense of pity? I don't profess any such motives. I simply did it because I love you, darling, and because there is nobody else in the world for me. When I saw you standing there I could not help it. I should have done it if you had actually been—well a kind of Miss—"

"But when I first told you, Cecil—"

"Yes, I know what you would say on that point. It was a great shock, Nest. I allowed my pride to over-master me. I could not think of anything but the fact that I was a Lugard. I didn't know what to say. I was only conscious of being utterly and abjectly miserable. Then I realised how impossible it was for me to do without you. That consideration disposed of all else."

"But you are under a solemn pledge to—"

"Oh, I admit it! I meant to bring John Blaydon to his knees, to hunt him down and make him publicly confess his misdeeds. I felt I could not rest till I had done so. But others have to be considered—Jack Barr, for instance, and Anita Givanni. Then there is that dangerous man—"

"Whom are you speaking of, Cecil?"

"The man who attempted your father's life. Who he is I don't know, but I am sure that Mascani and Givanni do. I was in court all the afternoon, and I came to the conclusion that the proceedings against

Anita are a sham. They were engineered by the police—instigated by the Italian detective, Paolo Tosca—for the purpose of making it clear that Blaydon and Sairson are one and the same man. Why? To prove that the attempt was aimed at Blaydon, not at Sairson. It is my belief that the police can lay their hands on the would-be murderer when they want to."

"It is very horrible and mysterious," Nest murmured.

"You would have been more convinced of that had you been in court to-day. I have heard a good deal of ancient history from Mascani and Givanni, who passes here as an exiled Italian with a fine skill for rearing flowers. Givanni has been a most important person in his time, and a maker of history. He belongs to a good family, and, unless I'm greatly mistaken is connected with the Belhams by marriage. When the whole thing comes out it will read like some topsy-turvy romance."

"With a dreadfully sordid side to it," Nest said.

"Well, we can't get away from that, dearest. You are alluding to your father, of course! I don't wish to say more about him than I can help. So far as I am concerned, I am disarmed. But your father must make amends for what he has done. What others may do—"

Nest sighed gently. Her eyes were full of trouble.

"Is there no way of settling this dreadful business?" she asked.

"It is very painful to have to talk to you like this, but it has to be done, Nest. When you are my wife—"

"You would like to stay in these parts?" Nest asked, with a blush.

"Of course, I should. Oh! these things are soon forgotten. I should like to have the old place back—it really belongs to me. You are a Belham, and have consented to become Mrs. Cecil Lugard. That will be more than sufficient for anybody. I don't suppose your mother has much love for a place where she has been so unhappy."

"Do you suppose she will ever be happy, Cecil?"

"We must make it up to her somehow. She is a noble woman. Let us hope for the best and be happy in the knowledge that we are together again. We have a great deal to be thankful for."

Lady Laurisdale was waiting on the terrace as the lovers came up. With her were Gosway and Sybil, with Major Renton in attendance.

"I suppose you came the longest way round," she laughed. "Well, there was a time when I liked the longest way round myself. I have 'phoned to the Grange, so that it will be all right. We shall have dinner on the terrace, and enjoy ourselves like children. Philip, take me to the rose garden and help me choose flowers for the table. I dare say these young people will spare us."

Gosway went off obediently with Lady Laurisdale. Somewhat later they had a very pleasant meal, from which all painful topics were excluded. The warmth of the night and the light of the moon kept them chatting together, but they broke off presently into couples. Gosway watched them placidly as he smoked his cigar.

"This is very jolly," he said, "quite like old times. I haven't had an evening like this for fifteen years or more, Blanche. It's very different from my cottage in London. You have to spend some of the best years of your life as I have done to appreciate this kind of thing. Well, if I sinned I have suffered, and perhaps I am now to have a little reward."

"You will have all you deserve, Philip, and that is a good deal," Lady Laurisdale said. "You were only foolish, like the rest of them."

"I was more than foolish," Gosway answered. "I did something criminal, Blanche. And all these years I have been under the thumb of that blackguard Sairson. When I look at these girls, and think that he is their father, I feel as if I were dreaming. Mrs. Sairson made her sacrifice for a brother who was, if possible, a greater blackguard than Sairson himself. One comfort is that Sairson must leave the country. He can't stay and face the constant exposure. His poor wife may enjoy a few years of happiness yet."

"Indeed, I hope so," Lady Laurisdale said fervently. "And so will you, Philip. You have promised to stay here and help us to save the property. Cecil says it can be done with care, and he will advise. You shall have the house the last agent lived in, and Major and Mrs. Renton shall be close by to see that you are not lonely. You have made up your mind to that?"

"I shall in time," Gosway smiled sadly. "It is a good match—he is a decent fellow and a gentleman. If I may be allowed—Hullo, who comes here? Mascani and Givanni!"

Mascani came up breathlessly. He wasted no time in ceremony.

"Maldini's missing!" he cried. "He has not been here? No? Well, that is a relief!"

"He hasn't been here!" Givanni echoed. "Then he is at Marlton Grange. I said we ought to have gone there first. Quick! for there is no time to be lost."

"I'll come with you," Gosway observed quietly. "I hope we shall not be too late, hurry up! There may be trouble."

CHAPTER XLIX

THE HOUR OF RECKONING

Sairson shouldered his way through the streets, sullen and defiant, as if the whole world were pointing the finger of scorn at him. He pushed defiantly along the pavement, not unmindful of the glances cast in his direction. He had never been popular here, or elsewhere, but there was an added hostility now, for the name of Blaydon was feared and execrated from one end of the country to the other. Everybody knew of the identity of the Sairson and Blaydon. A group of workmen jeered as he passed, and a boy yelled at him impudently. No doubt he has been notorious even at this distance from London.

He was out of the town at last, and on his way home. Somebody called him by name, and he looked round. Sebag was hurrying behind him. Sairson smiled bitterly.

"Your are a cunning devil," he said sourly. "You were wise to linger till the open road was reached. Didn't want to be seen in Cromer with me, eh? The dirty little Jew attorney and money-lender's tout ashamed to he seen with John Blaydon. I know you!"

Sebag smiled, not in the least put out by this tirade.

"Have it so if you choose," he said. "I always like to be on the safe side, Sairson."

"Speak to me again like that," Sairson answered furiously, "and I'll break your neck!"

"Oh, no you don't, Sairson!" Sebag rejoined. "You'll do nothing of the kind, my boy. In point of fact, even at the present moment you are making up your mind to ask my advice. I may be common and a Jew attorney, but I know my business, and at any rate I'm not John Blaydon. Why, you are ashamed of the name yourself!"

"I wasn't ashamed to tell the court the truth."

"Oh, you stuck to your guns! But you had to my boy, you had to! Much as you love money you would have given ten thousand pounds to have hushed up that business to-day. As John Sairson you could cut some kind of a figure at Marlton Grange, but as John Blaydon the country will be too hot to hold you. Even your brazen impudence will fail you. You'll not get a servant to stay in the house, nor a laborer to work on the estate. Wait till you have a month of it, my boy!"

"Why don't I break your neck?" Sairson ranted.

"Because you're afraid to. Why don't you tell me to go about my business! Because you intend to avail yourself of my services. There's precious ugly work to be done yet if you are to escape the dock. There's Lugard to be dealt with, not that he will be hard, for the sake of your girl. Then there's Captain Barr, back like one from the dead. You're in luck there, too, for I don't suppose he'll do much because of the other girl. But you'll have to fork out, old man. A lot of your beloved money will go. Then there's the Givanni business. All that farce to-day was arranged for her benefit. Do you imagine the police looked upon her as a criminal? Not a bit of it! Her friends will prosecute you, and Gosway will be one of the chief witnesses. He's staying at the Castle now. Oh, you're in a tight place, Blaydon!"

Sairson's anger had vanished, and he listened moodily to these taunts. It were stupid to suggest that Sebag was exaggerating in the slightest degree. Whichever way he turned the outlook was black. He realised that his criminal greed had overreached itself; that in his colossal contempt he had under-rated the ability of others.

"I can close Gosway's mouth, at any rate," he said.

"Can you? I doubt it! When in the witness-box he will be made to speak, and once an action is started against you, scores will be glad to keep the pot boiling. Better let me see whether I can compromise the whole business for you."

An hour or two earlier, Sebag's suggestion would have been repudiated with scorn. Now Sairson could only sigh moodily. There flashed into his mind a score of criminal transactions of which Sebag knew nothing. He had had his own way because his victims had no means of redress. Once the first dog was freed from the leash, the whole pack would be at his heels. Years of obloquy and curses had made him hard and callous, had rendered him indifferent to consequences. Now the day of reckoning was at hand, and the accounts would have to be audited.

"Better come home with me and have a mouthful of dinner," Sairson said at last. "Your suggestion is worth considering."

"Delighted," responded Sebag, carelessly. "Precisely what I should have suggested, my boy. You'll have to excuse my coming in this kit, because I have no dress togs here. Mrs. Sairson won't mind?"

"Mrs. Sairson won't be asked whether she minds or not. If you'll give me an hour or so after dinner, I can make the whole thing pretty plain to you. What these people want is their money. Let 'em have that and I shall hear no more of these threats."

"Oh, you've had some threats, then?"

"Well, it amounts to that," Sairson admitted. "There's Lugard. He's got hold of certain documents which he says prove all sorts of things."

Sebag wriggled uncomfortably. He had himself put Lugard in the way of finding these papers. He wondered whether Sairson had any inkling of the truth. Sebag's beady eyes studied Sairson's face intently. He was calm; apparently there was no danger. For Sairson was a violent man, utterly unable to control himself with anybody whom he deemed to be playing him false.

"That's rather bad," Sebag said seriously. "What has he found?"

"At present I know no more than you do yourself. Madame Givanni's solicitors were wrong, also. It's my belief Mascani is at the bottom of that. He would be glad to see me dangling at the end of a rope."

"Who are the solicitors you speak of?" Sebag asked.

"Curus and Wrex, of Lincoln's Inn Fields, if you must know," Sairson grunted.

Sebag whistled significantly. The name carried great weight with him.

"Then they must have a fine case," he said. "No chance of shaking these people off. Pity you offended them as you did two years ago over Smith's affair. They'd fight you for the sheer pleasure of it. I don't like this business at all, Sairson."

Sairson lapsed into moody silence, speaking no more till Marlton Grange was reached. He pushed his way into the study, followed by Sebag, and rang the bell twice. As no one answered it, he strode into the hall, demanding to know why the bell was not attended to. Mrs. Sairson came out of the dining-room, her face white, and her eyes red as if with much tears.

"There is no footman to wait upon you," she said. "They have both gone."

"Gone!" Sairson echoed. "Gone! Why? What does this mean?"

Mrs. Sairson followed him into the library. Sebag jumped to his feet and bowed.

"Delighted to make your acquaintance, madam," he said.

"This is Mr. Sebag," Sairson explained, "my lawyer—at least, one of my lawyers. He will stay to dinner. You'll excuse his dress."

Mrs. Sairson looked coldly at the smiling little man.

"It will make no difference to me," she said. "I shall dine in my own rooms. I am not disposed for company to-night. The girls are at the Castle, and will not be back till late."

Mrs. Sairson left the room, followed by her husband. He threw a very black and bitter look on her.

"What does this mean?" he asked. "I don't care two straws whether you dine in your room or not. If Sebag isn't good enough for you, that is no business of mine. Why have the footmen left?"

"They declined to remain," Mrs. Sairson explained. "One of them was in court to-day and brought back an evening paper. They have read the whole story in the servants' hall. They informed me that they wished to leave at once, and offered to pay wages in lieu of notice. The butler is packing his boxes at the present moment. But for loyalty towards me, they would all have gone. As it is they have all given me notice. I cannot stay here much longer."

Sairson crossed the hall to the library, where Sebag greeted him with a smile.

"Just as I expected," he said. "Domestic staff in a state of unrest. Too proud to remain under the same roof as John Blaydon. I heard what you were saving—difficult not to do so when you yell your head off. But don't bother about me; a glass of beer and a crust of bread and cheese will do for yours truly. The sooner we get to grips the better."

An hour or two later Sairson began to see things in a more rosy light. His face was flushed with the wine he had been drinking, and his teeth clutched a cigar. He wondered why he had not paid more heed to Sebag's advice before. He was receiving hints from him that aroused his cordial admiration. They were tricks and dodges of the vilest description, but Sairson recognised their advantage to him. When Sebag at length rose to go, Sairson was seeing his way clear.

"I'll meet you in London to-morrow," he said as he shook hands. "In the meanwhile, I'll take the steps you suggest. We'll show them yet what it is to meddle with John Sairson. My wife has gone to bed. Another drink before you go? No! Well, perhaps you are right. I've had a deal too much. Good-night!"

Sebag disappeared down the drive, and Sairson stood in the doorway, the cool refreshing breeze fanning his boated face.

He had turned the key in the lock before he remembered that the girls had not come back. They at least had their rich friends. So long as Lady Laurisdale was on their side the rest did not matter much, and the scandal would die a natural death. He must really make it up to Lady Laurisdale in some way. She was not a bad sort, and was a good fighter. If everything went well, her ladyship would be on his side yet.

He returned to the study in a more amiable frame of mind, and closed the door and the long French window which he had left open. The silence was broken by a chuckle that ended sharply in a high cackling laugh. Sairson turned with a shout.

"My God!" he cried. "It's Maldini! What—what do you want here!"

Maldini rose from behind a table; he had a shiny tube in his hand.

"I've come to finish it," he said. "I will make no mistake this time. No, don't you move; I am between you and the door. Mine is the hand that is ready for the reckoning. Dog! you shall die! I will rid the world of you, and the world shall say I have done well."

Sairson took a step forward, the sweat pouring from him at every pore. He needed nobody to tell him that he was face to face with a lunatic.

"Why—why," he stammered, "do you do this when I could—"

A wild cry of fury broke from Maldini. At the same time there came an answering shout from the garden. Maldini raised his hand.

"Too late!" he yelled. "Too late! The thing is done! Die, you dog! die a more merciful death than you have condemned others to. Now must I do my work."

As Sairson made a bound forward, the tube was raised. When the door was burst. Mascani and Givanni accompanied by Gosway, rushed in, and Sairson pitched head-long to the floor without a groan.

"I have done it," Maldini whispered, "as I always said I should. Victory! Victory!"

CHAPTER L

THE DEBT IS PAID

At the inquest on John Sairson, Mascani told how the money-lender had come by his death. From the very first it was plain to all concerned that Maldini was incapable of tendering evidence. There was history of insanity in his career, and after the commission of the crime he had been in a condition bordering on frenzy. It was equally obvious that he would not be in a fit state to stand his trial.

Maldini had always been eccentric—prompt to do anything for friends, but hating enemies with peculiar malignity. "I have known the man all my lifetime," said Mascani before the coroner of the inquiry, whose court was overcrowded on the occasion of the inquiry. "He was an Italian patriot in the old days, a fanatic, utterly reckless of his methods. He invented, long ago, a plan whereby liquid air could be employed as a missile, and a tube specially adapted for its use. There is no flash, no explosion, and, as a general rule, no sound; only a frightful concussion that destroys life if the missile touch a vital spot.

Madame Givanni's husband knew the secret—hence the trouble in which his daughter unwittingly found herself. The weapon with which the crime was committed is in the hands of experts, who will, if necessary, report on its working. It is very simple when it comes to be explained. It is easy to understand why the police suspected the girl, for her performance with the birds was accomplished by precisely similar means."

Very little more was to be said as to the history of the crime, and the mysterious manner in which it was perpetrated. Undoubtedly Maldini had anticipated science by the best part of half a century without arrogating any credit to himself. As a chemist, he might have attained to great fame; as it was, he was merely an anarchist visionary who, on many occasions, had escaped a violent death by sheer good fortune. Why, even after reason had deserted him, he had steadily and stealthily tracked Blaydon down, was never satisfactorily ascertained. Even Mascani could not solve that problem, despite his complete knowledge of the matter. Maldini might have been, and probably was, one of the financier's victims, and in any case Blaydon's insensate greed in making money out of the Cause, and ruining so many of its friends, stimulated this blind and unsleeping hate.

If Givanni had had any suspicions, he kept them to himself. Having regard to the circumstances surrounding the recovery of his beloved orchid, it is more than likely he could have named the avenger. But Givanni's veins were filled with hot blood, and he had his own reasons for detesting Blaydon.

For a long time the weapon continued to interest and puzzle the military community. The principles of the projectile of liquid air and its envelope proved to be very elusive, but some day it may be adapted to the rifle of a continental army. With its deadly force and absence of noise it will—in such case—add a new terror to warfare.

Apparently there was no wound on Sairson, at least no wound suggesting the use of a small arm projectile. There was a slight bruise on his forehead, but the skull was fractured. He had been killed instantly. Anita testified that she had learnt the secret from her father, who had been only less patriotic and less visionary then Maldini himself, but, with all respect to the court, she firmly refused to violate the pledge she had given to her beloved father and divulge the nature of its manufacture. She willingly explained, however, how she came to turn the weapon to account as a means of livelihood on the stage. Dudley Beaumont and his accomplices gave evidence also, but their testimony threw no light on the subject, and only served to illuminate their own unscrupulousness.

After Sairson was buried, things gradually reverted to their normal course. It seemed as if a terrible incubus had been removed from the house. As, strangely enough, the money-lender had left no will, the clearing up of the estate was troublesome, but in this work Gosway and Lugard proved of the greatest assistance, aided by Barr. It was not a bad thing, either, for Sebag, who found it the best stroke of business he had done in the course of his shady existence.

When the private books and ledgers came to be investigated, the position was much as Lugard had expected. Fortunately, there was more than enough to make restitution all round, and yet leave Mrs. Sairson a very rich woman.

"And now I fancy we can dispense with your services," Lugard told Sebag. "You have made a good thing out of this business, and are welcome to what you have made. Be satisfied with what you've got. Don't badger Mrs. Sairson suggesting this or that speculation, and don't forget that the examination of the books shows that you are not quite clean-handed. One or two transactions might interest the Incorporated Law Society. Keep away from us, and there will no trouble."

Sebag looked at Lugard with a smile of approval.

"Quite right," he said, "quite right, Mr. Lugard. In one way and another I have done exceedingly well. In the past I have had to struggle; every man has to who rises from the gutter as I have. There was a time when I had to take risks, but now I can afford to be highly respectable. In a few years my name will stand high in the profession. I mean to make the firm of Sebag and Co. one of the best in London."

"Upon my word," Lugard exclaimed. "I believe you will."

So far as Mr. Dudley Beaumont was concerned, Lugard's methods were curt and to the point.

"Your sister desires to have nothing to do with you," he said to Beaumont. "If you go Marlton Grange again, the servants have orders to throw you out. Mrs. Sairson sacrificed her life to save you, and she failed. Now that she has the opportunity to enjoy some years of happiness, I will not allow you to spoil them again. I have been making inquiries into your history, and if I chose could make matters exceedingly warm for you. Not to put too fine a point on it—I could land you in prison, and shall do so without a pang if you don't behave yourself. After what has happened, a further scandal has no terrors for us. You will be paid two pounds a week, on the understanding that you clear out of England for ever."

Beaumont raved and protested, but Lugard was firm. Finally he had the satisfaction of seeing Beaumont sail from Dover, and the eminent comedian passed out of the family history.

Mrs. Sairson smiled sadly as Lugard told her the story. "That was the beginning of my folly," she said. "I fondly imagined I could save my brother. I wrecked my happiness instead. My only consolation is that I have done my best to make amends for all the mischief caused by my husband. Everybody has been very kind—far kinder than I had expected. Friends seem to have sprung up around me in all directions. And now about the house, Cecil?"

"You will, we hope, be happy in it for years," Lugard said.

"No," Mrs. Sairson declared. "I could not stay here. It is a lovely place, but it has too many unhappy memories for me. Besides, it is yours. I hope to see Nest and you settled here before long. Angela tells me that she and Jack have taken a place. Well, the sooner the better. I was deprived of half a mother's pleasure in her children because of the taint in their blood."

"There is no taint," Lugard protested indignantly.

"Well perhaps I should not say quite as much as that," Mrs. Sairson smiled unsteadily. "But you know what I mean. They were John Blaydon's girls, and sooner or later knowledge of the bitter truth was bound to poison their lives. It poisoned Angela's for three years. It looked as if Nest's were to be wrecked also. Let me have the happy time of my life with my grandchildren. That is what I am looking forward to. There will be no stain on them."

"There never was a stain," Lugard said. "Besides, the thing will be forgotten. The public memory is short. So you have made up your mind to leave here? Where will you go?"

"My dear boy, this is your house. It was a Lugard's, and it is right that it should be a Lugard's. That my child is to marry a Lugard is a great happiness to me. When you have all married and settled down an old friend and I propose to indulge in a few months' wandering on the continent. I shall have that snug little place on the cliff which Captain Craven wises to sell. I shall be all right."

Cecil could not refuse to let her map out her own future.

On a lovely September evening two months later, Nest and he returned home after a delightful honeymoon. Barr and Angela had been back a week or more, and were at Marlton Grange to meet them. There was a gay smile on Angela's face; she was transformed out of all recognition.

"Nest!" she said, in shocked accents, "you are getting fashionable!"

"I'm not!" Nest protested indignantly. "But you are getting saucy. Jack, you must be careful!"

"I mean to risk it," Barr said happily. "Lugard, the place looks the same, and yet it is entirely different. How do you account for it?"

Lugard was unable to say. After dinner in the garden under the light of the big September moon, they alluded to the subject again.

"It is the atmosphere," Nest whispered, "the new atmosphere of love and trust and honor. I was never able to breathe here before, Cecil. Is that not the cause?"

Lugard said nothing, but fondly kissed his wife.

FRED M WHITE – A CONCISE BIBLIOGRAPHY

NOVELS (A-Z)

Ambition's Slave (1916)
The Argus Eye (1919)
Blackmail (1902)
The Blue Daffodil (1934)
The Brand Of Silence (1911)
A Broken Memory (1929)
The Bubble Reputation (1908)
By Order Of The League (1886)
The Cardinal Moth aka The Accused Orchid (1903)
The Case For the Crown (1918)
Claxton's Mill (1912)
A Clue In Wax (1930)
The Corner House (1905)
The Councillors of Falconhoe (1922)

Craven Fortune (1904)

A Crime On Canvas (1909)

The Crimson Blind (US title: The Mystery Of The Crimson Blind) (1905)

A Daughter Of Israel (1892)

The Day: Or The Passing Of A Throne (1914)

A Deal In Letters (1923)

The Devil's Advocate (1924)

Dropped From The Fast Express, or A Daughter's Sacrifice (1911)

The Edge Of The Sword (1907)

The Ends Of Justice (1906)

A Fatal Dose (aka Behind the Mask) (1907)

The Fight For The Child (1925)

The Five Knots (1907)

"Found Dead" (1930)

The Four Fingers (US title: The Mystery Of The Four Fingers) (1907)

A Front Of Brass (1910)

The Garden O' Dreams (1909)

A Golden Argosy (1886)

The Golden Bat (1924)

The Golden Rose (1909)

The Green Bungalow (1923)

The Grey Woman (aka Sinister House) (1928)

The Happy Exile (1920)

A Harbour Of Refuge (1918)

Hard Pressed (1910)

The Honour Of His House (1920)

The House Of Mammon (1913)

A House Of Sorrows (1911)

The House Of The Schemers (1906)

The House On The River (1925)

In Trust (1892)

Jim Crowshaw's Mary (1911)

The King Diamond (1927)

Lady Clara (1913)

Lady Edna's Awakening (1920)

The Lady In Blue (1915)

The Law Of The Land (1906)

The Leopard's Spots (1920)

The Lonely Bride (aka The White Bride) (1907)

The Lord Of The Manor (1907)

Love, The Foe (1910)

A Maker of Millions (1909)

The Man Called Gilray (1911)

The Man Who Found Christmas (a novelette) (1915)

The Man Who Knew (1932)

The Man Who Was Two (1921)

The Man With The Vandyk Beard (1925)

The Midnight Guest: A Detective Story (1907)

A Mummer's Throne (1910)
My Lady Bountiful (1905)
The Mystery Of Crocksands (1923)
The Mystery Of The Ravenspurs (aka The Black Valley) (1911)
The Mystery Of Room 75 (1922)
Naboth's Vineyard (1889)
The Nether Millstone (1906)
Netta, The Story Of Sin (1909)
New Century Calendar Clue (1948)
Number Thirteen (1914)
The Old Secretaire: A Christmas Story (novelette) (1887)
On The Night Express (1930)
The Open Door (1907)
Paul Quentin (1908)
Paul, The Sage (1910)
The Phantom Car (1929)
Powers Of Darkness (1912)
The Price Of Silence (1925)
The Psalm Stone (1905)
Queen Of Hearts (1930)
A Queen Of The Stage (1908)
The Riddle Of The Rail (1926)
The Robe Of Lucifer (1896)
A Royal Wrong (1913)
The Salt Of The Earth (1918)
The Scales Of Justice (1908)
Secret Of The River (1934)
The Secret Of The Sands (1911)
A Secret Service (1913)
The Seed Of Empire (1916)
The Sentence Of The Court (1913)
A Shadowed Love (1905)
The Shadow Of The Dead Hand (1926)
The Silver Stream (novelette)
The Slave Of Silence (1906)
A Society Jezebel (1917)
The Sundial (1908)
Tregarthen's Wife: A Cornish Story (1901)
The Turn Of The Tide (1923)
The Weight Of The Crown (1904)
The White Battalions (1900)
The White Bride (aka The Lonely Bride) (1910)
The White Glove (1910)
The Wings Of Victory (1919)
The Yellow Face (1906)

SHORT FICTION SERIES

THE MASTER CRIMINAL (1897-1898)

A series of 12 short stories featuring Felix Gryde, who describes himself as "a really clever soldier of fortune."

The Head Of The Caesars
At Windsor
The Silverpool Cup
The "Morrison Raid" Indemnity
Cleopatra's Robe
The Rosy Cross
The Death Of The President
The Cradlestone Oil Mills
Redburn Castle
"Crysoline Limited"
The Loss Of The "Eastern Empress"
General Marcos

THE LAST OF THE BORGIAS (1898)

A series of stories featuring Professor Victor Colonna, a vigilante physician who murders undesirable people with undetectable poisons.

The Scrip of Death
The Crimson Streak
The Holy Rose
The Saving Of Serena
The Varteg Necklace
The Three Carnations

DRENTON DENN - SPECIAL COMMISSIONER

Drenton Denn is a tough newspaper reporter on the payroll of The New York Post. His hallmarks are a straw hat, a Norfolk jacket, a perennial cigar, and a terrier by the name of "Prince."

The Yellow Moth
The Red Speck
Dust
The Fire Bugs
The Great White Moth

THE ROMANCE OF THE SECRET SERVICE FUND (1900)

This series features Newton Moore, the top agent at The Secret Service Fund.

By Woman's Wit
The Mazaroff Rifle
In The Express
The Almedi Concession
The Other Side Of The Chess Board
Three Of Them

THE DOOM OF LONDON

This sci-fi series of six stories describes a variety of catastrophes which ravage London.

The Four White Days
The Four Days' Night
The Dust Of Death
A Bubble Burst
The Invisible Force
The River Of Death

THE SAGE OF TYBURN (1905-1906)

Each of these stories was preceded by the header The Sage Of Tyburn.

No. 1 - The Chronicle Of The Yellow Girl
No. 2 - The Chronicle Of The Blue-Eyed Syndicate
No. 3 - The Chronicle Of The Inconsequent Princess
No. 4 - The Chronicle Of The Elderly Adonis
No. 5 - The Chronicle Of The Libelled Velasquez

THE DRAGON-FLY (1909)

Six stories about an impecunious but brilliant amateur criminologist, entomologist and ornithologist by the name of Horace Daimler. Each of the stories was preceded by the header The Dragon-Fly.

No. 1 - How Horace Daimler Got His Name
No. 2 - The Three Red Rats
No. 3 - [title unknown]
No. 4 - [title unknown]
No. 5 - A [illegible] Crime
No. 6 - The Mirror Over The Fireplace

REAL DRAMA (1909)

A series of stories published under the subtitle "Being Some Leaves From The Notebook Of A Late Theatrical Agent."

His Second Self
An Extra Turn
"Not In The Bill"
The Plagiarist
The Man In Possession
A Pair Of Handcuffs

THE TELEPHONE STAR (1912)

A series of stories about Keith Marrit, a star journalist working for a fictitious newspaper called The Telephone.

No. 1 - The Case Of El Hamid, The Seer
No. 2 - The Case Of The Genuine Counterfeit
No. 3 - The Case Of The Yellow Car
No. 4 - The Case Of Lord Wintercotte
No. 5 - The Case Of The Rusty Nail
No. 6 - The Case Of The One-Eyed Chauffeur

GIPSY TALES (1903-1916)

A series of stories describing the adventures of a wily British navvy with Romany roots, who is known only as "Gipsy." In his fantasies Gipsy portrays himself as a playwright, and tries to stage-manage the dramatis personae and the situations that feature in the stories.

A Matter Of Kindness
A Liberal Education
A Stranger In Bohemia
Drops Of Water
The Unpremeditated Curtain
Mere Details
Out Of Season

THE DIARY OF A LONELY SOUL (1915)

The Diary Of A Lonely Soul - Story 1 [title unknown]
The Diary Of A Lonely Soul - Story 2 [title unknown]
The Diary Of A Lonely Soul - Story 3 [title unknown]
The Diary Of A Lonely Soul - Story 4 [title unknown]
The Diary Of A Lonely Soul - Story 5 [title unknown]

A Captious Critic
The Case For The Prisoner
The Charlatan
A Christmas Bride
A Christmas Deputy
Christmas Cards
The Christmas Carol
A Christmas in Peril
A Christmas Star
The Clock Struck Twelve
The Colonel's Christmas Pudding
Compounding A Felony
The Convict
Coralie And The Pearls
A Corner In Elephants
The Courage Of Despair
Crossed Swords
The Dancing Shadow
The Daughters Of The Moon
A Daughter Of Nature
The Dawnstar
A Deal In Diamonds
Denny
A Derelict In Clover
The Desert Ship
A Dog's Life
The Doll's House
The Dormer Window
A Dose Of Quinine
The Doubting D, or, A Cranky Cryptogram
A Draught Of Life
Early Closing Day
An Eastern Princess
The Eavesdropper
The Ebbing Tide
The Egg Of The Little Auk
The Emsdam Dispatches
The Empty House
An Error Of Judgment
The Evidence For The Prisoner
Excess Profits
An Eye For An Eye
The Eye Of The Camera
The First Stone
The Foil
Forget-Me-Not
For Love's Sake
For Once In A Way

The Lesson The Ants Taught
The Livery Of Death
The Lonely Furrow
The Long Arm Of Bronze
Love In Aether
The Luck Of The Game
Made In England
The Man Himself
The Man Who Got Through
The Man Who Rang The Bell
The Man With The Eyeglass
A Masked Battery
The Master's Voice
A Matter Of Habit
'Merica
A Message from the Flood
The Midnight Call
The Missing Blade
The Missing Note
The Mistletoe Bough
Moray The Traitor
More Than Coronets
The Morning Glory
Music Hath Charms
A Musical Treat
The Mystery Of Room Five
Natural Selection
Nerves
The Night Express: The Story Of A Bank Robbery
The Northern Light
Not On The Records
An Object Lesson
The Odds On Zero
One Day With A Working Ant
One Foggy Night
One Of The Old Guard
On Peace Night
The Onus Of The Charge
The Orpheusia
Ostentation
The Other Man's Story
The Pardon
A Parrot Cry
The Path Of Progress
The Pawn And The Rook
Pearls Of Price
Photo By Lesterre
Pictures In The Snow (a Christmas story)

A Place In The Sun
The Platinum Chain
A Popular Novelist
Poste Restante
A Prize Crop
Proof Positive
The Purple Terror
A Queen In Hiding
A Question Of Money
Rachel's Seventh Year
Rawhide Science
The Real Dramatic Touch
A Record Round
Red Petals
Rob Peter—Pay Paul
A Rope Of Snow
Rose Of The Desert
A Royal Bag
The Royal Train
The Salmon Poachers
Santa Anna
A Satisfactory Reference
Saviour From The North
The Second Chapter
Second In The Field
The Shebeeners
A Single Hair
Sir Jeremiah's Big Shoot
Sister Louise
The Sixteenth Chapter
A Sleeping Partner
Sleeping Partner
A Sound In The Night
"Special" To The Telephone
A Stolen Interview
The Straight Game
The Stranger Within The Gate
Sub Rosa
The Substitute
The Superman
The Supreme Test
The Sword Of Justice
A Table Tragedy
The Thirty-Seventh Month
This Little World
A Thrilling Exit
The Throat Of The Wolf
The Ticket

To Be Let Furnished
Treasures Three
The Two Bon-Bons
Two Of Them
The Unbelieving Eye
Unbidden Guests
The Unexpected
An Unrecorded Crime
The Vital Spark
The Vital Spot
War Ribbons
The Waterwitch
The Western Way
When The Moon Set
The White Geranium
The White Spot
White Wings (1922)
The Wings Of Chance (1922)
The Witness (1920)
The World Next Door (1916)